PENGUIN BOOKS

That Certain Age

Praise for Elizabeth Buchan:

'This perceptive, beautifully written book brings fresh perspective to an age-old situation ... For women of all ages, a poignant, unforgettable novel' *You Magazine*

'In Buchan's witty hands, it is fate, the most satisfying entertaining mischief maker, which proves the undoing' *Sunday Times*

'Buchan is brilliant at creating memorable characters' *Sunday Mirror*

'Extremely readable, well-written, funny and sad' *Daily Mail*

'A compassionate and thoughtful portrait of a marriage in crisis and a woman bent on survival' *Woman & Home*

'Buchan's portrayal of Rose's emotions – from shock, betrayal and anger to a gradual acceptance of her situation – sets this novel apart from other tales of midlife crises' *Good Housekeeping*

'Bravo to Buchan's witty, wise and wonderfully readable novel' *Sunday Express*

'Buchan is a cut above the rest in this field' *Sunday Mirror*

'Fresh, compassionate and alarmingly perceptive ... I love it' Sian Phillips, actress

'What a terrific book!' Fay Weldon

'Intelligent and uplifting' *Sainsbury's* magazine

'Miss Buchan skilfully sets the serendipitous scene where hungry Nemesis hovers ... This is a compelling read' *Country Life*

'Bitter-sweet charm' *Sunday Tribune*, Dublin

'The *Revenge* is not about cutting up his suits or pouring away his collection of vintage wines, for Elizabeth is much too subtle a writer for that ... a resonant and excellent novel' *SW*

ABOUT THE AUTHOR

Elizabeth Buchan lives in London with her husband and two children and worked in publishing for several years. During this time, she wrote a biography for children: *Beatrix Potter: The Story of the Creator of Peter Rabbit* (Frederick Warne). Her first novel for adults, *Daughters of the Storm*, was set during the French Revolution. Her second, *Light of the Moon*, took as its subject a female undercover agent operating in occupied France during the Second World War. *Consider the Lily*, described by the *Independent* as 'a gorgeously well written tale: funny, sad, sophisticated', won the 1994 Romantic Novel of the Year Award, and *Perfect Love* was reviewed by the *Good Book Guide* as 'a powerful story: wise, observant, deeply felt, with elements that all women will recognize with a smile – or a shudder'. Subsequent novels include *Against Her Nature* ('a modern day *Vanity Fair* brilliantly done' – *Mail on Sunday*), *Secrets of the Heart* (Penguin), *Revenge of the Middle-Aged Woman* (Penguin) and *The Good Wife* (Penguin), which have been international bestsellers.

Elizabeth Buchan recently completed a stint on the committee for the Society of Authors, and was a judge for the 1997 Whitbread Awards and chairman of the judges for the 1997 Betty Trask Award. Her short stories have been published in various magazines and broadcast on BBC Radio 4.

For further information on Elizabeth Buchan and her work, please go to www.elizabethbuchan.com

That Certain Age

ELIZABETH BUCHAN

PENGUIN BOOKS

PENGUIN BOOKS

Published by the Penguin Group
Penguin Books Ltd, 80 Strand, London WC2R ORL, England
Penguin Group (USA) Inc., 375 Hudson Street, New York, New York 10014, USA
Penguin Books Australia Ltd, 250 Camberwell Road, Camberwell, Victoria 3124, Australia
Penguin Books Canada Ltd, 10 Alcorn Avenue, Toronto, Ontario, Canada M4V 3B2
Penguin Books India (P) Ltd, 11 Community Centre, Panchsheel Park, New Delhi – 110 017, India
Penguin Group (NZ), cnr Airborne and Rosedale Roads, Albany, Auckland 1310, New Zealand
Penguin Books (South Africa) (Pty) Ltd, 24 Sturdee Avenue, Rosebank 2196, South Africa

Penguin Books Ltd, Registered Offices: 80 Strand, London WC2R ORL, England

www.penguin.com

First published by Penguin Books 2004
1

Grateful acknowledgement is made for permission to reproduce the following:
Excerpt from 'Good-by and Keep Cold' by Robert Frost from *The Poetry of Robert Frost*
edited by Edward Connery Lathem and published by Jonathan Cape. Used by permission of
the Estate of Robert Frost and the Random House Group Limited.
Copyright 1923, © 1969 by Henry Holt and Company, copyright 1951 by Robert Frost.
Reprinted by permission of Henry Holt and Company, LLC

The moral right of the author has been asserted

Set in 12.5/14.75 pt Monotype Garamond
Typeset by Rowland Phototypesetting Ltd, Bury St Edmunds, Suffolk
Printed in England by Clays Ltd, St Ives plc

For Fanny

She felt the largeness of the world and the manifold wakings of men to labour and endurance. She was part of that involuntary, palpitating life . . .

George Eliot, *Middlemarch*

Acknowledgements

Two debts in particular must be acknowledged: to Geoffrey Wellum's remarkable and moving memoir *First Light* (Penguin), and to Frank Browning's *Apples: The Story of the Fruit of Temptation* (North Point Press). I have taken both detail and anecdote from them. Any mistakes are mine.

As always, I owe an enormous amount to my brilliant editors, Louise Moore in the UK and Pamela Dorman in the US, and their crack publishing teams. With especial thanks to Clare Ferraro, Hazel Orme, Carolyn Colburn, Judi Kloos, Katy Nicholson and Claire Bord, and last, but certainly not least, to my agent Mark Lucas.

To my friends and family: thank you.

Johanne Coker has made a generous donation to the NSPCC in return for naming a character in this novel.

Chapter One: Siena

I have so many laments filed away. *My hair is greying . . . I've lost my suppleness of mind and body . . . My figure is ruined . . . Never, never again will I feel as I used to . . .*

The cries of woman can be very loud. Plaintive and corrosive . . . grief-stricken and despairing . . . strident. We stay at home, crowded by yeasty little bodies, our oh-so-efficient captors, and weep noisy tears into the sink. We go out to work and shriek at the difficulties. Biology has arranged to keep tight tabs on us. Fillies at the rodeo, lined up to be broken in by ovaries and uteruses.

But as I explained to Charlie, my husband, thanks to science, biology can be handled. One can keep it at arm's length. So far, I had managed to ignore the ticking of the biological clock, with a clean, simple career schedule and, *please, Charlie*, let me keep it that way. He had asked me to keep the case under review, and added that men cried too: it was just that they were not heard.

This was not to say the issue between Charlie and me was resolved, far from it, but I held him close after he made that particular remark (not bitterly, but with his lawyer's matter-of-factness), whispering into his ear that I loved him.

'And I love you, too, very, very much,' he responded, and ran his fingers through my hair. But I knew he

1

was troubled. The question of whether we should have children – or not – was well-trodden ground between us, yet journey as we might over it, beating through the thickets of questions and arguments, we never agreed on the final destination.

'Am I cheating you, Charlie?' *Am I? Was I?*

I watched him carefully pack a parcel for his nephew's seventh birthday (a fake scar for the cheek, an inflatable cushion that emitted a rude noise if sat on and a starter pack of Meccano). He applied the last slick of Sellotape. 'Do you think I've made it large enough?' he asked. 'I want it to be a really big parcel and the most fun.' He sat down and wrote the card: 'To Nat, my favourite nephew, love, Uncle Charlie. PS Will you come paint-balling with me?' Then he drew a dinosaur on the back of the envelope, sealed it and said quietly, 'I have no idea if you're cheating me or not. I'll have to wait to find out.'

Why didn't I say to him, 'I have enough in my life. It's so full, so busy, so absorbing that I don't have room for anything else.' Because I know Charlie would have pushed back his floppy hair and replied, with one of his sweetest smiles – which seemed to embrace a secret vision of good things like a dog's wet nose pushing into your hand, sunlight falling on a cradle, 'We can make room. Of course we can make room.'

I envied Charlie his certainty and his immaculate generosity.

Lucy Thwaite (35) [ran the notes on my latest assignment] is a mother of three. Plans to return to work in catering. Needs smart, practical, adaptable wardrobe. The problem? Since birth of third child (5) she has put on weight and lost confidence. 'I'm at my wit's end . . . I hate my body, hate looking at it, and always wear baggy clothes . . .'

Lucy Thwaite's case notes had been sent over by Jenni from *Fashion, This Week* with the schedule, which gave me approximately four days to think over and sort out the said Lucy. The accompanying photograph revealed a woman whose features were set with a mix of exhaustion and fury. Even to the untrained eye, the sorting out of Lucy Thwaite would take more than a week.

Jenni, who hunted out my subjects and did the preliminary research, had spotted it too. 'Caged,' she said, on the phone, 'and battering bars to get out.'

In general, the spectre of unhappiness in my clients stirred pity – which made an uneasy bedfellow with the requirement in a fashion consultant to be frank. But life is a series of polarities, and I was the white knight riding to the rescue, bringing cheer and a little tough-talking on the point of my lance.

On meeting Lucy Thwaite at her home in the Midlands, it struck me that she had thought herself into the role of frump: she was prettier in the flesh and her skin had the lovely transparency that permanent fatigue sometimes gives women.

Lucy held out her hand, which was damp and soft when I took it. 'I'm so excited. None of my friends can believe it.' Her mouth twitched in a smile that did not reach her eyes.

Over the years I had made many mistakes, and to rely on first impressions was one of them, but I could not help recoiling a little from Lucy Thwaite's intractable aura of misery.

'You must come in. Do you want coffee? Mind the tricycle, that's Johnny's, my youngest, and – Oh, I'm sorry about the shopping. Just step over it.'

The house was a mess, as were many of the houses into which I stepped. A home was so naked, so revealing. Charlie and I hadn't allowed anyone into our flat until it was perfect. 'For better and for worse and *for tidiness*,' we joked with each other, for we shared the desire to remain hidden and private.

Lucy's kitchen was crowded with clothes, baskets and papers. She sat me down at the table and busied herself with the kettle and coffee. I cleared a space to put down my notebook among the cereal packets and papers, which included a cut-out of a small foot that had been glued on to a cardboard base through which laces had been threaded. It was a fragile thing, made in haste and inadequately gummed, but breathed childish optimism and determination. The label attached to it read: 'Centurion's boot, Hadrian's Wall, *circa* AD 200'.

Lucy gestured at it. 'I have the misfortune to send my children to schools that specialize in torture. Of the parents.' Her eyes were dull. 'Shelley came back last night and said she had to have a Roman sandal made by Friday. *A Roman sandal!* I don't know what one looks like, nor do I care – but what am I supposed to do? One thing's for sure, Derek won't be around to act as cobbler.'

4

I couldn't bear to make any comment, for I minded about that silly sandal.

Lucy dumped a mug of coffee in front of me. 'Will I be famous?' she asked.

I glanced at my watch – a gesture she understood instantly: she sat down at once. 'Lucy, let's talk about you. Could you tell me a little more about yourself?'

A shadow passed over the unhappy features. 'That's nice. I haven't been asked about myself since . . .' she rubbed her cheek '. . . since . . . I can't remember.'

She seemed genuinely taken aback by the invitation, and I wondered about the equation that had brought her to this nadir. Fatigue and motherhood, clearly. But was there also an unkind husband? A sudden lack of money?

Maybe it was simpler than that. Unhappiness was an everyday, plodding thing, and one got used to it.

I knew all about that.

I extracted a pen from my red Tod's handbag. Lucy's eyes rested on it covetously. 'That's the one thing I do indulge in,' she said. 'A nice handbag.'

No surprise there. Big women are frequently compulsive handbag (and shoe) buyers for a simple reason: a handbag (or shoes) brightens up the image and allows one to acquire a fashionable badge without the ritual humiliation of shopping for large-size clothes. *Vive* the accessory.

'In fact, I get through quite a few every year. Derek's always telling me off.'

'Better than getting through husbands, though.' I was never quite easy about being a second wife. *Ergo*, I made jokes about it.

Lucy Thwaite stared at me, and there were tears in her eyes. 'Is it?'

I smiled at her gently. 'Why don't we start?'

Twenty minutes later I understood more about Lucy Thwaite and her life than perhaps I wished to. The claustrophobic domesticity, perennial tiredness, lack of cash for little luxuries. I had encountered so many Lucy Thwaites.

Sometimes I asked myself what I was doing intruding into despair and these domestic muddles with my tough talking. It was so easy to rattle a few hangers in a wardrobe, issue strictures about cap sleeves (*not* for the older woman), colour and hems, then fly away on my magic broomstick, knowing I did not have to deal with them. And then I caught the glow of gratitude, a shy smile of pleasure, the tiny suggestion that a situation had changed and, suddenly, my contributions no longer seemed so clumsy, so witless.

I asked Lucy if I could check over her wardrobe, and she led me upstairs. On each tread there was a pile of folded (but not ironed) children's clothes. A pair of muddy football boots and a cot took up most of the space on the landing.

Lucy's wardrobe opened to reveal a full-length mirror inside the door. This is not unusual. It is positioned precisely so that women can shut away the image of themselves and, in many cases, contrive never to look at it.

'Lucy, come and stand in front of the mirror.'

She whisked the bedspread straight. 'Must I? Can't you just look at me?'

''Fraid not. It's part of the deal that you take a look.'

I took her by the shoulders and stood her fair and square. This was always a telling moment: revelation, breakdown or new dawn – I could never anticipate which.

She looked long and hard, and her plump shoulders tensed. 'I hate my body,' she spat at herself. 'It *disgusts* me.'

If I've had no opportunity to talk to my client, I can usually get the picture within five to ten seconds of sifting through her wardrobe. Funnily enough, smell has a great deal to do with it. I swear I can smell the quality of their lives. Expensive scent. Cheap scent. Expensive, careful dry-cleaning, or the masked aura of sweat and making-do with too little money and too little time as the owner of the clothes rushes to cook, shop, ferry and guard her children.

Big women tended to have fullish wardrobes for they buy clothes on impulse, promising themselves they will fit into them one day. Lucy Thwaite's contained less than I had calculated. Black trousers . . . tapered and too short. I pushed the coat-hangers this way and that. Embroidered cheesecloth blouse (relic from a Greek holiday?), a dress in an overlarge print with a front opening. A button was loose at the point where the material must strain across the bust.

'Is this a favourite, Lucy?'

She shrugged. 'It's a dress, I can get into it, and it does.'

I pushed it to one side. These were the clothes of someone who had no time, no breathing space, no confidence. *No joy*. Who had been brought low, and whose every waking minute was taken up by someone else. *Please. Come. Do. Make.* The voices swelled so hard and fell so harsh on the inner ear that they blotted out other sounds, including the still, small call for help.

The rail was buckled in the middle and the hangers clicked into a clump. 'I wore that coat in my twenties,' Lucy offered. 'Can't bear to throw it away.' She plucked at a pair of trousers with an elastic waistband. 'Bought these when I was pregnant and I wear them all the time.'

A thought slid across my sunny inner landscape, a cheap, unwelcome, off-the-peg rip-off that elbowed its way into the glitter and dazzle of my haute-couture dreams and projects: *This could be me.*

In my office at home in the flat at Embankment Court, so close to the river that the rooms seem to float over it, I checked my messages and post. My business – the weekly slot in *Fashion, This Week*, consultant on fashion shoots, regular demands to contribute think pieces to the glossier magazines and intermittent radio and television work – ensured there were many.

Dear Siena, Please help me. I'm going to university in the autumn and I look terrible. I don't have much money. Is there anything you can do to make me feel more confident?

I slotted the letter into the pending tray.

Dear Siena, We enjoy your column but we think you are often too harsh on your subjects. We are equal beings in the eyes of our

Maker and our outer covering is of little significance compared to what is within. We feel we should remind you of this point . . .

I held that letter over the bin, preparatory to dropping it in, but changed my mind, got up and pinned it to the noticeboard instead. I liked the idea of God watching over wardrobes and their custodians. In my experience, He had not seemed the sort of deity who would busy Himself with the cut and fold of fabric. But since I had turned thirty-five, a milestone just as worrying as forty, I had discovered that my opinions had not, after all, been set in stone. On the contrary, a great deal of nipping and tucking was going on.

Now I had to think about Lucy Thwaite and there was not much time (there never was). How could I transform her, make her happier for . . . oh, an hour or so?

The phone rang. 'Hi, India here.'

It was a sure-fire thing that if I was introduced to anyone called 'India', 'Paris' or 'Georgia', they were probably in my age bracket. Some maggot had worked into the collective psyche of my parents' generation, prompting them to discard the duller 'Caroline', 'Elizabeth' and 'Jane' in favour of naming their children after the wider world. It was nice, and we – the continents and cities – liked it.

India was my agent and she was thirty-five. 'Are you sitting comfortably? Big news. I've had an approach from Trimester Productions, the American company. They've spotted you in the mag and want to know if you'd do a pilot with them for a possible series over there.'

'Grief,' I said. 'America.'

'That's what I said, stupid. Early days, but listen up. This is what we have to do.'

Contracts, schedules, payment, publicity, anticipated audience . . . this was music to me: the andantes and crescendos of a successful career.

After the conversation had finished, I got up and went over to the noticeboard to which were pinned my time-tables, swatches of material, newspaper cuttings, and the photographs I needed to have around me – Charlie and I on honeymoon in the Himalayas, a family group of my parents with my brother, the *Crystal* (now defunct) fashion team and I on location in Sydney last year (we had been there for a week and the jet-lag was so bad that we decided we'd left before we arrived) and, last but not least, our friends Lola and Bill, in their New Hampshire orchard, just after the first spraying of the year.

Knowing that Charlie and I were paid-up members of the awkward organic brigade, Bill had been careful to explain in the accompanying letter that there was no way an apple farmer could grow successfully without intervention. 'An orchard is unnatural; it does not happen in the wild,' he wrote, and I found it touching that he minded so much what we thought. 'An orchard is a magnet for disease and unrest, and it infects itself, like politicians or extremists. We can't afford to rely on the weather or mountains to check the creep of bacterial and fungal infection. That is the price for a crisp, beautiful apple! Chemical vigilance.'

Fashion editor Lola and I met frequently on the circuit, and she and Bill had stayed with us at Embankment Court.

We were a good foursome – more than good: we were the kind of friends you know, instinctively, are for life. If I went to America, I would beg a visit to their country retreat and see that orchard for myself.

'Siena . . .'

I looked up from our dinner of noodles fried with ginger and spring onions. 'Yes?'

He smiled at me. 'Don't look so worried.'

'Not worried, just day-dreaming.' But I *was* worried. How could I work in America? How could I tell Charlie?

He put his head on one side and scrutinized me in a way that suggested he could see right through me, and beyond. 'You seem a bit Trappist tonight.'

'Sorry.' I pulled myself together. 'Tell me what happened today?'

Charlie acknowledged the *pro-forma* question by waving a finger. Judge-like (which is what I tease him he would like to be). He was defending a woman accused of murdering her six-month-old baby. He and a group of like-minded colleagues had set up Freedom Watch, a chambers that specialized in human-rights abuses, discrimination, and cases like this one. He had made a name for himself in championing the unchampionable and battling with the authorities. Compared to richer chambers, Freedom Watch operated on a shoestring, not least because Charlie, among others, insisted on taking on a proportion of legal-aid cases, which, as it happened, ate into our evenings and weekends. 'I'm lucky,' he had explained, when I first met him. 'My life has been clean, ordered and comfortable. I have to give something back.' It was an equation for which I loved him.

In this particular case, the baby had been found in his cot and the post-mortem had revealed bruising on his body. 'But the marks,' Charlie now pointed out, 'are consistent with bruising that might have occurred when the paramedics tried to revive him.' Noodles forgotten, he leant over the table. 'If Jackie, the mother, had killed her baby, I think she would confess to it. She has a kind of honesty about her.'

'So you believe she's not guilty.' It was a statement, not a question.

Charlie tensed. 'Absolutely,' he said. He pushed at a noodle. 'Jackie Woodruff did not kill her baby.'

I put down my chopsticks. Contrary to the front he put up, Charlie's reputation for brilliant defence and ultra-professionalism had not been easily won and those who admired (and hated) him for his ferocity and integrity might have been surprised. A constant war was waged in Charlie between his instinctive belief in the essential goodness of human beings, the perfectibility of human nature (with a little help from welfare, education and such agencies), and the evidence to the contrary presented daily in court.

He made one of his lightning switches. 'The best I can do for Jackie . . .' He paused. Charlie had in him his fair share of the actor *manqué*. '. . . is to nobble the clerk of the court to rig the jury.'

'Old joke.'

'They're the best.'

'So they are. Eat,' I admonished him gently. 'The noodles will get cold.'

'Bully.' He smiled at me and with such love that my heart danced.

A few minutes later I cleared away the bowls. They were white and satisfyingly thick, and I had devoted two weekends to searching for just the right ones. It was important to us that everything was just so in our flat, our home, and I loved to handle their rounded, pregnant curves and feel their weight nestling between my hands.

I stacked them in the machine and pulled a plate of fruit out of the fridge – neat groupings of blueberries and single raspberries, surrounded by slices of fresh pineapple and a quartered apricot. The effect of them on the plate, which was of a purer, more dazzling white even than the noodle bowls, was pleasing.

Charlie helped himself. A rivulet of pineapple juice ran down his chin and I reached over to dab it with my napkin. My excuse? We had only been married for five years and the novelty was still so sweet and delightful. Charlie was a source to me of endless fascination and, yes, pride; touching him for any reason gave me pure pleasure. Sometimes I made sure I bumped into him. Or I offered to massage his shoulders with the firm circular movements I knew helped him after hours spent hunched over a desk. Or I just kissed him, plain and square, on the mouth.

'Hey, what's that for?'

'No reason.'

'Tell me.'

'I don't want to make you bigger-headed than you are . . .'

We dined out frequently, for work or with good friends, which was fun. Yet it was fun, too, to be here together, following our routines. Supper, always well presented. Ten o'clock news, a discussion about what each was doing the following day, and who was on the shopping rota.

Then bed. That was not so predictable, and certainly not routine. The secret about sex – and I imagine there are many secrets about it, including that it happens less often than is imagined – well, my secret was that bed is the one place where sexual politics do *not* apply. There a woman can be entirely submissive, and a man entirely demanding, and each is thoroughly pleased with the other. Charlie and I were thoroughly pleased with each other.

Tonight on the television news we watched a posse of grey-suited politicians stride into the EU headquarters in Brussels on a mission to sort out landmines.

'Bet they were thinking about lunch,' I said.

Later, Charlie snorted at the cricket results. 'Why can't we win, for God's sake?'

'Give them a chance.'

'Siena, which planet are you on?'

I sank back on the sofa – large, feather-stuffed and upholstered in Bennison fabric.

'We're talking about the English cricket team,' he said, and wrapped up the case. 'Nuff said.'

I turned my head towards him. 'Charlie ... are you happy? With me?'

I knew it was tempting Fate to ask those questions for the ghosts of our previous marriages were there, white noise, if you like, in the background.

He shifted towards me, catching me in a near-stranglehold. 'Have I ever told you that you have the biggest blue eyes I've ever seen?'

'Not today.'

'When I look into them, I see a sunlit sea and . . .'

'And . . .'

'Stillness. Peace. Happiness.'

That was all right, then.

'Charlie,' I was propped up in bed with pillows, watching him undress, 'would you like the good news?'

'Tell.' He padded over to the wardrobe and hung up his suit.

'India phoned. I've been invited to make a pilot for a television series.'

Charlie shut the wardrobe door. 'Brilliant.'

'And the bad news?'

He sat down on the bed. 'What is bad news about my clever wife earning the accolades she deserves?' He looked at me steadily. 'It's good, Siena. I'm pleased.'

'Hang on . . . hang on. It's in America. Nothing's settled, and it may not happen, but I might have to go over there and jump through a lot of hoops and maybe . . .'

'That's the bad news? You'll have to do better than that.'

'A lot of money.'

'That's terrible.'

'It's a big break, one I'd never imagined happening.'

He hesitated. 'I know.'

After a while, Charlie got up and went into the

bathroom where I could hear him moving around. There was a splash of water, the sound of the electric toothbrush, then silence while he brushed his hair. He emerged and smiled at me. 'Early days, though.'

'Yup.'

He reached for his dressing-gown and tied the belt round his waist. 'You go to sleep. I've just got to check up on something and it can't wait.'

'Charlie, you're tired. Come to bed.' He was concluding a case involving a Romanian accused of being an illegal immigrant.

He shrugged. 'Not that tired. Don't worry, I won't wake you.'

He disappeared and I heard him snap on the light, the thump of his briefcase, and he settled to work.

He had a habit of working late into the night when he was troubled, angry, bothered. It was his way of dealing with it.

Chapter Two: Siena

I must have fallen asleep, for I found myself watching a dream television documentary about Bill and Lola's orchard. It had been transformed into an industrial factory field, patrolled by machine dragons. I was busy writing out headings in my notebook. Under 'Birdsong', I entered 'None'. Under 'Butterflies', 'None'. I added: 'No scutter of life in the grasses.' When I looked up at the trees they were hung with tidy, obedient, brightly coloured same-sized apples.

Confused, I woke up, rolled across to Charlie and slid my arm, oh, so gently, round his waist. Instantly I knew he was awake. 'I think I was having a nightmare about GM apples,' I said. 'They all looked the same.'

Silence.

'America's my big chance,' I said quietly. 'I might never get another. It will only be a one-off.'

'If it works,' Charlie murmured, 'it will not be a one-off.'

A girl may dream. First series, third series ... *tenth* series. Club and first class, weekends in the Hamptons, interesting people, interesting ideas, a new look at a different set-up ... So many possibilities were scrambling to take up residence in my head. 'It's difficult to turn down such an offer.'

'Yup,' he agreed, with the same controlled articulation, but he was not agreeing.

'*You* wouldn't pass it up.'

'OK, Siena,' he said quietly. 'How do we resolve this?'

More silence.

Charlie has learnt the art of holding silence in court, silences filled with more meaning than any words, but I was not so good at them.

'*When do we have children, Siena, when do you think?*'

'*Charlie, as soon as there's a gap in my schedule, then we can have a try. I'm so sorry but a book, an idea, a programme, a project, has come up . . . The magazine wants a weekly column, not a monthly . . . I must concentrate on that.*'

'*Siena, time is ticking past . . .*'

'I promise to think about it.'

Did he believe me? Probably not, for I had ducked and woven so often through the aforementioned thickets.

Charlie sat up in bed and switched on the light. He cupped my cheek in his hand. 'Do you mind me pointing out that you will be thirty-six next birthday?'

'Ouch.'

He reached for the glass by the bed and took a sip. I imagined the water trickling down his throat to a stomach churned by our late-night conversation.

'Charlie, I don't want to lose all the ground I've made.'

'But you'll gain,' he said, and stroked my cheek. 'You'll be a beautiful, wonderful mother.'

A flicker of impatience shocked me. That kind of thing was so easy to say – and took no account of my instinctive cowardice. I drew a deep breath. 'I'm frightened, Charlie.'

'But I'm here.' He put down the glass and sent me a grin: so wry, it was almost bitter, definitely mocking and . . . boyish. Like the son he craved. All I wanted was to make Charlie happy, which seemed simple enough. Except that it wasn't.

He bent over me, trying for the hundredth time to find out what held me back, trying to understand. 'Do you know what I think, Siena?'

'You're going to tell me.'

'I think men are the new women. It's one of the by-products and ironies of feminism.'

Joke.

My hand trembled a little as I turned off the light. The bedroom was plunged into darkness. Charlie touched my thigh. 'Consider . . .' (Whenever Charlie said, 'Consider,' I had a mental picture of him in his gown and wig, leaning on the court lectern with his bundle of documents, each significant step in the argument marked with a different-coloured Post-it.) '. . . you want to be at the top of your profession. I want a happy marriage and two point four children sitting at a table eating bowls of cereal, a drawer stuffed with drying-up cloths and a cat sleeping on the boiler. So I must be a new woman.'

Jay, my first husband, had been a great one for not putting things off. He did not put off marrying me – 'Why wait, honey?' – neither did he put off divorcing me – 'Why wait, Siena?' He had a point: he lived by the principle that all of us could go under a bus within the hour. He did not take note of the cool transition before dawn, or the ambiguous dusk in the evening. With Jay, it was either night or day. Charlie was so much cleverer, more subtle, infinitely more embracing of the nuances of mind and spirit.

I was too upset by our conversation to sleep, which had happened a lot lately. The result was dark circles under the eyes and a wholesale application of Touche Éclat (NB: no girl should be without it).

The dark was not the soft velvet Guinness black as it sometimes was, but jet ink. Experience had taught me that I would have to wait patiently, with burning eyes, until dawn diluted it to grey.

'Time is running out.' Charlie's voice, by my ear, startled me. 'It is . . .' He was placing his lawyer's finger on my 'thirty-five (but nearly thirty-six) which is twenty-five, these days, really' condition.

'I know.'

'Our children would be beautiful . . . perfect.'

'They're not accessories,' I flashed at him.

'Probably better if they were,' he came back, just as fast. 'You put a lot of energy and care into accessories.'

Calfskin or crocodile? Plastic or canvas?

'Not worthy, Charlie.'

'You're right. Sorry.' Abruptly, he sat up in bed, switched on the light. 'Siena. Open those big blue eyes of yours and take a look. You must think.' He looked down into them, searching for the Siena he wanted. 'Please, please, let's be sure we don't make a mistake.'

The trouble with seeing was that it meant you had to do something about it.

I reached up and brushed his hair off his forehead. 'Can we go to sleep, Charlie, please?'

Without another word, he switched off the light, lay down and turned his back.

Charlie was right, but all I could see were the wardrobes of Lucy Thwaite and her trapped sisters waiting to imprison me in their sad smells and capacious misery.

Soon Charlie's even breaths indicated that he was asleep, and I was glad – he needed it. I matched my breaths to his, a silly habit but it made me feel close to him, running parallel in a way that was impossible during the day.

There we were, then, breathing in tandem, the heads of a household of two.

Thank God, I slept.

When Charlie woke as the alarm clock performed its morning aerobics, I was ready with a cup of tea for him.

He struggled upright, groaned, and dropped his head into his hands. 'Were you a hospital matron in a previous life? Time?'

'Get-up time.' I sat on the bed and waited for him to surface properly. 'Hope today goes well.'

He blew on his tea. 'So do I.'

I watched him assemble himself for the day: clearing his head, straightening his limbs. Today the death of a baby would have to be accounted for. The case was going to be a long haul and the shadows cast by it were long and full of sorrow. I knew that Charlie would suffer if (a) his client was found guilty, (b) she had done it. The two points were not necessarily linked, and vice versa.

I hated to think of Charlie suffering, so I switched subjects. 'I'll be talking to India.'

'I expected you would.'

In the background, the phone rang in my office. I tensed, as if poised for flight. It would be the first of many calls and might be important, perhaps something I should sort out now, this minute.

Charlie read my thoughts. 'It can wait, Siena.'

'But maybe not.'

For answer he took my hand and teased each finger straight. 'Sometimes I think we're *addicted* to work.'

The answer-phone clicked on.

Charlie swung out of bed – long, strong, masculine legs, feet planted squarely on the floor – and padded into the bathroom. The radio was switched on, water ran, and I noticed that rain was lashing the window. I had forgotten to put on my slippers and my feet were icy. I inspected them. The nails were painted a pale pink, but it was time for a pedicure – the varnish had chipped. The palm-top diary was on the bedside table, and I 'leafed' through it. Maybe I could snatch one between lunch and the weekly visit to *Fashion, This Week*?

Again the phone in my office rang. Click went the answer-phone. With an effort, I stopped myself running into the office and closing the door against the unanswered questions.

A naked Charlie came back into the room, and dressed with his back to me. 'Are you going to stay there all day?'

The Cellophane crackled as he unpacked his laundered shirt.

'No.' I took my turn in the bathroom, which was steamy; the air-conditioner whined like an old dingbat. I got into the shower and ran it as hot as I could take, then cold. Good for cellulite, circulation and complexion.

A fully dressed Charlie appeared at the doorway. ''Bye, darling.' He shot his shirt cuffs. He looked washed, brushed, clever and wily – the Charlie who appeared in court.

The other Charlie, the softie, the loving one, who told me he was mine, lived here.

I couldn't bear to part with our differences still churning between us. I grabbed a towel and I kissed him and my damp hair dripped on to his suit.

He grasped me tight and kissed me back. 'I'll be late.'

The front door slammed.

I loved being alone in the flat. The solitude felt safe. Here, I could stretch and settle like a cat. I enjoyed travelling – who didn't? – but after a while, in Rome, Sydney or India, the call of where I belonged sounded in my ear. Lost in the Wild Wood, Mole in *The Wind in the Willows* lifted his face and sniffed the air: 'Home . . .' And so did I.

Embankment Court was a block of riverside flats, with a gym and a swimming-pool, necessities in our lifestyle. Our apartment had two bedrooms. 'One for the non-speaking nights,' I said, when Charlie and I originally inspected it.

'On non-speaking nights, you'll be with me in our bed

because if we have a disagreement we'll talk about it,' Charlie retorted, and ran his finger down my spine (which held up the practical discussions). The kitchen was small, which was not good, but the sitting room was huge, light and airy – a statement – and my office overlooked the river.

It was, of course, far too expensive and Charlie had last-minute doubts about it being too opulent, but I persuaded him that we could afford it. 'We'll manage,' I promised. 'I've got good money coming in.'

'We don't *need* such a smart flat.'

'You're allowed to live in a nice place,' I told him. 'Read my lips.'

He uttered a shout of laughter. 'I'd rather kiss 'em.'

That was all right, then.

Crypto-ascetic as Charlie might be, I could not help noticing he enjoyed living in the flat – almost more than I did.

The river provided daily theatre. Sometimes its water was sullen and crushed. At others it reflected dazzling starbursts of light and movement. Adjectives clicked along my descriptive abacus: captivating, changeable, unreliable, dangerous, spoilt. Today it was calm, nondescript and benign.

My first call was to India. 'Just going to bell you,' she said. 'Got your diary?'

I loved India, we were friends, but there was no question of my confiding to her any problems with Charlie. I reached for the palm-top. 'Go ahead.'

'Deep breath, Siena . . .'

Together we roughed out the schedules for *Fashion, This Week*, a couple of appearances on afternoon television programmes and the trip to New York. The year was blocked out with frightening speed.

'Now,' said India, 'I think it's about time you did a book.'

'Oh, my God.'

'No bleating,' said India, severely. 'Many girls would give their eye-teeth to be in your position. So wise up and let me put out some flyers.'

I wised up. Afterwards I worked through a pile of magazines that were delivered each week. It was my business to know what was going on in my neck of the woods and the magazines were the voices – soft-focus but ruthless, pretty but pretty tough – that issued invitations to step into a Never-never Land of perfect food, perfect surroundings and perfect clothes. I glanced over at the letter I had pinned to the noticeboard and managed to reread: '. . . our outer covering is of little significance compared to what is within.' Perhaps as we, the magazine readers, plodded towards an aspirational heaven of distressed houses and gardens and fragrant, purposeful wardrobes, the writer of that letter had spotted a flaw in the blueprint.

I leafed through one magazine that used cheaper paper and did not concern itself with the cutting edge or frills but concentrated on traditional fare – recipes for quick cheese meals, advice on how to lose weight without dieting, a hundred and one uses for Tupperware – and my attention was caught by an interview with a woman who had gone in search of her mother, who had given her up for adoption over four decades ago: 'My name is Kathleen but I didn't know who I was . . .'

Kathleen had found her mother who, it turned out, unmarried and disgraced, had been made to part with her baby. The photographs accompanying the piece showed the birth-mother as a teenager, in the tightly cinched skirt, buttoned blouse and hat of the fifties. The clothes far better suited to an older woman than to the girl who wore them badly. They imposed certain inflexible requirements on their wearer: a rigour of suspender belts, whalebone and modesty.

I touched the young, frightened, bewildered face with a fingertip. I had so many choices, and she had been permitted so few.

I checked my watch.

Running late.

The offices of *Fashion, This Week* hummed. A fleet of messengers whisked in and out of Reception and girls manoeuvred racks of clothes in and out of the lifts. Journalists in serious black talked into their mobile phones. The fashion brigade looked icy in cut-off trousers, and photographers wore uniform leather. The girl who was employed to maintain the plants in the atrium was cleaning the leaves of the *ficus* one by one.

On the third floor, I picked my way over piles of clothes, dodged racks and discovered Jenni ranting into the phone. 'Why the hell do we have to use free-lancers?' she was saying. 'They cause more trouble, more work, and we're perfectly capable of doing it ourselves, much better, actually.' She glanced up, saw me and reddened. 'Speak later,' she muttered, and terminated the conversation.

To say that Jenni disapproved of the freelancer was an under-estimation. Freelancers were a threat, a nuisance and a slur on the internal team's creativity.

'Hi,' I said, amused.

Jenni recovered her composure. 'Lucy Thwaite rang. She wants to duck out.'

'Hell. Why?'

Jenni examined a cuticle. 'You're the one who'll know. What do you want to do about the photographer? And who do you want to use as back-up? This is an arse, Siena.'

She was right.

Of course, Lucy's defection might have been my fault, which was what Jenni was implying. Her anxiety was infectious (and easily caught): she was worried that a glitch like this would reflect badly on her and it didn't take too many mistakes at *Fashion, This Week* before an outsider was transformed into an unemployed outsider.

'Let me phone her.' I dialled the number. 'Is that Lucy? Hallo, this is Siena Grant.' In the background, I heard a couple of the children screaming at each other.

'Excuse me,' said Lucy, and pitched her voice a professional decibel over the children's. 'Stop it, you lot.' She returned to the phone. 'Look, I don't think this is going to do me any good, or you.'

I took a deep breath. 'Lucy, if you're going back to work, it will help if you get some advice on looking your

27

best. It *does* help, I promise you, and I've got some good ideas that I think will be perfect.' Jenni listened as I cajoled and persuaded. After a couple of minutes, I sensed a thaw at the other end of the line and when I hung up Lucy had agreed to honour the appointment at the photographer's studio the following day.

'OK,' I reported to Jenni. 'She's up for it.'

'Well done,' she said, trapped between the desire to avoid a crisis and her disappointment at being defrauded of a little *Schadenfreude*.

We returned to the problem of Lucy Thwaite and spent the next hour or so working out how to edge past the barriers that, as a put-upon mother of three, she had erected, and to clothe her so that her lovely skin and neckline showed to advantage while her stomach and hips were camouflaged. Once this was achieved, who knew where Lucy Thwaite would go next?

After that Jenni and I checked photographs of next week's victim on the light box, marked them up and gave the all-clear to Production.

I told Jenni she looked fabulous in her black trousers and wraparound jersey top and she actually gave me a smile when I left.

I know that I have good taste but I cannot claim any credit for it since it was handed down to me by my parents. They came from families who, over the generations, had had time and money to develop and indulge it; the family houses and their contents were famous until recently when everything vanished: paintings, tapestries, trust funds and land.

My mother never talks about her family but my brother Richard and I were brought up in a small cottage close to our father's ancestral home, a beautiful Queen Anne mansion, which he had sold to a princeling from somewhere or other.

My mother derived huge amusement from the comic aspects of the situation and fired regular postcard bulletins to me in her overlarge handwriting. 'The orange trees died in the last frost, darling. No one took them in.' Or 'Mrs Fleet tells me the loo-roll holders are pure gold.' Or 'Guess what, Siena! A Porsche has been abandoned on the lawn.'

My father ignored the comedy. The wound of losing his family home never healed. From early on, I noticed that he took pains to avoid the big house: on his daily walks he made an extra loop to keep it out of sight. When I taxed him on this, he was genuinely surprised. 'Do I do that, Siena? I don't mean to.'

It is intriguing to analyse what we mean and don't mean to do, and my father's unconscious response to his loss made me wonder if we had any say over ourselves at all.

Consider (Charlie's word). I love Charlie. I want to spend my life with him and do whatever it takes to make this possible. These are my conscious aims and desires. But what are the fears — of oblivion and obliteration? — the wayward desires, the goblins of selfishness and ego that prowl through my subconscious to prevent me doing this?

'I used to search for my baby,' said Kathleen's mother, in that magazine article. 'Everywhere. I looked into prams, I looked at babies on the bus. Sometimes, I stood outside the local school playground, and thought: That could be my daughter. Everywhere I went, there was her shadow. They told me to forget I had ever had a baby, but that's impossible. Impossible.'

Chapter Three: Barbara

My Darling [wrote Ryder, in January 1941],

Have you forgiven me? It was a such silly, small thing over which to have a fight. Will you put it down to nerves — which I don't like admitting to, but they are there, and make me say stupid things?

I am writing this in the mess, having had a pint with Johnny, which is our way of putting off thoughts of tomorrow. The word is that things will be happening, so I wanted to prepare by making things right with you.

It was such an effort to leave you, and I feel part of myself peeling away when I do. But that is the only way I can work it.

This letter is all about me. It should really be all about you. But I wanted you to know that I have thought about you with love and gratitude. I want you to remember that, whatever happens. Please believe, I am your devoted husband.

Ryder was better at expressing himself on paper than in spoken words, and he wrote this letter to me eighteen years ago.

'And this,' said Bunty Andrews, my friend, with a look of see-how-clever-I-am-as-a-hostess, 'is Alexander Liberty, our new lodger, and here with us for a while because . . .' Bunty rolled her eyes, on which she had patched bright blue eyeshadow without reference to the shape of the lids, '. . . he is studying – What's it called? Psychoanalysis. Have I got it right, Alexander? Needs feeding up but he's very house-trained. Alexander, this is my great friend Barbara Beeching.'

Alexander held out his hand and I shook it. He was, I reckoned, twenty-three or twenty-four.

She did not wait for his response. 'As for Barbara, well, there's no better bridge player. A demon at the baize. Her friends love and hate her because she does everything so well, and her children are nice, too. Of course, her Roy had gone and got himself a serious girlfriend, which makes my girls very cross.'

This was the Andrewses' spring cocktail party and Bunty, cigarette in hand, was feverish and tired. She thrust a plate towards me. 'Have some. It's a new kind of spreadable cheese but I fear it's disgusting.'

Nevertheless, she was enjoying her moment of social triumph and, thanks to the gin, the party was humming. She melted away, leaving a residue of smoke.

'I'm sorry,' I addressed Alexander Liberty, 'you should be talking to the girls . . . I'm sure you'd prefer it.'

There were at least six girls, including my daughter Amy, and Bunty's Sylvia and Mary, clustered around the drinks trolley.

'Indeed I would,' he said and, for a startled second, I thought he meant it. Then I knew he possessed a sense of humour. 'Talking to someone such as yourself, Mrs Beeching, will tax me greatly.'

He was tall and thin, with the pared slenderness of the

youth who had not had time to bulk out into the grown man. Lightly tanned (where had he been?), with hair the colour of corn just before it is harvested, he looked clever, interesting, and just a shade vulnerable. He was rather shabby, too: his tweed jacket had seen years of service. As a housewife, I knew that sort of thing without thinking about it. He had cut himself shaving: there was a small, fresh nick under his ear. But he had a purity of profile, a smoothness of skin that reminded me of a Greek statue I had seen in the British Museum. Or was it Roman? Not being well educated in these things, I wasn't sure.

Returning my gaze, he raised an eyebrow, as if to say, 'You may scrutinize me as much as you like. In return, I will look at you.' But he was polite, too: he was waiting for me to initiate the conversation. Or perhaps he was making up his mind about what he saw. For the record, it was a forty-two-year-old woman in a green, full-skirted dress, black court shoes and red lipstick.

'Interesting name, Liberty.' I rolled my glass between my fingers.

'It's a corruption from the Polish. My family fled here after they fell out of favour with one king or another. I can't remember which. It was ages ago.' He touched a knuckle to his forehead. 'Actually, I do but it's not important.'

'I'm glad you weren't there during the war,' I said.

There was a small, hard silence. 'Yes, we escaped that. My family were lucky to have settled here.'

My gin and tonic had long ago lost its chill. I took a sip, and it was both bitter and oversweet. I had never liked alcohol very much, only the sensations that accompanied it. Not that I over-indulged as a rule, but Ryder was always bringing back whisky, gin and exotic liqueurs from his flying trips and we had developed preferences – or, rather, had come to discriminate, and the Andrewses' party gin was a cheap brand.

'Psychoanalysis,' I said. 'Does that mean you're a doctor?'

'Sort of. Will be. I've been training in London and Switzerland, and now I'm doing a stint at St Bede's.'

I noted his eyes were hazel, with long lashes. I was curious to know more. 'Psychiatrists try to see inside us.'

'Not "see" exactly. No one can do that.'

That was good, I thought. We range so far and deep in our secret lives and thoughts that it is best that we keep them to ourselves.

Disconcertingly, he suggested, 'Perhaps you're thinking that we need to keep our thoughts private. We *need* to keep a lot of thoughts private, but it is good to sort out what we mean.' I must have coloured, or looked taken aback, for a smile twitched his lips. 'Particularly when we need to understand a problem.'

His gaze slid round Bunty's sitting room, spacious but fussily fitted up. The girls by the drinks trolley chattered away like fledglings, and their skirts made a Constance Spry garden of pastels. Otherwise, the guests were mostly middle-aged, settled and established, pretty innocuous. Over by the window, a tweed-suited Major Blunt was discussing daffodil bulbs with Ryder, my husband of twenty-four years. Then he said, 'You're thinking I'm not old enough to know what I'm talking about.'

'Not at all. I was thinking it must be wonderful to be able to respond to problems in a fresh, new way. Before . . . one has become . . . well, bothered and changed by one's experiences.'

His reply took a little while and, when it came, startled me. 'And I was thinking how interesting it is to have experience.'

I thought of the years, where the seconds, minutes and hours were notched up in order. How I had stroked and groomed them with routines and quiet application. 'Yes, it is interesting,' I agreed.

This time I blushed properly. I pulled myself together and tried again. 'You're hoping to find out what motivates us?'

'*Yes*,' he said passionately, and I knew I'd touched a nerve, 'because it helps to heal and to understand. Sickness of body is not just physical. We need to know what part the mind plays, and how we respond to traumatic events. Or merely to our past.' He held up a hand. 'But, please, don't let me bore you.'

More than anything, I wished I could say something intelligent, something original he would think about later. 'Please – go on. Do we need to understand our past? Surely it's best forgotten in some instances.'

Unembarrassed, he studied my face and I knew he was trying to read me. 'Take the child. How does it resolve its conflicts with its parents and grow to healthy adulthood? We don't know. Freud, for example, believed that a child desires to possess the parent of the opposite sex, and to exclude, to kill, even, the parent of the same sex.'

'How – how inconvenient.'

'Are you laughing at me, Mrs Beeching?'

'No, I wouldn't do that . . . well, only a little.'

He held up a hand in mock defeat. 'I believe Freud and his theories have succeeded in changing the way we look at ourselves.'

'I'm sorry. I didn't mean to tease – I've always found that family life cannot be categorized easily. But I promise to think about it,' I added. 'Please call me Barbara and I *would* like to know more.'

His eyes widened a little at this shocking intimacy. 'I'd love to try and explain, but it would take too long.' He shifted the subject, and I was conscious of a reproof, a slight withdrawal. 'Mrs Andrews mentioned that you're a demon bridge player?'

'I hate most games, particularly physical ones. Ask me to play Monopoly, or Consequences, or worse, Charades, and I'll vanish in a puff of boredom and dread. But with cards, deal me a hand and I can divine the intention of my foe, the fall of the next card. Ryder – my husband – says that when I die, they'll open me up and find the suits engraved on my heart.'

'So, you *are* a watcher. An observer.' He inflicted the last word as if he had been considering what and who I was for some time.

And I felt absurdly flattered to be taken so seriously. 'Oh, I'm not afraid to go for the kill. I lose any softness and double my guile.'

'I'm terrified.' He flashed a smile, both shy and a little wicked. 'Do you play with or against your husband?'

'Occasionally I let him win,' I said.

The exchange was nothing, almost meaningless. But I had enjoyed it. Immensely.

At this point Ryder detached himself from Major Blunt and came over to me. 'Darling, should we be going?'

I introduced him to Alexander and explained what he did, and Ryder said, in the hearty manner he adopted when he was not sure of his ground, 'A trick-cyclist? I've always wanted to know what they *do*.'

'You know perfectly well what they do,' I said, and turned to Alexander. 'Ryder only pretends he has a tin ear and short patience for this kind of thing. In fact, he knows more about it than I do.'

I sensed impatience on the part of Alexander Liberty, and wanted to protest: *'No, no, my husband isn't like that really.'*

It was with relief that I saw Bunty bearing down on us. 'Alexander, I'm afraid duty calls.' She addressed Ryder and me: 'This young man is kindly escorting the girls to the cinema and they're anxious to be off.'

I laid a hand on my husband's arm. 'We mustn't delay you, then.'

The two men looked at each other. Once upon a time, Ryder had had the sort of . . . well, the *beauty* with which Alexander Liberty had been endowed – glowing, un-marked and flawless.

'Goodbye, then. It's been interesting meeting you,' said Ryder.

Embarrassed by Ryder – which did not often happen – I took care to shake Alexander Liberty's hand and he pressed my fingers as if to say, 'I enjoyed our conversation.'

'Thank goodness for that,' Ryder muttered into my ear. He put a hand on my waist and guided me out of the room. 'I want to go home.'

I woke early – with the birth of Roy and Amy, the habit of lying-in had vanished for ever. Now, when I opened my eyes, there was no luxurious slide into consciousness but a rush of light, sense and purpose.

It was Tuesday, four days after I had met Alexander Liberty.

At some point during the previous night, Ryder would have returned from his latest trip and, not wishing to disturb me, slept in the dressing room that opened off our bedroom. These were his 'duty' nights, as he put it. He preferred to have a little solitude and space in which to ease away the cares and responsibilities of flying the huge Stratocruiser. Either that, or his nightmares were plaguing him, which they did from time to time, and he took himself off in order not to wake me.

I admired Ryder very much. I always had. It takes courage and coolness to master a shuddering, whining aircraft and guide it to safety. I asked him whether he found it an intolerable burden having so many lives to worry about. 'It's different from flying solo and there's no excitement of the chase. Then, again, I don't have an enemy on my tail and there's no horrible feeling of uncertainty.' He dropped a kiss on the top of my head. 'I try not to complicate the issues.'

The remark was not intended as a rebuke, but it was a

neat encapsulation of our different personalities. Ryder was – basically – decisive and quick to act. I took my time: moulding, nipping and tucking, rolling something around in my mind until I felt I had made a shape with which I could work. 'Don't worry,' I reassured him, when I pointed this out. 'Our differences make our marriage more interesting.'

I got up and pulled on my padded satin dressing-gown, which was duck-egg blue and chosen, with Bunty egging me on, to flatter my colouring. I squinted through the crack in the door to Ryder's dressing room and was reassured by the sight of his uniform folded over the chair. Like many men, he looked good in uniform. A cunning eye at Headquarters had selected the dark blue and gold braid of the British Overseas Airways Corporation that set off Ryder's typical English looks and, now that he was a captain, his air of authority. Currently he was flying the Nigeria run: Frankfurt, Rome, Tripoli, then the big leg to Kano and, finally, the ease-down into Lagos. The journey took twenty-four hours, and the crew rested for two nights in hotels before the return journey.

'Tell me about these places,' I begged my well-travelled husband, more than once. He did his best. Frankfurt had a world-famous zoo. Rome was big and noisy. Tripoli, well – Ryder gave one of his little coughs – you had to be careful in Tripoli. 'And Kano?' I urged. Apparently Kano lay on the edge of the northern desert, and desert tribes, the beautiful Falani and Tuareg, rode into town to trade horse blankets and saddles. Lagos was humid, and the trees bloomed bright red and orange, the Yoruba wives ran the markets, and Ryder drank orange juice out of green glass bottles for breakfast.

'Is that all?'

'What more do you want to know?'

'I'm not sure.'

Ryder looked patient. 'Then how can I answer, my darling?'

'All right, then. What does it *feel* like to be in Africa?' Did the sun sear the skin? Did the spring smell different from our damp, horse-chestnut-blossomed one here? Where did the snakes live? How do Africans react to white faces?

'Silly, Babs. There are no seasons in the tropics.'

Ryder tended to stay put in the hotels: so many bugs waited to pounce on the unwary Anglo-Saxon and he had to be in tip-top condition. (I remembered a picture in *National Geographic* of the tuberculosis bacterium. A bright, elongated rod-shape that looked too interesting to be what it was.)

Ryder added, 'You can never be too careful in Africa. Dreadful things can happen in the rainforest, or on lonely roads. I've heard stories . . . One family hired what they thought was a reliable guard to watch the house at night and he killed them.'

What I had never confessed to Ryder was that I rather liked my 'duty' nights – only I called them 'off-duty' nights, when I was exempt from the intimacies of washing, sleeping and dressing in the presence of another being. When – unwisely – I had mentioned how I valued my solitude to Bunty, she was scandalized. 'Makes you sound like a hysterical old maid,' she said. 'You don't mean it, darling.'

I didn't refer to it again.

Now I crept down the passage to the bathroom. The water would be cold – Ryder had used up the last of the hot when he came in – and my feet cramped on the linoleum. I ran a small amount into the basin and scrubbed my face with soap. My skin responded by tightening over the cheekbones. The face, according to *Good Housekeeping*, had to be kept scrupulously clean.

The cold drove splinters into my shrinking flesh and I dressed as quickly as possible. Knickers, brassière, and the girdle that pummelled my stomach into shape. Over them went the tweed skirt made by Mrs Fellowes in Quarry Street, my favourite twin-set in coral lambswool and, finally, my stockings.

I twisted my hair up into its chignon – I was lucky for I was a pure blonde with dark eyebrows and brown eyes. No white hairs as yet, but even so ... 'By forty,' the wretched *Good Housekeeping* had also pointed out, 'a woman is settled and she cannot expect fireworks or to retain the glowing good looks of her youth ...'

No?

Apparently not.

Downstairs, Ryder's braided cap lay on the hall table, and I hung it up on the hat-stand, which had been a present from big-game hunter Uncle Victor. It was a tasteless thing with an elephant's foot as the base, but Ryder was fond of it so there was no question of getting rid of it.

I shivered. Being cold was so wearisome. *Dulling*,

because you could think of nothing else. I wished we had central-heating like the Sidneys, whose cottage was wrapped in delicious warmth. But even if we could have afforded to install a system, our home was a big Victorian villa with attics and cellars that would eat up fuel.

The kitchen still smelt faintly of my marmalade-making session, which was not unpleasant. I carried the coal hod by the Rayburn, which heated the water and on which I cooked, down to the cellar, shovelled in the anthracite and got warm that way instead.

The Rayburn was sluggish this morning – I didn't blame it – and I riddled away until it rewarded me with a gleam. I stuck the kettle on the top, snatched my garden coat from the cloakroom, let myself out at the back door and went to see to the hens.

A master confectioner had been up in the night, piping a skim of frost over the lawn, trees and the garden bench. It glimmered white and black, beautiful and harsh, wrapping the garden in silence. My feet left black prints as I walked past the tennis court and the tiny orchard beside it. It was not really an orchard for there were only five trees but they were heavy croppers. A poem said – and I can't remember who wrote it – that frost was good for apples.

> Keep cold, young orchard. Goodby and keep cold.
> Dread fifty above more than fifty below.

I went down the steps to the vegetable garden where the recently dug earth was frozen into chunks between rows of cabbages and Brussels sprouts – the handiwork of Herr Schlinker, who came twice a week to work there. My feet slid on the paving-stones and my breath accompanied me in clouds. A subdued clucking came from the hen-house, but when I let them out, the hens were not anxious to start the day either, and I had to shoo them into the run. The night boxes were warm from their bodies, and acrid with urine, but it was a good earthy smell. I parted the straw and searched for eggs. There were four: two alabaster white, tinged with green, and two yellow brown, stained and decorated with wispy underbelly feathers.

Cheeks glowing, I bore them back to the kitchen where I discovered Ryder, looking helpless. 'Didn't know what you'd planned for breakfast, Babs.'

'What do we normally have for breakfast?'

'Bacon and eggs.'

I favoured him with a look and reached for the frying-pan.

We always had breakfast in the dining room and the bacon was cold by the time I'd ferried the dishes through. I began on mine. 'Is your bacon cold, Ryder?'

'A bit.'

'Darling, why don't we get a table for the kitchen and have breakfast in there? Everybody's doing it and the bacon would be hot.'

It was a subject I had introduced every so often, for I had planned my table strategy. With Ryder, it was best to cast a stone into the pond and wait for the ripples. More often than he knew, and a campaign sometimes took a year or so, I achieved victory. The best and most productive were the ones where Ryder ended up convinced that my idea had been his in the first place.

'I don't want to lower standards,' he said. 'Kitchens are for cooking.'

'Says you.' I leant forward. 'I promise you, no standards will fall. But if you don't wish it . . . It's good for my waist-line, darling, to keep fetching and carrying, and now that Amy's away so much, I don't feel so tired.'

'Barbara, I hope you're not overdoing it.'

Satisfied with my progress, I finished my bacon, knowing that in the not-so-distant future we would have a breakfast table in the kitchen.

While Ryder read *The Times*, I tried unsuccessfully to read the front page, gave up, reached for my notebook and wrote, 'Cheese, butter, bacon. Cake – walnut?'

The day's shape unfolded – normal, quiet, busy.

Ryder handed me *The Times*. I smoothed it out: 26 February 1959. Today. Later I would read it from cover to cover, for I craved to know what went on in the world. For the present, I made do with the crossword. This was both a delight and an irritant: frequently it reduced me to frustration at my lack of . . . well, my lack.

First clue: 'Barbarians riding'.

I tsked, and Ryder looked up. 'For goodness' sake, why do you persist in doing it?'

'To get better.'

'Could you get better in silence, darling?'

The telephone cut in and I got up to answer it. A voice said, 'Not so chipper today, Mrs Beeching. I won't be in.'

'That's fine, Mrs Storr.' But it wasn't. The absence of Mrs Storr, who had been sent a little deranged and erratic by the loss of her only son in the Korean war, meant that I would be cooking twice today.

I leant against the hat-stand. Tuesday meant beef rissoles. (Monday was cold beef with pickle and mashed potato.) Wednesday . . . If Mrs Storr came in I would ask her to eke out the remnants of the joint in a cottage pie.

'Mrs Storr,' I informed Ryder, 'won't be in.' He didn't look at me. 'I don't think she'll ever recover from Kevin, you know.'

Now he did. 'Do you need more help? Should we get rid of her? If you *are* feeling overtired . . .'

'No.' I sat down and reached for the last piece of toast. 'I think women should run nations.'

'Wars are a necessary evil,' said Ryder, mildly enough.

I spooned marmalade on to my plate and inspected it. 'Isn't that rather defeatist?'

'If you like,' he replied, still cool and patient, 'but realistic. I don't doubt women's negotiating skills. And I don't doubt yours.' He smiled lovingly at me. 'But you have more important things to think about.'

I had to think about the shopping.

I put on my black hat with the feather, and my coat with the narrow rabbit-fur trim, picked up my shopping basket and called goodbye to Ryder.

'Don't be too long.' He leant over the banister on the landing. 'Otherwise I'll miss you.'

'Stupid.' I blew him a kiss.

Edgeborough Road was steep, and I walked to the top with tingling calves, turned right and went down the hill, past Mount Alvernia Hospital to the Epsom road, where I turned left. This was the route I took before I was laden with purchases. On the way back, I took the shorter one along the main road.

I passed the Odeon on my left. Alexander and the girls would have sat in the stuffy dark, giggling and eating popcorn. Before Amy had left for London on Sunday evening, she grudgingly disclosed that Alexander had been good company and she had enjoyed the film.

I crossed the street to the library and returned a book on the history of bridge. While the librarian searched for my ticket, I rifled idly through the volumes on the 'returned' shelf while I decided what to read next.

A voice said in my ear, Alexander Liberty's voice, '. . . a watcher. An observer.' And '. . . it is good to sort out what we mean.'

Then, suddenly, I was alight with excitement, impatience, *greed* to know more. I was licking my lips, metaphorically speaking, ready to bite into knowledge.

'Mrs Beeching.' The librarian handed me my ticket. 'Mrs Beeching? Can I be of any assistance?'

I smiled calmly at her. 'No, thank you,' and went to search through the non-fiction shelves for a book by Freud, who had such curious notions about parents and children.

Chapter Four: Barbara

Guildford was changing rapidly. We all saw it and sniffed it and remarked on the pace. The mood was quickening . . . The streets were becoming a magnet for shops and shoppers. There was an influx of new and ready money, a civic bustle, prising the city away from its sleepy past.

I liked it.

It was only ten thirty when I reached the high street but it was already crowded.

Recently, and to great excitement, a boutique had opened opposite Holy Trinity Church, which sold gramophone records in brown paper sleeves, and a larger one beside it, which specialized in electric lamps. Bunty and I inspected the window minutely.

'I'm going to have to buy one,' she announced.

'But you don't need a lamp.'

'I know, darling, but it's so exciting to have a choice.'

During the war there had been nothing much, apart from whisky and cigarettes. We made do and mended furiously, patriotically, and did not allow ourselves to think about colour, variety, the pleasure of making up one's mind. The appetite for those returned afterwards, in the dull, deprived, dun-coloured peace when there had been nothing to look at and nothing to buy. Now it was different.

As always, there was a queue in Sainsbury's and I amused myself by mentally replacing the brown packets of tea on the shelf with the blue sugar bags. Two cart-wheels of Cheddar and a mound of butter were being cut up by muslin-turbaned women. Yellow, satiny, rich, lush . . . painters had used those cheese and butter colours – the French painters who wanted to convey a new impression of what they saw. Throughout the war, my mother had worn a headscarf of that precise buttery shade because European Jews had been made to wear yellow stars, and she argued that solidarity had to begin somewhere. Busy with my children and focused on getting through the rationing and the bombs while Ryder was away on flying operations, I washed my hair in yellow camomile rinse to make it more golden and shiny. Surviving was all I could manage. 'That's fine, dear,' my mother said. 'Having principles is only possible when you're older.'

Next door at the counter of Fuller's tea-shop, there was a choice between a medium or a large walnut cake. Oh, the luxury of dithering, of weighing up the pros and cons. I hoped I'd never get used to it.

The shop assistant made a fuss of wrapping and boxing the cake (large), and I anticipated the texture of the thin, sweet icing and, underneath, the crumbling light-as-air sponge. A little impatient, a little too hot in my tightly belted coat, I glanced in the direction of the tables. The tea-room was full. Knives clinked on plates, conversation hummed and a queue waited for tables to empty. Then I saw him.

Alexander Liberty was sitting close to the window,

talking hard to a companion, a dark-haired boy of his own age. They were dressed in tweed jackets, ties and Fair Isle pullovers, and a half-empty plate of cakes lay between them.

'Madam.' The sales assistant gave me the cake box.

As I handed over the money, Alexander spotted me. He got to his feet instantly. 'Barbara.' He held out his hand. 'I was hoping I'd see you again. Was I rude to you at Mrs Andrews's party? Or, worse, *did* I bore you to death? If I did, I ask forgiveness.'

'No, no,' I protested, 'not at all. You gave me food for thought.'

'Good.'

He looked at me intently, piercingly, to see if I'd meant what I said, and – God help me – it was as if the shapes, objects and people of this familiar setting shifted and resettled, like the earth after a quake.

'Amy tells me you walked her home from the cinema the other night. Thank you.' I fussed with the cake box; its scent of spun sugar and walnuts sent saliva rushing into my mouth. 'Walnut cake,' I balanced it on my hands. 'We're fond of it – I eat too much, and I shouldn't.'

'Why shouldn't you?'

'No reason,' I said. 'Frugal habits from the war, I suppose.'

'Of course,' he said politely, and I wished I hadn't mentioned the war. It was so weary a subject, and it made me feel old. 'Would you join us?' he asked. He indicated his companion at the table. 'My colleague, Harry, would be delighted to meet you, particularly . . .'

'Particularly?'

'Particularly as I think you'd be interested in some of the ideas we're discussing.'

I would be interested. How delightful, and novel, it was to be included in such a conversation. Intrigued, I glanced down at the wretched cake box, and struggled with my conscience – there were chores to do at home. 'Don't be too long,' Ryder had said. I noted the intricate seaming of my brown leather gloves, but also my surge of excitement, and that I no longer felt a bit old.

'Thank you,' I replied, 'but no, I don't have time. I must get home.'

He seemed disappointed but not surprised. 'Harry and I were discussing Freud's theory of the memory slip, and we could have used you as a guinea pig. You could give us valuable data.'

I could not resist it. 'Such as?'

'The theory tries to explain why we forget the names or intentions of people and events that are quite important to us.'

'Excuse me.' A woman edged round us.

Alexander glanced back at Harry. 'It takes a little while to explain.'

'Then why don't you come and have Sunday lunch with us? Amy's coming down from London, and I – I mean I'm sure *she* would like to see you again.'

I found a woman's washbag once, on the beach at Teignmouth. It was years ago when the children were still small. We holidayed there every summer and, as often as not, we scooped up Sophie, Ryder's niece, and took her with us. She was the daughter of his brother, an only child, and her parents, Ian and Antonia, were unhappy with each other. 'I think it would be good for her if she spent time with us.' Ryder never alluded directly to the state of his brother's marriage, but I understood well enough.

A sweet, bold child, she was fearless, but accident prone. 'Sophie's cut herself'; 'Sophie's fallen down'; 'Sophie's fallen in' were daily cries, and I became expert in patching up her wounds.

'Aunt Babs,' she was weeping tears of pain after cutting herself rock-pooling, 'Aunt Babs, when I grow up I want to be just like you.'

The disinfectant I dabbed on her knees hurt her more than the cut, and I leant over and held her close. 'That's the nicest thing anybody could possibly say to me.'

Roy, Amy and Sophie were now adults, but Ryder and I still holidayed in Teignmouth each year. Sometimes they came too, but not as often as I would have liked. Ryder was fond of the town, and it suited his needs. He travelled so much, he said, that he couldn't bear the extra fuss of elaborate journeys. He just wanted peace and quiet.

We had discovered Blatchford's, a clifftop hotel, on our first visit and we engaged the same room year after year. It overlooked the beach, which had a wide sweep and plenty of safe sand, and a serenade of waves and seagulls sent us to sleep and woke us. Most mornings, we climbed down the steps cut into the red rock of the cliff, checked there was no train in sight, crossed the railway and dug in for the duration.

I was an expert, too, at managing the duration. In the early days, I learnt to wrap up sandwiches tightly in greaseproof paper so the sand couldn't get in. I knew that Roy would demand the green bucket and Amy would have to make do with the grey one. In the basket, I packed Elastoplasts for knees and toes, a packet of Spangles for bribes, and I made sure there were extra socks, clothes and towels for wet little bodies, and a library book for Ryder.

I had to be good at managing. It was my job. But, over the years, I had grown wary of using that word. Men, I noticed, were a little tricky on the subject of women and jobs. Being good at my 'job', though, bought me a little time and space, which I needed. If Ryder was busy with his book, and the children with their sandcastles, I was free to think – like the Japanese who, it was said, had so little space in their crowded country that their only source of true privacy was inside their heads.

That morning I felt restless. A couple of days ago there had been a storm and the sea was still angry. I checked the three children, who were busy with their sandcastles, buttoned my cardigan over my swimming costume and announced, 'I'm going for a stroll. Can you watch the children?'

Ryder barely looked up from his book. 'Don't be too long.'

I placed a finger against his cheek. 'What if I never come back?'

'Don't say that. Even as a joke.'

Skirting the high-water mark, solitary and deliciously

unfettered, I struck out along the beach. The weather was improving and there was even a suggestion of sun on my back. Sand, damp velvet beneath my toes ... seaweed draped over rocks, salt-encrusted driftwood. Then my foot struck a hard object and I looked down to see a plain white china cup and saucer and, beside them, a man's sock. Further along, resting above the tidemark, there was a small suitcase: brown attaché, well worn, and water-stained.

The boning in my swimming costume bit into my flesh as I knelt down and prised open the case. Inside there was a washbag in pink sprigged material, a small torch and a pair of scissors. I hesitated. Had someone died? I inserted finger and thumb into the sodden washbag, and drew out a box. I sensed that someone, a woman, *was* dead. I knew what that box – domed and rigid – contained. I had one too.

'Barbara!' Ryder's shout echoed down the beach. I looked up. He was on his feet, waving and pointing to Roy, who was hopping up and down, evidently crying. Quickly, I scooped up handfuls of sand and buried the box, a decent burial for a private thing, and hurried back to the children.

Roy had trodden on a weaver-fish. 'What do I do?' Ryder was trying to calm the frantic child. 'Is there anything we can do?'

I dived into the picnic basket, wrenched open the Thermos, and poured as much as I dared over Roy's wound – the warm tea would draw out the poison. Within minutes the pain had gone. 'That's what you do for a weaver-fish bite,' I informed Ryder.

That evening I inquired of Mr Ellis, the hotel proprietor, if there had been an accident. 'A yacht did go down,' he confirmed, 'ten miles up the coast, in the storm. Took with it the skipper, his mate and a woman.'

Had she been blonde or brunette? Married or with her lover? Did she feel that her life had been worthwhile as she fought in the cold water to stay alive, for she would have fought? Whatever she might or might not have been, how ironic, sad, inevitable was it that of all the things to survive her death it had been evidence of her fertility. Her femaleness.

Unexpectedly, Roy had driven down from London with Amy on Friday evening. 'Hope I'm not putting you out, Mother,' he had said, as he kissed me. 'I've asked Victoria over for lunch on Sunday.'

I had stood back to look at him. Already Roy had become the man he would be for the rest of his life. Rather grave, serious and nice, the sort of person who did not want to take risks but would drive a steady course down the middle. Was this a kind appraisal? Guilty, I kissed him twice and held him tight.

'All right, Mother!' He stepped away. 'You only saw me last week.'

Ryder had surprised me by reproving him for not giving me more warning. 'Phone your mother next time,' he said. 'She cannot be expected to conjure extra food out of thin air.' Roy looked discomforted.

Later on, he cornered me. 'Do I take advantage of you, Mother?' he wanted to know. 'You must *say*.'

I was up early on Sunday morning, riddled the Rayburn and fed the hens. Outside, the weather was melting into a warmer mood, with a teasing hint of spring in the whipped-cream clouds and softer air.

I dusted the sitting room. Big and gracious, it overlooked the front drive, and had a large fireplace and a bay window, for which I had chosen powder-blue curtains, the colour of an early-summer sky.

The ormolu clock on the mantelpiece struck eight o'clock, a lovely ripple of sound that slid over the seconds, the minutes and the hours. It was an Austrian clock and I was passionately attached to it, not only for its elegance but because it had belonged to my parents.

Two bronze cherubs flanked its face, leaning carelessly and happily against the casing. With a fingertip, I touched the one who was pointing at the dial. *You* don't care about time, I told it silently. *Not really*. The date on the clock face was 1781, the year Mozart had been in Vienna, and on the back was engraved '*Ich spüre nur die Zeit*', which meant, according to Major Blunt, who had translated it for me, 'I feel only time'. (Major Blunt spoke German, for he had worked in intelligence in Berlin after the war, so I reckoned he would have got it right.)

The clock always lifted my spirit: it breathed of the cultivation of the mind, of luxurious elegance, of fantasy and soaring imagination, and of a world where time mattered – of course – but not too much.

'Morning, Mother.' A dressing-gowned Amy put her head round the door.

Duster in hand, I swivelled round. 'Morning, darling.'

Her hair was tousled, her skin shiny with cold cream, and she looked drained from a long week in the ministry typing-pool. 'Darling, would Mrs Trant allow you downstairs in a dressing-gown?'

Mrs Trant was Amy's landlady. After much anxious discussion between Ryder and me as to the amount of freedom Amy should be permitted, we had given in when she pointed out angrily, 'When I'm twenty-one I can do as I please.'

'Don't worry,' Ryder had reassured me later, 'she'll knuckle down when she marries.'

Amy advanced into the sitting room. 'What's Mrs Trant got to do with it? When's everyone arriving?'

I brushed the snarled hair off her face. 'Usual time. Hurry up and get dressed – I need help.'

'Why can't Roy help you?' Amy's eyes were bright and hard with suppressed feeling.

'Is everything all right, Amy?'

'You haven't answered my question, Mother.' She sounded cool enough, but she was angry. 'Why don't you wake Roy?'

'Don't be silly.'

She shook her head. 'Not silly. Roy is as capable of helping you as I am.'

She left the room and went back upstairs. I gave the clock a final flick of the duster. A new, and baffling, obduracy had settled over my daughter. Gone was the giggling girl who had come home from school to confide, with innocence and a kind of earnest joy, the events of her day. Gone were the times when I had listened,

enraptured, to the battles and voyages of the schoolgirl –
replaced by the young woman who had put up a shutter
and invited no questions.

Later, having served the family breakfast and prepared
the lunch, I went upstairs. Ryder had opened the bedroom
window, and the stuffiness of night had been swept away.
I closed it. There was a whiff of mothballs from the open
wardrobe, a hint of vinegar where Mrs Storr had cleaned
the window, the residue of frying from my sweater on the
chair, which I wore when I was cooking. I folded it away:
for so much of the day my energies went into keeping at
bay the sweat, and smells, the evidence of living.

I sat down at the dressing-table and redid my hair. I
dabbed scent on my neck – its sweet, warm essence a
reminder that there were alternatives to scum on dish-
water, the creep of mould in the cellar, the miasma of
human bodies. Music, speculation, adventure and . . .
knowledge. On an impulse, I dabbed scent on my wrists,
just at the point where the pulse beat.

Although she had elected to wear her office skirt and
blouse rather than the dress I had bought her, Amy had
made an effort with her hair, which she had brushed back
from her forehead. It suited her better than the fringe
she preferred. Even so, beside Bunty's daughters Amy
appeared an awkward, solid figure; my anxiety for her
grew and deepened.

At the lunch table, Alexander sat between her and Mary,
and every so often the trio burst into laughter. Victoria,
who had arrived earlier and presented me with a bunch of

carnations and a box of Black Magic, was opposite Roy, who was well scrubbed and smartly dressed in a three-piece suit. Every so often Victoria sent him a melting look. Her hair was very short and tightly permed, and she was encased in a pink print – a pretty doll whom Roy evidently admired.

Bunty's husband, Peter, was placed, of course, next to me. 'Dreadful about the accident on the bypass.' He put another forkful of beef into his mouth and chewed importantly. 'What have I always said about that bypass?'

I fixed my eyes on Peter, of whom I was fond, and heard nothing. *Get on with it*, I wanted to say. *Can't we talk about something important?*

I overheard Alexander: '. . . and then I forced myself to climb back into college and impaled my foot on a spike.'

'Peter, what accident?'

'The racing driver on the A3. Going too fast.'

But I longed to know what had happened to Alexander's foot – in fact, it seemed vital to discover whether the smooth, golden skin and sappy bones underneath were now less perfect.

Peter pressed on with the uphill business of holding my attention. 'Would Ryder like a round of golf?'

I tried my best to focus on him. 'I'm sure he would. Let me see. He's flying all next week. What about the week after?'

Pink-centred, rimmed with brown, the slices of beef still lay on my plate. I could not eat it.

Peter extracted his diary from an inner pocket and checked it. 'Fine.'

'Tell me more!' Amy's voice rose, loud and amused. She had virtually turned her back on Roy, who was on her right. He was discussing central-heating with Bunty, who had the rabbit-in-the-headlights expression on her face.

'Amy.' I got to my feet, which was a signal for her to do likewise.

She contrived to ignore me, and it was Victoria who leapt up with a glad cry: 'Let me, Mrs Beeching . . .'

Victoria was neat and efficient, and I was grateful for her help. 'Apple pie, how lovely.' She darted round the kitchen, scraping and stacking plates. She emitted energy in waves, energy that was directed at making sure I liked her. 'You must give me the recipe,' she said. 'I so love collecting them for jams, chutneys, pies . . .'

I handed Victoria the dessert plates. 'Could you take these in for me, please?'

'Barbara,' she was examining the pie and said, with irritating helpfulness, 'some of the crust is burnt.' She bustled out of the kitchen and I heard her announce, 'Won't be a moment. A bit of an emergency.'

Knife in hand, I gritted my teeth and surveyed the kitchen. The wreckage was everywhere: dirty china stacked high, a tray of cooled fat on the sideboard, the table dusted with flour and bits of meat. The sink had acquired a frieze of cabbage. Hours of work would be required to restore it to order.

I shaved the offending scorchmark off the pie, and carried it triumphantly into the dining room. At my entrance, Alexander glanced up, and the brilliance and

59

mystery of his smile sent a shudder through every bone in my spine.

'When the weather's warmer,' Roy clapped an arm round Alexander's shoulders, 'you must come over and play tennis.'

Leaving Bunty, Peter and Ryder to cook by the fire, the rest of the party had adjourned to the garden for some fresh air.

'I'd like to very much.' Alexander mimed a swingeing forehand shot.

Roy imitated him. 'Let's do it.'

The party wandered down towards the hen-house, and the girls embarked on an egg hunt, shrieking and exclaiming.

'What's in there?' asked Alexander, pointing to the apple-house just visible behind the trees.

I explained what it was and we went towards it.

'Ah, the apple pie,' he said.

'The *burnt* apple pie.'

Alexander was amused. 'Not so very burnt.'

'But tell the truth, Bunty's apple pies are better than mine.'

He struggled a little with that one, and I could not stop myself laughing, which made him blush. 'Apple pie symbolizes the virtues we think are good about the family.'

'And are they good? Those virtues?'

'Well, that's it,' he said. 'I'm not sure they are for everyone. We're all so different.'

I shivered.

The apple-house was not beautiful. It was windowless and built of a cheaper red brick than the house but, inside, it was still fitted up with the original wooden slatted trays stacked up to the roof. It smelt of must and quite a few of the higher trays were damaged.

I pulled one out and displayed the rows of Bramleys and russets. 'It takes hours to rack them,' I picked one up, balanced it on my palm and held it out, 'but it's pleasant enough work. Try.'

Alexander took the apple and bit into it. 'Nice.'

I checked the tray, took out a couple of decaying fruits, and dropped them into the pail left outside the door for that purpose. Later I would empty the sweet-sour rot on to the compost heap.

I pointed to the damaged racks. 'I feel guilty that I let the children use it as a den, but they loved it.'

Alexander ran a hand up the slats. 'Grown-ups keep out. Not allowed.' He turned and grinned at me. 'Can't you remember what it felt like to rule a kingdom with no adults around? I can.'

I looked away. 'I don't think so.' I bent over and retrieved another rotting apple. 'But does one feel any more powerful as an adult?'

He dropped his core into the pail, and wiped his mouth. 'Depends who you are, and if you feel your life is going well.'

'Is yours?' The question flew from me, before I'd had time to consider it. 'Going well?'

'I hope so,' he said. 'And from what I see, husband, children, house, yours must be too.'

I smiled up at him. 'Women aren't powerful. They have to make do with little snippets here and there.'

'Oh, but they are,' Alexander contradicted, 'much, much more so than they think. They exert a terrible power.'

'Do they?' I considered the statement, its pleasing, teasing implications.

I turned and made to push the apple tray back into position. Alexander had the same thought. Our hands collided. His lay on mine.

Beneath his touch, my thoughts fractured into incoherence. 'Alexander . . .'

'Barbara?' With a little sigh, he snatched up my hand and kissed it.

What sort of courage had been required to do that I could not gauge, for I had never made such a gesture, or had it done to me before. But it was funny, and wonderful. 'How ridiculous.' Again, laughter trembled at the back of my throat. 'I could be your mother.'

He looked up at me. 'I'm sorry. No, I'm not sorry . . . but I owe you an apology.'

'No, no. It was a compliment.'

Together we stepped out into the garden. The whole episode must have taken four minutes, possibly five, but no more.

Chapter Five: Siena

'Listen up.' India bullied her way into my early morning. 'I've done a ring-round and Caesar Books are *very* keen – put me something together on paper. OK?'

I made the mistake of looking at my timetable. 'How soon?'

'Yesterday. Just do it, sweetie. Um?'

'Remind me to lower your percentage.'

'And you've been invited on to *The Frocks Quiz*. Interested?'

'Nope.'

'Thought not.'

'Bloody hell,' said Charlie, when I told him about the book offer. He had rushed home from court to change for a dinner in chambers. 'You'll kill yourself.' He pulled off his socks and danced around in his Calvin Kleins. 'But I suppose the money's useful and I'm a bit tight at the moment.' He squinted at the laundry basket and aimed a sock. Then he asked, carefully, for it was a slightly tricky area – no, not tricky, just not as straightforward as it seemed, 'Is it good money, Siena?'

I answered, just as carefully, 'Quite a lot of noughts for our running-away fund.'

'Our fund?'

'*Our* fund.'

Charlie knew I had several funds in which I squirrelled away money. They were my stash – my independence. Without them, I felt powerless, impotent.

I don't know exactly when and where a ratchet in my mind shifted from surprise at getting anywhere at all to determination to keep what I had. Yet it had. Roughly translated, this meant I had to grab what I could when I could. It was not greed, *per se*, though I dare say an onlooker might have been tempted to conclude that it was, but rather a distrust of the world. And Fate. And events. None of which was predisposed to be in my favour.

He looked at me steadily. 'I can't persuade you to trust me that I would look after you?'

'That's not the point.'

Suddenly he smiled. 'No.'

'You can never be sure,' I said, not for the first time. 'Things go wrong. Then you're dead meat. Too old, too over . . . There's only a nano-second in the sun and then it goes. Trust me.'

Charlie missed with the second sock. He ticked off the points on his fingers. 'One book. One trip to the US and possible TV series. One weekly slot to fill in the magazine. God knows how many appearances on chat shows, et cetera. That fills the next six months nicely. And then . . .'

'And then I'll be thirty-six.'

'That's *not* what I was going to say. I was going to say that our running-away fund will look pretty healthy.'

*

The subject of America came up again as we were driving down the M3 on Sunday morning. It was our precious free day, but this invitation was important.

To his surprise, Charlie had been sounded out by the head of a rival chambers. A vacancy might, just *might*, come up in the future. Nothing definite. Plenty of time. But if it turned out to be the case would Charlie be interested? It was a richer, plusher, more establishment set-up, and Charlie's first response had been 'No.' Then he had thought about it and told me I was on duty for lunch.

'Not so immune, then,' but I was only half teasing him, for this was a new, rather puzzling development.

'I'm trying to be sensible.' Charlie looked grave and loving. 'For both of us.'

But he had never been one for sense and prudence in the conventional way: his perspectives were bolder – and less practical. The old Charlie, alight with enjoyment at being alive and involved and crusading, which I found so irresistible, would not have considered selling out.

But what if I was driving him to compromise? The notion sat oddly – rather painfully – on my conscience.

Charlie was in his best grey suit and I was cinched into a hot-off-the-peg Izzy Athill dress, which Izzy's PR had tried to give me, but I knew better and had paid for it.

'Presumably Mike and Tony don't know about this lunch.' I had named a couple of Charlie's colleagues at the same level.

Charlie laughed. 'Better than that,' he said. 'They do know.' He reached into the glove compartment for his sunglasses and shoved them on. I leant over and pushed them up his nose. 'So? What's happening about the US?' he asked.

'I'm flying to New York for a preliminary meeting, a few days at the end of the month. Nothing's settled, Charlie. Everyone's just . . . looking.'

Charlie drove fast for another couple of miles or so. Then he dropped in, over the sound of the car's heating, 'Cimmie rang yesterday.'

'You never told me.'

'I must have forgotten.'

I looked away, out of my window. The reason Cimmie, Charlie's first wife, had left him, he had reported, was because Charlie had not taken her seriously enough. He had been busy with building up his practice in the chambers, which had taken all his energy, and Cimmie had been struggling to make her way as an interior designer. She accused him of not rating what she was doing, and of lack of support. He accused her of continual nagging, and of failure to understand how important it was that he had time and space to concentrate on his work. In this way, they circled each other, but the circles had become progressively wider until it was impossible for them to view each other.

'Afterwards I had an awful feeling that I had been playing at marriage,' Charlie rationalized. 'Trying it out for size. A sort of take-it-back-if-it-doesn't-fit.' The idea troubled him. 'I made so many mistakes. Never again.'

I had been the beneficiary of Charlie's determination never to make the same mistakes.

The last was an important factor in my decision to marry him. I carried the baggage of a failed marriage too, and the 'never again' declaration was what I yearned to hear. Our marriage would be cut and tailored seamlessly out of the waste and wreckage of our experience. That was the calculation.

'I've agreed to have lunch with Cimmie.'

'When?'

'I've forgotten.'

'Oh.' Charlie was a barrister, trained and sharp. As a rule, he did not forget things.

Charlie accelerated. 'You don't mind, I take it?'

I chose my words carefully. 'I didn't know you'd been in touch.'

Charlie took his eyes off the road to look at me. 'Did I ever say I wasn't?'

We drove along a river valley – a plush, manicured landscape in which nestled expensive red-brick Elizabethan houses and Georgian mansions with lawns sloping down to the river.

'Bet the Liversedges live in one of those.' I pointed to a perfect specimen of the latter.

They did.

On the phone, Sally Liversedge had said, 'It's only Sunday lunch. Small and intimate. Harry's so busy that big dos at the weekend just don't work.'

I gathered up my bag. 'Best behaviour?'

Charlie pulled on the handbrake and flicked my thigh with a finger. 'Best behaviour.'

We were greeted at the door by a beautiful young man

holding a drinks tray, and a second ushered us into a sitting room overlooking the river, decorated in pink and grey. 'So much for the intimate, informal gathering,' I hissed at Charlie.

Sally Liversedge detached herself from a group of ten or so and came over. She was a good-looking woman of approximately fifty-five, dressed in Timeless Elegance. Mistake. Timeless Elegance was ageing. I longed to coax her into a pair of wicked shoes, or to strip off the perfectly tailored blouse under her suit and replace it with a T-shirt.

Among others, she introduced us to a judge (Crown Court) and his wife, to a fashionable landscape gardener, who affected the crumpled-corduroy look, then a professor of jurisprudence and his wife. All of them were older than Charlie and me – and, at a guess, none would have read my column, which gave me an advantage. People could be snooty about fashion, but I say it tells us about ourselves in no small way. (Perhaps we don't want to listen, but that's another story.)

Ellen, the professor's wife, was dressed in a floral shirtwaister (not ideal for the thicker figure), cream court shoes and not a scrap of makeup. 'And what do you do?' she asked.

I explained, and a frown etched itself on her scrubbed countenance. After a pause, she said, 'How interesting.'

I asked her politely if she worked in the same area as her husband. 'I support my husband,' she replied aggressively. 'That is *work*, you know, but I'm sure your generation doesn't view it like that.'

'Of course,' I hastened to say. 'One of the nice things about being female today is that so many options are open. The choices are infinite.'

'If you believe that,' replied Ellen, 'then your generation is more stupid than I supposed.'

Thereafter the conversation flagged.

The windows in the dining room framed a vista of lawn and river, which was fringed by a couple of willows. We ate mushroom soup, lobster and *îles flottantes* served by the beautiful young men, who glided from guest to guest. At my end of the table, the talk was of an opera production that the judge had seen in Verona the previous summer, and the latest moves by the government to unclog the criminal justice system. I ate the excellent lunch and kept a weather eye on Charlie. Not unnaturally, he seemed a little tense and, every so often, I sent him a tiny smile. *You're doing fine.*

Afterwards we put on our coats and braved the chill to parade over the immaculate grass to the river, which was clear and free from weed. 'It's the flint,' explained Harry Liversedge. 'It filters the water.'

'Do you have fishing rights?' asked Charlie, and looked impressed when Harry replied, 'Of course.'

'It's like a film set,' he said, into my ear, but I caught the note of envy.

'Down, Rover,' I murmured.

'Now, you two,' reproved our hostess, 'you have all the time in the world to talk to each other.'

When we returned to the house, Sally drove the women into the kitchen to view the improvements she had been describing to us. The staff were decanting the leftovers from lunch and wiping down the surfaces.

'Of course,' Sally was smoothly modulated, 'we only had a new kitchen put in three years ago, but it never really pleased me, and I insisted that we try again. Harry was very understanding about the expense, so I'm particularly cross,' she pointed to a recessed wooden trim on the cupboards, 'that the builders disobeyed my instructions. It's all wrong.'

There was much tutting and exclaiming from the other women, but to my surprise I, who minded about perfection, experienced a twinge of . . . impatience?

'I dare say,' Sally might have divined my reaction, 'you probably consider that I'm being ultra fussy.'

'Not at all,' I said.

'When one is spending thousands and thousands, you expect everything to be *exactly* right.'

'Did Harry say anything to you?' I asked Charlie, on the way home.

'Plenty to think about,' he said. 'He was persuasive and flattering.'

'And?'

'I don't know,' he said. 'Could be tempted . . . depends. But nothing will happen for months – if at all.'

'Surely *not*, Charlie. You can't sell yourself out of your philanthropy into, well, not usury, but something that doesn't suit you.'

A set of traffic-lights flicked to red, and he stopped the car. 'Do you mean that, Siena?'

'Yes, I do.'

His face softened into tenderness. 'That's nice.' The lights changed and he put his foot on the accelerator. 'I'll bear it in mind.'

I reached over and grabbed his arm. 'No, don't bear it in mind. Stick to your ambitions.'

Charlie did not reply but I could tell he was pleased for he drove along whistling under his breath.

There was the usual M3 Sunday-evening bottleneck. (An evening wasted.) Beating up the motorway alongside us in the evening tide of traffic were four-by-fours, their boots stuffed with equipment – pushchairs and padded jackets, duvets covered in bright cotton – men with receding hairlines at the wheel and, beside them, women in Puffa jackets.

I began to compose the thank-you letter to the Liversedges, which must be written and posted tomorrow. To be any later was to demonstrate a shortfall in good manners, which might harm Charlie.

It was almost dark. I thought longingly of our quiet, water-lit flat – its space, its privacy and tranquillity. I looked forward to kicking off my shoes, and eating supper off a tray on the sofa. Cheese, biscuits, a glass of wine.

And so it was. After we had eaten, watched the news and flicked through the papers, Charlie peeled an apple and fed it to me, quarter by quarter.

'About Cimmie,' I gathered my courage, 'when are you lunching?'

Charlie dropped a coil of peel on to the plate. 'As it happens, when you're away in the States.'

*

Cimmie was not strictly beautiful. 'Oh dear,' she said, when I was introduced to her at my wedding to Charlie, 'I'm tempted to call you the second Mrs Grant.' She was there because Charlie felt it would be a noble gesture to ask her, and Cimmie wrote in acceptance: 'A good moment for closure?'

I suppressed an unworthy desire to point out that large breasts and halternecks were the worst combination. Yet there was allure in Cimmie's expression, in the way she held herself, that presented the illusion of beauty.

At the reception, she seized the first opportunity to come over to me. She took my hand and said thoughtfully, 'I can see why Charlie loves you. He tells me he does, very much.'

The pearl-drop earrings that Cimmie wore mimicked the movement of her head. She was being generous, but I did not want her generosity, which made me ashamed. 'Thank you.'

A little of my feeling must have registered with her, for Cimmie coloured and said brightly, 'I give him to you.'

'Such a good thing to have laid that ghost,' my mother commented, as she helped me change into my going-away outfit – a (fake) leopard skin Dolce and Gabbana jacket and leather skirt. 'One should always meet the first wife. Then you know what you're up against. Has Charlie met Jay?' She swivelled round and accosted Manda, my brides-maid, who had been supervising the dressing and un-dressing until my mother barged in. 'Have you been in touch with Jay?'

'Jay's in Hong Kong, making lots of money. He hasn't been back for ages, but I told him Siena was getting married again.' Manda smoothed the jacket over my shoulders. 'He was fine about it.' She leant over and kissed my cheek. 'You look lovely, Siena.' She held out my bouquet. 'Now, what did I instruct you to remember?'

I stroked the white roses, so beautiful, serene and unmarked. Soon, very soon, I would walk into a new future. '"The past is another country."'

She kissed me. 'Word perfect.'

I kissed her back. 'And what did I tell you?'

'"The wing of friendship never moults a feather."'

'Brilliant.'

My mother was looking on fondly. 'Any chance of your rejoining your guests?'

I repeated the gist of the conversation with Cimmie to Charlie while we were on honeymoon, walking in the Himalayas. I can picture it so well. Late afternoon, purple shadows spreading like oil over the mountainside, and our group was making its way towards Pokhara for the night. I was keeping up fine, but I felt rather low because I knew that no hot shower or comfortable bed lay ahead, only *ghee*, rice and a hard floor. Charlie, however, was in his element. Lean and bronzed, he had developed a mountain stride, a cross between a lope and fast walk, which meant he was always ahead. I know he enjoyed that tiny superiority and, because I loved him, I did too.

We sat and rested on a flat stone before the final lap into Pokhara and I chose that moment, targeted by the strong sun and chill wind, lapped by rocks and colour and unaccountably moved by the strangeness of the landscape, to inform him that Cimmie had given him to me.

Charlie extracted a wrinkled, tough-looking apricot from his rucksack, examined it and bit into it. 'Did she?'

On the opening day of Charlie's biggest case in his career, Cimmie had packed her bags and arranged for a substantial amount of their furniture to be removed from their house. She left a note regretting the inconvenience, but since Charlie was married to his career she felt that she got in his way. 'I see this as an unselfish move on my part,' she wrote, 'and you will be grateful.'

'Actually,' I added, examining my legs on which there were many bruises, 'I think Cimmie was fighting for survival.'

'To survive me?' Charlie was startled. 'I don't think so.'

'OK, Lucy. When you're ready.'

In the photographer's studio, Lucy Thwaite, Jenni and I stared into the triple mirror, which also reflected a makeup girl in the act of packing her holdall, and the photographer conferring with his assistant. A spotlight was trained on to the square of red paper taped down on the floor where, shortly, Lucy would pose.

What I saw in the mirror gave me enormous pleasure.

Jenni said, *'Great!'*

Lucy continued to stare at the woman in the dark-grey trouser suit, white silk camisole and suede ankle boots. Her hair had been cut into a feathery cap and her face was made up with a hint of olive eyeshadow and Mac's taupe lipstick.

'Is that me?' She seemed bewildered. 'Me?'

I slipped my arm round her shoulders and gave her a hug. 'Does it please you?'

Lucy's response was slow in coming and Jenni intervened: 'You look fantastic. Your back is *so* narrow.'

Lucy touched a feather on her forehead. 'Are you sure this colour suits me?' She tugged at a trouser leg. 'I'm not used to trousers that . . . fit like this. I don't know what Derek will say. Or the children.'

It was on the tip of my tongue to point out that it didn't matter what they thought, but I would have been wrong to say so. Of course Lucy saw herself reflected in her family. How else would she define herself?

She placed her hands on her hips and twirled. 'It does make me look thinner.'

Jenni and I exchanged a look. Whatever our differences, we liked this moment when the butterfly struggled out of the chrysalis.

Lucy burst into tears. Quick as a flash, Jenni drew her away from the mirror and made her sit down on the nearest chair. 'Lucy, Lucy . . . you'll spoil your makeup.'

The makeup girl reversed operations and began to unpack her stuff. I bent over Lucy, who looked up at me. 'I feel so tired,' she sobbed. 'I don't think I can cope.'

The makeup girl darted forward, brushed me aside and dabbed at Lucy's face with a tissue.

'Sorry,' said Lucy. 'Sorry, sorry.'

The makeup girl said, 'If you stop crying, I can do the repair work. It won't take a minute.' Her voice was soothing, her movements professional.

Eventually, Lucy relaxed. The photographer issued an order to his assistant, who adjusted the lights. I commandeered a second chair, carried it over to Lucy and sat down beside her. 'Is there anything we can do to help?'

Trapped and immobilized, Lucy muttered, 'It's fine. It's just . . . I had a bad night with one of the children. But I'm fine now.'

The session went without a further hitch and Lucy was packed into a taxi to catch her train. The photographer, Jenni and I huddled over the Polaroids.

'Close call,' said Jenni. 'Didn't think we were going to make it.'

The makeup girl carefully inserted her brushes into the roll-up holder. 'It happens. People get used to seeing themselves in a certain way, and it's a shock. Or it reminds them of what they used to look like, and that's a shock too.'

The photograph of Lucy that appeared later in the magazine was brilliantly successful. Far from the beaten, exhausted frump she feared, Lucy Thwaite sprang off the page: strong, glossy and cleverly dressed.

'How can I thank you?' she wrote to me. 'You have transformed me.'

I pinned up the letter on my noticeboard and thought of the Roman sandal that had been created out of cardboard and glue. It had touched me in the same way.

Chapter Six: Siena

When he introduced me to Manda, my first husband, Jay, said, in his easy way, 'This was the craziest girl in our year. Danced all night. Drank all night. Wrote the longest essays and got the highest marks.'

Manda held out her hand, sporting a ring in the shape of a skull. She was dressed in tight jeans and an artfully torn sweater on which the word 'Bitch' had been stamped in sequins. 'Jay exaggerates,' she said. 'He was the all-night drinker.'

'Can't remember,' said Jay.

'Precisely.' Manda's smile welcomed me into Jay's tight circle of university friends who, for his sake, were prepared to give me the benefit of the doubt, and I was grateful.

At that point (just post-university), Manda was fond of peddling the line that she could have worked in the City but preferred to do a job that meant something to people. Money should not dictate a life, she declared, a philosophy from whose principles she could not imagine deviating. But she had. Nowadays, Manda was more likely to drop into a conversation, 'To think I *could* have been earning telephone numbers!'

Unlike Manda, Jay had chosen the City and turned into one of the sleeker beasts in the corporate jungle. Out went the combat trousers and shaggy jumpers, the rag-bag of ideas and principles that made up his student mental landscape, and in came the made-to-measure suits, expensive leather shoes, a pile of shirts and a palm-top organizer that beeped at intervals during the day to remind him of where he was, plus a new set of attitudes to match.

'There are stages in life,' he said, when we talked over his metamorphosis from sceptic and socialist to raging capitalist. 'I've just moved on to the next.' He peered at me. 'Don't look like that, sweetie-pie. We can't stand still. No one can.'

We got married – white dress and veil, champagne, marquee, the full works – just after he received his first promotion, and honeymooned in New York. As it turned out, that was the last time I saw Jay for any length of time. I minded, and did not mind, for I was busy developing my own career. Yet his absences made our weekends awkward because, having lost touch in the interim, we had to work hard to find each other all over again. And, after a while, there were no more meetings of mind or body, and all I could have told you about Jay was a catalogue of his clothes, which I sorted and tidied each week.

I married Charlie and took a vow of vigilance – to watch myself, to watch for the spaces and silences creeping into the oh-so-together partnership, to sew them up tight when (if) I spotted them. I made Charlie stand beside me, and I drew an imaginary circle round us both and another interconnected one, so it formed a figure-of-eight. 'OK,' I said. 'This is us in this circle. In that one, we put all our bad experiences and mistakes. Now I'm going take a pair of imaginary scissors and cut the circles where the join is.'

'And?' asked a bewildered Charlie.

'We throw that bad circle away, up into the sky, and watch it fly out of sight.'

'You're mad,' he said.

The plan was for Charlie and me to meet Manda and her husband, Dick, at a restaurant on the river, then move on to a salsa club. (Dancing was the stuff of life, the lifter of spirits, etc., etc.)

Dick and Manda were late. 'Sorry . . . sorry . . .' Manda was breathless as she slumped on to the banquette seat. 'Babysitter –'

'– was late,' Dick supplied. 'And we were a bit worried that she'd been drinking.'

'Did you ask her?' Charlie was instantly on the case.

Manda and Dick exchanged a look. 'The terrible thing is that we so much wanted to get out – to see you two, I mean, we decided to give her the benefit of the doubt,' said Manda, and added, after a moment, 'I'm sure I smelt it on her.' She fiddled with the napkin. 'Or perhaps I didn't.' She turned to her husband.

It was up to Charlie to repair the anxiety he had helped to stir and he did. 'Is there a market for home breathalyser kits?'

Manda managed a reluctant smile.

'Dinner's on us,' I said quickly. 'No argument,' and saw them relax.

With the river running darkly outside, we ate roasted

cod with Puy lentils and asparagus tips, and drank a lemony white wine. Dick chatted to Charlie but Manda's conversation was slow in coming and, every so often, she paused, put down her fork or spoon as if she was listening for something.

'OK, Manda?'

She searched for the appropriate answer to prove that she was enjoying the occasion and was pleased to be out. 'Absolutely.'

'But?'

She fingered her hair. 'Rat's nest, but there we are. Haven't had time.' Then she gave in, and her shoulders sagged. 'It's been a bit trying lately. The childminder was ill, and Hetty got whatever it was and gave it to Patrick. Natch. Dick's father is in hospital and . . . the work is piling up. I've been dashing from pillar to post. I lied to my boss and told him I was ill so I could look after the children. *Don't* think he believed me. *I* wouldn't have believed me.'

Manda and Dick worked in publishing. Dick was a sales director – 'Unfortunately, unlike soap powder, books are only a small market, not a consumer base.' Manda was the editor of a popular fiction list for an ailing publishing house but she did not dare to look for an alternative job – 'I have to mark time while the children are so young.'

The news of the Caesar Books offer was received with the requisite amount of congratulation and a (heroically masked) degree of envy. 'How much advance did you say they were offering?' Manda assumed her professional look, and I could hear the noughts clicking through her mind. I told her, and she smiled at me. 'You deserve it.'

From time to time, I must plead guilty to a moulting feather or two from the said wing of friendship, brought about by (small) jealousies and a feeling of being less loved than others. Not pretty, I know. But this was never true of Manda, who strove to bypass negative feelings. Even while she was wishing desperately that a lump sum was winging its way into her bank account, she was looking out for me.

'It doesn't sound quite enough. Can't India bump it up? Go on, prod her. Make her earn her ten per cent.'

'Hey, whose side are you on?' Dick interjected.

'Won't I get royalties, if it sells?'

'Yes.'

Manda looked at me as if to say: 'You're doing so much better than me. Much, much better than me.' Yet – and this was the point at which our friendship had slithered into a puzzling phase – Manda had changed since she had become a mother. Or, rather, her interior landscape had changed and her points of reference no longer matched mine. She loved me no less (and I her), but there was a reservation on which I could not quite place my manicured finger, the suggestion that she possessed a private knowledge, a secret nourishment, which I lacked.

We fell to discussing developments in the book world, and of how something as small and individual as a publisher's list had been hijacked by accountants and huge retail groups.

'We have to go with it.' Dick's practical clear-sightedness had ensured that he made a success of his job. 'There's no going back to the bad old days when publishing was a cottage industry.'

'No more corner shops.' Charlie, who always championed the underdog, looked nostalgic.

Dick poked his arm. 'Hey, which century are you living in?'

The conversation moved on and Dick asked Charlie if he was working on a case or (ha-ha) 'resting'. 'Death of a baby,' said Charlie, his lips tightening. 'Mother accused of murder.'

'Oh, God!' exclaimed Manda. *'Don't.'* She pushed away her plate and looked at Dick. 'Should I phone?'

Dick shook his head, laid his hand on his wife's and articulated each word with care: 'Stop worrying. It'll be fine.'

'How can you bear it, Charlie?' Manda turned the full force of her concern on Charlie.

I glanced sharply at my husband. It was a question he asked himself often. How could one bear, day after day, the proximity to such frailty, violence and darkness? 'There is no answer,' he had said, 'except that repugnance is no response. Bite that lip and don't look into the void. Due process. Cool detachment.'

'I mean,' Manda went on, 'how can you bring yourself to defend her if you think she's guilty?'

'That's my deal,' said Charlie, and the professional light in his eye switched on. 'I can't write the plot, or the script, but I can make sure that her case is put as well as possible.'

But Manda had found a bone to worry. 'Charlie, if you *knew* she was guilty, would you defend her?'

Charlie slapped her hands down on the table. 'She's not guilty.' He shook his head. 'She's *not* guilty.'

I began to feel uneasy. 'Charlie—'

'I agree. She *wouldn't* have done it,' Manda cut across me. 'She wouldn't. No woman would. Not if she'd given birth.'

Dick said, 'Don't be silly, darling.'

Manda pointed at him. 'How do you know?'

And again I was struck by the sharpness and certainty of Manda's passion, and her denial – which I could not share.

Neither Dick nor Manda requested further details of the Jackie Woodruff case – they knew that Charlie should not discuss it. Not until it reached court, at any rate.

The waiter intervened to clear the plates and, by mutual consent, the subject was dropped. We searched for a topic less difficult, less unsettling. 'What's all this about changes at the law courts?' asked Dick, and he and Charlie settled down to a light, enjoyable ding-dong over jury cases.

Concerned, I noted Manda's hollow eyes. 'What are you going to do for a holiday this year?'

'Nothing. I think we'll just enjoy being at home.' She added fiercely, 'London is *such* fun in August.'

This was not the moment to mention the trip to Vietnam that Charlie and I were eager to make. 'Tell me about the children.'

Manda exhaled audibly, and looked near collapse. 'I love Hetty and Patrick so much,' she said. 'That's the main thing.' Short pause. 'I do hope the babysitter's OK.' She twisted her fingers together. 'I should have asked Janey, our neighbour. She'd have done it, but we're always bothering her.'

'Nice neighbours.'

'Lovely ones,' Manda agreed. 'Any new ones for you?'

I cradled my chin in my hands. 'The Scotts are opposite but they're tax exiles and not very often in London. Jenna Glossop lives with a pop-star one level up. We say hallo whenever we meet in the gym. Sometimes we have a gossip over fruit juice . . . Otherwise . . . I still don't really know any of them,' I admitted. 'It's not that sort of place.'

'You're missing out.' Manda searched in her bag for her lip-gloss, and smeared it on without looking. 'Truly.'

Was I? But what exactly was I missing? In my experience, dull gossip and bad coffee.

I leant over and wiped the overshoot of gloss from the corner of her mouth. 'Manda, would you like a makeover? It's easy to arrange, and we could have some fun.'

For a horrible moment, Manda's features registered revulsion and, even, humiliation. Then she recovered herself. 'You think I should have a makeover?' She wrinkled her nose at me. 'No, I don't think so. I've made a pact with myself. I'm not going to look in the mirror for the next five years while the children become human and then, *bang*, you won't see me for makeover.' I must have looked disappointed, and she added softly, 'Does it make sense if I say I don't feel up to it?'

'Sure?'

Manda's gesture embraced the expensive dinner table. 'The motto is: "Trudge on, darlings."'

We embarked on *panna cotta* with a raspberry coulis. Manda dug in and out of hers with staccato stabs of her spoon. But she seemed to be listening in to that other sphere. Finally she could bear it no longer. 'I'll just check up.' She went off to phone.

Minutes later, she reappeared. 'It's all fine.' She shot a look at Dick, who shrugged and resumed his conversation with Charlie.

'Actually,' said Manda, 'I think we'll give the salsa a miss. Do you mind?'

Dick concurred: 'I reckon it's best we go home.'

When we said goodbye outside the restaurant, I hugged Manda extra hard. Given ghostly prominence by street-lighting, the circles under her eyes looked even blacker, and she more haunted. 'Take care of yourself. I'm worried about you.'

'Same to you,' she said. 'You look a tad lonely.'

'Don't be silly. I have Charlie.'

'Yes.' She arched her eyebrows. '"Confucius, he say . . ."'

I nipped in: '"Marriage is a button on a waistband. It can work loose. Sewing it back on can result in bloodshed."'

'That was *terrible*, Siena.'

'It was. Every word.'

Ouch. But we both laughed and felt better.

As soon as we got back to the flat Charlie headed for his briefcase, but I collared him. 'Charlie. No.'

'Pot calling the kettle black?'

I placed my hands flat against his chest, trying to find his heartbeat and failing. 'Charlie, you're not getting too involved in this case, are you?'

Outside, the river glittered with lights and a neon orange glow bathed the buildings on the opposite bank. I thought of the centuries of perfecting that had gone into the system, the order and calm of its provisions, designed to sort out the terror, muddle and wrongly directed passions. 'Charlie, is it possible that Jackie Woodruff is guilty?'

He stepped away smartly, and turned on his heel. 'Oh, for God's sake, Siena,' he said, 'what do you know?'

A few days later I was scrubbing mussels at the sink, bought from the farmers' market on the way home. The cold water had shrunk my fingertips into raisins. Salt and ozone ... As the shiny blue-black heap mounted on the draining-board, I was reminded of family holidays at Whitby, shivery days spent rock-pooling and eating fish and chips out of newspaper, while the wind blasted sand into our faces.

The mussels felt hard, fat and smooth between my fingers. These days, I had to delve determinedly into the layers of memory to summon the texture of sand trapped between toes and thighs, the salty tightness of my cheeks, the wet armour of my swimsuit.

As a child, I had been oblivious to the fissures and cracks in our family. It was only later when I was a teenager that my parents' unhappiness became obvious. Point one, they never talked to each other directly, unless they had to: they talked through us. Point two, at home, they wore an expression I did not understand until I left: the expression of people geared up to endure at any price and until the bitter end.

'Hallo,' said Charlie, sneaking up on me. He put his arms round my waist. 'Hallo, Blue Eyes. Am I forgiven?' He sounded weary and despairing.

'Of course.' I snatched up a tea-towel, an expensive French waffle one, dried my hands, then put my arms round his neck. I so wanted everything to be right, with no shadows between us. 'What's up?'

He buried his face in my hair. 'Nothing, just end-of-dayish.'

'Truth, Charlie.'

He shook his head. 'Nothing.'

I knew there was more to it, but I was weary too. To be honest, I wanted supper. I kissed his nose, then his forehead and, for good measure, his lips. 'Why don't you cook the *moules*?'

He released me, then reached for the pan and the white wine; we edged round each other in the limited kitchen space. Charlie loved cooking, and it was the best diversionary tactic I could devise.

Before we ate, I put Enya on the CD player and, after a few mouthfuls, Charlie brightened. We discussed our plans for Vietnam, and it was clear that neither of us could find a spare week until the following October.

'October, then,' said Charlie. 'A hundred years away.'

It was no use avoiding the Jackie Woodruff case any longer so I asked carefully, 'What happened today?'

Charlie's shrug suggested nonchalance, but it didn't

fool me. The light sprang into his eyes. 'I interviewed Jackie and tried to make her understand what the prosecution are likely to pin her down on. What they're likely to do to her.'

'And?'

'I don't think she cares any more. They get like that sometimes.'

'She must care about her innocence.'

Charlie dropped the last shell into the bowl on the table between us. 'She cares only that her baby is dead.'

We cleared away the supper things and loaded the dishwasher. At last, the kitchen was wiped clean, its surfaces gleaming. 'I think I'll go to bed,' said Charlie.

'It's only ten thirty.'

He blew me a kiss. 'I'm tired.'

'I'll come soon. I just want to finish up an article.'

An hour later, I tiptoed into the bedroom but Charlie was not asleep. He had commandeered all the pillows and was sitting up in bed reading documents.

I fussed over my face and pulled a padded bomber jacket in metallic silver out of a carrier-bag. A guilty, but irresistible, purchase. Minus a body inside it, it looked ridiculous. 'What do you think?'

He wrinkled his nose. 'The words "mutton" and "lamb" seem to be sliding across my mind. I wonder why.'

That made me glance anxiously into the mirror. '*Thank* you.'

'Think nothing of it. For you, my advice is free.'

I picked up his discarded shirt and noticed the cuffs were fraying. 'Do you want me to find you a new one?'

'If you like,' he said carelessly, 'but no one notices things like that, and you don't have time.'

'Thanks for the vote of confidence in my job.'

There was a tiny silence. 'Any time,' said Charlie.

I climbed into bed. 'I order you to go to sleep,' I said, and switched off the light.

After a moment, Charlie addressed a question into the darkness: 'Would you like to move from here?'

'No.' I was startled. 'Aren't you happy with the flat?'

Charlie ignored the question. 'Wouldn't you like a garden?'

'We have the pots on the balcony.' His silence reproved me. 'Not good at digging, Charlie.'

'A dog? A cat? Anything normal?'

'Ditto, but substitute, "not good with fur all over furniture".' Another pause. 'Charlie, since when have you wanted dogs and cats?'

Beside me, Charlie tensed. 'We can't stay in one place for ever, Siena.'

'No law against it, is there?'

I knew perfectly well that Charlie was circling, the professional stalker marking out his objective. From having put down a marker in the distance, he was padding closer and the real subject of this conversation would – eventually – come to light.

'We'll soon be forty.' He pronounced 'forty' not so much with doom and foreboding as with surprise.

Not that again.

'Forty is the new thirty,' I said brightly, but I was ashamed of my brightness.

'Yup,' he agreed. 'Yup.'

I held him tightly. The clock on the bedside table clicked away digitally, recording the seconds, minutes . . . that would swell and grow into days and months. In the womb, a baby is marked off in weeks, in months after it is born and eventually, of course, in years.

Charlie was warm and firm in my arms. I closed my eyes, and my pulses quickened at the thought of the American trip and what it might bring. 'Go to sleep, Charlie.'

In the middle of the night I awoke with a cry. I had been dreaming I was walking along a beach, with the sea and wind howling in my ears. I had no idea where I was heading, and my steps grew heavier and heavier. My feet sank into the stones, which were sucked inside my high-heeled red shoes, and I was rocked by a terrible sensation of fear. Then the wind and the sea hushed, a suspension of sound and movement, and I looked up. High on the cliff above, Lucy Thwaite gesticulated at me.

I put a hand to my cheek and felt tears. But for what I had no idea – only that they had sprung from a dark, painful anxiety.

I edged close to Charlie, slid my arms round him and placed my lips on his mouth. He tasted of wine, and was warm and unconscious. I kissed his neck, and the place behind his ear that I loved. 'Wake up, Charlie!' I cried, desperate for his comfort.

He woke and protested, strongly at first, then with no conviction. He reached for me.

'I love you,' I said.

In the morning it was as if that whispered, passionate interlude had never taken place. A constraint had wrapped itself round us, throttling words and frosting the air.

'Look . . .' Charlie, who was eating toast standing up, broke the silence. 'I want to sort out a few things.'

A *few* things? 'Go on, I'm listening.'

He glanced at his watch. 'Let's agree to talk when you get back from the States,' he said.

I stirred my muesli, homemade, full of nuts, and fatigue triggered me into saying something I had not meant to say. 'You're not wishing you were still married to Cimmie, are you?'

Charlie looked stunned. 'Hang on. How does Cimmie come into it? We're talking about us, and our future.'

I got up and straightened his tie, a pointless gesture. 'Sorry.' I sat down again and picked up my spoon.

The phone rang in my office.

'I know what "a few things" means, Charlie, and I'll try to think about it, I promise.' I dipped the spoon into my bowl, and raised it to my mouth.

'I wish I could believe you.'

The spoon clattered on to the table, ejecting a spray of milk and damp oats. 'What a rotten thing to say.'

He stepped back, and away from me. 'I feel rotten.'

I walked distractedly around the flat. River? Murky but calm today, flowing hard out to sea. Weight? Fine, according to the scales. Work? Piling up nicely. Friendships? In good shape (I hoped). I was tempted to phone Manda and consult her on Charlie's uncharacteristic snippiness but I knew, at this time of day, her timetable included heroic feats of feeding and transport, and, to do so, would fail the category of friendship. Wardrobe? Perhaps the bomber jacket had been a genuflection too far to youth. (Even fashion consultants make mistakes.)

Marriage? My strike rate had not been a hundred per cent but, with Charlie, the odds had altered in my favour.

In sudden fear, I went into the sitting room and sank on to the sofa. *Please, let me find a way through.*

I was angry with Charlie that I was being forced to think like this and desperate not to *have* to. Then I remembered Jackie Woodruff and realized my desperation was nothing compared to hers. I tried to imagine what she looked like, how she spent her days. How did she manage to negotiate all those seconds, minutes and hours?

I leant back against the cushions. The slub in the material rubbed my cheek, and I closed my eyes. What I had never worked out before was that happiness has an isolating effect. I had withdrawn into my happiness because it was impossible to share. Unhappiness and doubt put one in touch with everyone else.

I opened my eyes, spotted a rogue scattering of crumbs on the carpet, sprang to my feet, fetched the dustpan and brush and swept them up.

Chapter Seven: Barbara

The days clocked up. Thank goodness, it would soon be proper spring. Even so, it was chilly in the bedroom, whose gas fire we lit only in emergencies. I got through my night routines as fast as possible. Underclothes into the laundry basket, my black dinner dress hung up carefully, hair brushed a hundred times, tasks easily performed and automatic. Nightly rituals I could not imagine being without.

'Is your book good?'

Ryder replied, 'Very. It's about Suez.'

'Ah, yes,' I said.

While I finished the hundred strokes, Ryder outlined the author's arguments, and added, 'Disastrous, the whole thing. For everyone. For the empire.' The former fighter pilot in Ryder would follow and analyse a military campaign. It was second nature to him. I gathered up my hairpins into the china dish Amy had given me for my birthday, and made a comment to the effect that all empires had to come to an end.

Ryder said, 'Darling, do come to bed.'

The pattern on Amy's dish was of tiny blue flowers through which a gauzy ribbon had been threaded. It was not her taste, but I cherished it because she thought it was mine. The hairpins chimed faintly as they hit the china.

I shook my head, let my hair drift over my shoulders, and got into bed.

The sheets were cold and I shivered as I reached for my book.

'What are *you* reading, Barbara?'

'It's on Freud and his ideas.' I held it up for Ryder to inspect. 'Listen to this: "There are three levels of consciousness: the conscious, the unconscious and the preconscious."'

'I'm all for the unconscious,' he said, abandoning his book. 'Lights out?'

I fiddled with my pillow, and made sure that my handkerchief was tucked under it. 'You might like to know that the pleasure principle drives the unconscious, which he thought meant avoiding pain and strong emotions.'

'Are you trying to tell me something, darling?' Ryder murmured. 'Is this one of your campaigns?'

'What campaigns, darling?'

'You know exactly what I mean.'

He was not entirely teasing. There was an edge to this conversation because of its subject.

I buttoned the cuff of my Viyella nightdress – practical and warm, but inelegant. 'Freud also says that we forget things deliberately when we want to cover them up.'

'Not in my experience.'

There was no chance of Ryder forgetting. By the end of the war, he said, the planes were full of ghosts. They crowded so thickly into the cockpits – young, joking, beautiful, brave and so very dead – that he had found it hard to sit at the controls.

We drank together, fought together and trusted together. We were that close. As close as crossed fingers.

I switched off the light and lay down. There were the little sounds of bodies settling for the night. A slither of sheet, a creak from the bedsprings, a sigh. Ryder reached out for a last mouthful of water.

'I'm all tuckered out,' he addressed the dark.

'"All tuckered out". That's another for Amy.'

Ryder picked up slang from other flying crews, particularly the Americans. Amy teased him about it. I could hear her now. 'Dad's all tuckered out, all tuckered out.'

'Sometimes I look forward to retiring.'

'Stop flying?'

The pillow rustled as he turned his head towards me. 'It happens, darling.'

'Won't they offer you a desk job at Headquarters when they take you off flying? Isn't that what happens?'

'If I wanted, but I rather like the idea of being at home, playing golf and bridge.'

'Oh.'

No fool, he picked up on my unease. 'Don't worry. I don't plan to hang around. I've been thinking. Travel might be something that people do more of in the future. Now would be the time to set up some sort of business to cater for it. In fact, Peter Andrews and I have been looking into the figures.'

'You never said anything.'

'Shall we say I forgot?'

I laughed.

His hand descended on my haunch. This was the usual

pattern: Ryder always took the initiative and this arrangement was how we dealt with that area of our marriage.

'I don't suppose . . .'

He always asked, never demanded. He was polite in his impositions. A slight headache nagged behind my eyes, but I got up and went into the bathroom, took out my diaphragm and did what was necessary.

It was always a reminder of how *separate* mind and body could be and I never ceased to wonder about their allotted powers. Sometimes, when my mind drifted, I worried that I was being deceitful, *unfaithful* almost. At others, I was taken aback by the pleasure that accompanied Ryder's flight paths round my body, and the desire that tightened my muscles.

But there had been times when I had young children and was rigid with distaste – not for Ryder, never for him, but for the activity, which had seemed so pointless. In those days, fatigue often made me light-headed and almost hysterical. Then, instead of the living, breathing Ryder moving above me, I saw only the captain of the plane, directing operations in a peaked cap and gold braid.

I closed my eyes and clenched the hand Alexander had kissed. It did not seem to belong to me any more, and it certainly did not belong in the marital bed.

I had no intention of going to Fuller's tea-shop. I had no intention of bumping into Alexander Liberty. But the following morning, on my shopping trip, I did both.

'Hallo again.' He seemed flatteringly pleased to see me, and looked so young and hopeful, his faint shabbiness so endearing, that a lump threatened to spring into my throat.

'Barbara, what a coincidence,' he said, and I knew at once that it was not and I wondered how long he had been there, and how many cups of coffee he had forced himself to drink. 'Could I buy you some coffee?'

'Aren't you working at the hospital?'

His gaze slid to his watch. 'Not exactly.'

We settled at a table by the window and there was a short silence. I busied myself by taking off my gloves and sifted through explanations that might be required of me later by anyone who happened to see this interesting duo. *We bumped into each other. Alexander wanted to thank me for lunch. He was doing some research.*

'You always seem so peaceful and untroubled,' he said. 'I admire that.'

'Thank you. What a nice compliment.'

He thanked me again for the lunch, and seemed unabashed by any memory of what had happened in the apple-house. Maybe, being a little foreign, he considered kissing an older woman's hand as part of the etiquette. Or perhaps he had felt I looked as though I *needed* my hand to be kissed. Whatever the explanation, I realized that the effect of the gesture was not unlike my throwing the stone into the pond when I embarked on a campaign. It had created ripples.

Coffee came in thick white china cups; it was a little too weak. Alexander asked me a lot of questions. How long had Ryder and I been married? Where had we met and how long had we lived in the house? 'Why do you want to know?' I protested.

97

'I'm interested.'

'But there's not much *to* know.'

'On the contrary. There's so much to know – in anyone's life. All of us.'

I don't know why but I found that moving.

I answered as best I could – I had met Ryder at a tennis club, I was eighteen when I married him . . . 'Are you practising on me?' I inquired eventually. 'The physician in embryo. Like the shape in the block of marble.'

He rested his chin on his hands. Suddenly he seemed older, bolder, more confident. 'Do you mind?'

'Not at all. But it's my turn now.'

He answered each of my questions fully and deliberately. 'My father was killed in the war, in France. I was eight. He volunteered to parachute behind enemy lines while the Allies were advancing. The trouble was, the authorities insisted that men like my father wore uniform because it was thought it would rally resistance quicker. He might have rallied the Resistance, but the uniform identified him as an easy target. A lot of them died as a result of that decision.'

'I'm sorry.' My hand lay on the table, the one he had kissed.

'I don't suppose I would have got on with him very well. My mother told me he was the sort of man who believed in dying for one's country.'

'And you don't?'

Alexander shrugged. 'It's not for everyone.'

'We believed in it,' I pointed out, with an uncomfortable sensation of being out of step, 'precisely so that your generation can buy bananas and sugar with freedom. And also to give you the freedom to tell us we're perfect bores.'

He looked up at me. Very serious and intense. 'And I'm availing myself of that freedom to tell you that you're far from boring.' He paused and we both looked down at my hand on the table. 'In fact, you're one of the most interesting women I've ever met.'

Every pulse in my body beat in response. A strange, wild and unnameable cacophony that was utterly foreign.

'It's true,' he said.

I removed my treacherously inclined hand and placed it on my lap. 'You're flattering me.'

'No. I'm not.'

I had the strangest feeling that a part of me had broken away, a lump off the iceberg, a separate Barbara Beeching, and was floating into another existence.

'Barbara . . .' In a felt trilby and the ocelot coat that should have been retired with Noah's ark, Bunty was observing us sharply, questioningly.

Alexander leapt to his feet. 'Hallo, Mrs Andrews. How nice! Will you join us?'

He helped her out of the coat and pulled up an additional chair. His manners, I registered, were perfect. Bunty peeled off her suede gloves. Her nails were painted bright red, but there was a chip on the little finger. From across the table, she raised an eyebrow at me.

The waitress brought fresh coffee and I poured it into the cups.

'Shouldn't you be at the hospital?' Bunty was polite and neutral – except that she wasn't.

'Yes,' Alexander was unrepentant, 'I should be but I bumped into Mrs Beeching and wanted to thank her for such a good lunch the other day.'

On the way out, he stopped by the till and handed over a ten-shilling note. 'I think he's paid the bill,' I murmured to Bunty. 'How very sweet. I'm sure he can't afford it.'

He vanished into the street.

Bunty said, 'Darling, you're looking so very well.'

I wasn't sure I could return the compliment: Bunty looked thin and worn. 'Any news?'

Bunty chatted about this and that, but her eyes roamed the room. Their telephone bill had been terrible . . . her widower father was giving her problems. 'The trouble is,' she said, 'he won't accept that I'm in charge now, not him, poor love.'

We drank our coffee. Bunty put down her cup with a decided clink of china. 'Barbara, darling, was that wise?' she asked severely. 'People do talk so quickly.' She opened her handbag, extracted her cigarette case and lit up. 'One's reputation.'

I did not require clarification. 'I'd hardly have been sitting in the window in full view if I was planning anything.'

'And what would you have been planning?'

I felt a flicker of irritation. 'Nothing.'

Bunty inhaled deeply and coughed. 'I can't think why not. I would. Any red-blooded woman would. It's not fair that I'm his landlady. I have to be extra careful. Think what might happen!'

We smiled conspiratorially at each other. Bunty and I

were both safe, married women-of-the-world and she didn't mean a word of what she had said.

'Talking of which, did I tell you about poor silly Tilly Field, who ran off with her husband's partner?'

'No.'

'She's been forbidden, by the divorce judge, to see her three children. Diana Warburton – you know Diana? She said she took her courage in her hands and went to see her. She found her cowering in a rented flat in Dorking. She looked ghastly. A wraith.' Bunty examined the chip in her nail polish. 'Is Ryder away?'

'For the week.'

After a moment, Bunty said, 'And Peter *never* goes away.'

We exchanged a look of perfect harmony, finished the pot of coffee and talked about vacuum-cleaners, fitted carpets and washing-machines with automatic mangles, all of which were high on our wanted list.

Bunty dropped her cigarette case back into her handbag and the big brass clasp snapped shut.

I bent over to retrieve my own bag and glanced into the street. There was Alexander, lounging with a cigarette and a newspaper by the window of the exciting electrical shop.

The unruly, tender bubble of laughter that was becoming familiar rose to my throat. It was too ridiculous. Who did Alexander think he was? And what did he think he was doing?

I took my gloves out of my handbag. 'Nice,' said Bunty, eyeing it. 'Where?'

'Ryder brought it back from Nigeria. It's python. The traders sell a lot of stuff by the roads and outside the hotels.'

I was thinking rapidly. Would I shake off Bunty? Would I head resolutely up the high street towards home? Or would I cross the road, tap Alexander's shoulder and say, *'You must stop this, now'*?

Or would I say, 'Hallo, again'?

I met Ryder at the tennis club. My mother had signed me up for a tournament, and dispatched a shrinking me in a badly cut tennis dress with the instruction 'to meet some nice people'. It was May 1935, a cold spring, and I was eighteen. Ryder was twenty-two, and had recently joined the RAF, after Prime Minister Stanley Baldwin had decided to treble its size.

From the first, Ryder overwhelmed me. Even his mistakes seemed to be advantages. 'I'm hellish at landing,' he admitted, over a pint of cider. 'Drives my instructor to drink. "Beeching, don't grab that bloody stick as if it's going to walk. It's going nowhere and, if you don't mind me bloody saying, nor will you if you don't make an effort to improve."'

He was so funny, so knowledgeable, so brave. Ryder had made the transition from the state of ignorance and foreboding in which I still floundered to a mature, enticing, grown-up world. He was so sweet over my shyness and talked endlessly to me about flying, the camaraderie of the mess room and the pleasures of driving through the country lanes in his open-topped car.

I appreciated his kindness, and his willingness to explain. 'But I like telling you things,' he said. 'I like that funny little frown when you're trying to concentrate.' It gave satisfaction on both sides: he liked to teach and I to learn. 'It's so easy to please you,' he said, and it was true for I was bewitched by drives in the car, light-hearted drinks in pubs, the way he pressed close to me at dances.

One afternoon, he came to pick me up in his car. He was pale, strangely tight-lipped, and there was an expression of what I could only call 'exultation' on his face. 'I did it,' he said. 'I've soloed. I was up there, fighting the slipstream, listening to the wires creak. I, Ryder Beeching, was in charge.' He jabbed a finger at the sky. 'Up there.' He grabbed my hands. 'You can't believe what it felt like – the power, being nearer . . . something.'

I raised my face. 'Ryder . . .'

The sun came out and flooded the car. As he kissed me, I closed my eyes and its light danced in a starburst behind the lids.

My girlfriends were envious, my status rose and my parents approved. With talk of another war, there was possibly danger ahead, but I clasped that notion close to me. It was part of loving Ryder and I did not question it. There was not a second of hesitation on my part when he asked me to marry him.

Two nights before the wedding, there was a knock on my door. 'Barbara . . .' My mother edged into the room in her dressing-gown and sat down on the bed.

The room was awash with clothes and tissue paper – it smelt of Coty's *Muguet*, of freshly laundered clothes, of soap and face powder and, faintly, of mothballs, which were kept inside the suitcases stacked on the luggage rack. There was a new satin nightdress case and a new silver-backed hairbrush on the chest-of-drawers, and four glass bottles with silver stoppers, a wedding present from my aunt.

My mother was oddly agitated. She rolled her handkerchief between restless fingers. 'Darling, I have to talk to you. I don't particularly wish to . . . but . . .' Her voice trailed into silence. Then she emitted a little gasp and said, 'Duty.'

I cast about for a way to extricate myself from this talk – I had a premonition that it would be torture for both of us. 'Don't worry,' I said. 'I think I know.'

My mother straightened. 'Do you?' she asked sharply. 'How?' She looked at me, hard and questioning. 'I suppose girls do talk among themselves.' She rallied and patted the space beside her on the bed. 'Sit down, darling. I don't think you do know.'

I thought of the kiss and the light behind my closed eyes, the way my body had trembled.

'You might not like . . . what men . . . do,' warned my mother. 'But it's best not to make a fuss. Some things in life are not exactly pleasant, but they do pass, and then one has the benefits of children to compensate.' She smiled wryly. 'You can think about something else, you know. It works . . . it worked . . .' She was unable to finish her sentence.

I shivered with anticipation and nerves – and a touch of fear. Not knowing where to look, I stared at the satin nightdress case, and wished I could summon Ryder's humour and confidence to buoy me up. 'Thank you, Mother. I'll bear it in mind.'

It was early September, and our wedding day was hot. I carried a bouquet of white stephanotis and green leaves and, pinned to my organza dress, the air force diamond brooch – Ryder's wedding gift. He wore his uniform and gave a speech about it being the happiest day of his life, which made me cry.

As for what men did? Undeniably it was messy and embarrassing, but I loved Ryder and its strangeness became sweetly familiar. Slowly, I became accustomed to married life, more experienced, willing to laugh. I slotted into the groove that had been provided, and made sure that I was, to quote Ryder, operational.

'Hallo again,' I said, with an eye on Bunty's departing back.

Alexander lowered the newspaper and stamped on his cigarette. 'I know this looks silly –'

'Not silly, but . . . unwise?'

The implications were not exactly precise, but they were there.

He pointed to a terracotta-coloured lamp in the shape of a classical amphora in the window of the lamp shop. Compared to the attenuated spikes and straight lines of the others, it was beautiful. 'I was contemplating buying that.' He looked uncertain. 'What's unwise about it?'

'If you were planning to give it to Bunty, she'd have fifty fits.'

'Of course she would,' he agreed, with a straight face. 'The design is *most* peculiar. Libertine, pagan and certainly not British. You can't trust anything or anyone from abroad, the filthy swine.'

I laughed, but I was faintly shocked. 'We're not that blinkered, are we?'

'Anyway, it was certainly unwise of you to come and say, "Hallo again."'

'Yes, it was, wasn't it? Look –'

'I am looking.' Alexander took a step closer to me. 'I'm looking at you very hard.'

'Please do – I mean *don't*.' I smiled. 'It's not polite.'

'All right, I won't. I'm looking away now but it doesn't mean I can't see. If it makes you feel any easier, I didn't come back to see you. I went to get some textbooks from the library. It was only when I spotted you and Mrs Andrews still in the window that I decided to wait.' He searched my face. 'Do you mind? Did you want to see me again?'

It would be stupid to pretend. 'A little.'

'Then I was coming back to see you.'

'Are you always so direct?'

'I try to be. Are you always so honest?'

'Only recently.'

Alexander was staring at me. 'That's a compliment? I hope it is.'

'Yes.'

He continued to stare at me, hungry and questioning.

'Goodbye,' I said, at last. 'Thank you for the coffee.'

I hastened away, heels tip-tapping, along the pavement, and did not look back.

In the kitchen at Edgeborough Road, the clock ticked on the wall above the Rayburn. I hung up my coat, put away the shopping and went upstairs to the bathroom to wash. I dipped my hands into cold water and splashed my burning face, conscious of my constricting underwear trapping the private areas of my body. I washed under my arms with lavender soap. The water was cool and cleansing, and the soap smelt reassuringly normal.

Mrs Storr had been in this morning, and I moved from bedroom to bedroom, checking them over. Bedspreads should be pulled straight, with the eiderdown arranged precisely on top. Window sills dusted. The floors brushed and waxed.

A duster lay on the floor of my bedroom where Mrs Storr must have dropped it. I ignored it and sat down on the bed. The door of the wardrobe was a little ajar. Neat and ordered, my clothes hung on the rack. My grey flannel suit, a Jaeger coat (so extravagant), the black evening dress . . . nothing too frivolous, but not too unfashionable either. The woman who wore these understood the limits and constrictions of her existence, and accepted them with gratitude. She understood about the arid patches, the domestic round of laundry problems, darning, smoking chimneys, the relentless march of meals, the need to polish glass fingerplates on doors. She could achieve an excellent standard for all these requirements and, while her fingers were busy, so too were her thoughts. They sustained and diverted her. Sometimes she enjoyed a private source of hilarity. Other people's antics *were* funny. So were the hens when they got broody. Other times, she wondered about huge, expansive subjects – God, the origins of the universe, and why the soul was called the soul. She puzzled over the crossword, and read easily digested novels and biographies from the library. She loved her family, and rejoiced in being of service to it.

After a while, I got up and shut the wardrobe door, picked up the fallen duster.

I wondered about that woman.

Chapter Eight: Barbara

When the cold weather finally eased, and the snowdrops and daffodils under the beech tree had come and gone, Mrs Storr and I embarked on the annual spring-clean. We dragged the rugs out into the garden and beat them. Mrs Storr polished door-handles and windows with newspaper dipped in vinegar. I turned out wardrobes, repapered drawers, and washed down paintwork.

This was all quite normal, familiar and unthreatening. But what if I was to wield a broom on myself, whisking in and out of the dark corners, the neglected alcoves, the out-of-reach shelves, winkling out dustballs that lurked in unexplained places? What would I find? The floating Barbara? I could not say 'the real Barbara', for what I presented to my husband and family was real enough and perfectly satisfactory. But say, just for argument, I wanted to go and find that other Barbara.

What then?

The buds on the trees swelled and grew sticky. Herr Schlinker's tulips flowered in a profusion of pink and white; I brought armfuls into the house and arranged them in vases.

Mrs Storr was never at her best in the spring. It made her think of death, more precisely the death of Kevin, her son. As she put it, Death had jumped the queue. 'Greedy bugger, if you'll pardon the language, Mrs Beeching. He should have taken me. I would have died gladly for Kevin.'

I listened to Mrs Storr and contemplated the strange and marvellous process of life. The tiny bundles of cells that Kevin had once been had stirred and multiplied into the painfully fair-skinned youth who had marched off to suffer terror, prickly heat and boils before extinction in the jungle, having had no time to live properly.

'Is it any comfort that he died for his country?' I asked her.

'None.'

I folded and refolded petticoats, brassières and girdles, mended sheets, darned stockings and socks, and cleared out the linen cupboard. I checked up on the pots of jam and chutney in the cellar. I emptied and washed Kilner jars and refreshed my precious stores of raisins, treacle, flour and oats.

I made lists: 'Do pantry. Do sewing basket. Do spare-room wardrobe.'

I hung out my 'Dos' like laundry on a mental washing-line.

On Ryder's birthday I gave a bridge party, followed by dinner, which involved a phenomenal amount of cleaning, cooking and starching. Perhaps it was the effect of the spring, but as I stepped into my black silk dress and fastened the belt, I simmered with anticipation and revitalized energy.

The conservatory had been swept and dusted, the bridge tables set up in there. Outside, a spring evening was on the wane and the stiff, formal beauty of the vases of tulips at each end delighted me.

It was no trouble at all to trounce Bunty and her partner. 'My goodness,' she said, 'the demon *has* been let loose.' The atmosphere at our table was polite but a little scratchy.

Seated at the one opposite, Ryder raised an eyebrow in my direction. *Perhaps not too clever, darling.*

My next cards were bad – a two, two fives, too many eights, a queen and a useless knave of diamonds. Normally I could have made something of them. Tonight I did something unusual: I softened my play, allowed Bunty and her partner to win, and was rewarded with an outbreak of positive geniality.

'I'm not sure I understand what you're up to,' muttered Bunty into my ear, as I led the ladies upstairs to powder their noses. 'That was too obvious.'

At dinner, I placed Fitzgerald Adams, a judge, on my right and Tony McEwan, who owned a couple of newsagents in the city, on my left. The latter was in high spirits. 'A new era in retailing is on its way, and I'm going to open a chain,' he explained. 'I'll stock the shops with other commodities too. You know, milk and sugar, the sort of things people forget and want at the last minute, and I plan to extend the opening hours.'

Energized by his vision, busy with the notion of prosperity, Tony talked without a break through the mushroom soup and roast beef about chilled storage cabinets and racking for newspapers. All that was required of me was to say, 'Yes,' at intervals in varying tones of appreciation. 'I admire your plans,' I ventured at last, and Tony gave me a swift, lustful look.

Judge Adams professed to enjoy the apple tart I had made (after consulting several cookery books) in the French way, with overlapping slices on a thin pastry base. The duty of a guest is to praise the food but I noticed he left what the recipe called 'frangipane' on the side of his plate. I asked politely if he was trying an interesting case.

He put down his spoon and fork. 'I'm afraid I can't discuss it.'

There followed a sliver of silence as I gave him the chance to ask a few questions about me, but they never came. I ploughed on with an old, trusted ploy. 'Where were you brought up?'

'Near Oxford.'

Aha, I had struck the gold mine. All I had to do was listen to a stream of reminiscence about the young Fitzgerald Adams and his family, and to keep a watchful eye on the rest of my guests.

You're one of the most interesting women I've ever met.

The notion warmed me. Keeping my gaze trained – as my mother had taught me – on the judge, I drank my wine. He didn't have a clue about how interesting I was; neither did he have any idea how I weighed and vetted him.

Later, Ryder and I undressed in a bedroom that was, for a change, relatively warm and cosy. 'Why do you suppose men never ask women questions about themselves? Is it because they're lazy? Or is it their mothers' fault for not teaching them?'

Ryder was wrestling with the studs in his boiled shirt. 'Adams must have been hard work. You *looked* as though you were enjoying yourself. Didn't you?'

'Fitzgerald Adams is only one of many men.'

He threw the shirt into the laundry basket. 'It's never bothered you before.'

Ryder's reply irritated me, and I said, more sharply than I had intended, 'Isn't it odd that a man of his position has no wish to know *anything* about anybody else? Does he ever question his assumptions? No, he doesn't.'

Ryder groaned, climbed into bed and lay with his face turned meaningfully into the pillow. 'Could we have this discussion another time?'

I looked down at him with black outrage. 'You might at least listen. You're no better than the judge.'

'Who minds what he thinks?' he murmured.

'I do. And you should mind, too, what other people think of me. You should mind that they don't bother to ask if I'm well, let alone what my opinions might be.'

Ryder opened his eyes briefly and shut them. 'They don't have to. You're far too beautiful.'

'Listen to me, darling. It does *not* happen to you.' Get Ryder into his uniform – no, even that wasn't necessary, Ryder in old corduroys and a checked shirt was sufficient to elicit a sort of glazed obeisance in people's faces. 'It's an important point,' I said.

At that Ryder sat up. 'I'm sorry, I'm sorry, I'm sorry. Will that do?' Again, he settled himself. 'For God's sake, go to sleep, Babs.'

To punish him, I reached for my manicure set and

trimmed my nails, slowly. On then did I switch off the light.

It was a small revenge, and not very satisfactory, wasted too, for Ryder's breathing indicated that he was asleep.

I did not grudge him his easy sleep for, where Ryder was concerned, sleep was neither easy nor predictable. His sleep patterns had been shot to pieces by the war, and the flying.

Ask most people alive at that time and they will tell you that sleep was rationed like everything else. The fighter pilots waited in the dispersal huts, or swooped in formation over the coastline, or dived into battle with a rattle of guns and chased their prey over the sea. Their wives, girlfriends and mothers pulled in their belts, tied on their headscarves and went about their business. *Hold on. Hold fast. Smile.* But underneath we were worried sick about the children, the bombs, the condition of our teeth and the lack of food.

'Sleep well,' I murmured, to the hump in the bed . . .

I had been up at the airfield, waiting to collect Ryder. The duty officer was cheerful. 'Back any minute,' he said, and cocked an ear. 'Have a cup of tea while you wait, Mrs Beeching.'

The tea was strong enough to dissolve teeth, and the milk on the verge of turning sour, but it was hot and comforting. Outside the huts, the maintenance crew were working on aircraft, and the field stretched away flat and unremarkable.

There was the noise of approaching aircraft, engines at

full throttle, an angry, dangerous sound. 'Christ!' said the duty officer, as the phone began to shrill. 'Enemy planes. Stukas. Duck.'

The sound of bombs falling tears the heart out of the chest. A sickening, flat noise. I found myself on all fours under the table, knees scraped, hands clenched.

Crump.

The hut shook. Glass crashed. The Stukas screamed. High above, a couple of returning Spitfires let loose with their guns.

Crump. Clods of earth sprayed the hut's window.

Fear, sickening and loathsome, clotted in my veins. My arms would not hold me, and I sank down full length and clutched my head. How was I going to get through this? '"A is for apple,"' I muttered desperately, '"round and red. B is for baby," my babies back at home . . . "E is for Eve, who ate the wretched apple . . . R is for Ryder . . ."' Where is he? Is he safe?

Dust filled my mouth, and spilt tea had leached into my skirt. I retched.

Then, suddenly, there was sweet silence.

'Are you all right?' The duty officer touched my shoulder. Slowly, slowly I got to my feet and dusted down my clothes.

'I'm fine,' I said, and my smile was false as Judas because my insides were liquid, and I wanted to cry hysterically. But I patted my hair and said, 'What a pity I haven't got my hairbrush.'

The duty officer picked up the phone and did some rapid talking. 'Offloading bombs on their way home. Yup.

Will do. Sure.' He smiled in my direction. 'Everyone's fine.' He slammed down the receiver. 'Only a bit of damage,' he said cheerfully. 'A crater on the airfield, and the outside lavatories have bought it. Nothing we can't cope with.'

Ten minutes later, Ryder flew in with the squadron. I watched them land, bump and skid towards the huts. Ryder leapt out of his cockpit and raced over towards where I waited, still covered with dust, stockings torn at the knee, wet skirt, hands shaking. 'Oh, God,' he said. 'I might have lost you.'

In a strange way, the two bombs flung out of those Stukas on their way home did me a service. After that I never underestimated fear. I knew its quality and shape. Its rank taste. Its ability to change one. I knew what Ryder had to go through. 'How do you stand it?' I wanted to know. How do you stay whole?

'I'm not sure I do, but if I do it's because of the beauty,' he replied, and it was then I noticed new lines etched round his eyes. 'Because when I go up in the Spit, I soar into infinity, towards God, if you like. And I'm free.'

Ryder's purpose had been clear and definite, but horribly dangerous. If one of his colleagues bought it, the others hid their grief with banter and prayed that Leslie or Pat or Jack had felt nothing and that the end had been quick and clean.

But let me use my newly discovered honesty. Their end was horrible.

My war purpose – to feed and protect the children –

had been filled with drudgery but had not been dangerous in the same way. I listened to the laughter, jokes, reminiscences on the airfields and in the messes, ashamed and confused by how much I envied my husband the purity of his purpose.

A couple of weeks later, Ryder came home from a trip complaining that he felt unwell.

I took his temperature: 101°F. 'Into bed.' I conducted him upstairs, and fed him aspirin and cold lemonade. 'Have you been taking your Paludrine?'

He was flushed and shivering. 'Don't fuss. I'm just tired. We ran into turbulence on the way out, and it was pretty hairy for an hour or so. But it was tiring, and it was too hot to sleep in Lagos.'

I stood by the bed to observe him properly. 'I'll ring Dr O'Donnell.' I fully expected Ryder to object, but he did not.

Dr O'Donnell said he was glad I'd called him out as one could never be too sure with tropical bugs. He fussed around an uncharacteristically quiescent Ryder and pronounced that he would have to go to hospital if he hadn't improved within three days. 'But it's probably only flu. Plenty of rest and liquids will sort him out.'

I spent the morning reorganizing the menus: boiled fish, mashed potato and – particular luxury – chicken soup. I phoned the butcher to ask if he had a chicken, but I was out of luck, which was dismal, as it meant Amelia, who had been off form lately, was top of the list for sacrifice.

Herr Schlinker was planting lettuces and potatoes in the vegetable garden when I went out to give the order. He wore his uniform of trousers and waistcoat with the peaked navy-blue cap that never left his head. He was working with his usual precision and delicacy – in his former life, before he had packed a suitcase and fled with his family from Austria, Herr Schlinker had been a master printer.

'Morning, Frau Beeching.' After more than twenty years in England, his accent was still marked. 'A good day.' He glanced up at a light blue sky with whippy white clouds.

'Mr Beeching is not well, and I would like to make him chicken broth.' I was a little hesitant, which was, perhaps, taking scruples too far. But having fled from a murderous regime, Herr Schlinker might not like acting as executioner to the hens.

He dug the fork into the composted black earth. 'Amelia? I'll see to it.'

'I'm sorry to ask you,' I said. 'It's a beastly job.'

He shook his head. 'Don't worry, Frau Beeching, I don't think about it.'

Amelia's sacrifice was not in vain. I made vast quantities of broth from her scrawny body and Ryder existed on practically nothing else for three days. I was plucking the final slivers of flesh from the carcass when the telephone rang. 'Barbara . . . is this convenient?'

'Of course. I have Ryder upstairs ill, but –'

'Would you like to come to a lunch-time lecture on Freud? It's being given by Professor Handley and is open to the public. He's a noted authority, and we've managed to lure him down. At St Bede's, tomorrow at twelve thirty? I thought it might interest you and I'd like to know what you think.'

'I have a dental appointment, but afterwards . . .'

'I've got two tickets and I'll save you a place.'

I returned to the kitchen, put the kettle on for Ryder's tea, made it, then carried the tray upstairs. He had been dozing. I plumped up the pillows and gave him the tea. 'Thank you,' he said gratefully. 'You make a chap very comfortable.'

His forehead felt cool for the first time in days. 'Dr O'Donnell says you can get up after lunch tomorrow. I'll light a fire and you can sit by it.'

'I haven't felt so weak for as long as I can remember.' He reached out and took my hand. 'Takes me back to childhood.'

'I can't imagine you small.' I stroked his cheek; stubble pricked my fingers. 'All scraped knees and conkers in your pockets.'

His dressing-gown – thick, woollen and tied with a cord – had fallen on to the floor and I picked it up, ran my hand over it. The material was thick and stiff from years of use. That – and his uniform – symbolized Ryder. Sometimes when he was away on a long trip and I had been worried or bothered or, merely, wanted him, I buried my face in the dressing-gown: it was the quickest way to bring him back.

'Read to me, darling,' he said.

A wave of tenderness for my sick husband washed

through me. 'You are a baby,' I murmured, sat down in the chair by the window, took up the paper and began on the leaders.

Except for my voice, the room was quiet, but for the occasional pop of the gas fire and a car in the road outside. Ryder drank his tea, leant back against the pillows and closed his eyes. Every so often, I adjusted my position and even that mundane gesture seemed to me to be filled with significance. I crossed my legs: my thighs slid over the smooth nylon and rested in the modest pose I was so used to assuming.

'Could I ask you to open your mouth, Mrs Beeching?' Mr Lester, the dentist, in the manner of many torturers, was unnervingly polite. 'Then I can see what the problem is.'

I had been up early to give Ryder breakfast, then changed the sheets and remade the bed while he had a bath. I had washed the sheets in the hottest water the electric tub could manage, heaved them out and put them through the mangle. They now hung, damp and dispirited-looking, on the line.

In preparation for Ryder coming downstairs, I had laid the fire, dusted the sitting room and polished the clock, which sang out the hour as I did so.

I was shown into Mr Lester's waiting room a few minutes before ten o'clock and leafed through copies of *Punch*. There was an arrangement of dried flowers in the fireplace; it might have been attractive once but it was now caked with dust. A picture of an Eastern girl in a silk tunic hung above the mantelpiece with a curiously green tinge to her complexion. It struck me as unfortunate for a dentist's waiting room.

'It's the top right-hand one,' I explained to Mr Lester. 'It suddenly began to throb.'

'You haven't been doing anything unusual, Mrs Beeching, eating-wise, I mean? Are you feeling particularly anxious about something? Anxiety affects the teeth, you know.'

I hadn't known.

He got to work with the probe. 'In fact, Mrs Beeching, the problem is not an upper tooth but a lower one. You've been experiencing what we call "referred" pain. It's quite common. I'm afraid I'm going to have to use the drill.'

Quite soon, sweat pricked in my armpits and coated my hands. The drill bored into my jaw, sending spirals of pain through it and a rush of tears to my eyes. I tried not to move.

'I'll be as quick as I can, Mrs Beeching.'

But the process seemed to take hours, and I wondered if dentists were the kind of people who liked inflicting pain. I had read about *them*. Then again, it seemed to me that I was submitting to this (admittedly) small agony greedily, and I had read about those sort of people too.

After a while, I tasted decay as Mr Lester carved it away from the healthy part of my tooth. 'Only a minute or so more,' he said, but the pain grew and I cried out. 'Steady,' he said.

He stood back. 'Have a rinse.' Tiny particles of decay clung to the drill, which he held up in front of my wet eyes. Torturer and tortured, eyeball to eyeball. 'Spit out all the nasty stuff.'

'Poor, poor you.' Alexander ushered me into the hall.

I sank down on a bench in the lecture hall. The rows were filling up with a mixture of students and doctors. There were a few determined-looking women in woollen skirts and blouses, holding notebooks.

'Is my cheek swollen?'

'A little. Was it very bad?'

My tongue fretted at the wounded tooth. 'When Mr Lester gets to work, I always try to think of something worse I've experienced.'

'Such as?'

I blushed. 'Having a baby is pretty bad.'

Alexander did not even blink. 'I expect it is. I don't think Nature made very good arrangements.'

'No.' I placed my handbag on the floor. 'Actually, I lost two after Amy.' It was rare that I confessed to that.

'I'm sorry,' he said swiftly. 'Very sorry.'

'I feel guilty about them, because although I adored Amy and Roy I dreaded having any more. The drudgery and everything . . . was daunting. Then, when I did lose them, I wanted them back.'

Alexander looked down at his folded hands. 'Of course I can't understand properly. I wish I could. And grief can be very lonely.'

His sympathy had a powerful effect on me. 'Ryder was disappointed. He wanted another son. We tried again, and this time I was thankful and looking forward to it, and did my best to make it happen. But it didn't, and I was quite ill for a long time afterwards. After that we agreed to let it be.'

'Do you regret the decision?'

I raised my eyes to his. 'It's not that simple.'

'I don't suppose anything important is ever simple,' he said. 'I'm just beginning to find that out.'

At that point Professor Handley, a large man with a pipe in hand, took the podium and spread out a stack of notes. Alexander muttered, 'Don't be alarmed, he's good on Freud and easy to understand.'

'I look forward to it . . . I've been reading a book on Freud, but struggling a little.'

Whether Professor Handley was good or not, I was in no position to judge. He ranged over Freud's early work, the development of his idea of the unconscious and his methods of analysis. Then he concentrated on the notion of sexuality in childhood, which was the route Freud had chosen to explain how the child matured into a social being.

I was by turns aghast and, I confess, amused. True . . . It was true that, at certain points, Ryder and Roy had not got on but I could not accept it was because Roy wished to castrate his father. And as for Amy's (apparent) rage at her lack of a penis, this struck me as ludicrous.

Then I thought about Amy. So cross, so jealous, so determined not to be fluffily feminine.

'So?' Alexander put a hand under my elbow and steered me outside into the sunlight.

I felt unequal to discussing the Oedipal complex. 'I was

interested in the idea that the individual often finds it difficult to live in society and to be happy because his desires are often contrary to what society allows.'

'Curious how most people latch on to that idea.' His grip tightened on my elbow. 'Do you find it difficult?'

When he kissed my hand in the apple-house, his mouth must have registered the pulse beneath the thin skin at the point where my wrist and hand are joined, felt its warmth, inhaled Coty's Muguet.

'No more than anyone else.'

Outside in the courtyard, I thanked him. 'You were kind and thoughtful to invite me.'

Alexander's lips twitched. 'There's another thing.' He spread his hands in a tentative gesture. 'I happened to be talking to Miss Raith, the almoner. She's looking for someone to come in one day a week to help her.'

'Why are you helping *me* so much?'

He shoved his hands into his trouser pockets and smiled. 'Because I thought it might be of interest. Because I hope we're friends.'

I intend to look up the definition of 'friendship' in the *Oxford English Dictionary*, which is in the library. Its precise meaning, the derivation of the word . . . and how . . . how it is not applied.

Chapter Nine: Siena

I stepped on to the plane to New York and turned left.

The group behind me turned right.

Nice.

The stewardess ushered me to my seat and fussed over me. Would I like this, that or the other?

So nice.

Safely buckled in, I rang Charlie. 'All well so far, I'll ring you when I arrive.'

I had caught him in chambers between interviewing clients and, in the background, there was a murmur of voices and the ringing of telephones. Presumably at his end Charlie could hear the whine of the aircraft's engines and the stewardess's chant, 'Drink, sir? Drink, madam?'

'Any developments on the Jackie Woodruff case?' I asked.

'None, except we know now that the prosecution will be calling in every bloody expert under the sun.'

'Charlie, I've been thinking . . . Have you looked back at the family history? Have babies died in the past?'

'Yup, we looked,' Charlie confirmed, and from where I sat miles away, I felt the chill. Normally, when things were going well and I made a suggestion, Charlie was sweetly grateful. It was a win-win thing. I wanted to demonstrate how much I cared, how involved I was in Charlie's professional life. He wanted me in there with him – but not too far. Just enough. That most of my suggestions were quietly binned was also normal.

'Good idea, though.' His voice crackled with impatience, and my heart sank. 'Nice of you to think about it.'

'*Charlie*, what do you mean?'

'Nothing, Siena.'

But he did, and there we were, wrestling with non-meanings where meanings should have been clear. Charlie was angry with me. Or, rather, he was struggling not to be angry with me because he believed that everyone had equal rights. No one should impose on anyone else. But he wanted to lay down the law like a good old-fashioned Victorian patriarch: *Siena, it is time to have children*.

And I was saying, *Not yet, not yet*. And, indeed, *Perhaps not*.

'Take care, Siena.'

'Love you,' I said, and every word was scorched into me. *I love Charlie: heart, soul and mind*.

Charlie did not reply, 'I love you,' which he should have done, but repeated, 'Take care.'

I closed my eyes, then opened them and glanced with alarm at the man who had sat down in the adjacent seat. He looked as though he might be a talker.

I took off my shoes, put on the socks supplied and fished out my notes and the itinerary India and I had gone through several times. With a bit of luck, a glorious six hours of silence lay ahead, one of the unsung perks of long-distance travel.

My mobile shrilled. 'Siena, have I caught you in time?' questioned Vita, the editor of *Fashion, This Week*. She never wasted time on chit-chat: she barely wasted time on breathing. 'Good. We've just been going through the schedules for the next quarter and I'm planning a change. I'd like you to "do" some men. OK?'

The question was a mere formality – the deed would have been done without my say-so. 'Fine.' More interesting were the reasons that had prompted Vita to put men on the agenda. She was a woman at pains to give an impression that, as a sex, men did not figure, except as a species of grub that lived under stones.

'I thought you'd have no objection.' Vita knew perfectly well that she would receive none. 'It will make us more . . . rounded, and rounded is where we're at. I'll get Jenni on to it at once.' She paused. 'The good news is that your column's readership is increasing. The bad news is that *Brewer's* is planning to run a rival one.'

A flicker of anxiety tightened my stomach, which was stupid. *Brewer's* did not have the circulation that *Fashion, This Week* commanded. 'No problem,' I said. 'They don't have the team.'

'No problem,' repeated Vita briskly. 'We'll bomb them off the page. Have a good trip. Contact me the minute you're back.'

She rang off. I switched off the mobile, and glanced out of the window at the grey airport buildings. Never very far away, anxiety swooped down. It was a thick, damp feeling at the back of my throat, which made me want to bite my nails. What was the *subtext* to Vita's call? Was there an implied criticism in her diktat? Was she saying, 'Sharpen up the act or else'?

I made a rapid mental reappraisal of the past weeks' columns. The prose had been snappy, the judgements spot on, the photos and the clothes first-class. So, too, had been the feedback, a judicious mix of praise (69 per cent) and how-dare-you-be-so-rude (31 per cent); the latter was necessary to give the operation spice and a whiff of danger, and to provide ballast for the (generally) sycophantic 'Your Letters' page.

Even if one made allowances for 'good' being a slippery concept, it was as good as Vita could get.

There was no Logical Reason for Anxiety. Yet anxiety, like freckles or eye colour, *was* omnipresent, a feature of life, a constant undercover reminder of danger.

Could I ring Charlie again? Did I dare? I looked out of the window. The fuel tenders buzzed to and fro. Wrong, wrong. There were plenty of logical reasons to be anxious. Status. Achievement. Money. Energy. All were finite; all were prone to develop spots of decay . . . like . . . like an apple.

The aircraft lumbered out of its berth and I was on my way.

I glanced at my watch and accepted a second glass of orange juice.

Think left-brain activity, such as sorting laundry – which was so necessary after working for long periods with the right brain. The television psychologist Taj Bindi ('His consultations cost a *fortune*'), whom I'd sat next to at one of Dick and Manda's publishing dinner-parties, had passed me the tip. For free. 'It's vital for inner health, Siena, to exercise both lobes of the brain . . .' he had placed a light hand on my bare arm '. . . to allow the subconscious time to work in peace.' Apparently, the subconscious only leapt into life while its owner was engaged in doing something mundane like ironing or cleaning the fridge.

At the time it crossed my mind that Taj's advice might have been a clever way of making sure women fitted in the housework along with everything else. Yet Taj Bindi had known what he was talking about. Those tedious, repetitive tasks were soothing. They permitted space, an easy drawing of breath. So, yes, as far as I was concerned, if the subconscious required left-brain laundry moments to function, then it would get them.

'Know thyself,' said the preacher – or was it the philosopher? The unexamined life was not worth living. (I don't know who said that either.) There we were, Dick, Manda, Charlie, I and the others in our circle, all rushing around trying to do precisely that.

'A successful career,' I hazarded, in one of Charlie's and my late-night discussions, 'is as much to do with "interior" knowledge as with the exterior factors.'

'True,' he agreed. 'Mastery over the self is the key. Between the *de facto* and the *de jure*.'

'Once a lawyer, always a lawyer.'

'Trot out that tired old cliché again, Mrs Grant, and I won't be responsible for what happens.'

We never finished that conversation.

The aircraft's engines roared into take-off mode. Charlie, I told him silently, the *de facto* is what I carry in me, the unwritten, unquantifiable instincts on which I call.

The *de jure*, that which is written down as the law, is what you work with.

So how does the mind fix the body image? I could tell you that. Why does it make you see what you see in a reflection of yourself in the mirror? *Big hips, small eyes. Ugh.* Of course, it should be . . . *Huge eyes, tiny hips. Beautiful.* I could explain that deliberate mis-seeing, too. But that's my business.

When I first encounter someone new, I know, within thirty seconds or so, certain aspects of them. *She is sad. He is telling lies.* I wish I could claim cleverness or superiority, but I was born with the facility, and I'm in the kind of job where it's sharpened with daily use.

But here I should correct myself. Lucy Thwaite had not been so cleverly handled. Or, for that matter, my first husband.

My mother also has the gift. 'Don't trust Jay,' she had warned me. But I had ignored her.

The aircraft got itself into the air, banked and headed for America. The man beside me drained his glass and picked a peanut out of the complimentary bowl. 'I'm Daniel,' he said, 'chairman of Easy Flex Systems. What do you do? Are you staying in New York?'

He's pleased with himself. He thinks he probably has an easy pick-up.

I opened my eyes very wide. 'I'm a housewife,' I replied, sweet and timid, 'at home with four children,' and watched his expression perform a lightning *volte-face* from interest into indifference and boredom.

*

New York was so cold. Steam billowed up from the gratings, and froze, icicles dripped from railings. I was protected from it as cars had been ordered by Trimester Productions to ferry me from airport to hotel and, the next day, to the studio – but not protected from gridlock on Lexington and Broadway where an army of double-parked delivery trucks were happily bottlenecking the traffic flow.

I was introduced to the team and the set, then informed that the audience would be housewives and students. The schedule was tight – so tight there was no chink of light anywhere.

On the first day we filmed for the pilot eight hours on the trot, with a similar session slotted in for the following day. I returned to the hotel with jet-lag gnawing at my edges, ordered room service and a film, then collapsed into sleep.

During the night I woke, stiff in the unfamiliar bed and masked by sweat. I turned over. The beat of the days slipping past sounded in my ears. In the dark, the terrors and anxieties massed and multiplied.

The phone rang at six a.m. It was the producer wanting to chew over a couple of different approaches. By eight o'clock, when I arrived at the downtown studio, Fersen, the wardrobe consultant, had already lighted on a couple of 'darling' alternatives to the clothes I had selected for my subject. He introduced himself by asking if I minded.

Go carefully, India had counselled. Be grown-up.

Fersen, slim and wiry, was dressed in tight leopardskin

trousers and a hooded velour jacket. He wanted Carole, a middle-aged black florist, to wear the same. They made him feel so liberated, not at all 'agey'.

Fersen's inner and outer self had met in the leopardskin trousers, but would this be true for Carole? I consulted my briefing notes on her and suggested tactfully, 'These are clothes that shout.'

'Pardon?' he said. 'Didn't get that. Your accent . . .'

'These are clothes that shout.'

'Precisely, Siena,' he said, his antagonism apparent, and his hearing perfect. 'I think Carole would appreciate a little shouting.'

Silence, while we absorbed the implications of the exchange. Fersen broke it first. 'And what do you do in England?'

I wheeled out the artillery. 'I have the consultancy, a magazine column, a book deal –'

He broke into this recital. 'Congratulations – a multi-hyphenate.'

'OK, OK, Siena . . . I'm with you now . . .' The makeup girl dragged me over to a table and mirror. 'Won't take long.' She dabbed and brushed. 'Looking good, looking good, Siena . . .' Then she stopped. 'Oh, my God,' she said. 'Your eyebrows are *so* English. Do you mind if I do some work on them?'

Did I mind? Were English eyebrows a problem?

'No,' I said faintly, and thought, Another damn thing to worry about.

Carole arrived with two bouquets she had made up that morning and presented them to Fersen and me. Fersen's was composed of dramatic colours and shapes; mine was of deep red roses into which had been tucked one white gardenia. Its smell was of velvet, luxury and beauty, and I knew at once that Carole was not a leopardskin trousers woman.

'OK,' I addressed Fersen. This was my first transatlantic negotiation. 'Let's try my version first, yours second.'

I emerged from those frantic few days feeling the white lash of exhaustion from coping with everyone's nerves, including my own.

'I'm a multi-hyphenate,' I informed Charlie, when I phoned him.

'Does a multi-hyphenate cook supper when it's at home?'

That was good. Charlie was making a joke. 'Not sure. I think it's probably too grand.'

I waited for Charlie to launch into a description of his day – whom he had seen, the progress of the case. But he didn't. There was a barrage of non-information. 'Was there anything in particular you wanted to say, Siena?'

'Not really. Just touching base. Few odd problems here. Nothing I won't get my head round.'

Marginal interest was displayed at the other end. 'I have no doubt you will. Listen, I have to go. Speak soon.'

Restless, I moved around the hotel room. A full fruit bowl had been placed on the table, a blisteringly white towelling dressing-gown hung on a peg, and plumped goose-down pillows edged with lace featured on the bed. There was not one but two leatherbound ring folders on the desk stuffed with instructions on how to negotiate the city. My eye lit on Carole's exquisite bouquet and lingered.

After all, I was in a different time zone and I had work to do.

London dweller that I was, I had no memory of real cold, the aggressive biting-into-the-cheeks variety that greeted Lola and me when we got out of the train at Franconia late on the Saturday morning.

'Don't worry,' said Lola, as we waited for Bill to pick us up. 'I have masses of spare clothes for idiots like you.'

We were old enough friends to call each other 'idiot'. Lola was fashion editor for *Chic* and worked 24/7, and Bill was an architect. He lived full-time at the Franconia house, and Lola preferred to roost in one room in TriBeCa during the week. 'It's a semi-detached marriage,' she explained. 'We like it that way. Took a bit of working out, but we got there.'

Muffled in a thick coat with a hat pulled down over his ears, Bill kissed me warmly and his wife lingeringly. 'You old hick,' she said tenderly. We bundled into the heated car and drove out of town for a mile or two, then turned on to a track at the end of which I saw a neat wooden house overlooking a valley planted with fruit trees.

In the spare room, furnished with rugs and antique furniture, Lola (or was it Bill?) had left a volume of Robert Frost's poetry on the bedside table. I picked it up and leafed through the introduction. The poet had lived here, in Franconia.

I looked out of the window. You could *see* the cold out there, and the quiet, and the landscape was what might be termed old-fashioned. It had neatness, precision, like an old sampler or woodcut.

'It's difficult to describe,' I said to Charlie when, after some debate with myself, I had snatched up my mobile and pressed the 'home' button. 'It sort of broods, but cleanly.'

'It's raining here,' Charlie countered. 'And the dustmen have gone on strike.'

A white blanket was folded over the line of hills and the dip of the valley. My breath misted the window-pane and I rubbed it away. 'I'm looking at trees and apple orchards.'

'Well . . .' Charlie spun out the word '. . . over here there's been an explosion of traffic cones, most of them at the end of our road, and the Circle Line has run once, an event to be commemorated with a Blue Plaque.'

'Listen,' I urged, anxious that Charlie should share in what I was seeing, 'there's something special here. It's so white, so quiet. So removed. You must come with me next time.'

'Since when have you been Miss Rural Paradise?'

Lola had laid out walking clothes on the bed, and I got dressed in them: corduroy trousers, check shirt and cable-knit sweater, which smelt faintly of bonfires. She hooted when I appeared downstairs, and I noted that she had retained her black trousers and cashmere sweater. 'Aren't you coming out, Lola?'

'I have lunch to fix and calls to make.' She ran her

fingers through streaked hair. 'I need a moment or two to hunker down. You know, to take off one skin and put on the other.'

Bill lent me a pair of boots. They had a rim of soft leather, supple toes and waxed laces. They were a fraction too big, but my feet felt good in them. 'Wrap this round your face,' he handed me a scarf and a hat, 'and keep your head covered.'

We stepped out into a brilliant, bitter world and I gasped – the cold seemed to peel the skin off my face.

Bill laughed. 'It always takes one by surprise.'

'I should have come prepared.'

He glanced at me. 'You don't know until you know.'

That was so like Bill. You wanted to tease him about his folksy wisdom and, at the same time, you didn't: you wanted to believe him.

He was not a big man and I'm quite tall. Even so, I had trouble keeping up for he was fleet and fit, and intimate with the land. We crunched over the iced snow, and walked up the slope to emerge on the ridge overlooking the valley, then dropped down towards the orchards.

'I've bought a couple of acres from the farmer over there, with apple trees.' He waved in the direction of a pink brick house further down the valley. 'It'll take me a few seasons to get them back into order as they've been neglected. But you can't prune apples too vigorously, as they go into shock.'

The grass was long, rigid with frost. We passed between the apple trees, suspended in winter formaldehyde, each twig, each nodule on the branch outlined in white hoar.

'These are the free-standers. I don't like dwarfs. Give me proper trees. For me, that's their point. Their bigness. Just as long as the rootstock is good.'

His drawl was comforting, almost sleepy-making. I stopped and gazed up through a latticework of branches at a hard, icy sky. 'What do you mean by rootstock?'

Bill tapped a branch with a gloved finger, and ice crystals fell to earth. 'Apples don't grow well on their own rootstock, so they're grafted.' He sent another shiver of crystal to the ground. 'I've planted Jonogold, which is a modern apple, and Katy, which came originally from Sweden. It has rosy cheeks, like a pretty Swedish maiden. Its parent was your English Worcester Pearmain.'

We ate an early supper of vegetable stew, cake and strawberry ice-cream in a kitchen fragrant with the smell of Bill's homemade bread.

When I woke on Sunday morning, a light snow had fallen during the night, masking our previous day's footprints in the drive.

Downstairs, Lola peered through the sitting-room window. 'This is the testing bit. I always imagine that I want to be out there communing with the Great Life Force, but when it comes to fifteen below zero, I back off. Why don't we just light the fire?'

'I'm going out,' said Bill.

'So am I,' I said.

'You're both mad,' said Lola, plumping down on to the sofa. 'On second thoughts, perhaps you're not. That leaves me to cook lunch.'

This time, Bill took a different route, and headed for a

clearing by an alder swamp, where some rabbits had come out to enjoy the sun. They sat in a group, scratching and grooming their winter coats. We watched them for some time – the play of muscle under their fur, the brightness of their eyes. The younger ones danced around energetically, making patterns in the snow. Their parents observed them. Indulgently? Affectionately?

We watched until the chill began to bite, then moved on past the swamp at whose edge the ice had melted into a dark, frozen slush. 'Looks like coffee granita,' I remarked.

'The city girl,' he said.

'Oh, God. Silly, vain and spoilt? Is that it?'

He uttered a bark of laughter. 'No, just different. Different points of comparison.'

He stopped, reached over and adjusted my scarf so that it covered my mouth. 'Charlie would be angry with me if I let you freeze,' he said. 'How is he?'

'The same. Busy.' We moved on. 'He wants us to start a family.'

'And?'

'I'm not sure. I wish I was a rabbit, and didn't have to think about it. It just happens or not.'

We reached the edge of the clearing, and walked up the ridge. 'Lola and I never wanted children,' Bill said eventually. 'Our families weren't pleased about it – she's probably told you.'

Lola had. She and Bill had been attacked from both sides: having children was a public duty, a personal pleasure, a function of men and women.

'At least you knew,' I said. 'And I *should* know. I have

138

– oh, how many? Thirty-two different kinds of mobile phone to choose from, forty-eight varieties of jeans, twelve airlines, a hundred and twenty thousand books, a hundred oils to put in my bath . . . I could go on. I should be good at making up my mind.'

'That's not choice,' Bill slipped his arm round my shoulders – he looked puzzled, 'that's consumerism. Having it all, whatever. Choice is different.'

To my surprise, Charlie was waiting for me at the airport on my return. I threw my arms round his neck and kissed his lips. 'How lovely.'

He kissed me back. 'Couldn't wait to see you.'

I breathed a sigh of relief.

As we let ourselves into the flat, I caught a whiff of trapped air, a suggestion of murky river, an eddy of city dust. Automatically I scanned the table by the door for the post.

'First thing you do,' Charlie teased. 'Don't worry, no one will have forgotten about you in a week. Check me over instead.'

So I did.

Later I got up and, in my dressing-gown, wandered into the sitting room and noticed at once the two glasses on the coffee-table, a dish of olives and some stones in the ashtray. I called out: 'You've been entertaining.'

A half-clothed Charlie appeared in the doorway. 'Yup. Cimmie came over.'

'Cimmie?'

Charlie picked up the glasses and the olives. 'In the end,

it was more convenient – and she wanted to see the flat.'
He glanced at me. 'Don't look like that, Siena. It was just
a drink.'

Chapter Ten: Siena

Cimmie had been in our home. That took a little thinking about. Yet there was nothing inherently treacherous in my husband sharing an innocent drink with his ex-spouse. Nothing to worry about at all. 'Of course that's fine.'

'So?'

I grabbed the first available thought. 'What colour is her hair?' Apparently Cimmie changed it as frequently as the seasons – it was a standing joke among her friends. (She had been in a blonde phase at our wedding.)

Without missing a beat, Charlie replied, 'Natural.'

'Which colour is that precisely?'

'Mouse.' He added: 'She looks glowing and it suits her.'

'Oh.'

Charlie hefted my abandoned suitcase from the hall into the bedroom. Only then he let drop the information: 'Cimmie has given up hair dye, booze and fags because she's pregnant. That's what she wanted to tell me.'

I handed Charlie his present, which was two expensive Brooks Brothers' shirts of the type he liked. 'Thanks, darling.' He put them down on the bed. 'I know how rushed for time you were.'

I unpacked. Shirts into the laundry basket, shoes into transparent boxes. Brush, hang and bag skirts and trousers in wardrobe. Stow underwear in drawers lined with lavender- and jasmine-scented paper.

Cimmie was having a baby.

We ate a meal of soup and cheese. Charlie had arranged the cheese on a bed of vine leaves; its white and cream looked beautiful against the sharp green. Outside, the river was flowing swiftly, swollen with winter rains. We talked about flying, airports and the baffling ways of customs officers, and hotels.

'I got them to change my room,' I said. 'Very nicely, of course. I told the manager I lived in a very special place and it was important I had a special room – that is, not the one they had allocated, which overlooked the street. He agreed with me and, quick as a flash, I was given a room at the back.'

It was the sort of trick I had picked up over years of business travel. Charlie rolled his eyes heavenwards.

I told him about Bill and Lola and the house in Franconia, and described the white, eerie, freezing landscape, the apple trees waiting patiently in their rows for the spring. I related anecdotes about filming for the pilot, and dropped in casually the information that Trimester Productions had signed me off with encouraging noises. 'I knew everything was probably OK when Dwayne, the producer, said the chairman of the network had approved the slogan "Siena's makeover for real people," and took me to dinner at the Four Seasons.'

Charlie's hair flopped over his forehead. 'Four Seasons, eh?'

'I was too exhausted to enjoy it. We'd spent the afternoon trying to find the right wedding outfit for a woman
who was size sixteen, a redhead. She fancied the camera-
man and wouldn't concentrate.'

'Yes,' said Charlie.

Our conversation petered out. We were talking about
the wrong subjects, of which the most pressing was rep-
resented by a half-empty dish of satin-green olives, and a
couple of glasses.

Across the table, Charlie raised his eyes. 'Go on,' he
said, 'let's have it out.'

I swallowed. 'Did you have to invite Cimmie here?'

He shrugged. 'Why not? She wanted to talk to me.'

'I'm sure she did.'

Charlie kept a straight face. 'She suggested that I divorce
you and make her an honest woman.'

Joke.

I experimented with a smile, but not very successfully.
'Bruce is the father, I imagine.'

'Yes. They're off to Australia as soon as they can get
married and the paperwork's been dealt with.'

'When . . . when is she having the baby?'

'Early autumn.'

'Season of mellow fruitfulness.' My hand hovered over
the cheeseboard, but I didn't want anything more to eat.
Whether Cimmie was married or not was irrelevant. She
was pregnant and I was not and, worse, Charlie minded
dreadfully.

'Sometimes I feel Cimmie lives with us too.'

'Jay isn't exactly absent from your thoughts, is he?'

I picked up my plate. 'Only as a reminder of what went wrong.'

'Crowded marriage.'

We exchanged a long look in which affection and understanding were minimal. It frightened me, and I went away to take a shower.

After flying, the skin requires careful cleansing and moisturizing. Tomorrow I had scheduled a manicure and pedicure, followed by a session with the aromatherapist. These were routine to a busy, successful, high-profile earner.

Charlie came in and sat down on the bed. I swivelled round from the wardrobe and peered at him. I had to try to understand who, and what, I was looking at. To see beneath the skin.

'I'd like to read you something,' he said heavily, and produced a letter.

'Dear Mr Grant, I want to thank you for what you're doing for me. Nobody believes I am innocent and, in a strange way, it doesn't matter very much any more. I don't even mind the idea of prison but I may feel differently in a couple of months. But if I can't have Rob, and he would have been a year old today, and I can't because he's dead, then I don't much care to carry on.

'I'll probably be beaten up if I do go to prison. They do that, don't they?'

I came and sat down beside him, and prised the letter away from him.

*When I was young, we lived by the river and there was a big
alder tree which I and my brothers used to climb. We dared
ourselves to crawl down the branch that hung over the water as far
as we could without falling in. I often ended up wet. I always
thought my Rob would do that when he grew up and I would sit
underneath and watch him.*

*Do you suppose ghosts grow up? I don't know. But I think his
little ghost will be there, climbing the tree.*

I took Charlie's hand in mine and chafed it. 'It's
unimaginable.' The death of a baby was unimaginable, and
I had no right to trespass on, or to pretend, any shade of
that grief. 'I'm sorry.'

'I've got a big job ahead on this one.' Charlie rubbed
his eyes.

'How do you think the baby died?'

His reply startled me. 'I'm not absolutely sure. The
child-minder, of course, swears blind she never touched
him roughly. He was a very bad sleeper, screamed a lot.
Jackie had been ill and had just started back at work. She
was still not properly recovered.'

I considered the information. 'It must be so . . . so
frightening,' I said. 'You're so tired, and busy, and rushed,
and there's this baby who won't go to sleep, who won't
let you alone. Maybe, maybe . . . you're driven to the brink
. . . Maybe . . . you do something terrible on the spur of
the moment.'

'And maybe not,' said Charlie.

In the bathroom, I gazed with jet-lagged features into
the mirror and smoothed cream into my face and chest

— don't forget the place between the breasts. It's a dead giveaway.

Our bodies bound Charlie and me, but mine came between us too, for it would be my body, not his, that accepted the business of gestation, delivery and . . . what came afterwards.

Startled and disturbed, I tipped my head upside-down and brushed my hair until my scalp protested.

I wished I understood myself.

I was still married to Jay when I booked a consultation with Ingrid Broadhurst, Life Coach, Therapist, with several sets of letters after her name.

Her office by the canal in Little Venice was flooded with light, but the seat to which she pointed me faced away from the window and towards a couple of pot plants that drooped from lack of water or attention. For the client, it was not an inspiring position in which to sit.

Ingrid was dressed in designer jeans and a leather blouson jacket, both of which suited her. She wrote my name on a form, took details about my health and cycle, raised an impeccably plucked eyebrow and asked, 'Why?'

'Why?'

'Why are you here?'

I tried to explain that when I woke each morning, I was conscious of an underlying, stubborn grief that would not go away, and that I could not fathom. It was like a piece of continually worn clothing – like the winter vest into which children used to be sewn for winter's duration, as itchy and malodorous.

'Is it loss? Is it fear? Can you be more specific?'

'OK, OK . . . Let me try. I'm twenty-seven, my career's going well, my husband's doing well. We've been married for two years. We live in a nice house in Chelsea . . .' In short, I had been given what I had asked for. But the real account of the past two years, the figures on the bottom line, showed a debit. 'Why,' I asked the life coach, therapist, 'does this not add up to happiness?'

Ingrid's eyes grew stern as she gazed into mine. 'No one is allowed to be unhappy. We shall get to the bottom of it.'

I had no idea how infinitely comforting it was to be taken charge of. I was not going to be *allowed* to be unhappy.

'Does he know you're unhappy?'

'I don't think so.'

'You haven't talked it over?'

'No.'

Ingrid was sterner. 'Siena,' she said, 'proper adult love is about telling the truth. It's about seizing the problems and shaking them by the scruff of the neck. You must schedule in a session with your husband.'

'I'm not sure,' I backed off hastily, 'that I want to take action. I just wanted to talk it over with someone who could put a finger on it.'

Ingrid wrote on my notes for a good two minutes. If I had been less scrupulous (or was it cowardly?), I might have been tempted to read her conclusions for I was skilled in reading upside-down. Finally, she put down her pen and glanced at the clock on the desk. 'Do you know what the root of evil is, Siena?'

I cast around. 'The seven deadly sins must play a part.'

Ingrid approved of my answer. 'Ah, but the greatest of these is sloth. Evil comes of laziness. An inner laziness that refuses to deal with issues.'

I returned home to Jay, burdened by my close proximity to evil and the sin of non-verbalizing. With respect to our marriage, this was a little ironic: Jay and I functioned on silly word games. 'Bugger off,' Jay would say, when he meant, 'Come and kiss me.'

Jay subscribed to the let's-have-our-cake-and-eat-it school. 'Let's do it now,' he often said, narrowing his small (his one imperfect feature) eyes. 'It only takes an earthquake, a terrorist's bomb, and the system collapses and we'll have missed out. We make money, we enjoy ourselves and take time out for each other.'

That was the Grand Plan.

Yet as Jay moved higher up the echelons of the bank and his pay trebled, I heard less about the Grand Plan and a great deal more about being a sleek beast in the corporate jungle. If I alluded to the Grand Plan during one of our increasingly rare suppers together, he would smile enigmatically and talk about share options.

'My two years of marriage seem to have been spent in striving.' On my second visit to Ingrid, I found myself addressing the potted plants as Ingrid took notes. 'Striving to please Jay and do all the other things, like keeping the house running and, of course, getting ahead in my career.' I added, with some pride, 'I've just been taken on as a fashion agony aunt for a trade magazine.'

'So? Your conclusions, Siena?'

'I've dressed my marriage up in the wrong clothes.' Yes, that was the best way to put it. I had dressed up my marriage to Jay in rainbow colours of hope, excitement and novelty.

'Undress it, Siena, and take a good look at what's underneath.'

'And what if I don't like it?'

Ingrid folded her hands. 'There are many things that we have to try on for size in this life,' she remarked, unruffled by my gusting emotions and neediness. 'Maybe marriage is one of them. If something's not right for *you*, then you must be honest and take it back to the shop.'

The cool certainty of her prescription took my breath away and the subsequent days passed in the confusion and clamour of an internal debate. What was I going to say to Jay? What did I want? I was so busy listening to the orchestra of voices that Ingrid had conjured up, so fascinated and absorbed by it, that I failed to initiate the actual debate.

Jay did it for me. Shortly after my fourth visit to Ingrid (a difficult session where we had worked on my 'blockage') Jay announced at breakfast that he had been offered a third promotion. 'But the deal is, I have to live in Hong Kong.'

'*Live* in *Hong Kong*?'

'It's not a salt mine, Siena. It's a civilized city.'

I bit my lip. 'But not my city. And I'm not leaving my work.'

Did I detect, or imagine, a look of relief on Jay's

features? 'You could do something along the same lines. Wise up. It would be good experience to add to the portfolio.'

'I don't think so,' I said.

Jay got to his feet and adjusted his tie. 'If that's how you feel.'

It was the moment for courage and for deblocking and whatever other nonsensical terms Ingrid employed. 'Surely you've noticed we've not been getting on lately, Jay. I think we should do something about it.'

He reached for his briefcase. 'Don't start, Siena. I've just enough energy to cope with this.' He beat his fist on the handle. 'OK? We'll sort out Hong Kong later.'

'I'm not happy, Jay. I don't know why, and I'm sure it's not your fault. But I don't think you can count on me coming to Hong Kong.'

A genuine battle appeared to wage in Jay's breast — between the imperative to get to work on time and the demands of his wife. A battle that encompassed the transformation that had taken place in him during our marriage from the old, charming, lovely Jay to the comparative stranger who stood before me in the kitchen, fiddling impatiently with his briefcase. 'So,' he said, with a flare of irritation and impatience, 'you'd better bugger off.'

I'm sure Jay regretted having uttered those words in the strained, stringent atmosphere of a rushed breakfast. And, for my part, I was racked by doubt as to the wisdom of following Ingrid's advice. The very concept of responsibility suggested that one took one's own decisions, and did not allow others to foist theirs on you.

But it was too late.

For the first and final time, Jay and I accepted that 'bugger off' meant what it said.

'*Lovely* to see you.' Manda's face was contorted with the effort of juggling Patrick on one hip, and trying to lay the table with one hand. 'Tell me *all*.'

It was Saturday. Charlie was working on the Woodruff case, and Dick was away at a booksellers' conference. Manda had to look after the children. There was a pile of manuscripts on the kitchen table, and the top one had been liberally splashed with orange juice. Hetty was crawling around the floor, singing to herself. She was wearing odd socks and a pink hairband. 'Don't mind Het.' Her mother nudged her with her foot. 'She's playing at being an Indian princess. Now, shoot.'

I launched into a description of Fersen's flounces, the free sample of Crème de la Mer in the hotel, the wooden house in Franconia, the blare and bustle of New York . . . and slithered into silence. Manda was not listening. It was not that she didn't wish to but that it was impossible. Patrick and Hetty were cross and vying for their mother's attention.

'I don't think they like Olga,' Manda admitted after she had – finally – put a quiche into the oven and slammed the door. 'They just don't seemed settled.'

'Hey.' I wrested Patrick from his mother and sat down. 'Don't play your poor mummy up.' I jiggled him on my knee. 'This is the way the farmer rides, Patrick. This is the way the bishop rides . . .'

Patrick favoured me with a quelling look and stuck his thumb into his mouth.

'Should I sack Olga?' Manda slumped into a chair. 'I don't have any real ground – and you need stacks of money for a nanny.'

'This is the way the poor man rides . . . clip-clop, clip-clop . . .'

Patrick gave a half-chuckle and took his thumb out of his mouth. He twisted round to look at his mother. 'Horsy.'

The curve of the bright, boyish head, the long lashes, the imperious toddler expression made me . . . made me catch my breath. This was what little boys looked like at his age . . . on the cusp of becoming masculine, no longer pretty. That moment of transition, I supposed, was the sort of thing a mother would notice.

'Thanks.' Manda buried her face in a hand. 'I'm so tired that I'm contemplating killing myself for some peace. It's the most attractive option I can think of.'

After the quiche, I insisted on taking the children to the park for an hour to give Manda a break.

That one (finite) hour stretched indefinitely into a month.

Every six metres or so, Hetty dropped her gloves. These had to be retrieved while I kept an eye on Patrick, who insisted that he wanted to walk. Every so often, he fell over and cried, and was propped upright and dusted down. He looked at me with suspicion and dislike. 'I want my mummy.' His wails were counterpointed by Hetty: 'My glubs, my glubs.'

A wind blew in from Siberia and our eyes streamed.

Hetty wanted to go to the swings so we plodded over to them. I pushed her to and fro until she was bored, with Patrick screaming in the pushchair. Then Patrick wanted a go on the slide, but panicked at the last moment. Both demanded ice-cream.

A calmer Manda opened the door. 'Mummy!' Patrick hurled himself into her arms. 'Mummy, I was sad.'

'Patrick Coker Scott! What a porky! You were having a lovely time with Siena.'

'My mummy.' Patrick put his arms round Manda's neck and turned to beam at me.

Manda laughed, a clear, joyous sound, and nuzzled him. 'What would I do without you two?' she said, and over the top of her son's head, her eyes, shining with tenderness, encountered mine. 'I couldn't *possibly* live without my Patrick and Hetty.'

Charlie was out at the gym when I returned home. 'Supper done,' he had scrawled on a note. I smiled. It had been, strictly, my turn but Charlie would have reckoned I was still tired (a week later) from the jet-lag. He was right, but he always liked to take over the kitchen. 'Men have few outlets for their creativity,' was the excuse when he elbowed me aside. When I pointed out (with reluctance) that most great artists, writers and musicians had been male, he replied, 'I'm talking about the bog-standard male, not the towering genius.'

I went into the office and checked the answer-phone. There were three messages, and I put out a hand to press the button.

Enough was enough.

I did not *need* to listen to messages. Listening to messages was addictive behaviour. An excuse to fill every minute of the day with work . . . and filling every minute of the day with work meant . . . I didn't have to think about other things.

But that was my secret.

I sat down on the floor and began the annual task of file weeding – papers, articles, theatre programmes on which I had scrawled notes on the costumes, a mass of stuff. As I flicked through the year's detritus, I couldn't remember why I'd chosen to keep most of it.

'Elegance is knowing when to stop . . .'

'"I paint dreams," declared Ziggy Patterson, frock-maker to the stars.'

'How to dress your identity . . .'

Charlie poked his head round the door. 'Hi.' He had damp, slicked-back hair and a scrubbed face.

I waved a cutting in his direction. 'Does your wardrobe have focus?'

He shook his wet head. 'I think that must be the most boring question in the world. Supper in half an hour.'

The 'Wardrobe with Focus' article joined the rubbish pile. I swept it up and binned it, then noticed my photo albums were out of order. There was a whole shelf of them, the latest in slick plastic folders, the earlier ones in bulky volumes interleaved with tissue.

'My Photograph Album, Home and School' was written on the first in silver pencil, and each photo was captioned. The grain of the paper was so marked that it broke up the line of writing. On the first page I had pasted in a group picture of the fifth form. I was in the back row between 'Ginger' Rodgers and Kelvin whom I'd kissed behind the music school. I looked untidy, sulky and cold.

A few pages on there was a blown-up family group. A range of hills filled the background, and in the foreground my mother and father sat with a rug spread between them and a coolbox surrounded by sandwiches, fruit and packets of biscuits. The caption read, 'Family Picnic near Chatsworth, 1978'. I had been ten, and Richard twelve.

The colour of the photograph had faded, lending the green of the hills a curiously muted texture; the blue and red of the tartan rug were almost obliterated. Richard was concentrating on his biscuit. I was examining the contents of a sandwich with apparent disgust and impatience. My parents were looking in opposite directions from each other.

I wondered who had taken the photograph and, try as I might, I couldn't remember the occasion. This was not surprising for I had not enjoyed my childhood. In my book, to be young was to be powerless, and without much laughter and comfort. I wouldn't wish it on anybody.

Charlie reappeared and I showed it to him. 'Remind me to ask your mother next time I see her if you ever smiled.'

Chapter Eleven: Siena

'This is Charlie Grant,' said my hostess at her noisy, chattery, candlelit dinner party. I barely knew her and her husband, let alone the guests – this unconnectedness entirely matching my new status. I was nervous, too, for I had lost the habit of being single.

'Hello, Charlie.'

He was tallish, dark, and had the kind of floppy hair that was probably a pain. He looked nice, but not remarkable or outstanding – which all goes to show.

Our hostess moved on, and he flicked up an eyebrow. 'I think we're the evening's good cause,' he said, 'but I've suddenly come over all supportive of the idea.'

The dining-table was too small for the number of diners, not that it mattered, and Charlie and I were crushed together and talked with our noses almost touching over pear and pecorino salad and seafood pasta.

He struck me at once as a man with a secret melancholy but he masked it with good, funny conversation. Yet I sensed it was there – I knew it was there, for it matched mine.

Liqueurs were served and I accepted one. 'You seem sad?' I said, brandy-emboldened. 'Are you?'

His hand tightened on his glass. 'I'm getting divorced.'

'So am I,' I said. 'In fact, I'm already divorced.' I looked into his eyes. 'I haven't said that before. I'm divorced. Three days and eight hours.'

We exchanged no more information than that, and the conversation between us moved on, but I registered the echo of coincidence and shared feeling.

Towards the end of the dinner, Charlie whispered in my ear, 'Why has our host shaved his head? I only saw him a couple of days ago and he had a full head of hair.'

I laughed. 'Ask him.'

Charlie shouted, 'Why the skinhead, Sherwood?' and Sherwood replied, 'I wanted authority. Bald is gravitas.'

'Nonsense,' called his wife. 'The children got nits and Sherwood went drastic.'

That dinner party took place on a Tuesday and Charlie and I met again on Thursday. That was the beginning of us, but progress was not straightforward. No, not easy and automatic at all. It took time, and hesitant steps.

'Getting divorced seems as easy as applying for a passport,' I said (or puffed at him), as we jogged together in the park. 'But it isn't.'

He laid a sweaty hand on my sweaty arm. 'I agree. I feel like I've fallen asleep on a train journey and woken up at the wrong station, miles from anywhere. It's dark, I have no money and, anyway, there are no taxis.'

I took myself back to Ingrid's office. 'I'm finding it difficult to go forward . . . I can't stop brooding on my failure with Jay . . . my *failure*, Ingrid.'

'Nobody fails,' she replied. 'It's not a term we recognize.' She had assumed her 'teacher' expression, which was deployed to suggest that a client was being obtuse or wilful. 'What do you want, Siena? Blood on the floor? You've got closure – won't that do?' She shuffled through my notes, which, considering the amount of times I had visited her, struck me as insultingly sparse. 'It can be argued that a first marriage is a learning curve.'

I stared at her. 'I don't think you're any help at all.' The words rushed out of my mouth, with the joy of a traveller arriving home from a long, arduous journey. 'In fact, I've decided you're destructive.'

For the first time that I could recall, Ingrid's lips parted in a delighted smile. 'But this is brilliant,' she cried. 'You've learnt my lessons well and triumphed over your inner laziness.'

As ever, Ingrid demanded the last word. In her book, neither unhappiness nor failure was admissible. But I had failed, and I *was* unhappy.

'So?' said Charlie. 'Why not say so? Be honest with yourself.'

Acupuncture was next on the list, but lying on a cushion stuck all over with needles did nothing for me. Neither did yoga. My thoughts were too chaotic, a raw mixture of grief and self-doubt, for me to concentrate on my *chakras*. This annoyed my teacher who took it personally. I sympathized, but as I explained to Charlie – of whom I was seeing more and more – alternative therapies were not for wimps. Like old age, they were for the tough and the strong. Furthermore I felt that plain old endurance – just muddling through each day – seemed the most promising plan for the moment.

Instead I had my hair restyled, and made a foray into Prada where I splashed out on a handbag in glistening black nylon and pointed black shoes.

'Very pointy,' Charlie remarked, when I met him at the cinema on the evening I wore them for the first time. 'Question is: are they sadistic or masochistic?'

As it happened, I was dying in slow agony from the blisters they had inflicted but my delight in such desirable objects combined with the pain to sum up my inner state quite perfectly.

Dear Siena,

    Will you help me? One of the last insults my ex-partner threw at me before she walked out was to say that I looked like a dog's dinner. I am just a bog-standard man. Stomach swelling a little – OK, more than that – recession on top. She left me six months ago, and it is only now that I am plucking up confidence to go out. Could you see a way of reinventing my image from the terrified slob that I am into a confident man-about-town?

    Yours, Joe Whattley

    PS I would not be honest if I didn't admit to a desire for revenge.

    PPS I know this letter sounds quite humorous but I can't explain what I really feel.

As a rule, I never revealed my clients' requests to anyone without their permission. But I made an exception and showed the letter to Charlie on our twelfth date (noted in my appointments diary).

'Know how he feels.' He handed back the letter.

I trod carefully. 'What would you have done differently with Cimmie?'

The reply took the wind out my sails. 'I wouldn't have allowed our differences to fester so much that I ended up hating her.' I looked sceptical, for the idea of Charlie hating anyone was difficult to take in. He added, 'I knew in theory that everyone is capable of hatred. And violence and murder. I deal with that all the time. But if *I'm* being honest, it's being faced with it in oneself that's a shock.'

'So how do we manage, Charlie?'

'I make the presumption of innocence. Or, rather, try to believe in the best. Despite my hatred, I loved Cimmie too and I wouldn't have left her. And she was wrong to say that I didn't take her seriously.'

He had gone a little pale. I reached over and touched his cheek. 'Hey.'

'And what about you?' he asked. 'Latest report in Life After Jay.'

Contrary. Puzzling.

I took a deep breath, which held more than a touch of healing and releasing. 'Deeply wounded that he gave me up so easily . . . All right, I was particularly anguished that he preferred a quick clean execution to a bloody fight to keep me. I don't understand, Charlie. I was unhappy and yet I wanted Jay to fight to keep me.'

We were stepping carefully, the pair of us. As Charlie put it, 'I'm not going to rush matters between us. Do you mind?'

'No.'

'We're friends.'

There was a suggestion of a question mark in the statement, but I was not going to debate the nature of friendship.

I was still too bruised and, if truthful, too busy. The consultancy was taking off and I had had an approach from *Fashion, This Week*. I preferred to view Charlie as the brother who held my hand as we waded out of the deep waters. I did not look to love him, only to like him, which I did very much.

The trick was not to expect happiness. I had made that mistake with Jay – of assuming happiness fills you, and replenishes, automatically, like an underground water-table.

Nine months later, Charlie took me out to dinner at Nobu. We discussed his latest case over green beans in balsamic vinegar: why a businessman who had been convicted of perjury had been given a longer sentence than a drink-driver who had killed his passenger. 'That's the way the law is coded,' said Charlie.

'And you don't mind that it's an ass?'

'Yes and no. But I ask myself, in a society that no longer has moral or religious restraints, what would happen if we didn't observe the law?'

I thought of my alternative therapies, and the church close to where I was living in a rented flat in Hoxton, which was virtually empty on Sundays. 'Point taken.'

Over the main course of (barely) seared tuna, the conversation slid into the intimate. 'Are you feeling better?' I asked him, surprised by a rush of tenderness.

'I am. I've worked out that the disaster of my marriage was not inevitable because men and women are at daggers drawn. It was merely – not merely, but you know what I mean – the result of misunderstanding and a build-up of resentment between two people.'

I watched the various expressions chase over his face. I had been wrong about him being unremarkable-looking. He was the opposite, and intelligent and full of feeling. I was surprised I'd missed it.

Charlie reached over the table, captured my hand in a sweet gesture and rubbed my thumb. That morning, I had made time for a manicure and my nails were painted an optimistic, confident red. (NB: scarlet should be worn only by younger women because it reflects badly on thinning skin.)

I looked up. Charlie's skin shone with health and youth, and his eyes, an intriguing green, were soft with emotion. 'You *are* better, Charlie. That's lovely.'

He continued to hold my hand. 'Siena, it *is* possible to make up one's mind to be happy.'

'Oh?'

'I read it somewhere, and it made sense.'

The waiters whisked to and fro. The table next to us got up and left. The room hummed with conversation and eating noises, a burst of laughter.

Up went my eyebrows. 'It's an idea with . . . appeal.'

'So? Shall we make up our minds to be happy . . . together, I mean?'

The old wounds threatened to break open, the fears and sadness of the past few years gathered at the back of my mind, but I pushed them away. I remembered the glitter, the optimism and the savagery of childhood fairy tales – the Prince Charmings, and Ice Queens, the Emperor without his new clothes, and the Little Mermaid, who walked on razors for love of her prince. Not all of them lived happily ever after.

'Siena?'

Charlie was not suggesting that we revisit childhood fantasies, but something quite different. It was a less absolute state of mind, more tentative.

Hunger stirred – for the completeness I had feared had died, hunger that, in the presence of Charlie, was proving almost more urgent than my doubt and fear. I returned the pressure of his fingers but, not quite there yet, I said, 'I don't know, Charlie.'

He surprised me. 'Nor do I, actually,' he said. 'Isn't that the point?'

'I hadn't thought.'

'I have, for both of us.'

'Bossy old you.'

'Joke.'

'Bad one.'

'Second time round?' he reminded me. 'Do you understand that's what I mean?'

'Yes, I do.' My fingers with their shiny scarlet nails reposed trustingly in Charlie's.

'Sure?'

'No . . . yes. Of course I'm sure.'

'You're willing to go through it all again?'

Think quickly, Siena. Think hard.

I twined my fingers round his. 'Why not?' and, because I could not resist it, followed up with, 'One's always better dressed at one's second wedding.'

Briefly, Charlie looked nonplussed. Then he threw back his head and roared with laughter. 'If that's the case I'll take you to Harvey Nichols at dawn tomorrow.'

The call came through from the States on Monday in early May.

'Ten programmes,' said India, briskly, when she relayed the news that Trimester Productions wanted to go ahead with *Siena's Prime Time Fashion.* 'To be filmed in two batches over the next six months. I'm just about to go into heavy negotiations over the contract and money, but I need your OK on this. Listen up, here are the details so far.'

I sat down in my office, filled with river reflections from the May sunshine, and absorbed the stream of figures – percentages and cuts of the profits – that were being held out to me. Of course, they were wrapped round tough clauses, linked to my availability, my willingness to take on a new market, to undergo publicity and live for weeks at a time in New York.

'Do you give me permission to go ahead?' India wanted to know.

'Yes,' I heard myself say. 'No, let me talk to Charlie.'

'Answer soonest.' India was severe. 'I mean it.'

I rang Charlie, but it was impossible to talk, so we arranged a snatch lunch at a café next to his chambers.

He arrived in a rush. I had already ordered a toasted

sandwich for him and (carb-free) bacon and eggs for myself. The toasted sandwich arrived first, which was a sore test – I would have given a lot to sink my teeth into it.

'Look,' said Charlie, 'let's get this straight. I don't want to stand in your way.' He took a bite, and said, with his mouth full, 'If I could have the baby, I'd do it. It would solve the problem. But I can't, and that's that. But I think we should decide where we're going.'

His black gown and white shirt made him seem older and sterner, which was, I suppose, the point. 'The contract only covers six months.'

'And what if there are more offers after it? If it's a success?'

'I could say no.'

Charlie's face was inscrutable. 'That would be unwise.' He finished the sandwich. 'Siena, the time has come for absolute honesty. Let's not have any misunderstandings.'

'Go on.'

But Charlie appeared to have changed his mind. 'Oh, I don't know.' He looked at me, almost as if he was seeing me for the first time. I hated the suggestion of an under-current of bafflement and sadness. 'Christ albloody-mighty!' he said, at last. 'It was easier in the old days. Man worked, woman stayed at home.'

I closed my eyes. 'Never thought I'd hear you say that.'

'No.'

'Charlie, you're not being honest. Go on, say what you want to say.'

'All right, Siena. It's make-your-mind-up time.'

Charlie's junior edged into the café, bearing a heavy briefcase. 'Could we have a word, Mr Grant?'

Charlie checked his watch. 'Give me ten, Roger.'

Roger seemed flustered. 'Sorry. It's urgent.'

Charlie looked thunderous and I glanced at my watch. 'I've got to go too, Charlie.'

'Don't expect me back for supper tonight,' Charlie said. 'Busy.'

'I wish you could come home.'

He softened. 'I wish I could, too.'

'Charlie, I'm going to say yes.'

He rose from the table. 'Sure,' he said. 'I never expected anything else.'

He looked so sad and disappointed that I almost wept. I almost cried out, *No, I won't do it*. But I didn't.

'You will back me?'

He didn't look at me. 'Of course.'

'You won't really,' I said.

'What I think seems to be irrelevant.' He bent over and kissed my cheek. Light and distant. Then he murmured, 'Don't worry about it.'

I watched him leave the café, and he didn't glance back or wave.

My appointment was with India, who was waiting for me. She led me upstairs to her room, which was dominated by a huge empty desk. When I first saw her set-up, I had entertained doubts about someone who did business without a single piece of paper in sight but I needn't have worried. India's brilliance was strategic and business was mostly conducted in her head.

Today she was dressed in pinstriped Armani. ('You paid for it,' she pointed out, when I exclaimed over it.) I explained the position between Charlie and me. She listened carefully, but without much sympathy. 'As I told you, Siena, Trimester need an answer, soonest. They don't hang around.'

We talked over the book for Caesar and India printed off a chart she had constructed showing (a) my schedule and income if the US deal went through, and (b) my schedule and income if it didn't.

'So, what do you feel, Siena?'

'Trapped.'

She shook her head. 'No, you're not. You just have to make up your mind. It's very simple.'

Not India too.

Unusually I chose to walk most of the way home. It was late spring, and we were past the hopeless time when, sick and tired of the cold and rain, it was impossible to imagine warmth and sun.

The muscles in my legs contracted and stretched. My breath quickened and I increased my pace, enjoying the exercise. I stopped to allow a woman with a pushchair to mastermind it past an overflowing rubbish bin on the pavement, and looked up to the poster on a building-site hoarding. It showed a photograph of starving children in Africa, tiny, with huge heads, and eyes that pleaded with the onlooker.

Half-way home, I shivered as I thought over the implications of my conversation with Charlie. What a joke God – whoever – had played on women. He had given them brains, wily social skills, longevity and, with a bit of luck, beauty. He had also given them a uterus. That was such a big black joke.

Once back in my office, I was safe and in control. This was my quiet retreat, my temple, fashioned to suit me. There were, to put it mildly, a hundred things to do. *Notes. Telephone calls. Research.* Inside my tights, one foot cramped. This was familiar territory in which all I had to do was work quietly and steadily through and, from time to time, clench my foot to relieve the spasm.

Actually, it was Voltaire who declared that it was possible to make up your mind to be happy. After Charlie proposed, I looked it up in a dictionary of quotations. But I also noted that Voltaire believed in making the best of all possible worlds, but I never mentioned that to Charlie. Instead I preferred to think about a quotation from Virgil on the opposite page. 'Love carries all before him: we too must yield to Love.'

But if I truly believed that why was I doing what I was doing?

Chapter Twelve: Barbara

I thought a lot about friendship, but all I could say for a surety was that Bunty was a friend, a good one, and Ryder's brother, Ian, and his wife, Antonia, were not friends, but relations. There was a difference.

Early in May they invited themselves over to spend Sunday at Edgeborough Road. They had a habit of doing this: Antonia hated cooking but was more than happy, eager, in fact, to eat other women's efforts.

Radiant and laughing, Sophie danced into my kitchen and caught me in my apron. 'Off,' she ordered, and tied it round her own waist. 'Put me to work, darling Aunt Babs.'

She was wearing a full skirt, a linen blouse and a patterned cardigan, and had tied up her hair in a ponytail. 'You look ravishing, Sophie.'

She nuzzled my cheek in the way she used to as a little girl. '*You* smell lovely. And you look so well. Have you found a new face cream? Will you tell me what it is?'

Whichever god had been present at Sophie's conception had been prodigal with gifts. As a child, her hair had been dark blonde, but it had lightened as she grew older, and was accompanied by huge blue eyes, a slender, almost too slender, figure. And she was possessed, too, of an intelligence that had helped her deftly evade any parental objections and got her to Oxford and a good degree. 'She'll be an old maid,' wailed Antonia, 'one of those fearsome harpies.' But there was no way the lovely, laughing Sophie would be branded a bluestocking and left on the shelf.

'Sometimes,' Bunty commented, in her sharp way, 'I suspect you love Sophie more than Amy.'

'Not true,' I protested. 'But I think I understand Sophie better.'

'Hum . . .' Bunty looked sceptical. 'Older women do *not* understand younger ones. Particularly daughters.'

Point taken. In the past two weeks I had asked Amy if she wanted to come to the hairdresser with me, go shopping in town, catch a play in the West End, have lunch together. And the answers had been 'too busy', 'otherwise engaged', 'no' and 'no'.

'Sophie is always so loving, and that makes a difference.'

'Sophie makes it her business to be loving.'

To paraphrase Alexander, I could 'see' into Sophie, sense the direction of her thoughts and moods. Sophie was like water in a chalk river – clear and sparkling – while Amy was a hidden lake, surrounded by bulrushes and tightly clumped willows.

'Where's Amy?' Sophie was asking.

'Upstairs, I think. The hot water ran out earlier, and she had to wait for a bath.'

In the early days of the Teignmouth holidays, Sophie had formed an alliance with Roy, who was exactly her age. Later on, when puberty asserted itself, and ignoring the tragedy of Amy being eighteen months younger, the girls formed a female cadre – not a powerful one for Roy took care to assert his boyish rights, but solid enough. The alliance had survived, despite Sophie going to university and Amy not. ('I'm glad for her,' said Amy stubbornly, tearfully, on hearing the news. 'Glad, glad.')

'What are you doing at the moment?' I hesitated to ask the next, crude question, but asked all the same: 'Any boyfriends?'

'Masses.' Sophie touched a strand of shining hair.

'Anyone special?'

'Good heavens, no.' Again, a strand twisted through her slender fingers. 'You know that Amy and I disapprove of being tied down. We don't intend to put our heads into the noose.'

I pushed a bowl of collard greens towards her. 'Chop them, there's a darling.' I watched her set to. 'You'll probably change your mind.'

'Unlikely.' A smile hovered at the corner of her lips.

I pointed my knife at Sophie's breast. 'I'll give you a year and when you do you must come and beg for mercy.'

She giggled and raised her knife, and we crossed (playful) swords. 'I promise, but you'll be waiting a long, long time.'

'That brings bad luck. Stop it.' Amy appeared in the doorway and I stifled a sigh, for she was dressed in a cotton skirt that lumped over her hips, an unflattering yellow blouse, and she had pinned her hair with a kirby-grip. Her eyes narrowed. 'Am I interrupting something between you two?'

Sophie turned. '*Where* have you been?'

Amy brushed past, knocking against me in her haste to kiss her cousin. Aware that the collision had been deliberate, I went away to chivvy the party to the table.

'Ian, dear,' Antonia fussed, as Ian accepted a refill of gin and tonic to go into lunch, 'the doctor did say.'

Ian's complexion suggested he lived a healthy, outdoor life but nothing could have been further from the truth. He was a bank manager who spent his days behind a large desk and his complexion was the achievement of many large lunches. 'Shut up, Antonia,' he said.

'Sophie,' asked Ryder at lunch, 'any luck with searching for a job?'

'Not yet, Uncle Ryder,' she favoured the table with one of her radiant looks, 'but I'm on a short-list for a job as a television announcer, which I think would be very interesting, and fun.'

Her father frowned. 'I should never have let her go to university. What on earth was the point?'

Antonia hissed in my ear, 'What am I going to do with her?' Her tone sharpened. 'It's ridiculous, Sophie. A ridiculous thing to want to be.'

After lunch, the women went upstairs to freshen up. Sophie disappeared into Amy's bedroom, and I was forced to listen to Antonia's litany of woe, which included a daughter who wanted to mix with dissolute people and refused to get herself a proper secretarial job.

Antonia applied her lipstick in angry slashes, and returned downstairs. In Amy's bedroom the girls were absorbed in their conversation – Sophie had let down her hair and Amy was brushing it (why couldn't it have been the other way round?). They were exchanging gossip and confidences that were not for my ears.

Sophie looked up and caught sight of me in the mirror hovering in the doorway. She sent me a conspiratorial smile.

'You don't disapprove, Aunt Barbara, do you?' she called. 'Of the television thing? You don't think it's silly?'

Instantly Amy's gaze fixed on me like a gin-trap.

'I don't know anything about it,' I said.

'Oh, Mum, you're such a *coward*,' said Amy.

Clearing out the apple-house was an annual ritual Ryder and I shared. Both of us hated it but, equally, neither was prepared to let the other take over. Ryder because he could not trust me – or, for that matter, Herr Schlinker, who was deemed (and this was not meant rudely) to possess a refugee's attitude to waste – to get rid of the rotting fruit. I wanted to make sure that no apple was discarded unnecessarily.

Sure enough, the arguments ran along the annual lines.

'We should cut out the good bits and use them.'

'You have enough to do,' Ryder countered. 'Don't we have enough apples? I don't want my wife apple-paring.'

He pulled out the first of the wooden slats; I sorted the fruit and emptied trays. Very soon the tin pails were filling with the rotting ones: greeny purple, blackish brown and deep purple-black.

Ryder dipped the scrubbing brush into a mixture of hot water and disinfectant and scrubbed the slats. The bristle scraped decisively against the wood. I looked up at the roof of the apple-house where the limewash was flaking and spiders' webs were clotted in the corners. Through the doorway the garden was framed like a painting and, in it, spring was at work sharpening colours, scattering flowers and leaves and blurring outlines – in contrast to the dead, musty atmosphere in the apple-house.

'You're very quiet these days.' Ryder's comment cut into my contemplations. 'Are you worrying about something?'

'No. Just busy, that's all.'

'No busier than usual.' He dipped the brush into the water and resumed his methodical scrubbing, one slat at a time. 'I'd be upset if you didn't tell me when there was something wrong.'

'Excuse me, darling.' I brushed past him with another armful of rejects. 'Of course I'd tell you if there was anything wrong.'

The pails were now full so I grabbed them and traipsed down the garden to the compost heap. It had rained earlier, a light, joyous spring rain, and my feet left imprints on the path. Herr Schlinker's onions and beetroot had already broken through the earth – a colour pattern card of emerald and olive. I always thought that the new greens of the year had a *fat* quality to them, plumped as they were by underground nutrients. Scratching around in the run, the hens clucked contentedly and, to my delight, there was the shy flash of a purple violet under the beech tree.

I bent over to take a closer look, easing back the layers

of leaf mould, and the earth curled under my fingernails. I sniffed, and the scent was of life and growth. It was a good, optimistic smell, and it made me feel happy.

Ryder had worked hard. When I returned, he was finishing off the final tray. 'We'll leave them to dry.' He stacked it against the others. Then, he smacked the question into the open. 'You're not ill in any way. Or . . . or pregnant, Babs, are you?'

The question startled me so thoroughly that, for a moment, I was bereft of words. What . . . when? Surely I hadn't made a mistake. I clicked off the weeks in my head, tracing the timetable of fuss and discomfort, followed by relief.

'No. No, to both, thank goodness.' I was emphatic. 'Not at our age, Ryder.' I slid my arm round his waist and kissed his cheek. 'It would be embarrassing.'

Antonia saying, '*My dear!*' and Ian raising an eyebrow in that suggestive, irritating manner. As for Roy and Amy, well, who knew what they would think?

Ryder dropped the scrubbing brush into the pail with a clang. 'Another son would have been nice.'

'Oh, Ryder, I wish I could have given you one.'

He was annoyed with himself for having – possibly – hurt me. 'Barbara, you gave me two children, and much else. But enough. Hand me the trays over there, will you, darling?'

We said no more on the subject.

By the time we had finished lunch, the sun had gone in and I lit the gas fire in the dining room. It was accounts day, and we spread our papers on the table. Ryder refilled his fountain pen, and held it poised over the columns of his ledger.

I fetched my notebook – a morocco-leather one with gold-edged leaves: I bought one each year from Biddle's in the high street. In it, I kept the tally of my housekeeping expenditure, a dull but, paradoxically, comforting task.

We worked companionably, checking and rechecking.

'Did we really spend that much on fuel?'

'Don't you remember we ordered in extra after the cold snap?'

'I never know whether it's summer or winter.'

This was a perfectly reasonable comment for a man who travelled in and out of time zones like a commuter.

'Groceries, five pounds and threepence. Cleaning materials, two pounds. Car repair, four pounds.' Then I admitted, 'New hat, two guineas.'

'Have I seen it?'

'It's for the summer. Pink flowers, very chic.'

Ryder transcribed the figures into 'Outgoings'. 'Do you need more money? Should I raise your allowance?'

'That's generous of you, darling, but there's no need.'

He gave me a penetrating look. 'Sure you're not short?'

I shook my head. I did not like, ever, to take advantage of my husband's generosity. This occasionally led to a shortage and shortfall, but it was a state of affairs I accepted.

'You have only to ask.'

I heard the clock ticking next door. With an inner ear, I strained to catch the quiet of the afternoon outside, the fall of the seconds and minutes of Ryder's and my life. The quiet between us, the murmured exchange of information, was normal, perfectly normal.

'Ryder . . .' I went over to his chair and slid my arms round him. 'What would you say if I did some work for St Bede's? In the almoner's department. Apparently they need help sorting out convalescent patients with transport and things like that. It would only be a day a week. It would be good work, and very helpful.'

He rubbed my hand. 'Provided you're unpaid, why not?'

'And if it was paid?'

Inside the circle of my arms, he tensed. 'I suppose that would be all right, but I wouldn't like it known. I don't want it thought I can't support you.'

'Darling, isn't that old-fashioned?'

'Maybe, but it's what I feel.'

'Everyone knows you earn a good salary,' I said. 'Captain.' I reached over and screwed the cap back on the ink bottle.

He smiled at the tease. 'Come back, Babs.' He put an arm round my waist and drew me close.

I looked down at the familiar head. I knew what went on inside it and yet I did not. Was it the case that the longer you lived with someone, there was less and less of which to be sure? I wondered, too, if Ryder was vanishing from my internal perspective. He was there, and not there, a constant presence but increasingly shadowy. We seemed to have leapt all the hurdles required of a long relationship – a war and all those griefs and terrors, children, and whether or not to eat in the kitchen. We had explored our love for each other, and accepted it.

'Ryder, I promise the hospital will not be paying me.'

That night at Bunty's bridge gathering, I allowed Ryder to trounce me and my partner, Jimmy Peters. Jimmy was gracious about it. Nevertheless, I caught his flash of annoyance. It could be argued that Jimmy triumphed on the golf course so frequently that a defeat at cards might be necessary redress, but men like him would not see it that way.

'Never mind, Barbara.' Jimmy helped me on with my coat at the end of the evening. 'It was a complicated game, and difficult to keep up.'

I prayed for Ryder to go away. I wanted the house emptied of family and the bustle of meals and washing. I wanted the spring air to sift through the rooms, cleansing and sweetening. I craved the solitude of the silent rooms in which to listen to the birdsong and hear my own thoughts.

Amy came and went at the weekend, wearing the yellow blouse and the awful skirt, which nothing would induce her to change. I pressed on her fruit cake, stockings and face cream. 'You must pay attention to your face, darling,' I told her.

She shrugged. 'Frightened that no man will want me, Mother?'

Ryder left on Saturday afternoon, and I waved him off from the front steps. On Sunday I woke with the dawn, to a day that seemed expectant, with light and sun.

I washed, sprinkled talcum powder under my arms, put on my light grey worsted suit with the fitted jacket, and my brogues with the leather tassels on the laces, snatched up a beret and set off up Edgeborough Road.

'Morning, Barbara.' I had almost collided with Phyllis Thomas, my neighbour. 'Are you off to church?'

'I thought I'd walk up to St Martha's. It's such a lovely day.'

Phyllis glanced at my brogues and my hatless condition, and there was an implied reproof in the scrutiny. 'Do take care,' she said, in her carefully modulated voice.

St Martha's on the Hill was a pilgrim church. Centuries ago on the way to Canterbury, the groups had stopped there to worship and beg sustenance. Not the best place for provender, for it was built high on the ridge, but it had become a stone beacon of their faith.

I went up Warren Road, then turned off to climb up through the trees that grew over the base of the hill. The going was soft, and the ground networked with roots. Either side of the path there were dense clumps of new bracken and the leafy arches of dog roses.

It was warm. The dreaded moisture sprang under my arms, and my shoes were soon coated with sandy soil. Half-way up I stopped, and used a handkerchief to wipe my face and armpits, but as I continued up the hill, the muscles flexing in my calves, my chest heaving under my jacket, it was impossible not to enjoy the sensation of being on the move.

I sprang up the final few feet to the top, and paused to regain my breath. It was a popular route, and walkers with sticks, rucksacks and dogs were out enjoying the weather and exercise.

There was a little time before the service started, so I sat on the wall and put on my beret. Up here, the shy wild flowers were free to grow where they wished in pastel groups. Below was the smooth, confident lope of the downland, pitted with outcrops of chalk and flint. And the breeze on my face felt like . . . it could hardly be called wildness and solitude, but something like that.

I checked the time. Whoever arranged church services did not consider wives. Either you were godly and attended Matins, or ungodly and produced a proper Sunday lunch.

I had measured out my life in Sunday lunches, in the snap and sizzle of roasting fat . . . in the hot smells of basted lamb and beef . . . in the duller odours of boiling cabbage and Brussels sprouts, in the visual architecture of whipped cream piled into a silver bowl, and the jewel colours of bottled fruit. I was an expert at setting out chairs round a table, in ironing napkins just so, in the placing of guests who came and went – and my power lay in my ability to assuage their hunger.

The congregation in the church was modest, to put it kindly, but I relished my anonymity and the straightforward, impeccably Anglican service. So safe, so sensible; so inimical to wild impulses of passionate, ecstatic fervour.

At school, I had had a Catholic friend, and she fascinated me with explanations of her faith's practices and beliefs, which had appeared impossibly exotic – and the veneration of the Virgin a compensation for bad treatment of women. We had lost touch, but vague memories floated through my mind as the vicar embarked on his sermon. What had been Mary's feelings when presented with the *fait accompli* of pregnancy and her subsequent harnessing into the divine icon of motherhood? Did the faintest suggestion of rebellion ever flicker through her innocence? Or was her sainthood perfect from the first flutter of her surprised body?

The vicar bade me a polite 'Good morning,' as I left the church. 'So nice to see a fresh face,' he murmured.

I pulled off my beret, and retraced with a light step my route down the hill. A shoelace had worked loose and I bent over to retie it. When I looked up, Alexander Liberty was coming towards me.

I was rooted to the spot.

He was dressed in corduroy trousers and a sweater, but no jacket or tie, and his expression registered surprise and pleasure. 'Hallo, Barbara.'

It was no use denying it. No amount of godliness stifled the jolt to my senses. 'Alexander, what are you doing here?'

He gestured to the walkers. 'Same as them. Making use of a fine Sunday and this is a well-known spot. I thought I'd take a look.'

'I hope you got my letter thanking you for the lecture.'

'I did.' Now he looked perfectly tranquil and self-possessed. 'Now that we've met, won't you join me?'

'Where to?'

'Does it matter? Newlands Corner. We could have lunch somewhere.'

'I put my money into the collection.'

Alexander searched his pockets. 'I don't have enough either. Never mind. We can do without lunch.'

'I should get home.'

'Should you?'

But he stood four-square on the path that led home, blocking it, and said, 'Come with me instead.'

So I did.

He led the way along the footpath. We walked in rhythm, quite fast, and we did not say much. After a while, the sun came out and I was forced to take off my jacket, conscious that my blouse was clinging to my skin. Alexander rolled up his shirtsleeves. We skirted the brow of the ridge, and plunged down a chalk path until we reached a bench, sited to take advantage of the view.

I sank down on it. Alexander remained standing, shaded his eyes and observed the scene below. 'Did you finish the book on Freud?'

'Not quite.' Sweat beaded my top lip, and I shifted out of the sun. I felt hot and awkward in my too-heavy skirt and blouse. 'I don't understand a lot of what he says, and some things . . . some things are so personal that they're difficult to read. But I wanted to ask you, how much do you agree with him?'

Alexander sat down beside me. Flushed from the exercise, glossy with health and youth, his beauty struck through me like a knife.

'There is an argument for saying that his theories are self-fulfilling, that any attack on them is proof they're true, because being aggressive about them is a result of repression.'

'But do you *believe* in them?'

'I don't know,' he replied simply. 'That's what I'm trying to find out. I don't know enough yet. I have a long, hard apprenticeship ahead, and I hope I make it through.' He hunched over and rested his elbows on his knees. 'Freud and his colleagues have made us question the old assumptions, and I believe that's right.'

Out of the corner of my eye, I stole glances at his profile so like the statue, drank in the sheen of his skin, and groped towards coherent thought. 'Won't that result in chaos?'

He looked thoughtful. 'Possibly, and it's a risk because we might end up destroying something we value. Rules are useful. But *why* are they there? Do we really know, or do we just accept them because we're too lazy to question them?'

'You've got your whole life to ask those questions,' I said. 'I wish I had. I wish I had time to learn.'

'But you have learnt. And there is time.'

There was a silence, but it was not the comfortable one of old friends who knew too much of each other to need to talk. Not a Bunty-Barbara silence. A fire raced under my skin.

I broke it by saying, 'This is a peculiar conversation.'

'Do you really mean, "This is a peculiar *situation*"?'

There it was again: Alexander's ability to catch some of my thoughts wrong-footed me.

He shifted to face me. 'Let's play a game.'

'Don't look so fierce,' I protested, laughing.

'Thinking of rules.'

'Which ones in particular?' A remnant of self-preservation made me add, 'Shouldn't you stop there?'

I took a deep breath, relishing its impact on my body. The moment was charged with dreamlike tension and my astonishment. Any second now, everything would return to normal. I would wipe my upper lip, touch the hair behind my ears to check it was in place, and I would sit on the bench, and continue to discuss the view with a pleasant acquaintance.

Alexander shifted. His eyes widened with the effort of marshalling – nerve? Courage? Playfulness? 'Barbara, if I *were* to break the rules, I would ask if I could become your lover.'

Chapter Thirteen: Barbara

'Are you shocked?'

The breath had fled from my chest. 'In theory . . . a little.'

I was about to be angry (with myself as well as him) because the question had altered everything, until I noticed that Alexander was shaking and I thought, You poor, poor darling, this is new to you. His youth and absurd courage brought laughter and tears at the same time. 'You silly . . . you foolish . . . wonderful . . . but I *am* going to tell you to be quiet.' I fumbled for my handkerchief.

'I know,' he said. 'But I wanted to ask it. I *had* to ask it. Dear Barbara, why are you crying?'

I laced my fingers together and felt the nails bite into my palms. 'Weren't you taking a risk just now? And in the apple-house? I could have made trouble for you.'

'I wasn't thinking about the consequences, I just did it – and if there were any it would have been worth it.'

Contemplating the row that might have resulted made me dizzy. 'But you did take a risk. If I had reacted badly, you could have been struck off the doctors' list or something. Or, at least, I could made terrible trouble.'

'Even so, I'm glad I did say what I said . . . It's out in the open.'

The fire raced and made free under my skin. 'I understand that it was only a *theoretical* question.'

'Yes.'

'It was just an example of questioning the rules,' I said. 'Now we shall forget it.'

He was not pretending I was irresistible, or magnetically beautiful, and I liked the simplicity of that approach. It was honest and bold. Anyway, at a previous meeting Alexander had confided something far more seductive. He had told me *I was interesting.*

Suddenly I was filled with an incredible sense of freedom, almost unbearably so. I *was* here, in the sunshine and breeze, smelling spring, and so was Alexander and I could think of, *consider*, nothing else.

'It was a lovely and flattering theoretical question, Alexander, and I thank you for asking it but it's not possible.'

'Anything's possible. It's whether you *want* to do something or not – oh, go on holiday, move house, whatever you care to think of. But I understand, Barbara, and if you want me to go, I will. All the same,' he leant towards me, 'I think you're a . . . remarkable woman.'

'You've made a mistake. I'm a conventional woman. I like a conventional life. Look at me.' I spread out my hands, with my wedding and engagement rings. 'Nothing special at all.'

'I don't agree.'

'How can I?' I whispered. 'I can't do anything to hurt Ryder.'

'I've no answer to that.'

I dug down on my lip with my teeth, and put a distance between us on the bench. 'Forgive me, Alexander . . . I know you study human behaviour, but I don't think you know . . . I don't think you have much experience in this area.' I looked away. 'Am I right?'

He sighed. 'Brothels are horrible places, and the average English maiden is pretty impregnable. Yes, you're right.'

His rather stumbling confession altered the balance. With respect to this subject, I knew more than him.

'I couldn't do that to Ryder, even if . . . even if I wished to progress beyond theory.'

'Of course,' he said, 'I understand –'

But I didn't think he did, and cut him off. 'You don't *know* how I've lived my life. It's been happy and peaceful, and I'm lucky.'

This was a cue for Alexander to get to his feet and retrieve the situation. He took it. 'I'm very sorry. Will you accept the apology?'

I pleated my skirt between fingers that would not quite obey me. 'There's nothing to be sorry for. How could I be offended by such a lovely compliment? In many ways, it made me feel a lot better about myself. But I couldn't have secrets from Ryder.'

Alexander squinted towards a clump of trees further along the path. 'We all have secrets, and we should be permitted them without guilt and worry, if that's what we want, otherwise they drive you mad.' He shrugged. 'Or that's where the psychiatrist comes in. We'll die from exposure unless we can be private in ourselves.'

'But not . . . this,' I said.

He turned his head and smiled at me. I found myself looking away.

'For me . . . It seems to me that sexual fidelity is not the same as fidelity. The body is different from the intimacy of the mind. That's the theory, anyway.'

It struck me as delightfully funny. 'That's one way of looking at adultery.'

'Don't tease, Barbara. Please.'

'All right.'

I rose to my feet and we retraced our steps along the chalky, flinty path with the green landscape glinting below.

Alexander rolled down his shirtsleeves and buttoned the cuffs. I watched the smooth flesh of his forearms disappear and said, conversationally, 'Freud argues that sexual satisfaction is the key to happiness and emotional balance.' Daringly, because I did not trust myself, I laid my hand on his arm. 'Alexander, you should find someone your own age. You should find someone to marry.'

'That's the crazy aspect. You shouldn't marry the first person you can persuade.' His laugh was rueful and a touch wicked. 'Harry and I spent an inordinate amount of time at college trying to entice girls into our beds. It was a nightmare. You thought things were progressing swimmingly and then the iron shutter clamped down – just about the region of the waist.'

The earth was soft underfoot, and slippery. Higher up on the bank, the cowslips were blooming. 'Even so, you should find someone your own age.'

Alexander stopped and I slithered to a halt. 'I don't want a *girl*. I don't want to find myself tied up with those rules.'

The temptation to draw close, to touch his neck, his cheek, trace their shape, was almost overpowering.

I stood with my hands held tightly by my sides, while Alexander wooed me. 'I can lend you lots of books . . . and we can talk about things too.'

How did I get home? I don't know. I think I flew, and arrived breathless, with a growling stomach.

I prowled the house. I flung myself into a chair and up again. I took the newspaper into the conservatory but it was too hot in there to read. I flitted through the garden, noting the fresh green of the new leaves, the shiny grey-white flints in the garden walls, the earth piled above Herr Schlinker's dug trenches.

Unable to settle, unable to eat, I went to bed early and tried to read a novel, but that was useless, too. In the middle of the night, I woke with a raging thirst, shrugged on my dressing-gown and walked down the passage. I came to a halt by the nursery door.

How often had I stood there in the past, straining for the reassurance of my children's breathing? More often than I could count. My senses heightened and troubled, I peered back down the funnel of those years to the shade of my former self – a protective maternal presence, per-petually watching and waiting.

In the kitchen, I filled a glass with cold water and drank it. The fumes from the Rayburn made my eyes prick in the gloom. I drank a second glass, hoping to cool the fever raging inside me.

Of course, I could say to Ryder in a worldly fashion, 'The time has come for a change. I have never inquired into your absences, nor would I dream of doing so. This . . . this would be nothing serious, a little diversion and I promise to handle it beautifully.' But it did not ring true. The argument was wrong.

I crept back upstairs. By the nursery door the white, maternal shade glimmered, but with every passing second it grew dimmer.

A couple of days later Ryder arrived home from his trip. 'Present,' he said, and deposited a raffia box decorated with cowrie shells in my lap. 'Cowries are used as currency in some parts of Nigeria. I thought you could keep your hairpins in it, Barbara. Or your lipsticks.'

The box was round and compact, solidly made. I thanked him, and wondered who had patted, plaited and fashioned it, and if they had wondered in turn as to whom it might eventually belong.

I held it up. 'I like it very much.'

Over a supper of beef and carrots, I asked Ryder what they ate in Nigeria. Our voices made a little echo in the dining room.

'Depends where you are,' he answered. 'But there is something called groundnut stew. And goat stew. They ball up rice with their fingers and dip it into it. It's quite an art.'

I looked down at the silver knives and forks Ryder and I were wielding. 'I must try to imagine.'

Later, as he tackled baked custard and rhubarb, Ryder said, 'I was thinking we should organize Teignmouth.'

I manipulated a lump in the custard to the side of my plate. 'Why don't we go somewhere else for a change?'

He looked startled. 'Whatever for?'

'I've never been abroad, and I'd like to go somewhere different.' Ryder was frowning, but not repressively so. 'If I'm honest, I'm rather tired of the same old place, year after year.'

'I had no idea.'

I had never much cared for rhubarb and abandoned it. 'With the children gone, we have an opportunity to explore. We should use it to look around, particularly if you're thinking about setting up a travel business. I'd love to go to France or Italy. We could take the car and drive wherever we wanted.'

'It would be expensive, but not impossible.' Ryder was being perfectly reasonable and thoughtful. 'Bit of an effort, though.'

'Ryder, I've never been out of the country. Isn't it about time?' I observed his reaction carefully. Studying my husband in a detached and analytical manner was new and rather exhilarating. Oh, the sloth and habit of a long marriage! I had fallen into the habit of believing that I was always thinking about Ryder but, in truth, I had been doing no such thing.

He sighed, pushed away his half-eaten rhubarb and custard – it was not Mrs Storr's finest hour. 'Are you warning me that we're getting stuck in our ways?'

'Yes . . . a little.'

'Is my wife telling me I'm useless? Or out of date?'

'No, nothing like that. Just that I'm in want of a little change.'

Again, he sighed, a weary sound, and my conscience was smitten. He looked up at me and smiled. 'Why not? Let me think about it.'

'While you're at it,' I threw in, 'I've seen a very nice table in McEwan's Antiques.'

'Table?' Ryder was bewildered.

I leant forward and smiled at my husband. 'For the kitchen, darling. Don't you remember?'

For a second or two, he looked at sea and helpless. Then his brow cleared. *'Barbara!'*

I repeated the gist of the exchange at tea with Bunty. She had greeted me with 'Darling, you grow younger every time I see you,' and led me into her fussy sitting room. 'How do I look?' she asked. 'New dress.'

It was a shirtwaister with a pencil skirt and wide belt. Her hair was freshly permed and she had made herself up carefully with foundation and red lipstick, but I was concerned to see that she had lost weight and was coughing more than usual. 'Smart.'

'That was the idea.'

Over my teacup, I observed Bunty, who was fiddling with the china on the tray, rearranging the sugar bowl and milk jug. How long had I known her? Twenty years? A little more. I watched the restless fingers and wondered if I had ever thought about Bunty properly. 'Are we becoming dull?' I asked her.

'Seconds?' She waved the teapot at me, and I shook my head. 'Perhaps a little, but safe, thank God. Think of the war. No, don't think of the war.' She shuddered theatrically. 'The idea of going through that again with young children! If we'd been single and able to have a good time, it might have been different.'

'I suppose the war has made us unadventurous.'

'Oh, stop it, Barbara,' Bunty said impatiently. 'I think we have to take what we get. And be thankful we have a roof over our heads, and food on the table.' She got up and extracted a cigarette from the shagreen box on the table. She lit it and emptied the full ashtray into the fireplace. 'Barbara . . . you're not going through the change early or anything?'

'No, no,' I said hastily, glad that her back was turned. I changed the subject. 'Tell me about the girls.'

'The girls.' Bunty straightened up and the bumps of her spine were visible under her dress. 'Daughters . . .' She took a thoughtful drag on the cigarette. 'They're different from you and me at that age. Or me, at any rate. I *certainly* don't understand them any more.'

'Has anything happened?'

'Sylvia spends most of her time in the coffee bar and Mary says she's in love with Elvis Presley.'

'Not so *very* different.'

'Ah, but you're wrong. They're different up here.' Smoke wreathed Bunty's permed head as she tapped her forehead impatiently.

In October 1941, wrapped in a coat and scarf, I stood at the end of the garden of the rented house on the edge of the airfield, straining up into the sky. It was evening, the temperature was brisk, and the squadron had scrambled over three hours ago.

Like the other wives uncomfortably encamped in lodgings close by, I was waiting for the boys to return. But since the bombing of the airfield, the women had been asked not to come up to collect the men.

Earlier in the morning, there had been a dogfight to the east. Judy Budwell and I had walked the children, and listened to the roar of the Spitfires, the judder of guns, and watched a pall of smoke billow and spread flatly across the sky.

Judy told me a trick about mending stockings. I said I'd give her a recipe for blackberry jam, and each of us laughed hollowly because there was no sugar for jam-making. She asked me a question about nappies. I asked her where her family lived.

Neither of us asked the important questions. Which of them would be stumbling home with holes ripped in the fuselage, and the telltale lurch of a wounded aircraft? Would one be missing this time? Ted? Bob?

Ryder?

Judy came out into the garden. She was pale and anxious, still weak from having had her baby. 'Tea?'

'Why not?'

We had agreed to sit this one out together and we went inside where I slapped on the kettle and wrestled with the gas-ring. Upstairs in the bedrooms our children were sleeping.

Each morning, I got up and reminded myself that my

duty was to be normal. Utterly, utterly normal. That was what Ryder needed. Normality meant a meal, a bath (such scrimping and planning for hot water), freshly laundered clothes and a waiting wife.

I smiled at Judy, who was perched by the window, trying not to look out. Neither of us would ever admit what an effort it was to keep things going. We hid our chapped hands, joked as we queued endlessly in the shops, and hitched in our belts as the rations got thinner.

Nothing to it. Piece of cake.

Instead I stored up the mundane to tell Ryder, to remind him of life on earth. The butcher had been caught selling meat illicitly, there had been a burglary in the pub, someone had snaffled some parachute silk and Nellie and Elsie Mottram were reported to be wearing silk French knickers.

It was important for our husbands to be sent back to the dispersal huts sated with normality.

'Barbara,' Judy had risen to her feet, a figure quivering with tension, 'I think I hear them.'

I switched off the gas and we ran back into the garden to gaze up into an opaline sky. The planes roared and dipped over us, dropping like graceful but angry birds over the airfield.

One, two, three . . . Five planes to a flight, so two were missing so far. Maybe they had run out of fuel. Maybe they had baled out over the sea.

Judy went even paler. 'I must go home,' she said. 'I have to be there.'

She ran inside the house, and scooped up Rudy, her

baby son, and carried the protesting child into the house on the other side of the street.

Judy's instincts were the right ones. At times like these it was better to be alone.

I wandered through the house, patting a cushion here, flicking at dust there. Sometimes, after going back for a spell of duty, Ryder wrote to me as he and the boys waited in the dispersal huts.

He had said how beautiful it was up there.

I thought it must be a marvellous thing to master such space and solitude.

In one letter he had written: 'You know there are no second chances. I worry that my instruments are unreliable, and I worry I don't have the courage to fly towards a pack of 109s. I worry that, if the time comes, I won't die well . . .'

There was the sound of a car drawing up outside the house, the slam of the door, a merry, beery exchange, and footsteps were coming up the path. 'Barbara!' Ryder surged into the house, bringing with him the smell of aircraft fuel, sweat and survival.

I ran into his arms. 'Thank God.' *Not this time.* 'Let me check you over. Are you hurt?'

'Just a scratch where I banged my head on the cowling.' He captured my hands and hooked my arms behind my back, standing so close to me that I felt every line of his body. 'Not so bad this one. One kill. One probable.' He kissed my lips and I tasted beer. 'Put your best dress on. Bit of a party in the mess. The flight sergeant's wife has offered to babysit.'

I flew upstairs and put on my evening frock, black with a sweetheart neckline, and filled in my mouth with my hoarded lipstick. It was part of my business to look good, to chat to the younger pilots who needed reassurance and a bit of mothering, to laugh and joke.

The mess room was crowded and smoky. Almost immediately Ryder was drawn into a group where an animated discussion went on as to how many pints of beer they could down. Having surveyed the figures at the bar for any lost souls, I scooped up Bill Droitwich (eighteen) and clucked over him. He seemed rattled and anxious, but after a while settled down and discussed eagerly what he saw as the advantages of the Hurricane over the Spitfire. 'The Hurricane's a flying gun platform,' he said, 'better than the Spit.'

'Careful,' I said, looking round. 'You'll be lynched.'

No one mentioned that Dickie Rose (twenty) had bought it. It had been his third flight.

Best not. Unwritten rules.

A roar went up from the group round Ryder. I set my face in a permanent smile and ignored the aching muscles. Sometimes I was reminded of the story of the Little Match Girl who pressed her nose to the pane of glass and looked in at a scene of happiness and warmth, while her feet froze on the pavement. That was how I felt when Ryder stepped out of the house and into his life in the mess, in the sky, in battle. Then he was entirely separate and disconnected, and there was no possibility for me of sharing it with him.

I had always imagined that jealousy is necessarily felt

about *someone*. But it isn't. The truth was that the painful, unsettled, *unworthy* feelings that I experienced were directed against the cosy camaraderie – the jokes, the slang, the togetherness, the shared but silent mourning for the deaths of those . . . boys – in which I had no place.

I chatted away and was rewarded by Bill Droitwich's beaming face. Yet every so often I glanced up or looked around and sought out Ryder. There he was: propped loosely against the bar, with a lash of iodine on the cut just below his hairline, in the act of lighting a cigarette, listening to Jack or Bob, and I would feel the deep burn of possession and love.

The success of my campaign to go abroad took me by surprise.

'Barbara . . . are you awake?' Ryder slid closer to me in bed.

A second or two elapsed. 'Yes.'

He placed a hand on my thigh. 'Sufficiently awake?'

Another, slightly longer pause. 'Yes.'

I anticipated Ryder making his customary moves and asking the customary things of my body, but he surprised me. He slipped an arm under my head, and nestled it on his shoulder. 'Comfortable?'

'Very,' I murmured.

'You're right about Teignmouth. We should go somewhere else. You got me thinking. We should take stock and make plans.'

I had anticipated him being calmly obstinate, charming

in his refusal, but implacable, so his capitulation took a moment to absorb.

The evening had been unremarkable. Ryder had listened to the radio, and I read without digesting anything. Only once before in my life had I felt so fevered, so alive, so . . . And this was both odd and different.

After the news, Ryder had got up, poured himself a whisky and taken up the crossword. Together, we had worked at the clues, swapping guesses. I went over to his chair and leant over it. Once I snatched the pen from him, and he said, 'Steady on, Babs.'

Now, he said, 'The world is opening up, Barbara. Soon a lot more people will be flying.'

He talked about the development of the jet engine, the need for more and bigger airports, daily schedules, the growing market for more pilots, air-traffic controllers and luggage-handlers. 'It's wide open, Babs, and I'm not too old to take advantage of it.'

He pulled the pillows around him as he liked them. 'So, what do you think? Not so stick-in-the-mud?'

'It's fascinating,' I replied. 'But it's going to be a much noisier world.'

'How like a woman to think of that.'

'How like *me* to think of that.'

'How like *you*, Barbara.'

I reached over and touched his cheek. 'Go to sleep, Ryder, otherwise it will affect your flying.'

I thought he had fallen asleep until I heard him mumble, 'Do you think about the old days at all?'

'From time to time.'

'I do,' he admitted, and I had an idea that he found it painful to say so.

'There's no need any more.'

'No,' he said. 'But I need to know that you haven't forgotten them.'

I thought of all we had been through together. 'No chance.'

'Good,' he said, and was asleep.

Chapter Fourteen: Barbara

Amy and I were in the kitchen, hulling a crop of strawberries that, by dint of coaxing and admonishing, Herr Schlinker had brought to triumphant fruition. I worked quickly and more or less neatly, and chose the moment to tell Amy my news. 'I'm going to work one day a week in the almoner's office at St Bede's.'

I swept up a pile of stalks and dropped them into the bin. If I had expected a response, I did not get it. I looked round. Amy was pulling at the fruit, roughly and without care, seemingly absorbed in the destruction she was wreaking and fascinated by it. 'Are you angry about something, Amy?'

That provoked her into saying furiously, 'I see. It's all right for you to have a job *now*.'

'Yes, your father's fine about it.'

'It suits you *now*, doesn't it, Mummy? Didn't suit you so well when I was growing up and thinking about my future.'

'I'm not sure I know what you're talking about. There was no question of me getting a job while I was looking after you two.'

She shook her head. 'I'm not talking about you. I'm talking about me. You never helped me. You never stuck up for me with Daddy. Daddy can't help what he is,' she added, in a kind of maternal way that was both endearing and funny – only it wasn't, for I was not netted into her mercy. 'I don't blame him but I always thought, I always hoped, you'd be sympathetic.'

That stung. 'Amy, when your father and I made our decisions, we thought that Roy would have to provide for a future family . . . and you would be provided for by a husband.'

Amy dismembered yet another strawberry and threw it on to the pile. 'Whenever I hear that sort of argument, I want to commit murder. Didn't you think about the unfairness? Hadn't you spotted that times have changed?'

I sat down heavily on a hard chair. 'Of course times have changed.'

'That's not an answer.' Amy pushed back her hair with a stained hand. 'You didn't consider that I'd love to learn all the things my brother learnt about instead of being fobbed off with needlework. Did it never occur to you that I might like to know about all those too, and not feel so *stupid* all the time?'

It was piteously spoken – an admission of self-doubt and . . . despair. 'Is that why you're so angry? Because you feel stupid?'

'Oh, I don't know, Mum. That's the point, I don't *know*. And that does make me feel stupid.'

She attacked another strawberry and I winced at the waste. 'If you can't do it properly, please don't do it.'

'Fine.' She stepped back immediately.

I assessed the mangled fruit and supposed I could make a strawberry fool instead of the flan I had planned. Amy swung away from the table, and wiped her hands on her pinafore.

'Darling, I'll have to wash that now.'

She sent me a look bordering on contempt. 'I'll do it, if it's a problem.'

'Amy, could we be friends and not at each other's throats?' Clumsily, I reached out to hug my puzzling, difficult daughter.

Amy avoided the contact. 'You always do that when you can't think of anything sensible to say, Mum. But it won't do any more.'

The threat of tears lay behind Amy's mutinous eyes and my own hurt was forgotten in a rush of pity. It was impossible to forget those feelings – baffled, raw and impotent. I know, because I had experienced them too. That was before Ryder had materialized, as it were, out of the sun, in a dazzle of light and promise, scooped up the unfinished, terrified eighteen-year-old and carried her away to begin a proper life.

'All right, Amy. What can I do?'

She turned a countenance on me so filled with rage and dislike that I found myself swallowing hard. But I summoned my wits, and any wisdom I possessed. 'Amy, it doesn't do any good to look like that. It isn't helping me to understand you.'

'How should I look, Mother? Like Roy's Victoria, all eager to please?'

'*No*,' I said involuntarily. 'Not like Victoria.'

We exchanged a reluctant grin. 'All right, we agree. Not like Victoria.'

Breathing easier with this slight chink in the wall, I fetched a bowl of cream from the fridge. 'Is Mrs Trant looking after you and are you eating properly?'

Instantly the chink closed. 'Mrs Trant is a stupid, nosy woman,' Amy almost spat the words, 'who doesn't have enough to do. You know the type. The world is full of women who have never had enough to occupy their minds, so they make mischief and bully others.'

The implication was that I belonged in that category.

'Amy . . .' I began to whip the cream and prayed for calm and sense as it thickened and draped itself round the bowl. When I was nursing Amy, I had held her plump little body close and dreamt that she would grow up and we would be *just like that*. Two crossed fingers. 'Mum, what do you think . . .' she would say, asking advice about clothes, boyfriends, how to do her hair. And I would reply, 'Let's do this,' or 'Let's try that,' and revel in our closed, conspiratorial intimacy. It should have been effortless, automatic. But it wasn't. I had neglected to ask the most basic questions. *What do you mean? What do you want?*

I abandoned the whisk and pushed aside the bowl. 'Sit down, Amy.'

Reluctantly, she obeyed. I drew up a chair beside her and took her hands in mine. 'Shall we try to have a proper talk instead of skirting the issues? I want to understand what *you* want. I want us to be honest. Shall we abandon the wretched Mrs Trant's lodgings and find somewhere else?'

Hardly a problem solver, but a beginning.

Amy hesitated – a sign that she was considering. I scanned her face for clues, for the tiniest crack in her defences, for a remnant of warmth. 'What can we talk about? When have we ever talked?'

'It's not too late. We can do something.'

But she pulled her hands away. 'You still don't understand. "Let's change Amy's landlady",' she mimicked my voice, 'and, *poof*, everything will be fine. But it's too late. You've done your best to make me into you, and here I am. Hope you're pleased.'

There was a streak of strawberry pulp on her face where she had rubbed at it, and her fringe had grown too long. I said urgently, 'I wanted the best for you, to give you a good home, and later on you would marry and have a family. That's where your energies and training will go. It has to be done well. It's not easy.'

'Oh, Mum. So wrapped up in this house that you can't see anything outside it!' She dug into the pocket of her skirt, produced a kirby-grip and pinned back the too-long fringe. The effect was awful.

I tried again: 'I understand that this is a difficult stage of your life, and you're not quite sure about anything, which is perfectly natural.'

Amy emitted a tiny, shuddering sigh. 'Easy to say.'

Oh, Amy, Amy.

Hunched miserably on that kitchen chair, she seemed so young, and youth was a mixture of vulnerability and promise. Was it possible that I could have spoilt that promise? And was it suffering that clouded her clear skin and imprinted lines on her forehead? Or just bad diet and fatigue? I reached out and smoothed away the frown with my thumb. For a second, she permitted me the gesture.

For a second, she was the baby who had nuzzled and clung to me for hours at a time.

Then she spoilt it. 'What you don't understand is that I don't want to be like you. And I'm frightened . . . I'm frightened that that's precisely what I'll be.'

We had resolved nothing further when I drove Amy to the station to catch the evening train. The only positive aspect of our confrontation in the kitchen was that we had opened up the subject – just a little.

I parked in the station yard, and gripped the wheel. 'What you've told me, Amy, has worried me very much. And I want to say I'm sorry.'

'Sorry?' She gathered up her shoulder-bag and twisted the strap round her fingers. 'At least you listened,' she said, and I was pathetically grateful for the bone of comfort. 'Sometimes I almost believed that you battled against me for the sake of it, Mum. As if it was something mothers did. Then I thought it was because you didn't like me.' She shrugged her shoulders. 'I know I'm not very likeable.'

'That's not true, Amy. *Please* believe that.'

She gave me a quick peck on the cheek and terminated the conversation. 'I'll see you next week.'

I watched her walk across the yard. Her skirt hem was uneven, and she hadn't bothered to brush her hair. She looked lonely and stubborn, and so very unsure.

She disappeared into the station without looking back.

I dropped my head on the wheel and cried.

The next morning in the almoner's office at St Bede's I surveyed the desk to which I had been ushered. It had a telephone on it, a couple of thick directories, and a pile of papers that Miss Raith told me were mine to tackle.

St Bede's was a complex of low buildings situated at the other end of the city from where we lived; the main flank comprised the wards and the outlying ones the administrative offices. The day was clear, the sky blue, and it had been a relief to step out of the front door and leave behind my accustomed routines. The exercise had cleared my head, and I had arrived at the hospital feeling better for the physical pleasure of walking.

It did not take me five minutes to discover my limitations and inexperience. This came as a shock for I had run my own house successfully for many years. In some despair, I leafed through the piles of papers. Some had been annotated: 'Speak to the health department.' 'Take up with BB.' 'Check budget.' Which was all pretty much Greek to me.

'Your first task,' Miss Raith tossed her instructions over her shoulder, 'is to organize Mr Clarkson's transport from hospital to the convalescent home.'

Miss Raith, the almoner, ran her department with zeal and an iron purpose. Dressed in a purposeful-looking skirt, blouse and lace-up shoes, she took in my green frock and high heels with an air of disapproval. Her opening gambit had been: 'You won't be much help to me for a couple of months, if that. I hope you're serious about this, and prepared to stay. Otherwise it's a waste of my time training you up. I warn you, I'm bound to be a bit impatient at times, but I take it you can cope with that?'

I read Mr Clarkson's notes. He was a widower, scraping

by on a small pension in a dank basement that did nothing for his health problems.

'The best we can do is secure him an extended convalescence,' Miss Raith said, 'then send him home to die of damp. At least he'll have had a little bit of comfort.'

'What should I do?'

She did not pause in the act of checking a line of figures. 'Get on the telephone, of course. Speak to the department responsible for social security and have some money allocated.'

Three hours later I put down the telephone, depleted and exhausted. My negotiating skills were badly wanting and I was unused to people who said, 'This is not my responsibility. I can't help you.'

'Does anyone ever take a decision?' I asked.

Miss Raith was searching for a document in the filing cabinet. 'Not if they can help it, so you'd better get used to that too.' She shoved the drawer shut with a clang and turned round. 'Welcome to the real world, Mrs Beeching.' She cocked an eyebrow at me. 'Willing to continue?'

It was dark in the almoner's office and cramped, and outside the sky had turned an even deeper blue. I glanced through the window, then dragged my gaze back to Miss Raith. 'Of course.'

I had missed lunch in the staff canteen but I wheedled something to eat and drink before it closed. I sat at a table by the window, ate a stale bun and drank bad coffee. The room was fuggy with boiled cabbage and cigarette smoke; I watched it empty. On the counter, the remainder of the buns sat under a glass dome beside a giant teapot. The canteen supervisor admonished a worryingly thin girl to hurry up; she lifted the heavy teapot and staggered out of sight.

At five thirty I walked down the asphalt drive to the road. Tap-tap, went the heels of my shoes, and I fancied they exuded a busy, optimistic, professional sound. Then I saw Alexander waiting by the entrance. He was more formally dressed than normal in a suit, and his hair was brushed back.

He was puffing nervously at a cigarette. 'Oh, good,' he said, when he saw me. 'You took your time.'

'How did you know I was here?'

'Mrs Andrews lets slip a lot of information over the breakfast table. I wonder if she realizes how much. "Barbara's first day as a working woman," she said this morning. "And it won't last long."'

I laughed. 'I can rely on Bunty for support.'

Alexander stamped on the cigarette. 'I've been thinking and thinking about you, Barbara, and you won't go away. That's the truth, and I'm not ashamed. So that's why I'm here. Do you want me to go? Just say and I will.' He grinned. 'You've got me running about like a dog after a stick. "Stay. Go."'

My eyes flew to his. Every nerve in my body pulsed. He lifted his eyebrows a fraction – a tiny message of what? Invitation? Perhaps appreciation. I experienced the seductive shock of having to think about it, and, yes, of my own response.

Alexander had told me I was *interesting*. He had also asked a theoretical question, which was not theoretical at all. If he had remained silent, I would have gone on my way, a little stirred up, a little flustered, but still essentially the same. But he had been bold and brave, and laid his wishes before me and there they were: demanding an answer.

'I'll stay, then.' We fell into step and walked down the road towards the station. 'Have you thought about me at all?' he asked.

'I have. I don't want to, but I have.'

He kept his eyes fixed ahead. 'If you knew how grateful I am. How happy I am.'

We moved on. Alexander's pace was too quick for me, and he was forced to slow down to let me keep up. We crossed the bridge over the railway line and I came to a halt. 'I must go and catch my bus.'

Evening commuters eddied in and out of the station and there was already a queue at the stop.

'Stay five more minutes,' he begged.

It did not take much persuasion, and we loitered on the bridge. Wreathed in steam, the evening trains pulled in and out of the platforms, disgorging men in dark suits and bowler hats. My bus came and went.

'It'll be nice tomorrow.' I looked up at the sky.

'Barbara, do you have a bicycle?'

'No, but Amy has. It's in the shed.'

'But you can cycle?'

'Oh, yes. I used to love it, years ago.'

'Then you must tomorrow. It's a wonderful thing to do on a summer's day. Say yes.'

'I'm not sure. I'm busy.'

'Too busy to enjoy a fine day? You're not allowed to say no.'

The doors on the trains clanged open and shut. I watched a woman chivvy two children across the bridge to the opposite platform.

'Say yes.'

'Well . . . yes.'

I waited a long time for the next bus to take me home, and amused myself by imagining what I must look like to an observer or a passer-by. Item: one unremarkable forty-two-year-old, shifting from foot to foot as the waiting told on her feet. But inside that middle-aged woman, there was springtime: light, joyous, and sun-filled.

The following morning found me peeling hard-boiled eggs; the shell and inner membrane were being obstinate. Fragments of the former clung to the latter, and part of the white had fallen away. I dropped it into the hens' bowl, then snatched it back. Hens eating their own eggs smacked of cannibalism.

I took the bread out of the bread-bin, a green enamel one that had become chipped in places over the years. The butter was softening by the side of the Rayburn and I spread some on the bread, then the mashed-up egg and slices of cucumber. I wrapped the whole lot in a square of greaseproof paper and tied it with string.

The announcer on the radio said, 'It is estimated in South Africa that up to fifty thousand black South Africans have rioted in protest against a slum-clearance scheme. The leaders of the riot were mainly women . . .'

The clock said twelve fifteen.

Upstairs, I changed into a skirt and short-sleeved blouse, brushed my hair and let it hang loose on my shoulders. At the last minute, I snatched up a scarf and a cardigan and looked into the mirror. I was not sure who was looking back at me. The woman was familiar, but not. She should be someone who did not normally act on impulse, not this creature balanced on the balls of her feet, sharply defined and vivid in the clear midday light.

Alexander had been right. Cycling on a fine summer's day was glorious. The wind rushed through my hair. I teetered, tested my muscles, clung on for dear life, careered down the hill . . . all with a sense of perfect release.

Alexander was waiting at the junction of the road to Shalford. When he saw me, he got back on his bicycle and I fell into line behind him. The sun stippled my arms, and the air was soft and fresh, the road well cambered. After three or four miles, he swung to the left and rode down an overgrown lane. Eventually, it grew too narrow, and we dismounted.

'Come on, Barbara.'

I was panting. 'I've never been here before. How can I have missed it?'

'I discovered it on one of my walks. The path leads down to the river and no one seems to know about it.'

He was elated by this, and I laughed as he helped me to prop up my bicycle, then took over the picnic basket. We pushed our way through the brambles and nettles, until the path opened up at the river where it curved back on itself, creating an oasis of turf and rushes, fringed by willows and oak. It was a verdant place, a modest, ignored paradise.

Alexander put down the basket and tested the grass with a foot. 'Don't think it's too damp.'

We faced each other. Alexander was tousled and flushed from the exercise, and shining with enjoyment at his cleverness. 'How was that?' he asked.

'An almost forgotten pleasure, but I'm going to be stiff tomorrow.'

'You don't allow yourself enough pleasure then. If I was Ryder I'd take you everywhere. Make you climb mountains but pamper you, too. Shower you with presents.'

He moved closer and I took a step back. 'I won't talk about Ryder.'

Alexander breathed in and out rapidly. 'Why are you here?'

'Friendship. Curiosity. I want to know what you're thinking. Which questions you're asking. You make me laugh. You make me feel . . . different.'

Then he kissed me. The sunlight fractured behind my closed lids, the river murmured, and Alexander smelt of sweat and heat. His lips moved over mine and I remembered Ryder kissing me for the first time. As I surrendered to the sensation, Ryder and Alexander merged and, for a second or two, I glimpsed the infinite layers of love and desire.

Somehow Alexander and I were on the ground. 'Wait!' I wanted to cry. But I didn't.

He fought to get inside the fastening of my blouse, and I had to help him. He found my breast but, having been so frantic to reach it, he lost interest and moved on.

He hitched up my skirt, and the material bunched awkwardly between us. 'Let me,' he murmured urgently. 'Barbara . . . please . . .'

I raised my hips and, again, I helped him. He sank into me with a brief, almost anguished, cry.

What followed was not graceful, or even subtle, only sensation: pure and vivid and intense. A root pressed into my back, my foot slid on the turf, Alexander's weight on me hurt; so did his extreme need.

It was over very quickly. He whispered my name, shuddered, gave a groan and his head sank on to my breast. I turned my head and a close-up of the grass presented itself to my dazzled gaze. An ant was climbing a blade and a cloud masked the sun. My throat swelled and tightened with gratitude for being alive.

I pulled Alexander closer and he murmured, 'Sorry. Far too quick. I meant to do so much better.'

'It doesn't matter.'

'Really?' He raised himself on an elbow and looked down at me, anxiously.

'Truly.'

He sat up and adjusted his clothing. My thighs glided stickily over each other so I cleaned myself up and fastened my blouse. I reached for my shoes and Alexander stopped me. 'Has anyone ever told you what beautiful feet you have? So narrow, so delicate.' He knelt down and ran his finger over the arch of my foot and up my leg. 'I'm going to tell you a hundred times a day. No, a hundred thousand times.'

Out of the corner of my eye, I caught a flash of blue as dragonflies swooped across the water. Further up on the opposite bank a moorhen scooted on the water, with drops of water like pearls running off its back.

My body throbbed, and there was a faint bruise on my arm where Alexander had grasped it. I felt absurdly, gloriously, almost childishly happy.

Alexander undid the sandwiches and sank his teeth into the egg and cucumber. He looked over to me, eyes alight with amusement, pleasure and greed. 'I'm hungry. Aren't you?'

I wheeled Amy's bicycle round the side of the house to the shed, and let myself in through the back door. I stepped into the cloakroom, with its familiar muddle of coats, and the house received me back. An ally? A refuge?

I hovered, irresolute, in the hall. I wanted to stay tousled and smelling of Alexander for as long as I dared. I did not want to lose any memory of those moments by the river. I wanted to relive the sun on my arms and the sound of the water. I wanted to drowse in those moments of illusion and luminous sensation.

My feet took me upstairs to my bedroom and I undressed with hands that shook a little. Discarding my clothes in a heap, I ran water into the bath.

Shocked by the change in temperature, I scrubbed until my skin turned pink. I dried myself and put on an entire set of clean clothes.

The phone was ringing as I returned downstairs.

'Darling, about bridge next week . . .' Bunty rattled on about dates and arrangements, and I agreed to everything she suggested. More than once she coughed: a harsh, disagreeable sound.

'Have you been to the doctor about that cough?' I asked.

'No, but it's driving me mad, so I think I must.'

'Do.'

'Barbara,' Bunty lowered her voice, 'you don't sound quite yourself.'

'Of course I'm myself.'

But I wasn't.

Chapter Fifteen: Siena

At seven fifteen a.m. the phone rang in my office and I picked it up. It was Charlie in chambers. He had been in such a rush that morning, he had forgotten the papers outlining his skeleton argument for the case next up after the Jackie Woodruff trial. 'I want Nancy to take a quick look. I know you're going to see Johnny. Could you drop it off?'

Nancy was a junior tenant in the chambers, but there was nothing junior about her ambition and her ability. 'Of course,' I said.

'Sorry about the trouble.'

But I took pleasure in it, an insignificant detour but charged, somehow, with intimacy and my gratitude to be able to *do* something for Charlie.

'Chambers' was too magnificent a term for the scruffy office block in Holborn that housed Freedom Watch – the architecture and concrete cladding could only be described as a fine example of Brutalism.

There was a queue at Reception and I waited. Two of the clerks were hovering outside their office. I recognized one, David; he had his back to me.

'Gone a bit mad on this one,' I heard him say. 'Demanding this, that and the other. Neo-natal statistics, genetic probabilities – it doesn't stop.'

I took the stairs two at a time (good for the thigh muscles) with an uneasy heart. They had been talking about Charlie, and I was not sure that I cared for the offhand tone of the remark, or for its implications.

I caught him in the middle of typing a document on a grubby computer terminal. The room was a tip – papers, boxes, books, strewn in abandon – and stuffy.

Charlie looked up at my entrance, pale and focused. 'Thanks, darling.'

I dropped the packet on his desk. 'Charlie, promise me you're not overdoing this one. Overcooking it.'

He smiled gently. 'Like you don't?'

I placed my hands on the desk and leant towards him. 'If I get too obsessed I make mistakes.'

'I can't legislate against making mistakes. But point taken. Don't worry, I'm in control.' His eyes slid towards the screen and cut me off. 'Thanks, darling. See you tonight.'

On my way out Nancy – tall, blonde, slender – passed me, clutching a large pile of papers. She looked serious and responsible. She stopped briefly, searched for a greeting and produced the one she thought would suit me. 'Nice jacket,' she said.

For some reason I found myself frowning.

Johnny (accountant, top-flight, expensive, suits custom-made) wore the plus-signs look on his face. Until comparatively recently, this had not often featured in our discussions and I took heart.

I had arrived at his expensive offices in Mayfair for my appointment, to find him working away on my figures.

'We'll be making you into a limited company if we continue to sail with this wind. You're nearly there.'

'How nearly? Ish?'

He glanced down at the balance sheets. 'A couple of years should do it. Meanwhile, my projections are for a healthy cash-flow.'

My smile encompassed a ripe and (excuse me) rich appreciation of this achievement.

Johnny and I now embarked on some pleasing calculations. 'I think we should go this way,' he said, more than once. Of course, the prospect of extra fees pleased him, but I think he took a pride also from the way my once tiny enterprise had built up.

'Johnny,' I was careful how I put it, 'if the figures are correct, I'm earning quite a lot more than Charlie.'

He looked up at me. 'Yup.'

'Ah.'

'Lucky Charlie, that's what I say.' Johnny clicked out of my file. 'I take it there's no problem?'

'No. No, of course not. Charlie's fine about it. It allows him to do his legal-aid work and I want him to be able to do that.'

Johnny and I wrapped up our discussion with a résumé on saving plans, pension tactics and tax, then bade each other a warm goodbye.

Back in the street, my mobile phone rang. 'Thank God!' said Manda. 'I need to talk to someone normal. Everyone in the office is either deluded or maddened by vicious ambition and Dick was away all weekend and I thought I'd go mad.'

I talked into the phone as I headed towards a coffee shop and, using sign language, ordered a large cappuccino. Manda's outpourings streamed seamlessly into my ear. *Children. Work. Au pairs. Children. Impossible to sleep, to think, to get thin (too tired). Nits. Children.*

'You're a darling,' she said eventually. 'It's all absolutely fine, but I needed an outlet for five minutes. I'm sorry it's always you. I'll do the same for you one day.'

For once, Manda's on-going drama left me a little impatient. 'You chose to have the delicious Het and Patrick.'

'True,' she admitted, with a catch in her voice, then added, infuriatingly, 'I know it doesn't sound like it but it was the best thing I ever did, snotty little horrors.'

I should have been taking up Manda's offer to help me broker a decision. Manda, please, help me to decide. Convince me my fears and anxieties are stupid, selfish. Teach me where to look for the belief. Help me to make it right with Charlie. He's the person I love best in the world (and who loves me best) and I don't want to give him what he most wants.

'So what are *you* doing, Siena?'

'Just been to see Johnny, and he tells me all's well, money-wise, and I'm feeling bullish and much more secure.'

'Yes,' she said, working furiously as always on the negative bypass. 'It's brilliant.'

'It's the power base.'

'Well, my power base, darling Siena, is taking a rain-check, but you wait. When the children are older, watch me.'

I dropped my phone back into my bag – a delightful Lulu Guinness number – and glanced at my watch. Technically, I should have been making tracks for home to work on the first draft for Caesar Books.

Coffee. Time. Expensive bag. Freedom of mind. Business shaping up.

Nice.

I watched the traffic swirl round Berkeley Square, and the newsagent on the corner had slotted a poster with the latest headlines on his stand. 'Ten Million Divorce Settlement for Film Star'.

How fortunate I was. I could sit here and appreciate the extravagance and richness of my city. For as long as I thought fit, I was at liberty to loiter in a coffee bar, sniffing the aroma and reading a copy of *Vogue*.

Oh, Charlie.

Ingrid would be proud of me.

That weekend, Charlie did not come home – in a manner of speaking. Yes, he slept in our bed at night but got up at dawn to go into the office and did not return until late at night. 'Sorry about that, but you understand,' he said. 'I have to have everything absolutely sure and worked out and checked.'

The case began on Tuesday, and I slipped with a huddle of other spectators into court number three at Blackfriars Crown Court. Hoping Charlie would not see me, I made for the back row.

The courtroom was a modern one: expensive wood panelling, comfortable seats and microphones in all the right places. The colours were light and pleasing, and yet it exuded an inexorability. I congratulated whoever had been in charge of the decoration for bringing off such a balancing trick.

My gaze flew to Charlie, who was conferring with his junior. His gown had slipped over his shoulder, and his wig was slightly askew.

Put it straight! I sent him the telepathic message. He must have heard, for he tugged at his gown and settled his wig.

Jackie, the defendant, already sat in the dock, flanked by a couple of women in prison officers' uniforms. Pretty, slight and desperately pale, she looked as though she had not eaten a good meal for months. She was wearing a short skirt (*wrong, wrong*: too short) and a boat-necked black jumper, but Charlie was right. She looked like the last woman in the world to kill her baby.

The judge arrived, addressed some words to counsel on a point of law, and the jury was ushered in. I saw Charlie appraise them minutely and knew he would be pleased that five were women.

Jackie Woodruff gave them a brief glance, as if they were of only passing interest, then stared ahead. Her expression was the most chilling I had ever seen, for it was devoid of sentience and emotion. It said: There is nothing you can do to me that has not already been done.

Charlie's notes and document bundle lay on the lectern. As always, they were marked with different-coloured Post-its – medical evidence, witness testimony, expert testimony. Etc. Due process of law, designed to clarify and explain the mess and muddle into which humans got themselves.

The indictment was read out. Robin Banstead, the prosecuting barrister, rose to his feet – a veteran, Charlie had said, and bloody too fond of himself and the claret (in no particular order). We listened to the circumstances, the injuries to the baby, the scene of death, the defendant's reaction. There would be evidence, he said, to suggest that Jackie Woodruff had been unhappy at the prospect of becoming a mother, and this was documented. He told us that she had had a difficult birth, and that details would be given. Having fleshed out the background more fully, he read out a list of the baby's bruises and one of the women in the jury covered her face with her hands.

Just then Charlie looked up and saw me. Not so much by a hint did he betray he knew me.

Then he got to his feet, tall and authoritative in his robes, the disobedient hair masked by the wig. Jackie Woodruff was a loving mother, he began, who had a supportive husband. The baby had been wanted but the birth had indeed been difficult, and Jackie's convalescence had taken longer than average; we would be given a detailed report by the midwife. There was not a shred of evidence, he said, to suggest that Jackie had harboured murderous thoughts or regretted her motherhood, but it was hardly surprising that, after a delivery which included an emergency dash to the operating theatre, a blood transfusion and a subsequent infection of the wound, she felt weak. 'Which mother among those here,' he asked, turning to the jury, 'would not feel daunted after such an experience?' Charlie paused. 'You might say that it was a perfectly natural reaction to feel beleaguered and not entirely in control, particularly as the baby was not a good sleeper. Those of you who are parents will perhaps remember what a shock to the system it is to have a new baby in the house, however longed-for. What would you have felt when, after a slow recovery when life is beginning to feel normal again, you go upstairs to your baby's room and discover that between the hours of two thirty, when you had put him down to sleep, and three fifteen, when you went to check him, he has died? It is unimaginable. So, too, is the subsequent scenario in which, rather than being taken in and cared for, given help and succour to struggle through the days and weeks, you are accused of being the person who brought about this devastating event.'

In the dock, Jackie Woodruff listened and lost the battle against feeling, for she trembled visibly. A woman prison officer took pity and handed her a glass of water. But Charlie drove on, riding over the horror and anguish – an advocate whose mastery commanded you to believe his version of what had happened.

'This *was* a longed-for baby,' he said, 'and we have evidence to support this.' He turned his head, and his gaze rested briefly on me. Then he turned back to the jury.

Charlie's voice soared and swooped – a persuasive and (cunningly concealed under the legal persiflage) passionate mediator for due process. I wanted to cry at the boldness and bravery of his endeavour in putting the world to rights.

*

The following Sunday morning I took charge. The day had dawned so sunny and inviting that I ordered, 'Up. We're going walking.'

'Fine,' he said, so we got into the car and drove out to Henley.

'Why were you in court?' Charlie asked finally, as he laced up his walking boots.

'I wanted to see you.'

'And?'

'I did see you.'

We digested this exchange as we climbed the hill and hugged the ridge for five or so miles. It was easy walking, undemanding and rhythmic.

Charlie stopped to consult the map. On our right in a field was a piggery, and the sows were taking advantage of the weather to wallow in the mud by the trough, their exposed pink udders shuddering with the movement of their large bodies.

'The footpath is supposed to go directly through the field, but I don't think the farmer feels too friendly about that.' Charlie pointed to the 'Trespassers Will Be Prosecuted' notice on the gate. The word 'Prosecuted' had been crossed out and 'Shot' scrawled over it.

I bent down to retie my bootlace. I felt good – muscles and complexion tingling with the exercise.

'Let's eat by the fallen tree over there,' said Charlie.

We loped down the slope to it. With the half-rotten trunk providing support, I opened my day-sack and pulled out Charlie's sandwiches.

'Not bloody tofu, I hope.'

'It's the new beef.'

Charlie raised a threatening eyebrow. 'If you've done that to me, Mrs Grant, you're finished.'

'Oh, Charlie, I so thought you'd like it.' I handed over the packet wrapped in silver foil. 'I went to enormous trouble to buy it.'

Half sceptical, half appalled, he inspected the sandwiches. 'Siena . . .'

'Cheese.' I took mercy on him.

Charlie gave his full attention to eating. I had lost my appetite but I was content to watch him dreamily. He ate quickly, ravenously. 'Careful, Charlie, you'll get indigestion.'

He looked at me. 'I eat on the run so often it's become a habit.'

The sun was deliciously strong, with a suggestion of the weighty mature heat massing for the summer. I passed Charlie a hard-boiled egg, with a packet of salt nicked from my plane trip to the States, and reached for the sun cream, which I massaged into my arms and face. Charlie was absorbed in peeling his egg, and I lay down with my day-sack under my head.

After a second or two, it struck me that he had gone quiet. I turned my head and squinted up at him. In one hand he held the egg, and in the other the salt packet with 'American Airlines' printed on it. He was staring at it, his expression unreadable.

I shut my eyes.

After a while, I asked, 'What will happen in the trial next week?'

'The prosecution will wheel out their case, starting with the midwife, and I will cross-examine.' He tossed back the packet of salt. 'My knives are sharpened.'

'Charlie, can I ask you again? You're not getting *too* caught up in this case, are you?'

'*No.*' He hunched over his knees. 'But I'm sure Jackie Woodruff didn't kill her baby.'

I edged nearer to him and dropped my hand on to his thigh.

He reached over and kissed me lightly on the lips, then with increasing fervour. There was the sound of voices and footsteps and he released me. A family group was toiling up the slope towards us, chattering to each other. The mother held a small son's hand, and the father toted a baby in a pink sunhat in a backpack. They looked young and fresh, and as they passed us the mother called, 'Afternoon.'

'Afternoon,' I replied, feeling Charlie's hold slacken. Once upon a time, Charlie and I wouldn't have cared if anyone was passing, but those early ardent days had gone.

I grabbed back his hand. 'You must tell Jackie not to wear such a short skirt,' I said. 'I can get something for her, if it's a problem.'

But Charlie was watching the family's progress up the grass slope. The little boy was finding it tough going, and his mother was coaxing him – 'Come on, Mikey.'

I don't think Charlie heard me.

Why did I go back to court number three?

I don't know exactly. Voyeur? Perhaps. Yet I was fixated

on Jackie Woodruff's ordeal. I needed to know: I wanted to look beneath that set white face, the trembling hands and the protestations of innocence. Where, if she was guilty, did one search for mercy, and forgiveness?

This time I had warned Charlie and, on my entrance, he sent me a private signal of a lifted finger.

Mrs Adjani was a good-looking, middle-aged Asian midwife with extensive experience. Robin Banstead asked her to describe Jackie's pregnancy and labour. 'Were they normal?' he wanted to know.

'Perfectly. Mrs Woodruff was rather sick in the first stages, and later developed back pain, which is also quite normal.'

'Did the defendant at any time express negative feelings?'

Mrs Adjani looked at her perfectly manicured hands. 'She did express some worry as to how she would cope with her job and the baby. In fact, on one visit I had to calm her down as she became hysterical.'

'And the delivery?'

'It was very difficult indeed. We hadn't anticipated any problems but Mrs Woodruff failed to dilate properly after twelve hours' labour, then bled very heavily.'

'And the aftermath?'

'It's fair to say that Mrs Woodruff was quite mutilated, her wound became infected, and she had to take several courses of antibiotics, which upset the baby.'

Later, Charlie got to his feet. 'Mrs Adjani, how normal is it for expectant women to express apprehension about becoming a mother?'

Mrs Adjani hesitated. 'Fairly normal.'

'Could you be more specific? Do one in a hundred women or one in five express such fears?'

'It depends on circumstances and temperament. Some women are not working, but of those who are, I've noticed about half express worry, some extreme anxiety.'

'I see.' Charlie turned over a page of his notes, which I knew was unnecessary: his line of attack was perfectly honed in his head. 'You say that you had to calm Mrs Woodruff down during one visit. How long had she been waiting to see you?'

'Over two hours, unfortunately, because we had a difficult case that needed immediate attention. The other mothers had to wait.'

'And was that a problem for Mrs Woodruff?'

'She did mention that she was missing an important meeting and was upset because she was worried about her boss's reaction.'

Charlie consulted his notes. 'And this particular appointment was scheduled for one o'clock – lunchtime, in fact. Was there any access to food and drink?'

'No, I'm afraid not.'

'So it would be fair to say that a heavily pregnant woman, who was upset that she was missing an important meeting and had been made to wait a very long time, was also unable to get any lunch, which, when one is pregnant, is rather necessary? Would you agree that an anxious pregnant woman with low blood sugar, which Mrs Woodruff would almost certainly have experienced, might well be weepy and overtired?'

Mrs Adjani looked straight at Charlie. 'That's correct.'

I fled back to my world.

Jackie Woodruff's life was being peeled away – her fears, her behaviour, her fitness to be a mother. We had been licensed to pry into every corner of her psyche, to monitor every shiver of her contractions, every stitch on her body. Her wounds, her weeping and her exhaustion . . . those areas that should be private, unseen and unrecorded.

Steve Matthews operates his own plumbing business. He spends most of his time in overalls and has lost confidence about what to wear out of work. Overweight. His wife complains that he is a complete slob and she is ashamed to go out with him. She says she wants to be married to David Beckham. Steve says he wants his self-respect back.

Steve would be the man hefting one of those workmen's bags from house to house. Hands battered but supple from the thick grease that plumbers use, a white-van man, with tools rattling in the back. Steve, I reckoned, was a free man, and I wondered if he knew he was being lined up by *Fashion, This Week* as a token.

He turned out to be surprisingly as I had figured, but with a great deal of charm and a number-one haircut. 'I'm good at my job,' he informed Jenni and me, 'but can't cut it socially, and my wife just goes out with her mates.'

'OK.' I circled him with my notebook. 'Tell me about your evenings.'

'Drink with the mates. Curry in front of the telly. Perhaps take the kids to the park.'

Summer was coming, and Steve had the sort of body that felt the heat. I eyed a disgusting T-shirt and badly fitting jeans. 'You should lose a bit of weight, Steve.'

'I know.' He took it good-naturedly. 'But I like my pint.'

Jenni wheeled out the rack of clothes, and I chose a short-sleeved heavy linen shirt in a clear blue, which could be worn untucked, and a pair of well-cut reasonably priced chinos. To those, I added an unstructured linen jacket that, after a little wear, was programmed to fall into flattering lines.

'Nothing too formal.' I prowled round Steve. 'Are you comfortable?'

He grinned. 'OK.'

Jenni adjusted the fall of the jacket, and brushed smooth the material over the shoulders.

'You look great, Steve,' I said. 'Pull back your shoulders.'

His grin widened. 'Nobody's said that to me for years.'

'I think we've got it.' I looked to Jenni for her reaction.

'Sure.' She was noncommittal.

While Jon, the photographer, set up his equipment, I got on with writing up my notes. Steve was ordered to sit in a chair and not move. Jenni fetched him a glass of iced water, and one for herself. I noted the omission.

'OK.' Jon beckoned Steve to the sheet of white paper pinned to the floor. 'Stick your hands in your pockets.'

Four hours later we trailed, exhausted, out of the building. On the pavement, Steve pumped my hand up and down. 'I'm dead chuffed.' He ducked his head. 'It's been good. Really good. I didn't think it was going to be, but it's been great.'

'I'm glad. That's what I'm here for.'

'No, really. I could do battle feeling like this. And the missus'll like it – but, best of all, wait till the kids see me.'

Steve Matthews. Typical male. Proud father. Confidence on the up. Pleased as punch.

'Course,' he added, 'it won't last. It's only a bit of fun and fluff, isn't it? Dressing up and all that. Like being a kid, really.'

Chapter Sixteen: Siena

I was awake for most of the night, strung tight with nerves and the fatigue of getting everything sorted out before the trip.

I counted sheep. I checked and rechecked my wardrobe, dozed and woke. I ran through the unidentified frozen objects in the freezer and hoped that Charlie would make sense of them, dozed and woke. Dozed again.

At six o'clock, the alarm shrilled and I threw myself out of bed thankfully. Charlie grunted and padded off in the direction of the kitchen.

I slid back the cupboard doors. Jumpers to the right on the shelves. Underwear to the left. *Ninety per cent of a wardrobe is never worn. Ninety per cent of a woman's wardrobe represents fantasies and despair.*

I ran my finger over a stack of white T-shirts, which rippled at the touch. Best to take five. Two pairs of trousers. Two jackets. One Diane von Furstenburg wrap-around dress for smart, etc., etc.

I sensed Charlie — dressing-gowned and tousled — watching me from the doorway. 'You'll be going out to dinners, then?' he said.

'Yes.' I inserted tissue into the sleeves of the dress.

'Right.'

'And I'm going up to Bill and Lola's.'

'Right.'

'There's plenty of stuff in the freezer but I'm not sure what it is. I didn't have time to check.'

'I can cook,' he said.

It was now seven thirty and the car for the airport was due in an hour so that I could catch the eleven-thirty flight.

'Looks as though you're going for much longer.' Charlie picked up one of my bras and let it dangle from a finger. 'What's happened to the capsule wardrobe?'

His tone was neutral, but I knew better. 'Wish you could come too.'

'Dream on.'

'Will you keep me posted on the trial?'

He shrugged. 'If you like.'

The bedroom was stacked with clothes. My open suitcase was on the floor, its contents shrouded in tissue. The flat seemed quiet, contained and, somehow, isolated. Charlie paced up and down the room. Had I got schedule, passport, tickets, insurance?

When I could get a word in edgeways, I admitted that I'd forgotten to ring my insurance broker, but promised to do it from the airport.

'How stupid is that? What have you been doing for the past few days?'

'Charlie, you're not in court now, you know.'

'Doesn't negate my point.'

There was a new tautness in the way he held himself, a withheld anger. 'Has something gone wrong?' I asked.

'Did I tell you the forensic pathologist testified that the

odds were ten million to one that Baby Rob died naturally?'

'You did. Last night.' I transferred a pile of underwear to the bed. 'Darling, could you get out of the way?'

He stepped aside. 'How about a sort-out of my wardrobe? Would that get your attention?'

'Stop it.'

Charlie nudged a pair of my shoes with a bare foot – high heels, backless, peep-toes. 'They look impossible to walk in.'

'They are, but they're to-die-for gorgeous.'

He looked at me steadily. 'Do they really matter? Do they *really* matter?'

'No,' I snapped. 'They don't *really* matter, but they're there and part of my business.'

I packed the final items of clothing into the suitcase and shut it. On cue, the doorbell rang. The car had arrived and I instructed the driver to wait.

'I'm off,' I said unnecessarily, and reached up to nuzzle Charlie's cheek. He smelt of sleep with a faint tinge of last night's garlic – familiar and loved. 'Aren't you going to wish me luck?'

He kissed me lightly on the lips. It was not a cold kiss, neither was it full of regret at the goodbye, but detached – and in that detachment lay danger. Charlie had taken himself off my case, and was leaving me to sink or swim on my own.

Furious, I shook him, and said the first unguarded thing that came into my head: 'OK. OK, you win. I'll give up everything and become a *hausfrau*. I'll stay at home, mother a parcel of children, fetch and carry for your lordship.'

That roused him. 'Stop it.'

'Isn't that what all this is *about*?'

He pawed at the tousle of his hair. 'What have we been doing all these years? Struggling to sort out discrimination and inequality. It's my job, or hadn't you noticed? So why should I want to inflict the things I battle against on my wife?'

'That's what you *say*, Charlie. You know as well as I that what people say is not necessarily what they believe.'

He laughed, but it sounded more like a bark. 'I'm hardly likely to spend my life working for one thing and practising another.'

'Why not? Most people in public life do precisely that.'

'And what evidence do you have on my double life?' Charlie had switched into the positively cold and feline, and now answered his own question. *Court trick.* 'Zilch.'

I glanced round the bedroom, still wreathed in our shared night's sleep and muddle. A half-full glass of water on the bedside, a thick white towel on the floor, a discarded nightdress. If I had not been going away, it would have been purged and sparkling by nightfall, a cleansed place where, maybe, he and I might have settled the disputes between us.

Instead . . .

Charlie cast off his dressing-gown and flung on a pair of trousers and a T-shirt. 'I'll carry your luggage down.' His voice was neutral and his face studiedly vacant.

I backed down. 'Aren't you going to say something?'

He zipped up his fly. 'What could I possibly say to that one, Siena? You've accused me of living a lie. You're about

236

to fly half-way across the world to dress up a bunch of prancing clowns and tell them they're wonderful, and there's no time to discuss it properly.'

'They are *not* prancing clowns. They're ordinary people, trying to feel better about themselves. OK?'

Charlie was silent. He didn't have to say anything: the silence – the perfected art of the courtroom silence – said everything he felt about my job.

Airports. Planes. New York. Schedules ... Before it had even begun, my trip was being undermined by confusion and the upset of my private life. The quarrel would affect us both, and I did my best to make reparation. 'I'm sorry, Charlie. I shouldn't have said it.'

He shook his head. 'Don't keep the driver waiting, Siena. He probably killed himself to get here in time.' He picked up the suitcase, brushed past me and went out of the front door.

On the pavement outside, he handed me into the car and shut the door. 'Goodbye, Siena.'

'Goodbye.'

All the long journey to the airport, I tried not to cry. If I had not accused Charlie of double standards, the phrase 'prancing clowns' would not be ringing in my head. Why could we not have dealt with each other in a straightforward manner and how could I, supposedly an expert, have handled Charlie so badly? How could *he* have been so arrogant? The car hummed along the motorway, and turned left into the airport where it came to a standstill in a traffic jam. I gazed out at the line of brake-lights, and my misery intensified.

We had never said goodbye to each other like this before.

New York, 3rd June. Dear Parents, Here I am again. No time to breathe. It's hot, noisy and frantic. Will ring on return. Love Siena

New York, 4th June. Manda, Hotel right in centre. 5th Ave two blocks away. Spotted divine Chloé dress. Hold tight. Best love. Sxxx

'Hi, darling,' went the message I had left on the answer-phone, 'I expect you're wrapping up for the day. Just to say I'm thinking of you. Please phone.'

So far Charlie had not replied.

The hotel air-conditioning was fierce, and a blast of recycled air played over my face as I propped myself upright on the pillows and reached groggily for a glass of water. I felt dreadful: still attenuated with the jet-lag, that seemed to have got me. Neither the arnica pills nor the melatonin had worked.

I pulled back the sheet and padded into the bathroom – a tasteful assembly of marble and gold fittings – took a long, cool shower and felt marginally better. It was six thirty in the morning.

Later I called the hotel concierge and checked that my car would be there to take me to the hairdresser, then on to the studios near Battery Park. While I was waiting, I leafed through the schedules and the itinerary. First I was to meet my two subjects for the programme – a single mother of two called Pearl, and Angela, a black public-relations consultant.

Pearl is twenty-two, blonde and unemployed. She wants to smarten up in order to enter the job market . . .

Pearl turned out to be both pretty and pouty, had issues, and resisted most of my suggestions. No, she did not want to wear trousers and a jacket. 'That's not my image.' When I pointed out that we were trying to change her image so that she could move on, she fixed me with angry eyes. 'Who says?'

I caught sight of a hovering Fersen in skin-tight black leather trousers. He seized the moment to step in. 'Pearl, honey,' he said, 'just calm. A little calm.'

After a moment, she asked me, 'Where are you from?'

'London.'

'Huh,' she said.

We spent an hour trying to persuade Pearl into the outfit that had been chosen, and while I coaxed and petted her, Fersen kept saying things like 'It's to-die-for, Pearl,' and 'Why, hallo, Pearl, you're beautiful.'

Prancing clowns?

'Pearl,' I said. 'Come and look at yourself.'

I got on with the task in hand, but a voice in my head pointed out that Charlie regarded this petting and coaxing of the Lucys and Pearls as a frivolity, an adjunct to the real business of existence, which was graver and weightier.

'Yup. I suppose that's OK.' Pearl thrust out a leg in

the manner of a model to admire the cut of the trousers.

'Siena,' Fersen draped a scarf round Pearl's neck, and whirled round, a leather-clad dervish, 'don't you think this looks just darling?'

It didn't. 'Fersen, I don't think so . . .'

I smiled winningly at Pearl, who had come to a standstill in front of the long mirror and had, apparently, taken cheer from its reflection. She had also woken up to the fact that she was in the temple of a television studio. 'Hey, guys,' she said, 'I'll give you my phone number in case an agent calls in after the show.'

Dwayne, the producer, materialized out of the darkness on to the lit set. 'Siena, I need you to deal with a couple of points.'

The lighting engineer called, 'Can we rethink those last few shots?'

A makeup girl darted forward and fiddled with my hair.

There was so much to think about, so much here that was easier to deal with: I forgot Charlie, I forgot our quarrel and concentrated on my job.

I had devoted a lot of thought to Angela and her clothes. She required outfits that offered a variety of possibilities. Her problems were diffidence, and dislike of her body. 'My ass is colossal.'

I knew that one – I'd been there so often before. 'It's a very nice bum,' I said patiently, 'and the skirt does it justice.'

'Look, lady, you can't do anything with it.'

'That's why I'm here, Angela.'

I heard a mutter from some of the studio crew, who were standing by to do a dry-run shoot for tomorrow. Inexplicably Fersen chose this moment to render a modicum of support. 'Looking good, Angela.'

I flashed him a look of gratitude, and muttered, 'Thanks.'

Next up was Angela's objection to the neat little sweater I had picked out for her. 'Red makes me feel like a political statement.'

'Red gets you noticed,' I pointed out, 'which is useful in your line of business.'

'There's red and red,' said Angela.

'Just wear it for a few minutes, and see how it settles on you.'

'Nope, I don't think so.'

'OK, how about the pale yellow one?'

Finally we persuaded Angela to try the red sweater. She looked fabulous, which, finally, she grudgingly acknowledged. The camera team swung into action but, just when they were ready to shoot, a vital piece of equipment blew. There was much hysteria and rushing round to find a replacement.

Angela looked at her watch. 'I've got to go,' she said. 'My children need picking up from school, and my mother is sick.'

By late afternoon, the crew had had enough. There was a final conference on what would happen tomorrow, notes were exchanged, opinions given. The team had run down. The energy had vanished. We were all wilting, it was hot in the studio, and I was more than a little shaky.

We rolled out of the studio at six thirty. As I was shrugging on my jacket, Fersen came up. 'Fancy some pizza and a beer?'

Above anything, I longed for the solitary sanctuary of my hotel room. 'Sure, that would be nice.'

'You know,' he said, after we had installed ourselves at a table in the nearest pizza parlour, 'some of us can't quite figure why we need someone from the UK to do this gig.'

I inspected my tuna salad, which came with doughballs soused in garlic butter. Not good for close contact in the studio, but they tasted good. 'Cultural exchange. We're one big happy family, these days.'

Fersen took a large mouthful of pepperoni pizza and chewed. 'Families can be dysfunctional. I should know. Mine is the alpha dysfunctional family. Father a lush but loaded. Mother a demented career woman. You're speaking to the original Park Avenue Princess. I even had initials on my potty.'

'Are they still alive?'

He stared at me. 'I'm not in touch.'

Outside in the street, New York glittered with lights and roared with traffic. The heat smothered the city in an evening wrap, but inside the pizza parlour the temperature hovered just above icy. A group of Hispanics sucked at bottles of beer, two beautiful Italian girls chattered away and a man in chinos and loafers studied a financial journal. Under the table, my foot (shod in L. K. Bennett) tapped a rhythm on the floor. It was the beat of zest in this city, triumph that I had got there.

Fersen pushed away his plate, the pizza half eaten. 'I have to watch my figure.' He took a tiny sip of his beer. 'Are you quite comfortable with everything, Siena?'

Under the table, my foot stilled. 'Sure. Perfectly. Just one thing. Could we have a bigger range of clothes to hand? Just so the choice is bit wider?' Fersen's eyes narrowed unpleasantly, and I added, 'No criticism, but I've learnt over the years.'

'So have I.' The remark laid bare the hunger to succeed, and the struggle to get there. 'When you're gay,' he added, 'you have to work at it just a teeny bit harder.'

The following morning when I arrived at the studio, Dwayne hustled me into a side room. 'I gather you have issues. Why didn't you mention them to me?'

Astonished, I stared at him, and realization dawned. 'I only suggested to Fersen that we had a wider choice of clothes to hand. Just in case. That's all.'

'I take it badly. Let's put it this way, if you have any worries, Siena, come to me. I'm the one to deal. OK? Don't talk to the team.'

'OK.' I had been here before, too, with Jenni.

When Fersen slid into the office, in baggy cargos and hair tied back with a velvet scrunchie, I launched an offensive. 'You look good,' I said. 'Thanks for last night. It really helped, listening to your opinions.'

'No trouble.'

'No, really, it was great getting to know you better.'

His nostrils flared. Was this for real? Could he trust me?

Well, yes and no.

Later, I said to him, as we re-dressed Angela, 'What do you think about the necklace, Fersen?'

'Drop it,' he said.

I regarded Angela thoughtfully. 'You're right. Drop it.'

The filming was exhausting. The up-side was that both Pearl and Angela performed beautifully, and their transformations had the right Cinderella quality, which elated the onlooker and brought a lump to the throat. It was good viewing.

Afterwards the team reassembled to take a look at the next two guinea-pigs – a trucker from Kansas and an executive from an electrical company.

'It's going bust,' the latter confided to me, 'and I want to be looking up to scratch when it does. Anyway, I like the cred of having been on your show.'

'Cred' meant pulling power, and he winked at me.

At the close of the session, I sought out Fersen – I had spotted he didn't approve of the suit I had selected for the electrical executive. 'I was thinking,' I said, 'that I didn't make the right choice with the Sebastian Jones suit. I'm thinking maybe a Chuck Coates would be better.'

'Why, Siena?'

'Chuck's tailoring is less aggressive.' I banked on the probability that Fersen would take the opposite line to what I said, whatever his private opinions. 'The Jones is too sharp, too in-your-face.'

'But that's what he *needs*, Siena. He has to make his way.'

'Persuade me.'

Fersen launched into a list of Sebastian Jones's advantages, which, considering it was not his choice, was impressive. I stacked my notes, slid them into my briefcase, nodded from time to time. 'Maybe you're right,' I said, at one point.

A little later, I hitched the strap of my briefcase over my shoulder and conceded, 'You've convinced me.'

There was a hint of gratitude, of shy pleasure, of backing down, in the way Fersen flipped back: 'I thought you Brits always insisted on your own way.'

'Depends on the Brit.' I touched his arm briefly, and we said goodnight.

I returned to the hotel with a knot in my stomach. Nerves. Spent adrenaline. Fear.

Sometimes my confidence suddenly, and without warning, slips away. Then a profound struggle ensues to keep going, and to hold my nerve. Then I needed Charlie.

But I didn't have him.

Perhaps he didn't want to talk to me anyway. Perhaps I couldn't talk to him. I wouldn't be able to bring myself to say: 'Charlie, you may be right . . . there *may* be something in my business that doesn't quite do the trick. Perhaps I'm using it as a blind thrown down in order not to look beyond.'

I wandered round the hotel room, picking up objects here and there. Why had he not rung? The bowl of fruit on the table had been replenished, and I bit into an apple. It was well past its best, without taste or texture. I threw it into the bin.

Earlier I had rung my parents.

'It's warm,' my mother had said. 'Thank God.'

'Hot here,' I said.

My father chose a different tack. 'I don't like the way the pound's going against the dollar.' This was his way of expressing concern for me.

'It's fine, Dad. My expenses are paid.'

He clicked his teeth in disapproval. 'We're taking a short break in the Highlands,' he said. 'Ardoit. Last time we were there, you and your brother decided to re-enact the Jacobite rebellions.'

'I seem to remember we defeated the Hanoverians and went on the run for a week.'

'You were wretched nuisances,' said my father. 'We didn't know where you'd got to.'

I laughed, and felt more normal.

During the night, the air-conditioning failed, and I woke up bathed in sweat. The air smelt frighteningly stale and my mouth was tinder dry. As a result, I left for the studio with a headache that had not responded to paracetamol.

Confidence was the modern woman's second name. Creamed, toned, colour-co-ordinated, creative, effective, powerful. Earning money was confidence. Attitude was confidence. Loving was confidence.

So where had mine gone?

Charlie hadn't phoned.

Chapter Seventeen: Barbara

I woke with a start, heavy headed and confused. 'Ryder? It's all right – hang on, darling.'

He was thrashing around in the bed. 'End of the line . . .' he shouted. 'Black . . .'

I rolled over, wrapped my arms round him and tried to quieten him. 'It's all right. It's all right, you're at home.' He bucked and thrashed, and muttered, and I smelt rank terror on him. 'Ryder . . . Ryder . . . come on. Wake up. Darling, come on . . . gently.'

His eyes flew open. He swallowed. 'Barbara?'

'Ryder.' I pressed my body against his, willing my every-day, familiar normality to bring him back. 'You're home. You're with me. Do you understand?'

'Oh, God,' he was dazed, 'am I?'

I cradled him for a long time, until I was sure he was calmer. But when, craving his customary comfort, he reached for me, I shrank away.

'What's wrong?' he asked. 'What have I done?'

'Nothing – nothing.' At that moment I was sickened by myself. Yet I could not have given Ryder what he wanted and needed. 'Darling, I'm going to switch on the light now,' I said, and the brightness dazzled us. 'Ryder, I'm going to get you some tea. All you have to do is stay quiet. I won't be long.'

When I returned, he was staring up at the ceiling. He was drenched with sweat, so I made him change his pyjamas, wiped his face and put him back to bed. I sat down on his side and handed him the tea.

'Sorry, darling.' He was still dazed, and refused to look at me. 'What a . . . *pest* these nightmares are.'

'Which one was it?'

He grimaced. 'In the Spitfire, and there's a battle. Then I feel a tremendous pain in my leg and I know I'm shot, and the pedals have jammed and the Spit goes into a dive, and it keeps on diving and I'm braced for the impact, but it never happens – and I'm desperate for it to hit the ground just to get it over and done with.'

I reached over and caressed his cheek. 'Bad one.'

'Stupid, isn't it?' He stared into the teacup, suffering and ashamed of his suffering and, after all the years, of allowing me to witness it. 'The images still come out of the dark. Even after all this time . . .'

'Ryder . . . I've noticed they've been a bit worse lately. Would it be a good idea to go and talk to someone who specializes in that kind of thing?'

Ryder tensed, then frowned. 'What have you been reading, Barbara?'

'That book on Freud. But it's an idea worth considering. Will you think about it?'

'If the airline ever found out, I'd be done for.'

'So you will consider it?'

'I didn't say that. We've been through all this before. I don't like psychiatrists. My nightmares are just nightmares. Look, all I have to do is pack the bad dreams into a box and stick them on a shelf in my mind. Then it's fine. Dealt with. Put away. If you jaw on about these things, they do become a problem.'

'What happens if the shelf breaks?'

'I hate that kind of stuff.'

'I know you do, but you might be surprised by what happens.'

There was a long silence, and Ryder tapped the teaspoon against his cup. 'If my nightmares bother you, Barbara, I can always sleep in the dressing room.'

'Listen,' I reached over and stilled the rattling teaspoon, 'part of a dream is remembered, and part is called latent, which means the conscious cannot remember it and it needs to be called up. That's where the psychiatrist comes in and sorts it out.' Outside, the dawn chorus was beginning, a light medley at first but gathering in volume. I was edging the subject along nicely, but it would have to be handled in small doses. 'If you've been overdoing it, Ryder, you must say.'

'Do you think if I wasn't perfectly confident I'd allow myself to fly a plane full of passengers?'

We were drifting back to sleep when Ryder asked, 'How on earth *is* it possible to forget, Barbara? You can't just wish away a war and what happened to us all. You can't blot it out.'

He had never said anything remotely like that before.

He was right. Nothing could compare with the struggle to be normal while the bombs fell. Nothing compared with the queer, awkward excitement of surviving yet another day. The nervous strain. The heightened responses.

The superhuman concentration. In Ryder's case, the struggle to offer up a life and not to mind. To wake up, half-way through the war, and realize youth had gone.

But all that was past . . . over. I pulled the pillows into a cradle for my head. The remedy was to think about now, and the future. Alexander had been right. It was possible to make changes. We were free to do so. We were not imprisoned in a mental time warp. If science and medicine meant anything, if having a mind meant anything, Ryder and I could prove we were not useless at living in the present.

And Alexander? Whose bold, brave words and inept lovemaking had woken a mixture of passion, sweetness and longing that were – puzzlingly – quite separate from what I felt for my family. And myself? How could I have done what I did? How could I have not known that I was capable of getting on to a bicycle and riding down a country road to meet Alexander?

'About Teignmouth . . .' Ryder sounded reassuringly drowsy. 'I've cancelled it, and arranged for us to fly to Switzerland. But I'll leave you to sort out the details, as I haven't got time.'

'Ryder.' I laid my hand on the curve of his back, and he shifted to acknowledge the caress. 'That's wonderful.'

'I thought it would please you.'

In the dark, I blushed scarlet with guilt and shame and astonishment at myself . . . yet none of these responses was adequate.

*

The weekend was going to be busy. Amy and Sophie were due to stay, Roy and Victoria were coming over on Sunday, and Sylvia and Mary were bringing Alexander for lunch.

Amy surprised me by walking into the kitchen on Friday evening. She had a smudge on her nose from the train, and looked exhausted.

I was making a steak and kidney pie and my hands were floury; there was a white drift over the lino too. 'Amy! I wasn't expecting you tonight.'

'I wanted to talk to you.' She watched me wipe my hands on my apron. 'Mum, you told me off for doing that.'

I laughed. 'So I did. What do you want to talk about?'

She planted herself squarely in front of me. 'I wanted to tell you that I was sorry . . . about what I said.'

'I'd almost persuaded myself you didn't mean it.'

'But I did mean it,' she contradicted me. 'I have to be honest, I meant every word, but not in the *way* I said it. Not angrily and meanly. Did I hurt you, Mum? I want you to be honest with me, really honest. I think it's important we understand how each other's mind is working.' She added less confidently, and rather stiffly, 'Relations will be better between us.'

It was Amy's quaint way of putting it. Yet this conversation was more honest and open than any we had had for a long time. 'All right.' I grasped the nettle. 'Yes, you did hurt me. Very much.'

Amy gave me a tough and questioning look. 'I thought I did, and I wanted to put the record straight.'

I felt for a kitchen chair, and sank into it. 'Feel free.'

Somewhat to my surprise, Amy fetched a dustpan

and brush and swept up the spilt flour. 'I want to make absolutely clear that I wish to do something serious with my life.'

'I understand. But before you go any further, looking after a family *is* serious.'

'Please don't interrupt. Looking after a family is not enough.' She tipped the contents of the dustpan into the rubbish bin. 'Sophie and I do not accept your way. We've discussed it often. I'm not prepared to spend my life in a typing-pool, dying of boredom. So . . . I've signed up at night school to study, and then I'm going to apply to the civil service. They take women. I've decided to aim high and – and I'm not going to let you and Dad talk me out of it. If I fail, it's my business.' She shut the rubbish bin with a decided tap. 'There!'

On Sunday afternoon the cry went up for a game of tennis, and Ryder was persuaded to join in.

As usual, Roy took command and organized the hunt for racquets and balls and demanded that lots should be drawn as to who played first.

Victoria fluttered her eyelashes at him. 'I'll man the lemonade station, and hold your towel.'

She and I sat on the bench and watched the game. 'Doesn't Roy look wonderful in his whites?' she said.

I observed my son, efficiently manning the back line. 'Yes, he does.' He was certainly at his best on a court – he loosened up, lost his customary stiffness.

For the first match – three sets only, to make it fair, said Roy – Roy and Ryder played Sophie and Alexander.

Sophie was twirling her racquet, and danced across the court. Alexander loped easily from side to side, fit and lithe, clearly an experienced player.

Victoria said softly, 'Alexander is very good-looking, but I think Roy has the edge. Roy is so intelligent and strong.'

'They both are.'

Victoria looked astonished that I hadn't rushed to the defence of my son – and, of course, she was right. 'Not in the same way,' she maintained stoutly, and I gave her full marks for loyalty.

I settled back on the bench.

'Come on, Dad.' Roy was impatient with Ryder's failure to run to the net.

'Well *done*,' cried Sophie, after Alexander dashed forward and hit a spinner of a backhand into the corner of the court.

Amy and Mary were ball-boying and Sylvia umpiring. 'Fifteen–thirty – no, I mean thirty–fifteen.'

'Make up your mind,' Alexander shouted good-naturedly. His gaze flicked towards me, and I busied myself with the jug of lemonade.

Alexander sent a serve spinning over the net and raced back to the base-line to wait for the return. But Ryder merely hooked the serve off the ground, halved its velocity and dropped it just over the net. 'Well done, Mr Beeching,' cried Sylvia. 'Brilliantly cunning.'

'Absolutely, sir.' Alexander did not look at Ryder, and changed position. Sophie ran up to him, placed her hand over his ear and whispered into it. Alexander replied in a low tone. Sophie touched his shoulder and said, with a naughty glance over her shoulder, 'Make Uncle Ryder run.'

I didn't dare to look at Alexander.

Victoria called, 'Go on, Roy.'

Alexander did his best to make Ryder run, but Ryder was an experienced tennis player, and knew how to foil that particular tactic. 'No, you don't,' he said, and sent a low, hard forehand to the back line. 'Move, you two.' He sent Alexander and Sophie racing round the court to his bidding – and the score crept inexorably to the advantage of father and son.

Again it was Alexander's turn to serve. He sent the ball spinning over the net.

'Out,' called Ryder.

'But, sir, I don't think . . .' Alexander lowered his racquet.

'Out,' repeated Ryder.

'I don't think so,' said Alexander.

'He's right,' said Roy, waving a finger. 'It was out. Miles out, in fact.'

Alexander froze. For a moment, it was touch and go. Then he shrugged gracefully, smiled and said, 'Of course.' He walked to the back of the court.

Ryder tossed a ball into the air, and looked pleased with himself. 'Life in old dogs,' he said.

Alexander served two double faults in succession. I watched and knew that he was angry, and that the anger made him try too hard. Then he served an ace, and Ryder missed it.

After three sets, there was a break for refreshments. Victoria handed round the lemonade. Ryder gave his racquet to Amy. 'Here, I'm all tuckered out.'

'Poor, poor Dad,' Amy teased. 'So tuckered out you've just thrashed the opposition.'

Victoria was dabbing at Roy's face with a towel. 'You're so *hot*,' she cooed.

'Good game.' Ryder's gaze rested thoughtfully on Alexander.

'Yes, sir.'

'Tactics and experience are what get us chaps through. Wouldn't you say?'

Alexander's smile flickered briefly.

Play resumed. Sophie missed a ball. Amy drove one hard across the net. Alexander served another ace. The wood-pigeons were sounding off in the trees, and the summer light invested the scene with a magic, shimmering quality – the breath caught in my throat.

'Nice to see the young enjoying themselves.' Ryder was relaxed and genial.

He raised a hand to shade his eyes. Under his short-sleeved shirt the muscle was still there, strong and marked but with a suggestion of stringiness, and I remembered the smooth, golden beauty of Alexander's arms wrapped round my body by the river.

Ryder was saying, 'They're so educated and accomplished, and ambitious. Do you know, and I shouldn't say this, I feel jealous of them? Sometimes.'

The admission was startling. 'Do you?'

'It's not so odd. Probably our parents were jealous of us.' He slipped an arm round my waist. 'I'm looking forward to our holiday.'

Later, over tea in the conservatory, Ryder took

Alexander aside. 'I'd like some advice on where to go in Switzerland. You studied there, didn't you? I'm taking Barbara on a well-earned holiday.' He fetched the atlas, and the two men went into a huddle.

Sophie plumped herself down next to me. 'What do you think of Amy's plans?'

I was watching Ryder and Alexander. 'I'm getting used to the idea.' Exertion on the court had made Sophie's hair curl at the temples. Enchanting little wisps.

'I approve of what Amy's doing so much, Aunt Barbara. I think she's being wonderful. It's not a criticism of you or anything, but I think women have a right to lead useful, serious lives . . .' Sophie was using much the same words as Amy; I recognized them as their adopted, chosen vocabulary, their language.

'We *must* earn our living, and not become drones. Have our own money.' She placed a hand on my knee. 'I couldn't *bear* to be at the mercy of anyone for money.' Having delivered the manifesto Sophie turned her attention to me. 'How are you getting on at St Bede's?'

'Miss Raith has made it perfectly clear that I have a lot to learn but I'm enjoying being stretched.'

'You see what I mean?'

I wasn't fooled. Sophie wasn't interested in me and my job, but in watching Alexander, who had planted a finger on the atlas and was gesticulating with the other hand.

'He's awfully nice, isn't he?' She managed to be wistful, hopeful, awkward, ravishing, vulnerable and irresistible all at the same time.

'Yes, he is. Very.'

She edged her chair closer and dropped her voice. 'I like Alexander so much. Don't you?' The blue eyes sparkled. 'I *think* he likes me.'

I couldn't look at Sophie. I didn't want to look at her. I swivelled round to check the tea-tray . . . anything.

'Did I say something, Aunt Babs?' Her voice tugged at my ear. 'You look odd.'

Reluctantly I turned back to her. 'Just a twinge — nothing. I must have eaten too much cake.'

'You looked as though something had hit you.'

'No, nothing,' I got out between dry lips.

After a moment, she resumed: 'Do you think I have a chance, Aunt Barbara? See what you think.' She smiled trustingly. 'You're the only one I really talk to.'

Alexander rang up the next day to thank me for the lunch. 'I have some names of hotels.'

I fetched my notebook and wrote down 'Hôtel de la Montagne, Crans, and Hôtel du Lac, Montreux'. 'Do you know them?'

'I've stayed at the Hôtel de la Montagne. I took a short break from study, went up into the mountains and spent a night there.'

'I never asked you if you liked Switzerland. What did you find there?'

'It's stuffy. Beautiful, and civilized, too. And the course was exciting and up to the minute.' He paused. 'We're still friends?'

'Yes. Always friends.'

'Good girl.'

I gave a stifled gasp. 'It hurts, this opening up of the mind. It hurts what I've done to Ryder. And there's all the other people I might be hurting.'

'Do you *want* to see me?'

I closed my eyes, and recollected the sweet rush of passion and delight. I smelt the river and the reeds, felt the sun on my face and the wild, unexpected exhilaration. 'Yes, I do, but I'm not going to.'

'Is that final?'

'Alexander, whatever happens – No, sooner or later this . . . would have to end. I'm not afraid of that. And why not now? I'm not afraid of suffering for it, and I'm not going to leave Ryder. It was just a moment, a lovely, lovely moment. But I'm thinking of you. Think of other girls . . . think of Sophie or Mary.'

'If I put this phone down and never spoke to you again, would that mean I was out of your life? Would I disappear? Would it stop?'

'No.' Tears spilled down my cheeks. '*No.* Yes, yes, it would.'

'What do you mean?'

'I don't know, Alexander. *I don't know.*'

I sat in the canteen at St Bede's and dutifully ate ham and salad, tasted nothing, and sifted over the conversation with Alexander, assessing each word as if it was the rarest caviar or vintage wine. Later I walked back through the city on feet that ached from unsuitable shoes, carrying my cravings and guilt, my response to the intensity, the surprise and rawness of what I had done, and thought I would die from the burden of the knowledge.

The aircraft banked sharply over Lake Geneva, feathered its wings and began the descent to the airport. In the seat beside me, Ryder muttered something. I put my hand on his knee. 'You're not flying this,' I reminded him.

'I should be,' he countered. 'That was bloody awful.'

'They're nervous because you're on board.' Ryder had made himself known to the crew before we had settled into our seats.

Below us the lake, dotted at the edge with towns and villages, glittered with an unfamiliar light. What kind of different life was lived there? I observed the white wake from a boat moving across the water, the flash from a car window as it sped down a road, the panorama of rock and sky.

Ryder was still analysing the finer points of the flight when we stepped out on to Sion station, which was filled with holidaymakers in shorts and shortsleeved shirts. Ryder was in his suit, and I was wearing a shirtwaister, which was far too thick, and a navy blue jacket to which I had pinned the wives' BOAC badge. I wished I had not.

The taxi took us up the mountain to the hotel in the village of Crans where we would stay for three days, and the manager ushered us into a clean, comfortable room that smelt of pine. It overlooked the valley and the mountain range opposite.

Ryder poked at the duvet on the bed. 'I'd forgotten we'd have these here. Will you manage?'

I picked up an edge between finger and thumb. Covered in a white cotton cover, it was light and soft. 'It feels so luxurious.' I slid back the window on to the balcony and stepped out into the fresh air and sun. 'This is wonderful.' I turned to face Ryder. *'Wonderful.'*

He laughed. 'You looked transformed, Barbara, quite different.'

We ate a late lunch on the hotel terrace, with that bright, hard unfamiliar sun streaming round us, and my blood quickened at the strangeness and novelty. I chose an omelette, which, when it arrived, was made with an unfamiliar cheese, and salad, with a dressing I did not recognize. Ryder ate ham wrapped in pastry, and we drank a thin white wine.

Afterwards I put on a pair of slacks and my sensible lace-up shoes, and Ryder and I followed a path up through the mountain tree-line. An hour later we emerged into a meadow of flowers – in blues, yellows and delicate pinks. Higher up, there was a hut and a flock of sheep scrabbling over the rockfaces; their bells sounded sweet and clear. The air was sharper at this altitude but, if anything, the sun was stronger. On the range of mountains opposite, there were pockets of snow on the summits and a marked, undulating tree-line of dark pines.

'Like it?' Ryder leant on his stick. He was panting, but flushed and looking younger than I'd seen him for years.

'I do.'

'Thought you would.' He moved closer, and I smelt sweat on him, fresh and familiar. 'I should have brought you here a long time ago. I'm sorry, Babs, I think I've been a bit selfish in the past. Got into a habit.'

'It doesn't matter,' I murmured. 'We're here now.'

Chapter Eighteen: Barbara

We slept dreamlessly under the unfamiliar duvet. The cotton was crisp, with a hint of lavender, the goose down enveloped us, a soft, luxurious second skin. Before we went to sleep, I opened the window and the mountain air poured into the bedroom, with a whisper of pine, snow and grandeur.

Ryder woke me at dawn. 'Come on,' he said, but I drew back.

I did not want this. I did not want Ryder.

I made to get out of bed – *go to the bathroom, do what is necessary. Escape his touch a second or two longer.* But Ryder prevented me. 'Pretend we're at the beginning.'

I'll try, I thought. *I have to try. I owe it to him.*

Ryder whispered my name.

And it was like returning to the beginning. My shrinking body wooed into compliance, the descent into pure sensation, the discarding of rational thought. As Ryder had coaxed and summoned my responses then, so he did now . . . until I no longer knew what was now, what was then . . . what was Ryder, and what was Alexander. As Ryder lay spent and quiet in my arms, I was shaken by the breadth of this experience, by its capacity to be so many things: loving and deceitful, desired and yet not. Exclusive, but not.

In the morning, Ryder worked out another route up the mountain, this time approaching it from the north. The gradient of this path was much steeper and more treacherous and, furthermore, we were facing into the sun. I was not unfit but I was forced to stop frequently as my chest heaved and my leg muscles protested.

Ryder walked ahead and I was at liberty to observe him with new (sharper?) eyes. Broader and bulkier, yes, but not so very different to look at from the day he had stepped out of the sunlight and into my life.

It was dangerous being up so high. The air up here on the mountain played tricks – elemental and magical in its clarity and sharpness, a sharpness that acted as a window . . . for if Ryder had happened to glance back at me, I had the oddest feeling that he would have seen straight into my soul.

After a good two hours' hike, we stopped to eat lunch on a slope beneath the summit. Already my forearms were reddening and my face was burning. I flung myself down, gratefully, and inhaled keen air.

Ryder shrugged off his rucksack and offered me the water-bottle. 'Next time we come we must buy you proper boots. I should have thought to do so.'

I inspected my shoes. 'They're holding up.'

'It never does to underestimate the mountain.' He knelt down, tipped up my chin and said earnestly, 'You could lose your life for the wrong pair of shoes.' He glanced up at the summit and at the hut visible beneath it. 'Next time we'll get up there, but for now we'll stick to the path.'

The water was warm and not really thirst-quenching.

Ryder sat down beside me, and spread the map over his knees. 'I reckoned that if we head east from here,' he pointed, 'we'll hit Bourges where we can have tea, then catch a bus back to the hotel.'

My sandwich consisted of the unfamiliar cheese between dry slices of bread. I teased him a little. 'You're thinking of walnut cake.'

Ryder bit into his sandwich, and leant back against the rock. 'If I'm thinking of anything, it certainly would be walnut cake.'

I squinted up at him. Settled back against the rock, shirtsleeves rolled up, he looked relaxed, easy, at peace.

We talked lazily of nothing much until Ryder brought up the subject of Ian and Antonia. 'They're each other's bad habit, which they refuse to turn into a good one. Poor little Sophie, caught squarely in the crossfire.'

'Like our daughter, Sophie's against marriage. Broadly speaking. So they say. Amy informs me that marriage was invented by men to ensure their comfort from cradle to grave.'

Ryder said lazily, 'They'll learn.'

'I think Amy's absolutely right.'

Ryder poked the soft part of my thigh with his stick. 'You do, do you?' A little later, he asked, 'Can you see me setting up a travel business, Barbara?'

'I don't see why not.'

'We might have to sell the house to release capital. I don't want to make you do something you don't wish to do, so I need to know how you'd feel.'

Ryder was spreading his wings, and I saw now what

I was up against. Rashly, I had thought there might be a glimmer of an opportunity to duck under the net and try my hand at . . . what? Studying psychology? Becoming Miss Raith's right hand? I envisaged myself, dressed in smart suit and hat, leaving behind the jam-making and polishing, the racking of apples, and stepping into an office where there would be a desk with my name inscribed on it.

Hasty correction: instead of needing me less as we grew older, Ryder would need me more. Breakfasts, lunches, dinners, ironed shirts and cleaning routines, moral support – all would be required in regular spadefuls.

I ate the sandwich slowly, thoughtfully. When I had finished, I lay down and closed my eyes. 'Actually, I don't think I want to go back,' I murmured. 'I want to stay up here for ever, and become a goatherd or a mountain ranger.'

'Steady on,' said Ryder, and laid a hand on my thigh.

The heat and weight of his touch on my flesh was an anchor – and he meant it to be.

The shop windows at Bourges were enchanting. Chocolates, bread – domes and plaits, cottage loaves in wheat, rye and maize – jams, great cartwheels of cheese, pitted with holes and laced with blue veins, creamy white and butter yellow, lace, shoes of every shade and description, the colours, shapes, profusion, *choice* . . .

Eventually Ryder shovelled me into a tea-shop and we sat down at a linen-covered table to eye a trolley groaning with cakes the like of which I had never seen.

We ordered hot chocolate and I chose a choux bun

filled with cream. I plunged in my fork, lifted the first mouthful and let my tongue slide over the cream. 'Lovely.'

The tea-shop was full of other walkers in bright clothes and boots, and women in well-cut suits and gleaming shoes. 'Those are the sort of boots you need.' Ryder indicated a particularly stout pair sported by a beefy man. For a moment I thought he was serious. The air hummed with conversation, the chink of china and, in one corner, cigarette smoke drifted above a table.

'Happy?' asked Ryder, who had already demolished most of his cake.

'Perfectly.' Ryder's pleasure in my pleasure made us both happy, and I thought what an easy position it was to be in.

I wrinkled my nose at him. 'You're a good man, Ryder. Not many are as good as you.'

I persuaded him that it would be fun to walk back to our hotel. 'Ambitious,' he said, 'but what the hell?' We arrived back, almost mute with exhaustion, bathed, changed, ate dinner overlooking the hotel terrace and went to bed early.

I woke in the early hours. Ryder was motionless, breathing deeply. I slid out of bed, pulled my sweater round my shoulders and let myself out noiselessly on to the balcony.

In Sion below, a dozen or so lights cut into the pitch black, and were echoed in the villages on the mountain range opposite. The flag on the hotel's pole flapped, sounding like wet laundry and, in the distance, a solitary car made its way down the mountainside.

The wind blew directly into my face, and my feet curled

with the cold. High up in the mountains were glaciers, sheets of ice – as unfamiliar as I was now to myself.

This utter aloneness, confusion, surprise, was exhilarating, and should be experienced at least once. 'Barbara,' I found myself murmuring, 'you have allowed your life to go on without too much thought, and that was wasteful.'

The words slid away into the keen air.

Everyone is allowed secrets.

True, for I belonged neither to Ryder, nor to my children . . . nor to Alexander. I belonged only to myself.

'What *are* you doing, darling?' Ryder stepped out on to the balcony. 'You'll catch your death. Come back to bed.'

He placed his hands on my shoulders and smiled down at me, trying to read what was going on. Speechless, I gripped him tightly. After a moment, he bent over and kissed my cheek. 'Whatever it is,' he said, 'it's no use worrying about it.'

We ordered coffee and croissants for breakfast on the terrace, and were served them under a striped umbrella – already, the sun was bright and brilliant. 'Look,' I pointed up at the mountain, stippled in shadows and grey rock, 'the snow is so bright and clean.'

There was a splash from the swimming-pool, and the staff were dragging the sun-loungers out on to the terrace beside it. A trio of early walkers were making their way down the hotel drive with rucksacks and sticks. The day already seemed *en fête*, careless and rosy with summer. Ryder and I had nothing to do but enjoy ourselves until, in due course, we packed up and travelled to Montreux.

I refilled our coffee cups, and raised mine to my lips. 'Are you happy?' I asked Ryder.

'Of course,' he said.

'There's no "of course" about anything,' I whipped back.

The hotel in Montreux was on the edge of the lake. The town was a mixture of nineteenth-century buildings, which suggested a vanished heyday, and more modern villas. It had an edge to it, a precarious run-downness, almost a seedy air, but perhaps, as I pointed out to Ryder, that had something to do with the number of men who favoured raincoats and fedoras.

We checked in to the hotel, and the concierge said, 'Monsieur Beeching, there is a message.'

'Oh, my God!' I exclaimed. 'The children!'

Ryder read it. 'It's from work. They need me back. They're two down. Illness.'

'Is that all? When?'

'Now.'

I felt under no obligation to be well-mannered. 'Wretched, wretched nuisance.' Then I sighed. 'At least we're packed.'

'Yes . . .' Ryder reread the message. 'But you're not going home.'

'Of course I am.'

'Stay here,' he said. 'You'll be all right for a couple of days. It's all booked and you were looking forward to it. Visit the art galleries, do some shopping, take a boat trip. It's all good research, Barbara, and you can take notes, which we need to do. Look around. See what tourists *do*.'

'No, darling. I really think I should be with you. We can come another time.'

'No argument,' he said. Then he was asking the concierge to make the arrangements and, in a remarkably short time, it was settled.

After that we took a bus along the lakeside, observing the water, which was a green crystal in places, dusted with foam in others, and exclaiming, like the tourists we were, over the Château de Chillon. We stopped for lunch in a café and ordered grilled veal chops and coffee. I struggled to eat mine, and to keep Ryder amused.

He noted my lack of appetite. 'You're not nervous, are you, darling, about being on your own?'

'No, no, not at all. Thank you for spoiling me,' I said.

'You deserve it.'

After lunch, I saw him on to the train to the airport, burdened with luggage for he had insisted on taking some of mine home with him in order to make my travelling easier. 'Hand over all those bottles,' he had said, and I packed up the cologne, the rosewater for my face and the domed box similar to the one I found on the beach at Teignmouth all those years ago. 'I suppose,' he kissed me goodbye, 'you'll think of this as an adventure, but I hope you won't want to have too many without me.'

I whisked myself back to the café on the waterfront, ordered coffee and watched the water while I decided what to do.

A little later, a woman sat down at the table beside me. She was dressed in a light duster coat, which had seen better days, and a faded blue felt hat under which her dark hair was greying. She placed a pair of darned gloves on the table, and ordered coffee in fluent but unmistakably English-accented French.

'Excuse me,' I leant over, 'I think you might be English. I wonder if you could tell me which are the best museums and picture galleries in Montreux.'

She gave a start of surprise, but told me of a small but excellent gallery, and I suggested we drank our coffee together.

She introduced herself as Anne Abercrombie: she was a widow and was living in Montreux because it was cheaper than England.

'An exile. You must miss your family and friends?'

'Exile has its compensations,' she said quietly. 'I enjoy my own company.'

We talked about the town and the gallery, and she explained that the collection had been donated by a French businessman who had fled to Switzerland during the war and wished to show his gratitude. I explained that I was doing reconnaissance for my husband who was thinking of setting up a small travel business, and asked her if she ever went back to England.

She raised her eyes to mine. 'I wasn't quite truthful. I'm not a widow, but divorced. It happened a long time ago, but things are not easy for a divorced woman back home, as you will know. It's always rather difficult so I prefer to remain here.'

'And what about your husband?'

She picked up her darned gloves. 'My husband divorced

me, and it was easier for him. He got a job in a different part of the country. And a new wife. But I've not had a bad life, considering. It was not an easy position to find oneself in, but not impossible. In fact, I wouldn't have it any other way. I hope you enjoy the paintings.'

We bade each other goodbye, and I watched her leave the café, her air of mystery and hesitancy explained.

Despite the warmth, I shivered.

The gallery was in a white building with a portico. A myrtle hedge ran up to the entrance, which was flanked by two bay trees in pots. Inside, there were four galleries and the windows were shrouded with muslin to protect the paintings. They were predominantly French, mostly cosy interiors and provincial landscapes.

The pictures in the fourth room were different, late nineteenth century, and concentrated on narrative. *Awaiting News from the Battlefront* showed a young woman with two children clutching her skirts watching a telegraph boy advance up the drive to their picturesque cottage. *The Prodigal Son* caught him looking the worse for wear as he collapsed in the street outside his father's house.

I had never cared much for this style of painting, and many of the pictures were over-detailed. Yet one arrested my eye. It showed a well-built young man in armour on a white horse in a forest. Some of the trees were in blossom. Rabbits played in the undergrowth, and a fox and a badger watched the rider. A turreted, fairytale castle surrounded by a briar thicket, rose in the distance. It was by William Lennox, entitled *In Quest of the Sleeping Beauty*.

I examined it carefully, the flash of primrose and violet,

the pink tree blossom, the flutter of the rider's banner and the gleam of light on his armour. Did he know towards whom he rode? Or was he propelled by faith, hearsay and hope? There was a steady, fixed blindness in his progress, and he looked to neither right nor left, ignoring the beauty of the forest.

The artist had seen to it that the transaction about to take place – in return for her rescue, the maiden would give years of unstinting service – was disguised by the romance and colour of the escapade, of that precise moment.

Now I understood why I didn't like narrative paintings. They did not reveal the whole story.

'Barbara.'

I whirled round from paying off the taxi at the hotel. '*Alexander!*' He was dressed in a linen suit and light brogues, which gave him a slightly foreign air that fitted perfectly with the surroundings.

My purse, full of change, dropped to the ground and Swiss francs rolled all over the place. Alexander bent over, collected them up and pressed them into my hands. 'Have you gone mad?' I demanded.

'Possibly. And I like the feeling.' He grinned. 'Good research.' He grew serious. 'I couldn't bear knowing you were here and I was here and . . . so I asked for you in the hotel. They said Ryder had checked out but you were still here. Then I knew I could wait.'

Behind us, the taxi pulled away and the doorman

stepped forward to usher us inside. 'You must go away, this instant. Why are you in Switzerland?'

Alexander stood aside to allow me to go first into the lobby. 'You were in one of my favourite places in the world, so I got on the train. Rotten journey – the carriage was far too hot, and my companion snored.'

Struggling between intense joy and irritation, I said, 'It didn't occur to me that neither of us was to be trusted.'

'I wasn't going to let you know I was here. I was just going to look and then go away. There was plenty I could do and, anyway, I wanted to look up one of my old professors.'

Other guests in the lobby were busy with luggage, reservations and travel arrangements. In the terrace restaurant, lunch was coming to an end, and coffee and cigarettes were being consumed in the sunlight.

His hand lay on my arm.

'Barbara ... actually, I'm not taking anything for granted. Could you make time to be with me? Will you have dinner?'

'You mean ... will I go to bed with you afterwards?'

He looked at me steadily and without pretence. 'Yes, I do.'

'No college girls, then?' I murmured.

Alexander removed his hand. 'I'm restless and desperate without you.'

How many people were watching this exchange? Porter. Waiter. Guests? I don't know.

For the hundredth time, I noted his beauty, realized

with a shock how much I had demanded from myself since I first met him.

Alexander was breathing fast, nervous but determined, unsure of success, frightened of humiliation, but willing to take a chance. And I loved him for that courage.

'Dinner then,' I said.

In the hotel bedroom that evening, I took a long bath and dried myself on towels so crisp they reddened my skin. I rubbed scent into the folds of my elbows and knees, between my thighs and breasts. I stepped into silk underwear and rolled silk stockings up my legs. The whisper of materials sounded a muted arpeggio of desire. I blackened my lashes, but not too much, powdered my face, outlined my mouth carefully with lipstick and filled it in.

My dress was black and full-skirted. I pinned a diamond clip at the corner of the neckline, and swept up my hair into its chignon.

Thus scented, powdered and cleansed, I settled at the window in the hotel lobby, which overlooked the lake, and waited for Alexander.

Chapter Nineteen: Siena

'Hey, you look wiped out.' Lola kissed me and picked up my bag. 'I am. The heat in the city nearly killed me.' Actually, Lola didn't look anything like wiped out, but cool and fresh in a pair of cut-offs and a sleeveless T-shirt. 'Everything's waiting for you. Shower, cold drink, nice meal.' She stowed my bag in the car, then eased out of the station and headed in the direction of the house. 'Bill's looking forward to your arrival. He reckons you take more interest in his wretched orchard than I do.'

There was no trace of jealousy or bad feeling in the remark, just affection. 'Darling Lola. What's it like to be a saint? Tell me your news.'

Lola required no second urging. She opened her mouth and out streamed a skein of brilliant gossip and specu-lation. Some of the finer, insider detail escaped me, but I grasped the essential gist. Gossip in New York and London was two sets of peas in the same pod.

Bill must have spotted the car bumping down the lane because he was waiting in the drive. 'Hi.' He opened the door and the heat slapped my skin. He was in shorts and a pair of old sandals, and his feet were smeared with dust. He hefted my case into the house and up to the spare bedroom. I breathed a sigh of relief as I followed him up.

'It's great to be here.' I crossed to the window and

looked down at the landscape with its nicely rolling hills. The sun was already drying everything, and by the end of summer, it would be brown and brittle out there. But now the prospect was still essentially green and lazy, a vista that made one think of messing about in boats, and tipsy picnics under oak trees.

Lola rustled up a lunch of tomatoes and basil; we mopped up the dressing with fresh bread, then drank coffee on the porch, our seats pushed against the wall of the house in the shade. We lazed away much of the afternoon, but at four o'clock Bill put down his paper and said, 'Time for a stroll. Siena?'

'Leave the girl alone,' Lola protested. 'She should be sitting here with one of my smoothies.'

'She can do that later. It's up to you, Siena.' But he beckoned bossily with a finger, which meant the opposite.

It was the hot and still part of the afternoon, the moment before the sun begins to slide down towards the horizon, before the air stirred in preparation for evening. Bill and I headed up for the orchard past maples and hickories.

And there was the orchard, so quiet and patient. I looked, and absorbed, and what I saw crept like balm over my frenzy. 'What I remember most about this is its peace.'

Bill shook his head, wiseacre fashion. 'Not really. Not if you had special listening equipment. If you pressed your beautiful, delicate ear to this trunk, or down on the grass, you would hear the roar of battle for the life of the trees.'

'Roar of battle?'

'For starters . . .' He stopped by a tree. It was in full leaf and the buds on the leaders were swollen and ripening into infant fruit. 'At any one moment, aphids, codling moth . . .' he ticked off the points '. . . airborne diseases, moulds, anything you care to name, are waiting to pounce and get their share. And I'm standing by to make sure they don't. It's a night-and-day vigil.'

'It sounds like the battle for Middle Earth or a world war.'

He took my hand, his touch friendly and reassuring. 'An orchard is artificial. Apple trees in the wild don't grow in swathes, but singly, or perhaps in twos. It's a good survival technique. In that way, they give themselves a chance to develop resistance to local diseases and microbes. But an orchard,' Bill dropped my hand, leaving me curiously bereft, 'an orchard is a beachhead for diseases and bugs.'

He parted the leaves and pointed out the apple buds. Round and . . . pregnant-looking. 'There's probably some moth larva curling up inside a juicy leaf as we speak.' He bent over to examine the leaves more closely. 'For them, the apple tree is a permanent salad bar.'

The long grass under the trees curled over my sneakers. Inside them my toes flexed and slid over the sweaty soles.

Bill moved on to the next tree. He snapped off a leaf and held it up to the light. 'Just checking for disease.' He bent down and scraped the bark with a fingernail. 'You look as though you could do with a long rest, Siena.'

'Everyone I know could do with a rest.'

He turned and sent me one of his slow smiles. 'I'm lucky. I have plenty of time for that here.' He tapped a bud experimentally. 'Yup. You're ready for the next stage,' he informed it. 'Get going.'

I tucked my arm into his. 'How does it work with you and Lola? Aren't there times when you're both in the wrong place at the wrong time and the strain tells?'

'Yes,' he replied, 'but there you are. Either you work through it or you don't.'

With that I had to be content. Bill and Lola kept their private areas private.

We quickened our pace to walk up the slope to the top of the ridge, leaving the orchard behind. Hot and sweating, I reached the top, halted and stretched out my arms until the joints in my elbows and fingers cracked.

Bill stood beside me and shaded his eyes. 'Speaking of which, how's Charlie?'

'He should be here. He'd love it.'

He *should* have been here, observing this landscape, this busy, noisy, incredibly fecund, secret world. My skin pricked with longing for him. I wanted him to be standing beside me, to breathe in his smell, to link my arm with his and listen with him to the microbes, moulds, seeds and fruit doing battle.

Bill touched my arm. 'You didn't answer my question.'

'He's fine.'

'Charlie rang,' Lola informed me, when Bill and I came into the house a couple of hours later.

278

I bent down to remove a stalk of grass that was embedded in my shoelace. 'Any message?'

'Sorry that he missed you but he'll catch up next week. He's away for the rest of the weekend.'

'Oh.' Charlie had failed to mention that he was planning to be away. I straightened up and encountered Lola's raised, questioning eyebrows. 'That's *fine*,' I said.

Later, when she had presented me with a glass of cabernet sauvignon and we were tucked up on the swing seat on the porch, I said, 'It's good that Charlie had last-minute plans. He needs a bit of a break. He's been working too hard.'

Lola took a sip of her wine. 'And?'

I turned my head sharply. 'And?'

'You tell me, sweetie.'

'It's good to get out of the routine sometimes. Take a break and come over here to work.'

'Says you,' said Lola.

Before I left, Bill drew me aside. 'Do I detect that you and Charlie have . . .' his mouth twitched '. . . issues? The ones we talked about before?'

'The same.'

'I'm not the one to talk, Siena, about the rights and wrongs of having or not having a family, but would it be useful to point out that you haven't definitely said no?'

Whoa! I was up against it. It was one thing for Charlie, with all his love and longing, to punch with a velvet glove, and another for Bill to do so – and that made it all the more powerful. 'Is that fair?'

279

'Entirely,' he replied, and kissed my cheek. 'Send my best wishes to Charlie. Tell him we want to see him next visit.'

I had never worked so hard in my life. I was used to pushing myself, but these days were something else. I became accustomed to waking up in the hotel bedroom feeling dreadful, and equally dreadful when I flung myself back into bed at night. Yet the dreadfulness was, curiously, not unsatisfactory. It was a consequence of pulling with the team to make something.

By the end of the second week of filming, it was clear that we needed more time. There were frantic phone calls all over New York, and across the Atlantic. There was a balancing act to be done with everyone's schedules, made almost impossible by the fact that most people on the team were booked to move on to something else.

'OK, OK,' said Dwayne. 'We do a raincheck to this one, and reassemble later in the year when I've had a chance to take an overview. Would that suit you, Siena?'

It did not suit me. 'Of course. No problem.'

On the day before I went home to the UK, the team assembled to take a look at the rushes. Some were good, other bits worried me.

The programmes held a nice variety of the touching and the productive; the guinea pigs, the Pearls and Angelas, appeared to go away looking better and happier, which was what it was all about – somehow, I had detected a cowering psyche, dusted it down, reclothed it and sent it out into the city feeling better. Surely that meant something?

At home Steve the plumber had said it was only fun and fluff – but I'd been thinking about that. Doctors and psychiatrists have the edge on most of us – that I concede. They stitch up wounds, perform skin grafts on body and mind, but not everyone, thank goodness, requires or wishes anything so drastic. Some of us need fun and fluff. And fashion catches the moment. Pins down the fragile second. Holds up a mirror, admittedly small, and shows us who we are.

The bad bits? One or two shots caught me in mid-instruction, or circling my subject thoughtfully, a hand crossed over my midriff, the other cupping my chin. It was perfectly normal – it was my thinking pose – but I couldn't help concluding that the Siena Grant in the television rushes looked too thin, too hollow . . . insubstantial.

It was raining in England and the temperature was ten degrees lower than it had been in New York, but Charlie was at the airport to meet me. He whisked me back to the flat where he had laid out a late breakfast of croissants and coffee. 'I hope you brought a video,' he said, handing me the strongest and most welcome coffee I could remember, and I appreciated the effort behind his request. 'I'd like to have a look. See how you work. See what it was like.'

'That's nice of you.' I gave him his present, a rucksack for day-trekking bought downtown.

In the past, Charlie's comments had sometimes been too critical. Being Charlie, he failed – sometimes – to cotton on to the idea that there was criticism and criticism, and that extreme honesty and negative appraisal were not always required. But in the name of togetherness I had bitten my lip.

He examined the rucksack – 'Great, love it' – and pulled me close. 'It was bloody lonely here without you.'

'So what are you going to do about welcoming me home?'

'Make you another cup of coffee, of course. How else would I welcome you home?'

'*Charlie!*'

Later he said, 'That was nice. I feel I haven't seen you for months.'

I rested my cheek on his shoulder, and tried to tell him about the apple trees, and the secret roar of warfare, and the idea that a divine spark flickered in that landscape. 'I wanted you there to show you.'

The arm tightened round me.

Even later, I asked, 'Will you be seeing Cimmie again?' I pictured her, bulging and oh-so-generous to the second wife. *I give Charlie to you.*

'Probably not,' said Charlie.

I was busy unpacking when he let slip, 'Jackie Woodruff admitted she hadn't slept for two nights before Rob died, and her boss had issued her with a first warning for lateness.'

Aghast, I whirled round. 'Charlie, how could I have forgotten? What else has happened?'

'One of the jurors was taken ill and had to be hospi-
talized, briefly as it happened, but the summing-up had to
be postponed for a week.'

'And?'

'Who knows? The jury have had time to rethink their
initial impressions. They forget the impact of what people
look and sound like, and think about the evidence. Which
is the point, of course . . .'

'Are you worried?'

He shrugged. 'No more than usual.'

'And Jackie?'

Charlie put his head on one side. 'I try to understand
how it feels if your baby has died, and you're on trial for
his murder, but I can't.'

He picked up the tray with the half-empty coffee cups
and went into the kitchen. I heard him slam the dishwasher
shut, which meant he was very worried.

I pinioned him against the sink. 'What else, Charlie?
There's something else.'

He sighed. 'OK. When they checked little Rob's X-rays,
they spotted what they think might have been an earlier
fracture of his arm.'

My first port of call was *Fashion, This Week* where I was
summoned to Vita's office.

She was talking on the phone but gestured that I should
take a seat. That meant: long talk. The office was large
and airy, stacked high with copies of rival magazines. Vita
was in a wide skirt, cinched in tightly at the waist (which
must have been hell), and a pair of very high heels.

'Sorry about that.' She had finished her conversation and smiled warmly at me. 'Welcome back, you're quite a star. *How* was the States?'

She questioned me minutely and I answered as fully as possible. It struck me that Vita's angling for information had an ulterior motive. 'Are you thinking of heading Stateside?' I asked.

She shot a furtive glance round the room. 'No, but British editors are not unknown over there.'

We exchanged a look of perfect understanding.

'One always has to keep the shock absorbers in trim.' Vita poured out a glass of mineral water and handed it to me. 'Critics are hell and the first rule of life is, they never let up.'

I laughed. The warning applied as much to Vita as it did to me. 'How's circulation?'

'Good, as far as I know. And your slot is holding up.' She pulled a dossier towards her and flipped it open. It was filled with figures and graphs, and she ran her finger down the table. 'Yup. It's holding up well. But we have to think "future". Always onwards and upwards. Let's widen the range a bit, otherwise it'll get samey. Do you get my point?'

I drank some water. 'Of course.'

'Perhaps we should think there isn't too much "future" in the column. It has a finite life.'

'True.' I did a lightning mental overview of the possibilities, trying to assess what might be coming next, and how I would deal with it.

'We want you on board, *star* that you are, but we want

284

you to think about change and the next big thing. Keep on your toes. Even stars have to do that. It's a cliché, but nothing lasts for ever.' She shrugged self-consciously. 'Not even me.'

Vita was right, but thinking 'future' had its dangers. One needed the right muscles in tip-top condition. Charlie was thinking of the future, Vita was thinking of the future . . . Everyone was thinking of the future.

Even I was.

Before I left the office, I sought out Jenni. She was sitting at her desk, marking proofs of the next edition. 'Hi,' she said.

'I've brought you something from the States.'

She glanced at the parcel (Carolina Herrera scent) that I placed on the desk top but did not attempt to open it. 'Thanks. I'm glad you're here. I want to tell you I'm leaving.' She couldn't contain her satisfaction. 'I'm going to work for *Vogue*. I have my future to think of, and I'm off next month.'

Charlie called me on my mobile. 'Look,' his voice was rushed and urgent, 'we've broken for lunch, but the jury have sent word they've reached a verdict. Can you come?'

I glanced at my watch. Book, magazine, catch up with correspondence, research, phone call to Dwayne – the categories of 'must-do' were stacked up like my T-shirts in the wardrobe.

But Charlie needed me. I knew he did. 'Give me five, and I'm on my way.'

I got to court number three just in time and slid into

the back row. My knees felt peculiar, weak and unsteady, and I was thankful to be seated. It is far, far worse being nervous for someone you love than for yourself and, for Charlie's sake, I wanted to behave perfectly.

He was in his usual position, his junior behind him. Notes were being passed between Robin Banstead and his junior. The clerk of the court muttered into his phone. The judge arrived, and the jury bailiff ushered in the jury. One of the women gave a hacking cough as she sat down.

Jackie Woodruff sat in her place between the prison officers. She wore a white blouse and a black skirt, which covered her knees. She looked ordinary and unmurderous. Perhaps my advice had been of some use.

I did not like to stare at her too openly but, from time to time, I snatched a quick look. She was paler than I remembered, her lips dry and cracked, her face rigid. She reminded me of a painting, a modern expressionist crucifixion – a face set in agony and despair glimpsed among the crowd.

An air of menace hung over the court. A baby had died, and his life had to be accounted for. I remembered Charlie once saying, 'The law is blunt and imperfect, but it's all we have got.'

The jury foreman – a small, blonde woman – was invited to stand. When she was asked for the verdict, she clutched her hands together. 'Guilty,' she said.

'No, no, *no*!' Jackie Woodruff's husband lurched to his feet.

In the dock Jackie retched.

Robin Banstead did not permit himself to smile. After all, this was about a dead baby. But he was pleased, I could tell.

There was a muted scream from the gallery and a woman clutched her neighbour. Then uproar.

This, then, was where Charlie's journey had ended, and there was an inevitability about the finale. This was the pay-off for the long hours, late nights, the investment of his belief. He had tested the prosecution's case almost to destruction, but not quite.

It took me a good few minutes to reach him, and I had to dodge round the court bailiff to do so. But I knew I had to get hold of him.

'Charlie!' I touched his arm. He looked round but I don't think he registered who I was. 'Just a minute,' he said. 'I have to speak to the defendant.'

He reached up and laid his hand on the rim of the dock where Jackie Woodruff was still sitting. 'I failed you,' he said. 'I don't know how to say sorry.'

She lifted her face to his. 'Oh.'

'I know this is the wrong verdict. You must appeal.'

Jackie looked away – I suppose into her bleak future. 'I must, must I?' she said, and I was taken aback by the venom in her voice. 'What do you know, Mr Grant? What does a well-off *man* know about – about – any of it? Being so tired that you want to die, and your baby never, ever shuts up. No, like most sodding men, you think you know exactly the position.' She plucked at the material of the black skirt. 'It's over now, and you can go home.'

Chapter Twenty: Siena

Technically, Charlie's next case appealed in every possible way to his libertarian, egalitarian and combative instincts. A black boy (several convictions already notched up) had died in the showers in a remand centre and no one, but no one, was talking.

I did my best. Had there been a camera in the showers? I asked Charlie. If not, why not? Had anyone admitted to being in the area at the time of the death? Any record of a prison officer having patrolled?

Charlie replied politely, but there was no spark. No metaphorical licking of his lips. He seemed to be labouring under a deep inertia, an unwillingness to elaborate on the case.

He was gentle enough with me, but distant. 'You were right,' he admitted at one point. 'I was too involved in the Woodruff case. I let it get to me.'

Charlie's sister rang: wasn't it about time he honoured a long-standing promise to take Nat on the London Eye?

I said, perfect, and it was arranged for the following Saturday. I cancelled a planned outing with Manda, and Charlie, Nat and I set out on a sunny afternoon.

Nat, bright, tousle-haired and knobbly-kneed, insisted on wearing the fake scar Charlie had sent him. It kept slipping off his cheek.

'I'm seven,' he informed me, and I told him I already knew that. He slipped his hand into Charlie's and chattered away while we waited in the queue.

'How old were you, Uncle Charlie, when you first went up?'

'Very old,' said Charlie.

'But how old?'

Charlie laughed. 'I don't remember.'

Nat looked appalled and the fake scar slipped down to his chin. Charlie bent over and prised it off. 'You might frighten someone,' he said. 'Why don't I put it in my pocket?'

'I want some chips,' Nat announced, casting a weather eye at the nearby café.

'So do I,' said Charlie. 'Why don't we have them afterwards? Otherwise we'll lose our place.'

Nat pressed home the advantage. 'And Coke.'

'Sure.'

At this point, Nat looked a trifle shifty. 'Uncle Charlie, Mum doesn't like me having Coke.'

'Ah,' said Charlie. 'Why don't we forget to mention it to her? Then she won't have to worry.'

Nat considered this proposition and found it acceptable. 'Thank you, Uncle Charlie. You're very nice.'

'Nat, I'm on your side,' said Charlie. 'Remember that. I'll never not be on your side. If you see what I mean.'

Nat's little face was a study in relief and cockiness, and the pleasure of having his uncle hanging on a string.

I watched them. Maybe the shadow of the Woodruff case was lifting, for Charlie was happier than I had seen him for a while. Nat, chatty and disposed to confidences, was entirely at ease.

The capsule transcribed its arc. Charlie and Nat stood pressed together, watching the panorama. And I could decipher in Nat's thin, unformed body, shades of Charlie as he would have been. And in Charlie what Nat would become.

They shared a joke and Nat shrieked, 'Uncle Charlie, that's naughty!'

Charlie bent down and whispered, 'Don't tell Aunt Siena.'

'*No*,' said Nat, flashing me a cheeky look.

Again, Charlie's arm snaked round his nephew and held him . . . as if he was the most precious thing in the world.

The capsule finished its descent. But I did not register the river, the road, the miniaturized buildings. I was fixated by the closeness and trust between a man and little boy.

Marybelle Hammond (50) is a high-profile investment banker recently returned from the Far East. The Problem: she feels she is out of touch with UK fashion. She is cash-<u>loaded</u> [Jenni had underlined it] but time-poor.

Marybelle Hammond was a thin woman, wearing a black trouser suit and a white blouse. 'I took a lifetime to achieve this look,' she said, within minutes of our first meeting. 'I can't remember when I last ate a carb. Of course, it's a battle against bad-breath ketosis.'

I took a step back. 'I admire your control.'

Instinct (and experience) alerted me that we were about

to conduct a conversation that went along the lines: *'I'm so fat.'*

'No, you're not, just look at my stomach.'

'I got on the scales last night and I'd put on two ounces.'

'Really? You'd never know.'

Mercifully we did not. I'd been wrong. Marybelle Hammond was not the usual sort of woman. Even so, she sneaked the first opportunity to assess the state of my hips. 'It's easy once you've decided. Then it becomes lifestyle.'

She lied – and in this I was correct – for every line of her tortured body suggested she was engaged in a perpetual bitter battle with her desire for a square meal.

We perched on chairs in the *Fashion, This Week* studio and drank mineral water. I asked Marybelle to tell me a little about herself. She extracted a Mac foundation compact from her crocodile Kelly and flipped it open. 'I began as a secretary . . .' She waited for me to respond with 'How amazing,' and dabbed at her nose with the sponge. '. . . but I was promoted within six months and the climb just went on and on, ever upwards.' More dabbing. I longed to reach over, still the restless hand and say, 'It's enough, you look fine.'

'Was it a struggle to get to the top?'

Experience (my own) had also taught me that this was a question successful women did not answer honestly. I sat back and waited. The war waged in Marybelle's features was between the desire to shrug off her progress as effortless because of her innate brilliance, and the equally strong desire to be admired for her dedication to the fight. The result was compromise. 'I kept my wits about me.'

I checked my notes. 'Would there be any problem with your new employers about publicity? A lot of people read the slot. And your family? Sometimes they don't like it.'

The answer shot back: 'I don't have a family. Parents died some time ago and I'm not in touch with my sister.' She dropped the Mac compact back into the Kelly. 'She lives up north.'

'North' was inflected in a way that suggested profound alienation or, at least, profound contempt.

She smoothed her hair. 'So, what's on the menu?'

'Working clothes, work entertaining, leisure, in that order.'

'I don't do leisure, so there's no need for that. And I don't have any friends.' Her smile contained a challenge: question that if you dare. 'But I have money and independence, and that's enough.'

'OK,' I said, after a pause. 'What you're really after is a wardrobe centred on work.'

'You've got it. That's my life.'

I made Marybelle stand in front of the long mirror. 'First, you should try not to wear black. It's ageing.'

A crack appeared in Marybelle's demeanour. 'Ageing . . . ageing . . .' she repeated. 'It hadn't occurred to me.' She gave herself an extra long appraisal in the mirror. 'Now you tell me I'm ageing.'

The sun reflected the river into the flat. Today it was hard and bright and unyielding. I chucked my briefcase on to the floor in the sitting room, and opened all the windows: the room was stuffy.

I sat down on the sofa. Think preparation for the Marybelle Hammond piece. Think colour, shape, situation . . . the considerations that were now automatic, second nature. Plot, plan, research – and move, seemingly serenely, through the various necessities and parameters of the job I knew so well.

The voice in my head was saying: *You're free to do as you wish. There are no constraints. You earn money, good money, which keeps Charlie in his laundered shirts and you in padded bomber jackets. The money's so good that you're heading towards the creation of your own company. Unlike your mother, or your grandmother, you're free to make decisions, to step on a plane, to pay attention to yourself.*

Actually, it's your duty to yourself, Siena, to strive and achieve.

I scribbled a couple of notes. Then I got up and wandered over to the window. And, for the first time, I wished it was possible to step out into a garden. I thought of Bill's orchard drowsing in the summer heat.

I leant my head against the pane.

'No, no, *no!*' I could still hear the cry of Jackie Woodruff's husband.

I could still see, so vivid, so sharp, Jackie's hand fly towards her mouth, and the pucker of her mouth as she retched, the foreman of the jury sinking back into her seat, her neighbour reaching over and patting her hand. I could hear the uproar from the press seats as the journos fought to get outside.

I could picture minutely my husband's shocked face.

'Did you do it?' I asked the figure in the dock silently.

As it happened, Jackie had turned her head and looked in my direction.

I don't know. I was so tired. I didn't know what I was doing.

After a while I went into the bedroom, and sat on the edge of the bed. My head was jangled, my stomach uneasy. I needed the equivalent of a spring-clean, a trip to the car wash. On my bedside table, there were bottles aplenty of echinacea and omega oils three and six, and Imedeen for the complexion. I had not taken any of them for days. By my chair, still designer-bagged and wrapped, there was a pair of new shoes. High-heeled, strappy beauties, and I didn't care if I ever saw them again.

For Jackie Woodruff it mattered only that the cot upstairs was empty and the yellow plastic duck with the bright red beak on the side of the bath no longer floated in the water. There were no creases in a small plump body to dust with talcum powder, no little toes to tickle. No whisper of: *Who's my beloved? Who's my best boy?* No tucking and wrapping in nappies and shawls. No struggle to make a routine out of the days, no exchange of information with friends, no hanging over a cot to listen for the quick breath of a sleeping son. Her arms cradled emptiness, and her stitched, battered body had nothing to show for all that effort, waste and grief.

She was guilty.

I raised my hand to my cheek . . . It was wet. In fact, tears were running down my face.

*

Marybelle Hammond plucked at the skirt of the Dolce & Gabbana suit I had selected. She wrinkled her forehead, took a step back, put her head on one side.

'It suits you, Marybelle. It puts you firmly in "smart".'

It was true. The suit softened her, yet gave her edge. It was not Timeless Elegance but cleverer. The violet, the colour of a summer day at dusk, of purple rainclouds, suited her skin tone perfectly.

'I'm not quite sure, Siena.' I realized she was finding it difficult to take direction from someone such as myself. Or anyone.

That made Marybelle Hammond vulnerable.

'It brings you up-to-date, is very classy, and much less ageing than what you usually wear.'

She didn't like that. To be fair, neither would I but, when all was said and done, I was the white knight riding to the rescue, bringing cheer and a little tough talking on the point of my lance, etc., etc. Her eyelids, brushed with the (wrong) green eye-shadow, lowered over a hostile expression.

'You wanted my help.'

'I don't have to accept it.'

'Would you like to take it home and show it to a friend?'

'I told you I have no friends.'

Unusually for me, for I relished a small fight, I cut my losses. 'OK. Let's look at something else.'

She rang me at eight thirty precisely the following morning. 'Is that Siena?' She was crisp and sounded as if she had already taken several important decisions. 'Look, I'm sorry about this, but I don't want to feature in your column . . . for various reasons. You were right. Top banks don't like the publicity. But I would like to hire you in a private capacity. Could you come over to my house and overhaul my wardrobe?'

Before I could reply, she said, 'That's settled. Midday, at my place.' She named a fee, and I flushed at the size.

At a quarter to twelve, I parked my car in a narrow Chelsea street and rang the doorbell of an equally narrow town-house, which must have cost a fortune. A woman – cleaner? housekeeper? – led me upstairs to the sitting room, where Marybelle was presiding over a coffee tray. 'I don't normally drink coffee, but I thought you would.'

The room was plainly but expensively furnished and I was not surprised to observe that there were no photographs, only a vase of perfectly arranged peonies and one or two pieces of good china.

She looked rather pale. 'It's been quite a year, changing job and country.'

I didn't have much time to spare, neither did I wish to be there. I drank my coffee quickly. 'What do you want me to do?'

She seemed surprised. 'Set me up.'

All of a sudden, I understood why I didn't like this assignment. Marybelle was handling it as a transaction for which she would pay me a great deal, but nothing more: there would be no pleasure, no joy in it and, for that matter, no thanks. Perhaps I had been spoilt: I wanted more from my work than the crude debit and credit of a bank transaction.

Her bedroom was super-clean, super-comfortable and decorated in yellow and white, with a touch of powder blue here and there. She flung open the double doors of the wardrobe, which was the sort with rails that could be pulled out.

'There you go, Siena.'

I leafed through the hangers. The clothes were badly hung, and not in the best of condition. Marybelle gave them a perfunctory glance. 'They belong to another life. I'm going to get rid of them all.'

It was neither here nor there to me what Marybelle did with them, but I was intrigued by the implication that she wished to discard her former life. 'Not these.' I rescued a black skirt cut on the cross and a pretty peplum jacket.

I worked my way through the rails, and saved about a quarter. We argued over a sheepskin coat but, in the end, she gave in. Afterwards, she insisted on offering me some salad and water, which the housekeeper served in a tiny dining room.

Our conversation consisted mostly of Marybelle's fantastic career. 'It's a question of making up one's mind. My first boss made the mistake of thinking that, because I was a woman, he could walk all over me.' She flashed me a shark-toothed smile. 'As it happened, I ended up his boss.'

She pressed a second helping of avocado and mozzarella on to my plate, and took nothing for herself. But she watched me eat, and the flow of information was relentless. The time she had single-handedly saved a deal from crashing and the loss of millions . . . the crack team of corporate wizards she had masterminded that was the talk of Hong Kong. Not once did she inquire about my life or opinions, and I was nagged by a sense of familiarity. Then

I remembered. It was how Jay had talked and behaved.

'And what are you hoping to do with the new job?'

Marybelle looked amazed. 'Run the show eventually. What else?'

The publicist from Trimester Productions rang. 'Hi. I'm Carrie. We didn't get to meet when you were over, but we will next time. I am *so* pleased to be working on this project with you.'

We fenced around for a few more minutes, then got down to business. 'I think your programme is *so* fascinating. I need to know a little about you, and a bit about your work in the UK.' She fired off a string of questions. Where did I begin? How did I develop my approach? Is straight talking essential? 'It's *so* important that I understand how you work, Siena. I need to understand the concepts.'

'She and me both.' I shoved the box of popcorn at Charlie. We had met at the local cinema playhouse to catch the early-evening performance of *Désespoir et Amour*, which I wanted to see. 'What are the concepts?'

Charlie chewed a piece of the popcorn. 'Do you fancy a drink?'

As usual, the cinema bar was packed. It was a cross between a pub and a wine bar, and sufficiently confident to get away with it. We went there often, just hanging out before a film.

I found a table in the corner. Charlie edged the popcorn on to it, then pushed it away with his finger. 'I want to talk to you, Siena.'

'Get me a glass of wine first, Charlie, please.'

I felt the weight of the past few months settle on my shoulders – the travelling, the worrying, plotting and planning, and I thought of Bill's orchard where none of that had seemed to matter.

I watched Charlie at the bar. Tall, assured, exchanging pleasantries with the barman.

'OK, OK . . .' I clinked my glass of red wine against his white.

He drank a mouthful, swiped a hand over his mouth, took a second mouthful, leant forward and said, very seriously, 'How would you feel if I gave up law to become a plumber?'

I felt the electric prickle of shock. 'Charlie!'

'Could choose my hours, Siena, and it's a nice little earner – there's a national plumbing crisis. England expects —'

'Charlie.' I stared at him.

Again he wiped his mouth and sighed. 'Don't think I'd be any good with U-bends.'

'OK. What is it?'

'How about I take up Harry Liversedge's offer to join his chambers? After . . . after the Woodruff case, I reckon I need a change.'

He couldn't have been less enthusiastic, but I knew he hadn't made the suggestion lightly. 'OK. Point number one. It's not your kind of chambers. Two, you'd be giving up the work in which you believe. Is the thinking that because you'd earn more we wouldn't be so reliant on me?'

'Clever girl.'

'So, if we started a family, I wouldn't need to be so worried over money?'

'Precisely.'

'Charlie, you don't get it.'

I wished I hadn't said that. Charlie blinked, and I caught a flash of real hurt and anger.

'Yes, I do,' he countered, his expression unreadable. He thought for a moment. 'Are you sure, Siena, you know where you're going?'

Lucy Thwaite, Marybelle Hammond . . . I could take my pick.

I looked up at the clock on the wall. 'We'll miss the film.'

Charlie's hand descended on mine like a steel trap shutting down. 'Forget the film, Siena. We're going to have this out.'

'You're bullying me.'

Charlie lost patience. 'We've been tiptoeing round this subject long enough.'

'A little more time,' I begged.

'I'll help you, I promise.' He pulled my fingers roughly, one by one. 'These days, it's a two thing, not a one thing any more.'

But I was truly frightened, panic-stricken. 'How many men have said that?' I pulled away my hand. 'What's the betting that if Harry Liversedge so much as lifts an eyebrow there's no going home to see your son or daughter in the nativity play, is there? Or to help out with the homework.'

There were a couple of mats on the table – rushwork, which looked African – no doubt made by workers who were paid fair-trade prices. They exuded fairness but they knew, and I knew, that nothing was fair and equitable. Particularly not biology.

I abandoned my half-finished wine. 'I'm going home.'

I shouldered my way out of the bar and left Charlie to it. The long evening was waning, and the light thrown over the streets was muzzy. I struck out for the park, which was the long route home but the nicer one.

It was filled with activity: skateboarders, joggers, walkers and couples sitting on the grass with bottles of wine and beer, all doing their thing in a scene that symbolized summer cheer.

I halted by a clump of laurel bushes, which were overgrown and matted – the perfect den and, indeed, the ground had been beaten flat by countless feet; on it lay a couple of smashed birds' eggs. They were blue and speckled with black. Perhaps a child had stolen them from the nest and dropped them. Perhaps a predator had sneaked through the mother's defences, sucked out the contents and left the shells for her to see.

Footsteps came up behind me. 'Siena . . .'

I swung round.

Charlie spread his hands. 'I want you to know I've come to the end. I've tried every tactic. I've asked you nicely. I've asked you in anger and in sorrow. I've promised what I could . . . but I can't – *can't* – turn into a woman. Anyway, now I've had enough of the whole damn subject. And that's that. Finish.'

He turned on his heel and walked away in the opposite direction. He didn't come home until very late. I didn't ask where he had been.

Chapter Twenty-one: Barbara

The hotel was getting ready for the evening. At the bar, the cocktail shaker was in constant use. The lift gates clanged open and shut, disgorging guests in evening dress. There was an air of anticipation, of mystery – what might the night yield in the way of pleasure to the woman in blue silk, the man in the bow-tie? What would they discover? The foreignness of the men and women – their elegant clothes, unfamiliar-smelling cigarettes, their smooth, tanned skins – made me long to be one of them.

A watcher, an observer . . . had been Alexander's verdict on first meeting me, and that was how I judged myself. I nipped and tucked, shaped and moulded things in my mind, and took my time. I was the foil to Ryder. That was my role. Yet, here I was – gowned, perfumed, apparently tranquil – and the enormity of my recklessness, my daring, took my breath away.

I distracted myself by rifling through the morning papers, which were still laid out on the lobby table. As they were in French and German, they had their limitations. A copy of French *Vogue* was more enticing, and I retreated to a seat by the window, and was instantly captivated by the breathless, intense prose. From what I could gather, there were references to 'the soul' and to 'confidence'. (Did we have 'soul' and 'confidence' at home?) 'A woman should be more important than her clothes,' Coco Chanel was quoted as having said.

I looked up and Alexander was threading his way through the lobby. I could not stifle my pleasure at the sight of him.

He touched my hand. 'Hallo. What have you been doing?'

I pointed to a picture of a sleek, rangy model in *Vogue*. 'The emphasis is on youth, on longer hair. Fossilized attitudes are out. And the freedom to be wittily critical of the past is in. Apparently we should laugh more at ourselves.'

'Exactly.' He kissed my cheek. 'You look beautiful.'

He had brushed back his hair severely, which emphasized his facial bone structure and I wondered if he knew how attractive he was. He did not seem aware of the picture he made, for his attention was on me.

'So do you,' I said.

For a second or two, our fingers clung together.

Alexander handed me my wrap, and we hailed a taxi. He told me he was taking me to the restaurant, not far from the Château de Chillon, to which his tutor had taken him. 'Wolfgang was on a mission to teach the English how to enjoy themselves. He also thought they were the most snobbish race on earth, and their women were either dull housewives in awful clothes, or shrieking bluestockings with neglected hair.'

'I own up to some dull clothes.'

'You're not dull. Never that.'

I looked out of the taxi window into the street. Large

and rather desolate-looking, many of the houses, built in a more optimistic era, had seen better times. Paintwork flaked, the windows sagged and roofs required attention. After a moment, I asked, 'Am I dreaming, Alexander?'

'If you are, I hope it's a good one.' He touched my cheek. 'Should I analyse it?'

We smiled at each other, and the taxi came to a halt.

The restaurant was small, with long curtains and tables arranged for maximum intimacy. It looked expensive. Through the window, in the distance, the dusk lent the château an (unearned) ethereal quality.

We ordered drinks – a martini for Alexander, gin and tonic for me. I faced him. 'I have a confession. I don't have enough money to pay for this. Or, rather, I couldn't account to Ryder for the sum.'

'Would he mind you going to a restaurant?'

'Not at all. He's very generous. He'd admire my boldness in doing so alone, as he would think, but I couldn't use his money for this.'

'Barbara . . . of course. I'll pay.'

'You have enough?'

'Yes.' He glanced at the other diners. 'How many other men here are not dining with their wives? Quite a few, I suspect. No one will make a fuss, or blink an eye.'

The waiter unfolded my napkin and spread it across my knees. Its whiteness was almost blinding, and the banquette was soft, and I was suspended, outside time and place, in a world I recognized only from dreams. It was a place of huge seductiveness, for the rules were different: there, you were free to do as you wished. Indulge as you liked. There were no strings, no duties.

'Didn't Freud say that civilization demands huge sacrifices from individuals?'

'Something like that.'

'Because, he reasoned, underneath we're aggressive and violent? Even dull housewives.'

Alexander grinned. 'Especially dull housewives.'

'I've been thinking. It isn't such a huge sacrifice. In fact, it's an easier way of existing. If we stick to good manners and good behaviour, we're released from having to think too much. But, for you, it must be different. You have to cope all the time with the fall-out, with nastier truth and behaviour. I hope it doesn't change you too much. I hope it doesn't make you too sad.'

'That's the nicest thing anyone has said to me.'

We ordered melon and trout, and while we ate the melon, Alexander talked about his friends in Switzerland and his studies. I told him about Anne Abercrombie and the painting by William Lennox. The conversation drifted on to the subject of Roy and, finally, to Amy and her struggles.

'I didn't think having a daughter would be so difficult.' The confession did not come easily, even when I made it to Alexander. 'I assumed I would teach Amy what my mother had taught me, and that would be that. But it didn't turn out that way. Amy proved me wrong, and there have been times . . . when I know she's hated me.'

The trout was superb, but Alexander ate little and

pushed aside his plate. 'I'm sure when Amy finds out what she wants to do, she won't be so angry. I was like that. Promise. I think . . . when you find the right path, you bowl along it.'

Not entirely, I thought. All the same, Alexander was comforting. 'Once Sophie said something rather like that.'

'Sophie?' Alexander drank some wine and considered. 'Sophie's very clever. She's quite something.'

The clatter of dishes and cutlery, the luxurious and unfamiliar setting, the smooth, glittering expanse of the lake outside, which reflected a million points of light, contributed to my sense that I was trying on another woman's life. Alexander reached across the table and took my hand. I smiled at him, said something. He laughed and kissed it, and everything was magical between us.

If I ever confessed about Alexander – and to whom would I ever confess? – I would emphasize that it was the small details of this meeting that left an impression. The starched linen on my lap, the taste of my lipstick, the mark it left on my glass, the pinch of my left shoe, the brush of his mouth on my skin.

It would have to be the small details because the wild feelings, the perfection of those moments, the pleasure and delight, the surprise that it was happening, its mixture of elation and terror, would be impossible to describe.

After dinner, Alexander took me back to the hotel. I was a little drunk, but wildly happy.

He closed the door of the room behind us, leant against it, pulled me to him and buried his face in my neck. 'I can't believe this.'

'Nor can I.' I shifted closer to him, trying to feel his heartbeat, to match my body to his. I did not know if this was love – it was too complicated for a single label – but what I felt was passionate, and deep, and irrevocable.

Someone had turned down the bed. The curtains had been drawn, a glass and a jug of water placed on the table. The unseen hand had turned on a lamp, which spilled a muted, diffuse light over the bed.

After a moment, Alexander turned me and, one by one, undid the buttons of my dress, then eased it off my shoulders. It slid to the floor and I stepped out of it.

'Until I met you,' he murmured, 'I didn't know about myself. I thought I did. I knew nothing of what it was like to long for the days to pass because you *must* see someone again.'

We lay facing each other on the bed. All of a sudden, Alexander seemed paralysed – by emotion? Anxiety? I stroked his cheek. 'What is it, Alexander?'

'I don't know,' he replied. 'Only all this is so much and it hurts. And I hadn't imagined I'd feel like this.'

'You're so sweet.'

'Sweet? Is that all?'

'Isn't that enough?'

'Don't tease, Barbara. Please.'

His appeal caught at my heart. 'No. I won't tease.'

He drew in his breath, a long sigh of relief. Still he made no move, and I caught a gleam of anxiety, of fear even, that he would not live up to his expectations. Or mine.

I bit my lip. 'Alexander . . . I know I'm not perfect. You won't mind?'

Immediately, his face cleared and he reached for me. 'Stupid, darling Barbara . . .'

Around dawn, I woke up. Alexander was sleeping on his side, turned away from me. I stretched out a hand and touched his thigh, gently, so as not to wake him. Then I settled to watch him, tallying every breath. For with every one . . . the tick of the clock . . . morning came closer.

At that moment, suspended between unconsciousness and the proper waking, I talked with my secret self . . . examined my hoarded joys and sorrows . . . peered into the rag-bag that contained fragments of my past.

Yes, what they say is true. The light of dawn is cold and clear.

Ah, Sophie, I heard Alexander say in my ear. *She's quite something.*

What Sophie possessed was something I would never have again.

One blazing hot day before the war, Ryder took me up in the Tiger Moth. My first flight. 'Had to butter up the flying officer,' he said, 'but I finally persuaded him it was important that brides-to-be had some idea . . .'

He was so pleased with himself, so excited at the prospect of showing me what excited him, so handsome and assured in his uniform. Simply to look at him – his fine, capable hands, the wide mouth, the way his hair grew on the back of his neck – triggered a physical response so powerful that I could think of nothing else.

He drove us at high speed down the road in his beloved

car. I remember that the dog-roses bloomed in the hedges and, after spring rain, the verges were brilliantly green.

'Here we are.' He turned into a field and parked alongside two planes, on which the mechanics were working, and jumped out of the car. 'Aren't they beauties?'

He helped me out of my seat. I was wearing trousers and a thin blouse, and he handed me a leather jacket, fussed over me as I put it on. 'I pinched it off Johnny. You're so slender, darling, it will probably fall off you, but it's cold up there.' He peered at me. 'Nervous?'

'Not a bit.' It was true. Normally so unsure, the prospect of flying did not trouble me.

A mechanic said, 'All ready, sir,' and Ryder showed me the controls. Joystick – push forward to dive, pull back to climb – altimeter, rudder bar. The mechanic helped me into the back seat; Ryder lowered himself into the front and gave the thumbs-up.

I didn't know what to expect, and hadn't anticipated the boneshaking rattle of the plane, or the skidding sensation while Ryder corrected the swing as he taxied into position for take-off. I smelt acrid exhaust, my teeth chattered and my stomach leapt into my mouth as the nose of the aircraft poked skyward. I was pushed back into my seat.

We were up, circling and climbing. Almost immediately, the noises dropped and the sensation of speed fell away. I craned downwards, and saw a river flowing through the meadows, its waters so clear that I could almost make out the weed on its bed.

'Glorious, isn't it?' Ryder's voice issued through the speaking tube.

'Glorious!'

'Hang on, then . . . I'm going to fly you to the end of the world and back.'

Were we close to God, Ryder and I, on that special, inaugural flight? Certainly we were as close as we could be to each other. Like crossed fingers. Taking me up with him was Ryder's way of cementing our partnership. It was a token of his perfect trust, his belief in me; in putting my life in his hands, I gave him mine.

That golden afternoon I flew with Ryder into an untainted future. There were no nightmares yet. No awkward, painful cards had been dealt. We were poised on the blue edge of infinity, borne up and cradled by forces greater than we, and everything – anything – was promised.

That day I understood happiness. Pure, almost spiritual.

I woke Alexander. 'I don't want to say this, but I think you must go.'

Instantly he was alert. 'If you want me to, of course, but I don't think there'll be any problem with the hotel.'

He wrapped his arms round me and I lay there savouring the peculiarly intense sensations – the early-morning light, the warmth of his body, a sensation of floating through a vast space.

Morning sounds . . . The gravel was being swept outside. Trolleys clinked in the corridor. Vehicles arrived and departed. Alexander propped himself against the headboard. 'I love the way you look, Mrs Beeching.'

Involuntarily, I turned my head away – the morning light would not be kind. 'Thank you.'

Alexander got out of bed, washed and dressed. Trousers, a now crumpled shirt, jacket. Eventually the older, more formal version of him, with damp hair and unshaven stubble, sat on the edge of the bed and took my hand. 'I will be discreet. Promise.'

'Alexander . . .'

'Darling Barbara . . .'

'We must not meet again like this. For many reasons, most of which you know already.'

'Are you saying what I think you're saying?'

'Yes, I am.'

I felt him tense. 'I see. I didn't expect . . . not so soon at any rate.' He stroked my fingers thoughtfully. 'Was there something last night?' He avoided my eyes. 'Don't you care for me?'

That made me smile. I gazed at the corn-coloured hair, and the profile in which I took such delight. 'Far too much, as it happens. But I have a life to which I must return.'

'I wasn't asking you to leave Ryder.'

'No.'

'Then why?'

I threw back the duvet, reached for my dressing-gown and went to the window. A horse-drawn milk float was pulling out of the hotel entrance. 'You have changed how I think and feel, Alexander.' My hands were trembling and I was forced to hold on to the sill for support. 'But there are other things to consider.'

'I know what you're going to say.'

I dared to look round. Alexander was hunched over his

311

knees. 'I don't think you do.' I turned back to the window. 'It's no use either of us thinking we can cope with two lives. It isn't possible.' He made an inarticulate noise of protest and hurt, and I went to sit beside him. 'You must be free to find someone else. Not at the moment, perhaps.' I placed my hand under his chin and made him look at me. 'The point is, sooner or later you will, and then this will turn sour. I'm listening to my instincts and they're good ones. One day, you'll know just how good. As for me, I must think of Ryder, and try to make reparation.'

'But if you weren't happy, you owe it to yourself . . .'

'Oh, I was happy,' I countered. 'That's the point. I don't regret you for one second and, hopefully, Ryder will never know, but I see so clearly now that I can't have you. It's not part of what I am, what made me, what made Ryder and me.'

Alexander got to his feet. 'I'm not sure I understand,' he said angrily.

'I think you will, eventually. You, of all people, will understand.'

He bent down and picked up some loose change that had fallen from his pockets on to the floor. 'Are you saying it was a waste? That it meant nothing?'

'Oh, no. Not that,' I cried. 'It was the opposite. My decision has nothing to do with rules and conventions, the things you question and study. And you were right, fidelity is not necessarily to do with the body, but with the mind. *That*, too, is the point.'

'Right,' he said, and jingled the change in his pocket. Misery and humiliation registered in his face, in the way he dug his hands into his pockets. 'It was my fault, wasn't it? I made the running.' He smiled ruefully. 'I should have known when Ryder beat me at tennis what I was up against.'

I got up and took his hands. 'Listen. It wasn't a waste. Not for me. I'll carry with me what you and I said to each other, and our times together, for the rest of my life. I shall think of them . . . thankfully.'

'Oh, God,' he said. '"Thankfully". I wanted more than *that*.'

I looked down at our clasped hands. 'I shall think of you with love, with great love.'

When Alexander left, he turned back at the door and said, 'I know I owe you a debt, Barbara.'

'Where will you go? You'll be all right?'

He smiled at me, and made an effort at jauntiness. 'What do you think?'

I looked at him. 'You'll be all right.' My voice was steady. 'I know you will.'

His smile faded. Then he was gone.

I sank down on the bed and strained to hear the last of his footsteps going down the corridor. He walked fast, impatiently. The sound faded.

I reached out and placed my hand on his pillow, searching in vain for the indent of his head, some residual warmth. Then I beat my hand on the mattress.

After a while I got up and went into the bathroom. I bathed, dressed and brushed my tangled hair. But instead of sweeping it into its customary chignon I allowed it to hang loose over my shoulders. Then I dusted my face with powder, noting the smudges of exhaustion under my eyes, and put on my lipstick.

I packed carefully and efficiently, easing my shoes into the shoe-bags, and inserting tissue paper between the clothes. I counted the remainder of my Swiss francs . . . some for the taxi, some for a cup of coffee and a roll at the airport. The remainder for tips. To the last penny, everything must be – would be – accounted for and entered in the household accounts book.

There, it was done, and I rang the bell for the porter to collect my luggage.

In the airport lounge, I drank a cup of coffee and ate a sandwich. It tasted of sand, but I couldn't bear to waste it and forced myself to swallow every mouthful.

Once I thought I heard Alexander's voice calling, 'Barbara,' and started up, out of my seat.

I finished the coffee and longed for a glass of water, but in my heightened state I felt too unnerved, too noticeable, to fetch one. Surely anyone looking at me would see that under my skirt, jacket and linen blouse my heart beat wildly at variance with my neat appearance.

'Poor silly Tilly Field,' Bunty had said, 'looks like a wraith.' Her husband had divorced her for taking a lover. It was possible, if Ryder ever found out, that I, too, could end up in exile in Dorking or Montreux.

Yet those reflections were not the truly frightening ones.

I must face Ryder. Become a mother again. Resume a

normal life. I must sit with my husband and say: 'Tell me your plans and let us work something out together.'

Note. Make mint and redcurrant jelly. Pick raspberries. Bottle tomatoes and, later, the plums. Talk to Herr Schlinker about autumn planting. Ring Miss Raith.

I nerved myself for the future where I would have to draw long and deep on my reserves. I would be cunning and guileful, loving and deceitful. There was no help for it.

I know I owe you a debt, Barbara.

Had I detected a frisson of relief in his voice? Perhaps I had. Perhaps I had wanted to hear it. But it hurt.

Chapter Twenty-two: Barbara

The house in Edgeborough Road had the stale, static feel of emptied life, except for the ticking clock in the sitting room.

Mrs Storr had come and gone, leaving a plate of scones on the kitchen table and a note: 'Mrs Andrews coming for tea.'

It was warm outside, with the softness of summer. In the run, the hens were chatting to each other. They clucked at my approach. I bent down and poked a finger through the wire. 'Hallo again.'

They observed me with bright, indifferent eyes and I rested my head against the wire.

After a while, I straightened and went indoors to unpack.

'You look ravishing,' said Bunty, when she arrived, kissing me on each cheek. 'That's the way they do it abroad, isn't it?'

Just to see her made me feel better. I placed my hands on her shoulders. 'Let me look at you.' Very pale. Sallow, almost. Far too thin. 'Have you seen Dr O'Donnell?'

She ducked her head. 'Yes . . . No. No.'

'Right.' I swivelled her round and marched her to the telephone. 'I'm standing beside you while you make the appointment. And I'm coming with you.'

Bunty obeyed. When she put down the phone, she said, 'Thank you, darling. I needed you to make me do that.'

I carried the tea-tray into the garden where the doves were busy in the trees. Coughing and talking at the same time, Bunty followed me. 'The girls are off to Cornwall with some friends. Sophie's going too and, surprise, Alexander will be joining them for a couple of days. It's all been arranged at the last minute.'

I offered Bunty the plate of scones. My hand was perfectly steady. 'Some of our strawberry jam?'

'Goodie.' But I noticed that Bunty only took one mouthful of the scone and left the rest. 'I have an idea that your Sophie has her eye on Alexander, which leaves my poor girls in the shade. Just something Sylvia hinted.'

I poured milk into her tea. 'Goodness, things have been happening in my absence.'

'"Goodness" has nothing to do with it any more, Barbara darling. With the young, I mean.' She shot me a look. 'The young . . . they're different. Love affairs, and I mean love affairs, are quite the norm. God knows what my girls are getting up to.'

'The pot needs refilling, Bunty.' I fled back into the house, leant on the rail of the Rayburn, and clenched it until my fists turned white.

Ryder returned home loaded with parcels of gin and whisky. He surged in, chucked his cap on the hall table and rifled through the post. 'Lots of bills.' He kissed me soundly on the cheek. 'No problems getting home, then?

317

Seasoned traveller.' He stepped back and quizzed me: 'Are you well? You look it. Did you enjoy yourself? Tell me everything.'

I braced myself, stowed the bottles and ran a bath for him. He called me to come and scrub his back, and I teased him about his tanned face and white chest. He splashed about, sang under his breath, and demanded a warmed towel from the airing cupboard.

We ate the lunch Mrs Storr had prepared (Tuesday: beef rissoles) and afterwards I made coffee, which we took into the conservatory. Ryder snaffled the crossword.

'The red rose is no maiden . . . nine letters. The red rose?'

'Belle Dame,' I said.

Startled, he looked up. 'Have you been practising?'

I held his gaze, cool and steady. 'Not really.'

'You must have.'

'Worried I'm catching up, darling?'

'No. Absolutely not.'

I laughed and, for a moment or two, everything was normal.

The phone rang and I answered.

'Mum?' It was Roy. 'Are you busy?'

It was unlike Roy to ring, let alone during the day. 'Is everything all right?' I asked.

'Yes.' He was a little guarded. 'I have something to tell you both. Victoria and I are getting married.'

'Good grief – I mean, congratulations! How . . . wonderful.'

'Can we come and see you? To talk over arrangements?'

'Of course, of course. Roy . . . are you quite sure?'

'Yes, I think so. No, I'm sure so. Look, I must go.'

I put the phone down and went to tell Ryder. '*Marrying* Victoria,' he said. 'Oh, God.'

'Ryder. We have to try and like her.'

We spent the rest of the afternoon discussing the development. Ryder and I were united by our mixed feelings and discussed anxiously Roy's comparative youth and whether or not Victoria might have bullied him into it.

'He's only twenty-three and not that well paid.' Ryder raised an eyebrow. 'Should we stop it before it goes further?'

'I don't see how we can interfere.'

Ryder favoured me with one of his direct looks. 'Since when has that presented a problem for you?'

'What do you mean?'

'Barbara, your cunning ability to plot while protesting innocence is one of the wonders of the modern world.'

Roy had offered to come over that evening. He was touchingly anxious to secure our approval, and Ryder and I did our best to provide it with champagne and congratulations.

Victoria looked radiant, and sported on her left hand a ring with a minute emerald, flanked by two only marginally larger diamonds. 'I took ages and ages to choose, but Roy was so understanding and patient.'

To the sharp maternal eye, Roy seemed a little shell-shocked and, at the first possible opportunity, I drew him to one side. 'Give me the information. When, where and how?'

'I hope you're pleased Mother.' He grasped my hands. 'It's such a big step, but I think it's the right one. She's a marvellous girl, and will keep me fed and watered.'

'But do you love her, really, properly?'

'Yes, I do.'

'Do you want some thoughts on marriage?'

'Yes – no.' He laughed self-consciously. 'I don't like all this emotional stuff, Mum.'

'Marriage is a bit like discovering a continent. Much of it is mapped out – you can see the coastline and mountains – but a lot of it is akin to what Christopher Columbus must have felt when he was searching for America: he knew it was there, but had no idea how to fill in the detail.' I searched my son's face but he looked bewildered. And I thought: *He* would have known what I was talking about. Then: That wasn't fair. 'Both of you have to be prepared to navigate into the unknown, and you might be surprised by what . . . by what you find.'

Roy grinned. 'Didn't know you were so poetic.' He clapped a hand on my shoulder. 'Good old Mum. But you'd be better off talking to Victoria about that sort of stuff.'

As the weeks passed, the weather grew hot. The garden shimmered in the heat, forcing Herr Schlinker to discard his jacket – he was sighted only rarely in his shirtsleeves.

The garden had never been so productive. There was a swollen quality about it – swelling vegetables, the hard acid green balls expanding into ripeness. The strawberries had cropped heavily. In the fruit cage, raspberries multiplied like stars and redcurrants dripped on their glowing trusses. Every day I dug up a fistful of tiny new potatoes, and harvested carrots and peas, which we ate with mint and butter. They tasted of earth and sweetness.

Ian and Antonia arrived to spend a night. 'So long since we've seen you.' Antonia cut through my words of greeting. 'It's ages since I talked to you.' The implication was that I had been ignoring her.

'Congratulations on Roy,' said Ian, heavily. 'Wish Sophie was in the same boat and safely accounted for.'

He went into a huddle with Ryder to discuss money, and I was left to field Antonia, who was preoccupied with the recent death of her mother: or, more specifically, the will, which had favoured Sophie, the granddaughter, over Antonia, the daughter.

'Course, I couldn't have expected anything else.' Antonia looked long-suffering and tragic. 'But I was the one who spent hours reading to Mummy and organizing her nursing care. Sophie never went near her. Or not as much as I did.'

'Antonia.' Ian turned round. 'There's no point. Your mother did as she thought best. You should be glad for Sophie.'

'If you say one more thing, I'll hit you.' Antonia's mouth tightened. 'I should be allowed to say what I feel on the subject. The truth is Sophie never really did a hand's turn, and I did, and she gets the proceeds. I needn't have bothered.'

'Oh dear,' I heard myself say. 'That's the best argument I've heard in favour of neglect for a long time.'

Ian looked shocked and Antonia glared at me. The narrow, discontented face had grown a beak, the bony shoulders wings, her summer dress feathers. She was a bird of prey, with too-bright lipstick.

'Barbara!' protested Ryder, but not without a glimmer of a smile.

Then Antonia turned the tables. 'Even if I am horrid about it, it doesn't mean I'm not *right*.'

'Although Antonia has a point, I was thankful to see the back of them,' I confided to Bunty, when we got together the following day. 'She gets more disagreeable by the month.'

'And we don't?'

We were in the fruit cage, picking away, nails and fingers purple with juice. Out of the corner of my eye, I registered Bunty's thin, stooping figure. Thank God for her. I battened freely on her warmth, her sharp, funny wit.

'Darling,' she straightened up and wiped her hands on her handkerchief, 'I thought you'd like to know that the girls are back, having had a wonderful time, brown as berries. Apparently Sophie and Alexander *did* hit it off.'

'Just a minute . . .' I reached for the final cluster of raspberries and added them to the bowl. 'There.'

'I thought you should know first.'

I turned round. 'Know what first?'

Bunty gave me a level look. 'Just filling you in on the gossip, darling.'

'Yes.' I was a little dizzy and . . . nauseous. 'Yes, just gossip.' I leant against the door to the fruit cage.

'Are you all right, Barbara?'

I managed a smile. 'Perfectly. Bending over made me dizzy.'

It was no surprise to me when Sophie rang. 'Can I come and stay? Please, it's important.'

She arrived the next day, the blue eyes dancing and shining with an emotion I hadn't seen in her before. But I recognized it at once.

'We had such a good time in Cornwall . . . such an odd place, full of ruined mines, and such folk-tales. And rain – but the sea was wonderful.'

I had prepared a cold beef and salad lunch, and she picked at it like a bird. 'Sorry, Aunt Babs, not very hungry, these days.' She drank glass after glass of water.

We took our coffee into the garden, and drowsed in the afternoon heat, not saying very much.

I knew what Sophie must be feeling – a heightened response to the birdsong, to the sway of the leaves in the trees, to the vivid splashes of red lobelia and white roses, the smooth contour of the lawn.

I knew.

Sophie roused herself. 'My parents should never have got married, should they, Aunt Babs? They never suited each other. Not like you and Uncle Ryder.'

'They may have done once. People change greatly.'

'That's what Amy and I don't like about it.' Sophie poured me a second cup of coffee. 'I think men and women should love each other on equal terms. If it doesn't work out, they should be allowed to bow out gracefully. Alexander says that was one of the things that attracted him to study Freud, because Freud believed one should be down-to-earth and objective.' She settled back in the chair. 'Actually, I think Freud said a whole lot of stupid things and I told Alexander so. He'd be better to study Jung. Freud was very unscientific.' She smiled wistfully, mischievously. 'We had lots of arguments.'

I fumbled in my pocket for a handkerchief, and pressed it to my forehead. 'It's so hot.' I gathered my wits to focus on Sophie. 'Would you have liked it if your parents had separated?'

She smoothed down her cotton skirt. 'Frankly, yes.'

I drank my coffee. It was bitter and threw my stomach into greater turmoil. Inside the house the clock struck two. Surreptitiously, I watched Sophie's beautiful face, registered her occasional staccato remark, watched her fall silent, grow dreamy, yearning, troubled.

I feel only time.

'I want to talk to you about Alexander . . .' She leant forward, drowsiness vanished. 'I'd like your advice.'

I put down my cup. 'What advice could I give you, Sophie?'

She flushed. 'If it's a bore.'

'No, no, of course not. Why don't you talk to me while I rack some apples? Herr Schlinker will never forgive me if I don't do something with the Worcesters.'

She jumped up and held out her hand. 'Come on, then.'

We crossed the lawn and went into the apple-house. It smelt musty and of old fruit, which hit the back of my throat and made me retch.

'Are you all right?' Sophie placed an anxious hand on my arm. 'Perhaps it's too hot.'

'No. It's fine.' Herr Schlinker had picked two pails' worth and I emptied them on to the grass. 'Let's grade them.'

The apples were faintly warm to the touch, proof that they should be stored at once. We worked efficiently to discard those whose skin had been roughened by disease, or by rottenness because a worm nestled in the flesh.

'Look . . .' Sophie balanced an apple on her palm. 'Perfect.'

So it was . . . with a regular shape and unblemished, a red blush suffusing the skin.

'Can I eat it?' She plunged her white, even teeth into it, and chewed. 'Delicious. A fresh ripe apple is unlike anything else.'

I continued with the sorting, using Ryder's system — small apples on the high racks, eaters at the back, cookers (which came later) in the front. The medium ones went on the middle racks, the largest at the bottom.

Sophie fetched the stepladder from the shed, and climbed up to the top racks. 'Hand 'em up.'

'Be sure they don't touch, and you must push the rack back very gently.'

She busied herself, and sang out, 'Ripeness is all.'

'About Alexander . . .' I handed her up the next load. 'What did you want to ask?'

Sophie had her back to me. 'I don't know . . . I thought I did and I wanted to ask you . . . if you approved of him. But . . . one moment there's something between us, I'm sure there is. You *know*, don't you? Then it goes . . . It's almost as if something's blocking it. Some obstacle. In Cornwall we spent a lot of time together, talking, walking, having fun. Arguing, as I said, but in a good way. He seemed to seek me out, but in the end it came to nothing.' She examined a last apple, then positioned it on the rack.

She backed down the stepladder. 'Aunt Babs, I need to ask a favour. Would you allow me to invite him over here? Then I think I could make some sense of it.'

'Is that wise?' I said involuntarily. 'Won't he think you're chasing him? Men don't like that.'

'Aunt Babs, I don't *believe* in that stuff. If a girl likes a man, she's perfectly entitled to make an overture.' She picked up an empty pail. 'It's difficult at Mrs Andrews's. There are so many people in the house, and she does patrol so. It's impossible to have a private conversation. And I *can't* invite him home.'

'Is that why you came?'

She swallowed. 'Yes.'

I got up early and boiled a ham, which I glazed and decorated with honey and cloves. I made a redcurrant fool, and the lightest sponge cake I could manage, then sandwiched it together with homemade strawberry jam.

It was still so hot, and Sophie and I laid the table under the tree with a white linen cloth and my best wine glasses.

Sophie clasped her hands. 'That's just how I wanted it,' she said. 'Like France. You know, in the paintings with long tables under trees and a big house in the background. Thank you, Aunt Babs.'

I turned away.

Alexander arrived punctually. I was upstairs when I heard the doorbell ring, the patter of Sophie's running feet, a murmured exchange, and the sound of her excited chatter as she led him into the garden.

I sat on the bed, my hands folded. The pain I was experiencing was primitive in its intensity and I had not expected it. But it was something that had to be got over, that I had to endure. And I knew I *would* endure it, then emerge the other side.

Eventually I got up, patted my hair, which was loose, and dabbed cologne on my wrists.

I was proud of myself as I walked across the lawn to Sophie and Alexander: I was perfectly in control. They did not see me at first, for they were talking hard. Alexander's eyes were fixed on her, and she had ducked her head, charmingly, trustfully. 'So you see . . .' she was saying.

Alexander registered me first. He raised his eyes . . . and our gaze locked for two, three, even five seconds, but no more. 'Barbara,' he rose to his feet, 'how are you?'

'Thank you, very well. What a lovely day.'

'I didn't know you were going to be here. I was hoping to hear about Switzerland.'

'Oh, it was lovely.' I looked at Sophie. The chatter, smiles and trust had been replaced by a horrible, frozen astonishment. 'Sophie, I came to see if you needed anything before I went out?'

She seemed to shake herself. 'Yes,' she replied. 'I mean, no.'

'You're going out?' Alexander inquired politely.

'I'm cycling over to Shalford where I'm seeing a friend who will be shocked by the bicycle. But I've rather taken to it lately. I like the exercise. Your lunch is ready. All you have to do is carry it out. Sophie?'

She turned her head to look at me. 'Thank you, Aunt Barbara,' she said. She might have been addressing a stranger.

Alexander offered to help me get the bicycle out of the shed, then wheeled it into Edgeborough Road. He leant it against the wall, brick with grey-white flint glinting in the sun, and checked the tyres. 'How are you?'

'Fine.'

'I was angry with you at first. Now I'm not, but I miss you.'

'Yes.' I grasped the handlebars. I was not at all practised in ending affairs but there was, I perceived dimly, a certain honour in trying to do it well. 'Alexander, be careful with Sophie. You mustn't treat her badly. And you must never come here again.'

I had not lied about the bicycle. I had taken to its freedoms, and I loved the way it stretched and exercised my body. It took me back to the time when I hurtled down country lanes with schoolfriends, some sandwiches, a bottle of orange squash, and a compass that didn't work.

I pedalled up Warren Road. My only conscious thought was of the fresh air, sun, and the breath bursting in my chest. At the Shalford junction I turned left and, within minutes, I was wheeling the bicycle down the overgrown lane towards the river.

There had been no rain for weeks, and the level of the river had dropped, exposing brown residues of cracked mud and rotting, pulpy vegetation. It smelt too, of the rot and brackish water.

I went and sat on the bank, and stared into the water. I remembered the sheen of Alexander's skin, the curve of his back. Inside that body, the older Alexander was beginning to emerge. One day, he would wake up and demand an egg boiled for precisely five minutes, a clean shirt, his own armchair. His movements and (probably) his thoughts would have gelled into the recognizable and (probably) the predictable. I knew because it had happened to Ryder, to Bunty . . . to me.

My head was swimming, and the heat was stifling. I stumbled upright and walked along the bank, which was slippery with dry, baked earth. Midges rose above the water and cabbage whites dipped over the rushes. In an attempt to feel normal, for my body seemed peculiarly weightless yet leaden, I swung my arms round. I walked on, the blood tingling down them and into my breasts.

When I got home, the kitchen was as I had left it. The dishcloth was folded over the tap, the floor swept. There was no remnant of lunch, no china waiting to be washed, no sign that a meal had been shared and enjoyed.

I went to find Sophie. She was sitting quietly in the shade under the tree, her hands folded in her lap.

'Sophie?'

She didn't look at me. 'I've sent him away, Aunt Barbara.'

Chapter Twenty-three: Siena

Dakota Pierce is forty-five. Four children, ranging from 7 to 18. She is president of Mothers for Dignity and Status, which is an important influence in sun-belt states with a building membership. She needs a capsule wardrobe for her frequent lecturing trips, for fronting up the organization's public face, and for entertaining at home. The keywords are: modest but elegant.

Fersen met me in the television studio, his expression more or less welcoming. 'Hi – good trip over? Great. Let's go. Technically, this one is all apple pie and rosy cheeks,' he said, 'but don't be fooled.'

'I thought a jacket and skirt, taupe linen maybe . . .'

Fersen laughed. 'You haven't got it, Siena. This "modest" means glam. And a bit of bling-bling flung in, too.'

'Ah . . .'

'Guys, we'll just run through the routine,' said Dwayne. 'Pay attention.'

The air-conditioning in the studio was going full blast, and everyone was sucking at bottles of water.

'Just a few notes, guys.' Dwayne held up his hand. 'It's great news that we're all gathered once again. Let's make it a special occasion and get these final two editions into the can.' He ran over points from previous programmes. Too much hand-waving, Siena, darling. Try to keep them out of it. Camera team: not enough focus on the clothes. If the subject cries, focus on that. *Emotion is good.* Remember the tricks – bad lighting, etc. – so that the 'before' and 'after' are clearly distinguished. *Don't be afraid of animosity.*

Dakota Pierce possessed a china-doll complexion, ankles that looked as though they might snap, and a spirit that – clearly – would do anything but. She spoke with a southern lilt and there was a steel-trap determination in her eyes.

She flipped open a capacious handbag, and sprayed her face with Evian water. 'I speak up for motherhood, which is undervalued in our society. Women have been made to feel that if they stay home with their little children they aren't much better than the family dog. We, my sisters in motherhood and I, aim to change all that. We want dignity for the role, and recognition for our hard work.'

Fersen and Dakota were not destined to be natural allies and Dakota addressed any remarks intended for him through me.

'Do you have children?' she asked. 'I thought not. Well, as the representative of the family . . .' she gave a little laugh '. . . the foundation stone of our society, after all, I have to be careful not to project the wrong image.'

Fersen made the mistake of insisting (through me) that Dakota put on skin-tight trousers with a scoop-necked top. Result: point-blank refusal. 'I don't think you get it,' Dakota told the members of the team, who had been drawn – flies and moths – to the epicentre of this argument. 'I have a responsibility not to present women as sex objects.'

I segued into action. 'Dakota, why don't we try the top with this skirt?' I produced a DKNY jersey number. 'Oh, *yes!*' she said, and turned her back on Fersen.

Fersen and I exchanged looks. *You win some, you lose some.*

I glanced at my watch. Three o'clock. Back home, Charlie would have struggled to work through – what? A late-summer city day, possibly damp, with English rain, a hint of old pollen, and ripening berries on dusty bushes? Was today a court day? If so, he would have robed up, stuck on his wig, picked up his papers and reminded himself: *I'm not here to take a view on a client – it doesn't matter what he or she might have done. I'm here to be their advocate, not their judge.*

What else did Charlie say? *If there's wickedness, and I know there is because I see it, it must follow that there is goodness and love.*

'Siena, could we have your attention?' Dwayne was annoyed.

Equally annoyed with myself, for I was usually one hundred per cent on the case, I snapped to attention.

'OK.' I surveyed Dakota. Around five foot ten, size sixteen on top, fourteen hips. Long legs, which needed emphasis. Bad posture, stomach needed to be brought under control.

It would take all my skill, but I could bring out her beauty. Out must go the shapeless round-necked jumper and too-formal suit (dated). Substitute knee-length skirt, belted chiffon jacket and peep-toe court shoes.

Slowly, slowly, a glamorous woman took shape. The statue inside the block of marble. The woman inside the mother. The mother as part of the woman.

At nine o'clock that night I was driven back to the hotel and deposited at the entrance. It was just beyond dusk, and the city was humming, growing brighter.

The old Siena would have rushed up to her room, showered, thrown on trousers and a skinny top and gone out into the hum and bustle of the night. Instead I lingered on the sidewalk, craning up at the overhead skyscraper vista, tension tightening my shoulders and neck.

When I reached my room, the bedspread had been pulled back and a chocolate placed on the pillow. The bowl of fruit on the table had been replenished and two bottles of mineral water stood on the tray. Fresh white towels hung in the bathroom, more expensive toiletries, and fresh soap in the dish on the marble bath.

All that a girl could wish for.

Earlier that day I put a call through to Charlie. His mobile was switched off. I rang the clerk in his chambers. 'He's not here,' Michael answered, 'but we're expecting him.' The phone in the flat rang and rang, a desolate noise. An hour later, I'd tried it again. Nothing.

I ordered Caesar salad from Room Service, climbed into bed and chose a video. 'We will not mention the title on your bill,' was the reassuring message on the screen – in case I had plumped for pornography – and I watched a romantic comedy with a sentimental ending without much interest. Didn't stop me crying, though.

At three o'clock I rang Charlie. No go.

At four, I rang Charlie. No answer, nothing.

Sleep? Difficult, oh, so difficult . . . I tossed and turned and found myself, in a dream, at the picnic in the photograph.

The tartan rug was worn and scratchy on my bare thighs, the breeze nipped sharply at exposed flesh, and the taste of margarine in the sandwich was vivid. (God knows why my mother used margarine.) Even in the dream, I knew I hated being a child.

Richard and I were whispering to each other. We were planning our latest campaign to restore the Stuarts, and we discussed in great detail the problem of wounds and fevers.

Our parents were sitting on either side of the rug. They each grasped a plastic mug with a tiny nip of sherry in it. The alcohol had brought a flush to my mother's cheek. They neither spoke to nor looked at each other. Instead they watched us. An amused smile softened my father's normally grim countenance and my mother's eyes were indulgent. 'Look at you both,' she said. 'Quite mad.'

It was only a moment, the exact sequence and context forgotten, yet my subconscious had seized it, stored it and, for whatever reason, trotted out a replay.

I woke up. Dreams are so over, Ingrid had informed me at one of her consultations. Evaluation of the *here and now* was what counted.

OK, Ingrid. Here it is. No money to speak of, unhappy with each other, not much to anticipate in old age . . . my parents were not the most settled or the happiest of people. Yet they had known that the point of having children was what they could bring to the task: what they could give us.

Did this make sense? Charlie would have a view, and I wanted to discuss it with him. Out of habit, I reached for the phone but did not pick it up. I knew, without being told, that he had decided to take a break. It was radio silence.

Before I had left for New York I cornered Charlie. I had switched off the phones and the radio, and we were sealed inside the beautiful, airy flat. 'I can't go to New York like this.'

He looked at me, slightly sad, a little mocking, not himself. 'Is that you speaking, or Ingrid?'

'Stop it.' I sat him down on the sofa. 'Charlie, I want more than anything to make you happy.'

He softened. 'And I you, Siena, truly.' I took his hand, and held it. After a moment, his fingers closed over mine. 'OK,' he said. 'My fault. I've been too busy to think.'

'Well, I've been thinking.' I closed my eyes. 'You know I'm "thirty-five, which is twenty-five really".' Charlie snorted. 'Charlie, the "twenty-five really" is a game we play. Or I play, because it might be too late. What if we try and nothing happens? And you'll blame me because it's likely to be me. Biology again. You won't put it like that because that's not you. But you'll think it. And I'm not sure I could cope.'

He looked down at our hands and removed his. 'Isn't it worth the risk?'

'You took a risk with Jackie Woodruff. To believe in her, I mean, above and beyond what was required. And see how miserable it made you.'

'I was doing my job.'

'Were you, Charlie? Darling Charlie. Are you absolutely sure you weren't convinced a woman couldn't murder her baby because – because we're in the middle of this battle?'

He started to his feet. 'Below the belt, Siena.' He began to pace the room. Then he swung round to face me. 'Siena. You can have as many dresses, pairs of shoes, dinners in restaurants as you want. And I wish you well of them. But I don't want them any more. From being a bloody fool with Cimmie, I've moved on.' At the mention of her name, I felt a freezing chill go through me. 'Maybe Jackie Woodruff did kill her baby. I don't know. But I gave it my best shot because if there's wickedness, it follows there are also sweetness, goodness and love. And because I know so much about the former, I know the latter is doubly important.' He turned back to look out of the window. 'OK. You were right in one thing. I made a mistake,' he admitted, slowly and painfully. 'I got too involved.'

I hid my face in my hands. 'That's what I'm so frightened of. If it goes wrong. If I can't cope.' What happens if sweetness, goodness and love are not on tap? And if one is blundering around, with a baby, desperate to locate them? What happens then?

Answer: Jackie Woodruff happens.

'I don't know, Charlie,' I cried. 'I don't know what to do.'

'If you're not willing to jump,' Charlie said, 'I can't help you, Siena.' He added bitterly, 'Jackie Woodruff thought I was a fool. And I am.'

*

336

My eyes were burning and my feet had lead soles attached to them as I stepped into the car, which proceeded to fight its way downtown to the studio. A day of negotiation, retakes, private little feuds lay ahead – a switchback of expectation and taut nerves.

Siena Grant, I thought, this is what you *wanted*.

If it was possible, Dakota Pierce looked even fresher-faced than she had the previous day. 'It's been great. The hotel was mobbed with calls when word got out I was in town. I hesitated before taking them – this is my private life. Then I talked to God and He told me that what is private is also public.'

I handed Dakota a black cocktail dress with a sweetheart neckline and wide skirt. 'How fifties! How darling, Siena! I love it. I've got three evening engagements next week alone, and it'll do perfectly.'

'You must get tired.'

Dakota stared at me, amazed. 'Tired? But I'm in the service of motherhood and the family. There's no time to get tired.' She winked at me. 'I've been put on this earth and entrusted with the precious task of bringing the message. Tired doesn't come into it.'

At lunchtime I escaped from the studio and headed in the direction of Battery Park. I sat on a bench as close to the water as possible, ate a hot dog (disgusting, but nice) and drank a smoothie. I consulted my guidebook. 'Now roofless, Castle Clinton was built to protect Manhattan from the British . . .'

The sun danced over the channel, and a grey heat haze loured over the city. The bins were overflowing with rubbish, and the gulls swooped and foraged in it.

The ferry came in with a screech and a wash of white water. I glanced at my watch. *Where was Charlie? What was he doing?*

It was time to dress Dakota Pierce and, with camera and lights, achieve the transformation. I leant over to drop my rubbish into the bin, and my foot nudged the bags stacked round it. One split, and out rolled three apples, badly bruised, brown-fleshed, decayed. They had been there for a while: insects crawled over them, and drunken wasps feasted on the sweet, oozing juice.

These were the city windfalls, the urban equivalent of the apples that, in Bill's orchard, dropped too early and rotted in the long grasses under the trees. 'Bit like life,' Bill had joked. 'Wasted opportunities, missed chances. Bruised flesh.'

The smell of the apples pricked my nose. Sweet and sour, heated and fermented. I closed my eyes and pictured piles of windfalls, oozing a substance I could only call despair.

'You walked,' exclaimed Fersen, when I made it back into the studio. 'You *walked*? Where was the car?'

'I'm not doing entourage today,' I said.

'More fool you,' said Fersen.

That made two of us, Charlie and me.

In the middle of (my) night, I rang Manda. 'Just checking up on you.'

'That's nice, darling. Nobody does that any more.'

'Any big excitements at work?'

She named a couple of authors of whom I'd never heard, which I know disappointed her. 'They're very good,' she said accusingly. 'You're such a cultural desert, Siena. You *must* read them. Anyway, what about you? If you're ringing little old me, you're feeling homesick.'

'Got it.'

'Who would have thought it?' She giggled. 'Somehow I must summon the energy to sympathize with my fabulously successful best friend who's having a jolly in New York.'

I considered putting down the phone. 'Don't, Manda.'

'Sweetie,' she picked up my distress and, instantly, she was on the case, 'I didn't mean that. Shoot.'

'I'm feeling a bit odd about everything. I can't locate Charlie, and he's fed up with me. The baby issue. I can't make up my mind, and I'm mucking him about.'

Manda tsked. 'You must choose,' she said. 'That's all I can offer.'

'It ain't much.'

'That's the way it is, Siena. Darling Siena. If it's any comfort, peace comes with making a choice. And I've never regretted mine.'

The programmes were in the can. Dwayne declared himself pleased, and the team packed up ready for dispersal.

Fersen was busy on his mobile, finalizing his next assignment. 'Oh, my total God,' he said, making hand signals at me to indicate the speaker was a complete loser. 'The nightmare . . .'

Dakota cast him a look of intense dislike. I handed her some notes I had written for her.

Wide-legged trousers to detract attention from broad upper body, jackets to slim down chunkiness, wrap-around cardigan feminizes too-square torso.

She pressed her card into my hand. 'This has been such a pleasure, Siena.' She was wearing the red Armani dress with a white jacket that we had picked out. She gave herself a once-over in the studio mirror. 'The message hasn't changed, but the messenger looks a great deal better.'

'That's good.'

'Well, yes and no,' she said. 'Let's not get things out of proportion. A lot of my mothers would like to get their hands on you. If ever you're over in Virginia, you must call me.' She pressed a kiss on my cheek and whirled away.

'Apple pie?' I asked Fersen.

'Apple pie with fangs.'

I held out my hand. 'It's been good working with you.'

'Hey,' he said. 'You'll be coming back. I have good vibes about the series.'

'Here's hoping, Fersen. Please call me if you're ever in London.'

He leant forward and kissed me. But it was not the mwah-mwah that I had grown used to: it was a proper kiss on the cheek.

That pleased me.

I put on a pair of sneakers and headed back uptown

through the heat. Why do this, Siena? Answer: I want the exercise, and to tire myself out. I had twenty-four hours before my flight home – the margin of error built into the filming schedules – and now that I was released from Trimester and about to go home, I felt a rush of affection for the hot city streets.

Washington Square was practically deserted, except for a couple of pitiful-looking stray cats that lay outstretched in the shade. The heat had bleached and dried anything green to brittle brown.

I passed on through. Up Fifth Avenue. My back drenched with sweat, my feet slipping inside the sneakers. As I walked, my body took on a different rhythm. I felt every pulsebeat, every rush of blood through heart, lungs and groin. My body appeared to be shifting in focus, softening, becoming weightier – as if it was anticipating, or waiting for, some new stirring.

I plodded on.

There was no message for me at the hotel.

What could I do?

Take in a movie? Phone Lola and Bill? Sleep?

I had a long, cold shower, sat down at the desk in my room, shuffled through my papers and checked my diary for when I got home. Reshape book schedule. Email India. Assemble final material for book from case notes: Lucy Thwaite. Should I choose the photograph at the moment when she had turned to say something to me? For a couple of seconds she had looked pretty and happy, taken out of herself. Or should I go with the tired, unhappy, real Lucy? Which Marybelle Hammond? The classy, successful businesswoman? Or the woman who confessed, 'I don't have friends'?

What was my business exactly? To peddle dreams, or put another gloss on existence because that was the most anyone could do?

Charlie, I might say to him, it's true that I dress up appearances, and sometimes it helps with sadness and despair, but you do the same. (What's more, you dress up to dress it up.) And I know he would answer: Jackie Woodruff taught me we need more.

Later, I hung up my clothes. I did a few stomach crunches on the floor. I creamed and patted my face. I went into the bathroom, hovered in the doorway, went out.

Time to sleep. To renew the skin, the energy, the spirit.

I went back into the bathroom, stretched out a hand to take up my packet of pills.

Left them.

Again I dreamed vividly, *so* vividly it hurt. I was trying on a pair of trousers that were far too small and a great, black panic snapped its jaws. Then I was standing in front of a mirror beside Lucy Thwaite and I was as plump as she was. I stared hard at the unfamiliar me, trying to piece together the clues for – apparently – I had become as marked and battered by children as she. This metamorphosis was so convincing that, racked by disgust and worry, I hid my face in my hands and then ... I felt a strange, sweet explosion of what I could only explain as joy.

I woke.

The digital clock said 5.30 a.m. (10.30 a.m., UK time, Charlie time). The roar of the city was already gearing up. Cars. Lorries. People. Heat.

I reached for the phone. I rang the flat, the chambers, the mobile. Nothing.

I tried not to cry, because crying was disastrous for the lines around the eyes. Diane de Poitiers had dictated that a woman should neither laugh nor cry for that reason, and she was one of the most beautiful women of her age (and the best dressed). Still, following that line of logic, no woman could ever display any emotion.

So there I lay: Siena Grant, successful, good at her job, high earner – with her English-now-American eyebrows – leaking tears, emotion and fear in equal measure.

Chapter Twenty-four: Barbara

'Why did you send Alexander away?'

'We quarrelled, Aunt Barbara. Does that surprise you?'

Sophie's utter stillness was unnerving and, I think, new to her repertoire. The scene looked so normal: pretty garden, lunch table, two women dressed in bright summer frocks. But it wasn't, and of the many possible indictments in this affair between Alexander and me, the count of having summoned into Sophie's blue eyes a darkness and guile that had been foreign to her was – almost – the greatest.

'Sophie, I'm so sorry. You'll be disappointed.' I gestured to the table on which sat the folded napkins, the polished glasses and the untouched food.

Sophie leant towards me. 'Yes, it is disappointing,' she said flatly. 'Because we quarrelled about you.'

It was perfectly in keeping that, once a suspicion had rooted, Sophie voiced it. It was her nature, and in her adopted philosophy. Speak the truth. Be open. She did not, as yet, value silence.

'I saw the look you gave each other and I accused him of . . . liking you, and of you . . . liking him back. It seemed the explanation for . . . the strange . . . whatever it is – I can't put my finger on.' She shrugged. 'He said, of course he liked you but if I was implying anything else I was talking rubbish.'

'I see.'

'I'm not a fool, Aunt Barbara. I can tell when a man and woman have secrets between them. Looking back, it makes sense of a lot of things. Little remarks. The way he talks about you.'

I heard all this from a distance and I spoke calmly. 'Be careful what you say, Sophie. You could do a lot of damage.'

She struck out wildly: 'But it's *true*, isn't it?'

'Because I know you're upset, I will overlook that remark.' For something to do, I gathered up the glasses. 'As we get older, things and situations appear less and less straightforward. I think you will find that too – and, yes, I am fond of Alexander. I find him challenging and interesting. And attractive.'

Sophie picked up one of the napkins, and plucked at the rolled hem. 'If it's untrue, why haven't you thrown me out? I've just accused you of – of God knows what.'

I stood over her. 'Because I love you, Sophie. I always have, and I always will.' This was the one honest statement I could permit myself. 'You sound like Amy sometimes, Sophie, and you get things as muddled.'

Sophie was struggling between suspicion and her longing to think the best. 'Do you want to know the joke, Aunt Barbara? Alexander was always preaching honesty and openness. We both absolutely agreed on that. When I asked him, he said he was interested in me and he was free.' She paused. 'But I'm sure he lied to me. I'm sure of it.'

'Is it the lying you are worried about or that Alexander may have been involved with someone?'

'How do I know?' she spat.

'Sophie, I don't know what you and Alexander have between you, but if you feel as you do, it can't be negligible and you must go and sort it out.'

Sophie pressed her fingers to her mouth. 'I thought he agreed that we were perfectly matched. Or he was beginning to. In Cornwall . . . it was . . . it was going to be all right. Apart from . . .' She threw down the napkin. 'I slept with him, you know. Wasn't that proof enough that I loved him?'

'Ah,' I said. 'That was brave. And a risk. You don't know each other very well.'

'I liked it,' she said. 'It was strange, but wonderful and . . . puzzling.'

I wanted to cry out: *I know that.* It was impossible to sit down, take Sophie's hands in mine and talk to her as I longed to do – about the hunger and delight, the discovery, the joy in the senses and the curious unexpected torments. Impossible.

I did what I could.

'Sophie, you say you advocate sexual freedom, and not being possessive, and you distrust convention.' She looked away but I pressed on: 'It's so different from how I was brought up . . . it would have been unthinkable. But I respect those differences. And, surely, if you adopt those principles, you must expect both you and Alexander to have adventures. You have to accept what happens. And if you've fallen in love with him – and I can see why you might have done . . . He is quite . . . unusual –'

Instantly Sophie stiffened. 'So I'm right.' Her customary

346

sweetness of expression had vanished, replaced by the hard, accusing look. 'He does like you.' She peered at me. 'And you like him, whatever you say.' She ticked off the points on her finger. 'The classic situation. Older woman, younger man. Younger woman made to look stupid and out of place.' There was a long pause. 'I always *believed* in you, Aunt Barbara. You were a sort of . . . rock in my life. My mother, really. I was so happy that Uncle Ryder had you. And everything in this house was so settled and ordered and lovely. But it wasn't, was it?'

'You are presuming to know what goes on between your uncle and myself?' My voice was ice cold.

She flushed angrily. 'You were supposed to hold things together.'

'As a point of theoretical interest why am I not allowed your kind of freedoms – if I wanted them?'

'Because,' she beat her hand on her thigh, 'because . . . Oh Alexander . . .' Her hand clenched into a fist, and I flinched at the note of hurt and longing, almost savage, almost feral.

'Sophie, if you want Alexander you must go and talk to him.'

Sophie sprang to her feet. 'I could tell Uncle Ryder.'

'And what on *earth* would you tell him? That you have this feeling? This idea? You do not have one shred of evidence *and* you have insulted me. How do you think you would deal with his reaction?'

She swirled round, and the breath seemed to collapse out of her. 'Am I wrong? Have I got this badly, unspeakably wrong?'

347

Lying is quite an art, and I was a good, rapid scholar. 'Yes, you have. Very, very wrong. And now you must say you're sorry.'

'I wish I could believe you.'

'Well, you must,' I said, 'and I will do my best to forget this conversation. Now, go and find Alexander, talk it through and see what happens. And it is best that you don't come here for a while.'

'Not come *here*?' Sophie looked ashen. 'Yes, you're right. I'll go and pack.'

She threw down the napkin, and walked away across the lawn and into the house. I picked up the tray, then put it down because my hands were shaking too much. I tried again and succeeded in carrying the plates of uneaten food into the house.

I was putting away the glasses when Sophie reappeared in the doorway. She had put on a cardigan, and scraped her hair back into a ponytail. Her eyes were red, her lips swollen, and there was desolation, and grief, reflected in the way she held herself.

'Goodbye,' she said. 'No, don't see me off. I shall be fine.'

'Your case is heavy. I'll give you a lift to the station.'

She warded me off with her hand. 'No, don't.'

'Sophie?'

She gave a strangled laugh. 'I wanted to be like you once, but I'm not sure any longer.'

There was nothing I could do to prevent my sharp intake of breath. Sophie heard it and absorbed it. Then, she smoothed her skirt and, unbelievably, a knowing smile curved the corner of her lips for she knew she had dealt me a wound.

'Still, you are so much older than I am, Aunt Barbara . . .' She left the rest unsaid.

I had to make sure that Sophie went away with my anger ringing in her ears. 'How dare you?' I blazed. 'If you want to be an adult, behave like one, Sophie. How dare you put on to me your own failings and problems with Alexander? Go and ask him if you like, get him to explain the theory. It is the most basic form of displacement, and a refusal to acknowledge that you have not dealt with a situation.'

Tears began to run down her face. 'If this is what falling in love is about, I don't want it.'

In not being allowed to wipe away those tears lay a great punishment. For I longed to draw her close and soothe and stroke and kiss her into calm.

She was weeping properly now, with little gasps and wails. 'It's full of deceit and pretence. I imagined it would be so beautiful, so happy. So straightforward. But it isn't, is it?'

My reply was the felt, experienced, pared-to-the-bone truth. 'No, it isn't.'

I kept my promise and accompanied Bunty to see Dr O'Donnell and sat patiently in the waiting room. Eventually he ushered her out of the surgery. Bunty looked defiant, but relieved. Dr O'Donnell looked stern. 'Repeat after me,' he said, 'in front of Mrs Beeching. I am giving up cigarettes as from today.'

349

Bunty's gaze slid between Dr O'Donnell and me. 'It's only a chest infection that won't budge,' she said. 'You said it's all right.'

'You've been lucky so far,' Dr O'Donnell pointed out. 'But your lungs are not in good fettle and they need a break. If you don't give up, I must ask you to find another doctor.'

Bunty bridled and fiddled with her handbag. 'You don't know what you're asking.'

Dr O'Donnell folded his arms.

'Fine.' Bunty threw in the towel, and I breathed a sigh of relief. 'I'm giving up cigarettes.'

A couple of weeks later, still troubled by certain symptoms, I went to consult Dr O'Donnell myself. He hummed and hawed, prodded and asked pertinent, embarrassing questions, which I answered as best I could. Yes, I had been abroad. Yes, my stomach had played up and had not settled since I had returned.

Eventually he said, 'We'll have to see, Mrs Beeching. It's probably some foreign bug or other making free with your stomach. But it is possible you're having a baby. Come back and see me next week.'

I closed my eyes, and leant back in the chair. 'You don't mean it?'

'Well, yes, I do. I know it's a shock.'

'Yes, it's a terrible shock,' I whispered.

'Well, then?' Dr O'Donnell waited.

'Do I have to have it?'

An expression of revulsion spread across his features. 'Mrs Beeching, I did not hear that. And not only did I not hear it, but I never want to hear it again.'

The doctor's face wavered across my vision.

'I never imagined . . . I thought all that sort of thing was over.'

Dr O'Donnell frowned. 'Come,' he admonished me. 'Married women do have babies. Even at forty-two.'

'Would you mind if I sat in the waiting room for a little while?' I asked. 'I feel a bit faint.'

He looked more sympathetic. 'If I had a penny for every time it happened to a woman of your age, Mrs Beeching, I'd be a rich man.'

Afterwards, I met Bunty for coffee in Fuller's tea-shop. The weather was still glorious, but she was dressed in her autumn tweed suit, green mixed with purple, which was religiously exhumed, whatever the weather, in September every year. 'Why haven't you rung me?' she demanded.

'I've been busy.'

'Now, why do I think you're not telling me something?'

To deflect Bunty, I diverted her with the latest family news. Roy and Victoria had settled on a date in December for their wedding and I was being inundated with plans by Victoria and her mother.

'Do you like Victoria?' Bunty wanted to know. She reached over and snaffled a piece of walnut cake. 'Can't stop eating since I've given up. It's ghastly.'

I had gone off coffee and pushed away my cup. 'I'm getting used to her. Did I tell you that Amy has changed jobs? She's been promoted into administration and has moved into a flat with an old schoolfriend. She seems much happier. Her studies begin in a couple of weeks.

She rang up the other day and wanted to know how to clean an oven.'

We discussed daughters and weddings, and the right kind of hat for the mother of the groom. Eventually Bunty dropped into the conversation, 'I've decided not to take lodgers any longer. They're more trouble than they're worth. I'm getting too old and tired to make breakfasts and cope with sheets and linen. I told Peter we'd just have to manage.'

'So no more . . . Alexanders?' It was difficult to articulate his name.

Bunty reached over for the coffee-pot, and poured herself a second cup. 'That cake was delicious. Alexander's going back to Switzerland. To study. He's off at the end of the month.' She paused. 'Jolly good thing, too, if you ask me. He was playing havoc with all the girls.'

There was a pause. Bunty clinked her spoon against the cup. 'Sorry, darling, I know it's irritating, but I have to fiddle with something . . . Barbara, you're still not telling me something. Own up.'

What could I tell Bunty? All manner of things. The sadness was that if I told her about Alexander everything would change but, equally, if I didn't tell her everything would change too.

'Go on,' she urged.

Sharp, nosy, lovely Bunty. 'I think I may be pregnant.'

'Oh, my God, Barbara. How simply awful.'

I dreamt of Alexander boarding a train in Paris, laden with suitcases and a bag of textbooks. He was dressed in his corduroy trousers and tweed jacket, and was hot from the heaving of bags and the urgency of changing stations and trains. But he was not bothered by trivial inconveniences. I knew this for, in the dream, I could see straight into his head. He was thinking of his work . . . of how he could best forward the boundaries of his understanding and experience. He was telling himself not to be lazy in pursuing these ambitions, not to be deterred by timidity or lethargy. He was also thinking of lovemaking, and the boundaries broken and imposed by feeling and desire, and of how love embraces many subtleties.

I hovered over him in the dream. 'I so admire you,' I told him. 'I approve of what you want to do, what you want to be, and I think some of it has rubbed off on me.' And I watched him for a long time, to the last second of my unconsciousness, in order to savour his beauty, energy and determination.

I woke and, downstairs, the clock was chiming. My stomach churned, and I had an overwhelming desire to fill it with sweet, starchy food.

'Oh, my God,' said Bunty. 'How simply awful.'

She was right.

The doorbell rang when I was in the garden, sweeping up the windfall apples. A substantial number had already rotted, and the wasps were having a field day.

Mrs Storr answered the door and ushered the visitor into the garden.

'Barbara?'

I placed my hand on the small of my back, which ached,

and eased myself upright. Alexander was walking towards me with an outstretched hand. He looked lean and fit but he had also filled out (Bunty's meals?), and had lost that diffident, bookish, vulnerable air.

'I've come to say goodbye.'

'Bunty told me you were leaving.' I scanned his face. 'You're going to Switzerland.'

'I've enrolled at the clinic in Zurich for a two-year course. There's so much going on over there, and I want to progress and work on recent developments.'

'Does that mean you're dismissing Freud?'

'Not entirely, but I need to study his work in a different context. I've already discarded one or two of his ideas.'

'Yes. Yes, I think you have.'

'Barbara . . .'

'Don't look at me like that.'

'How am I looking at you?'

'Wrongly.'

'All right.' Alexander fixed his gaze on the ground. 'I wanted to say that I don't regret anything. That I'm sorry if you've been hurt or worried or compromised.'

I folded my hands across my stomach. 'I'll be all right,' I promised.

We drifted back across the lawn towards the house. Alexander cleared his throat. 'Sophie told me about your conversation, and about her suspicions . . . It was difficult, I did my best to calm her down, but I feel badly that she's so upset and embarrassed for something that's not her fault. I shouldn't have responded to her invitation . . . quite yet. It wasn't as easy as I thought. And I feel rotten that I couldn't be open and honest. But there wasn't any choice.' He stopped and took my hand. 'In a couple of months, when everything has settled down, Sophie will come out and visit me. Maybe something will come of it. I don't know yet.'

'Alexander, you must promise me not to hurt Sophie. If you don't think it will be . . . it will work.'

His grasp tightened. '*Have* I hurt you, Barbara? I wouldn't have done that for anything. Please say you're well and fine.'

I looked up into the countenance in which I had taken such delight, glimpsed infinite, and snakelike, convolutions of mourning and loss. Begun in a Swiss hotel, the process of separation was almost complete. Seconds passed and, finally, I said, 'I'm well.'

'I can't bear it when *you* look at me like that.'

'We were talking about Sophie. Promise me.'

Alexander released my hand. 'She says she can never live up to you. And she's frightened she can never make it up with you.'

The sun was warm on my skin, my hair felt soft, heavy and shiny. 'Don't get too wrapped up in your work.'

He nodded. 'I worry that I took advantage of you, Barbara.'

That was difficult to stomach. 'What I did with you was of my own free will. I won't have *that* taken away. Now, you must go.'

I watched him walk away across the lawn, turn right under the trellis arch and disappear down the drive. I made no move to follow him.

I returned to the windfalls. The wheelbarrow was heavy and I was out of breath by the time I had manipulated it to the compost heap and begun shovelling.

A smell of decay and must, not unpleasant, rose from the compost heap. Green, yellow and brown, the apples lay on the top, ready for the decaying process to get to work – turning them first to pulp, then to the moist, velvet, friable compost that the garden needed to resurrect itself in the new year.

After a while, I turned my back on the golden afternoon, and returned to the dim, cooling house.

Ryder returned at the end of the week, tired and tetchy. In Lagos, he had been struck down with a stomach bug, and the hotel's air-conditioning had failed. The flight back had been delayed by twelve hours.

'God, I'm weary, Barbara.'

I had ensured that the water was hot, and I made him take a long bath. Then I served him supper of chicken and beans from the garden, then plum crumble with homemade custard.

Afterwards I took the coffee into the garden. It was just warm enough and we sat together in the darkness, listening to the night sounds.

'Ryder, I have something to tell you.'

'What?' He sounded drowsy.

'I think I'm pregnant.'

'Good God!' He shot upright in the chair. 'When?'

'April . . . I think. The dates are a bit hazy, but I think April.'

'So, Switzerland? We should have been more careful.'

'Dr O'Donnell said that it's not unknown for women of my age to have a surprise pregnancy. The body begins to be a bit irregular and unpredictable, and mistakes are made. I'm sorry for the shock.'

He put down his coffee cup. 'It is a shock, Babs, but I'm pleased. Perhaps we'll have another son.'

He got up, crouched beside me and seized my hands. 'I'd better get you a glass of hot milk.'

'It might put paid to your plans,' I pointed out, 'for the new business.'

'I don't see why it should. You'll be less on board, but there are plenty of others who could come in on it.'

I could not help it, but I had to disentangle my hands from Ryder's – I could not bear to touch him. Not yet, not quite yet. 'Of course, there's a chance I'll miscarry. Like before. I must warn you that Dr O'Donnell said older mothers do have problems.'

'No sitting around in the chill, then.' Ryder straightened and pulled me gently to my feet. 'Go to bed and I'll bring the milk up.'

I took the stairs slowly, each step leaden with questions and the weight imposed by the necessity of silence. I would never know whose baby it was, and the not knowing was part of my sentence. In all the years to come, I must bear the unknowing. I must close my lips, seal up my thoughts, know that the unknowing would stretch indefinitely. Sometimes it would be bearable; at others it would try to break me.

I sat at the dressing-table and gave my hair its customary

hundred strokes. Ryder appeared with a glass of hot milk on a tray. 'Into bed, darling.'

He tucked me in and handed me the milk. 'Thank you.' I had never liked hot milk, but for his sake I made myself drink it.

The autumn crept on and the days grew shorter and colder, the shadows longer.

Herr Schlinker was putting the garden to bed: digging, weeding, pruning, making bonfires. Reluctantly, I cleaned and oiled Amy's bicycle, put it back into the shed and closed the door on it. I would not be riding it for a long time. I would not be free to ride down a road, with the wind in my hair, and my muscles straining. Not for a long, long time.

In the evenings, I lit the fire, and when Ryder was home, both of us read. I had embarked on Freud's *The Psychology of Love* and earmarked *Studies in Hysteria*, which had been reserved for me at the library.

The bridge parties had begun again, and I attended as many as possible. But pregnancy had softened my brain: I was too busy calculating what was going on behind the faces of the players to keep tally of the fall of the cards.

'Goodness,' said Bunty, after one session at which I had lost spectacularly. 'How are the mighty fallen.'

Every day I woke and reiterated my article of faith: I will master myself.

I had a baby to think of, and as the weeks went on, it became clearer and surer in my mind and in my body. Nothing was more important. And I had years of a woman's experience on which to call – and I would use those skills, my knowledge, my *interesting* mind, to cradle, nurture and protect my family.

Yet sometimes, when I threw open a window to watch the last rays of the sun, and caught a flock of birds wheeling south, I felt pain and misery creep through me and I longed for the comfort of laying down my secret . . . I longed for the freedom to get up and leave behind the mistakes, to go somewhere else. I wanted the relief of knowing.

But I couldn't have it.

Chapter Twenty-five: Barbara

May, 1943

Ryder came home unexpectedly. He walked up the front path of the rented house by the airfield and into the kitchen, where I was trying to make a Woolton pie for supper. Disgusting war food.

All day the Spitfires had come and gone, and the traffic to and from the airfield ferried men and women in blue uniforms. There was a big show on somewhere. I heard the Spits' engines leap into life, saw the clouds of smoke and the flicker of flame. *The aircraft comes alive*, Ryder had told me, *as if it's straining to get into the air.*

Soon after, there was the throaty growl of the Merlin engines, and the planes flung themselves up into the air.

The wives and girlfriends stood in their gardens and gazed into an innocent-looking sky. Good luck, Johnny, good luck, Robin . . . Neil, Jacko and Tommy . . . Please come back, all of you.

God knows where they were going. *Into battle over the sea? Over the London docks? Sky full of aeroplanes. Junkers and Heinkels diving and sweeping. 109s with guns blazing, and our boys fighting for height and surprise. Break formation. Enemy up your chuff. Turn hard to starboard. A Hurricane dives to earth with a devil's forked tail of black smoke. A Heinkel screams to its death.*

Now, in the jittery interim, the women were waiting and I busied myself with the usual tasks.

'Barbara . . .'

Wooden spoon in hand, I whirled round. 'Ryder, darling, I didn't hear you come back.' He was pale and shaky. The spoon dropped to the floor. 'What is it? Has something awful happened?'

'I'm going to be sick,' he said, and dashed for the outside privy. Five minutes later he returned. 'Sorry about that.'

I wiped his face with a damp towel and checked him over. Flying kit damp from perspiration, a faint smell of vomit, pale, sweating, but no wounds. 'How many lost?'

'Ken and Tim. We think.'

'I'm so sorry.' Ken was twenty-one, and Tim just nineteen. Babies, both.

'I saw them go down. Ken's parachute didn't open. Poor wretch.'

Ryder turned on his heel and went into the other room. I heard the clink of the whisky bottle and a glass. I shoved the pie into the oven and joined him. Ryder was looking out of the window, swirling the whisky in the glass.

'You're not telling me everything.'

He rubbed at a smudge. 'I've been taken off ops. For the foreseeable future.' He gave a harsh, wry laugh. 'For my own good.'

I struggled hard not to show my relief.

'Go on, say it, then, Barbara.'

'No, I won't.'

'But you feel it. You're glad. You're *bloody* glad. You can't wait to have me at home, running about like a tame dog.'

The unfairness of the accusation was hurtful, but I knew that he was lashing out at the easy target.

He examined his whisky. 'Isn't that what all the women think?'

'Of course they do. What do you expect? Most of them don't complain. And don't say anything.'

Ryder said hopelessly, 'I don't know what I'll do if I can't fly.'

The switch in emphasis and tone was as frightening as his invective. I touched his sleeve gingerly. 'After a few weeks' rest, they'll put you back on. You need to do nothing for a while, Ryder, you know you do. We'll go to your parents'. Walk. Sleep. Eat properly.'

He shrugged. 'I don't know.' He drank some whisky, then more. 'Can't help feeling I've let the squadron down.'

I cast around for something, anything, to help him. 'The regulations say you can only do so many ops in a row. Why do you think that is? Because they realize you wear out. Fighter pilots wear out. No one can stand it for too long.'

But Ryder wasn't listening. 'I should try and get round it.'

'No.' I touched his cheek.

He jerked away. 'Don't.'

Suddenly I was angry. 'Do you want to die? Do you want to leave me and the children?'

Eventually Ryder stirred himself. 'I'd better go back

and clear out my locker so some other lucky bastard can have it. Then I'd better show myself for a last pint in the mess, and they can jeer at the finished, over-the-hill bastard that I am.'

Occasionally the wives discussed what to do with broken men who came home. We weren't very good at it. 'Ryder, have courage. Darling, it may be only for a few weeks, and if you concentrate on getting well and taking care of yourself, you'll be flying very soon.'

He rubbed his face, and I could see the thoughts slipping and sliding through his tired brain. 'I'd better get the children,' I said, because I couldn't think of anything else. Because I was helpless in the face of his distress. 'They're with Judy.'

That night, Ryder had his first nightmare. It took me a couple of minutes to rouse him as he shuddered and gasped. 'What? What is it?'

I pulled his head on to my shoulder and cradled it. He was hot and sweating, still tense. 'Tell me what you were dreaming.'

'I'm up there,' he said reluctantly. 'And it's where I want to be. Tommy's on my right, and Bob on the left. The rest are behind. We're flying in tight formation. Tommy waggles his wings, and Bob sends me a thumb's-up. Good boys, both, tried and tested and seasoned, and I'm happy we're friends. The sky is blue, with tiny white clouds, and in the distance the sea is glittering, blue and glassy. It's so peaceful and beautiful and I know that I'm nearer God than I'm ever likely to be again.

'Then I hear the voice on the R/T. "Dorniers and 109s

above." I do a quick recce – the sky's filled with the bloody things. I've never seen so many enemy and I know it's going to be a bloodbath. I swing into my drill. Reflector sight on. Gun button to fire. Airscrew pitch to 2650 revs. Press the emergency boost override. Lower seat a notch . . .'

I continue to hold him, massaging his back with circular movements, and pressing my fingers into the tight muscles in his shoulder. I listen – and I'm up there with him, skidding through the thin air . . . readying for battle, my stomach twisting with nerves and anticipation.

'And then . . . and then, Barbara, I've broken formation, turned the plane and headed away from the battle, leaving the others behind. That's my nightmare.'

I raised myself on my elbow and bent over him. 'Ryder, you didn't do it. You did *not* abandon them.'

He gazed up at me. 'But I wanted to . . . Because I've lost my nerve and they can see it. I'm scared blue and witless, and I don't want to go up there and fight any more.'

But he did. Ryder went back, and survived. But nothing was the same. That was the war. It took Ryder – the golden, invincible boy who kissed me in a burst of sunlight and flew me to the edge of infinity – and wrung him dry. It took me – the silly, dazzled eighteen-year-old – and imprinted lines round my eyes and, for a long time, dullness in my heart.

The war brought us face to face with ourselves, and Ryder's nightmares were the scars of honour, a victory roll. We were bound together by it, he and I. All the same,

364

it stole our youth and I think I've been searching for mine ever since.

New Year's Eve, 1959
After supper, I sat in the sitting room at Edgeborough Road. I was bulky and a little fretful: the pregnancy so far had not been easy and I had been sleeping badly.

A log snapped on the fire, and the clock struck half past ten. Ryder looked up from the crossword. 'Should you go to bed, Babs?'

'I'd like to see in the new decade.'

'But you're tired.'

I smiled at him. 'So are you.'

'Got it!' Ryder pounced on the crossword, and wrote in an answer. 'Babs, I've been thinking. I might just give that idea of yours – to see someone about my sleeping – a bit of a go. Perhaps there's something in it. And I need to be in good shape with the baby coming.'

His tone was light, noncommittal. Don't make too big an issue of this, it warned.

'Good idea,' I replied.

'Right, then.' He stood and came over to me. 'Up you get, darling. No argument.'

I was getting so large that he had to push me up the stairs. Laughing and exclaiming, I got to the top and Ryder pulled me along the landing to the bedroom.

While he got changed in his dressing room, I moved around the bedroom, readying it for the night. I turned down the counterpane, hung up my dress, put my shoes in the wardrobe.

On the way back from the bathroom, I paused by the window. A white and ghostly light lay over the garden and I could – just – distinguish the block of the apple-house and the spiky shadows of the apple trees. Herr Schlinker was talking about planting new ones. 'It's important that we get the best rootstock for the grafts,' he had said. But that would depend on whether Ryder and I sold the house and moved away.

Downstairs the clock struck eleven o'clock.

'Barbara,' Ryder called out.

I smiled and turned back from the window. 'I'm here.'

I was, and I wasn't. Carrying my burdens – of life and unknowing – I went back into the bedroom, where Ryder was waiting, and closed the door.

Chapter Twenty-six: Siena

I woke with a start. Someone was knocking at the door of the hotel room. Dimly, I registered the *whoosh* of the lift, the discreet rattle of a trolley in the corridor and, again, the knock. I struggled upright. 'Come in.'

The door opened, and my hand flew to my mouth. 'Charlie!'

Weary and travel-rumpled, he was there, hair flopping over his forehead, suitcase in hand, keycard in hand. He walked in, set down the case, shut the door with his foot. 'Do I get a kiss?'

I was out of that bed like greased lightning. 'My God! Where have you come from? Why? Why? Why?'

His arm snaked round me. 'It was a question of wanting to see you.'

I clung to him, laughing and crying. 'And I wanted to see you.'

His arm still round me, he nudged his case further into the room. 'Do you think I'll manage to stay awake until ten tonight?'

'Depends what we do.'

He sat down on the bed with a thump. 'My God, I *am* weary. I was in court until the last minute, then I ran for the plane.'

I knelt up behind him to massage his back and neck.

He swivelled his head round. 'Apart from the sheer delight of making this absurd journey and sitting in a cattle truck of a plane for six hours, I've come to tell you something.'

I slid my arms round his neck and pressed my face against his. 'Tell.'

'Cimmie has had her baby. A girl called Heloise. They're doing fine.'

I reared back. 'You came all the way to New York to tell me that? I think not.'

Charlie wagged his head from side to side. 'And I took so much trouble – and it was *so* expensive.'

Cimmie? I stared at him. Then I got it. My lips twitched. 'I'm glad for Cimmie and Bruce.'

Charlie stroked my cheek. 'They've gone away, and they won't bother us any more.'

'True.' With a lilt of surprise, I realized it was. I pulled him down on to the bed and settled myself beside him. 'So . . . why are you here?'

'Harry Liversedge has now formally invited me to join the chambers and I've accepted.'

'Ah . . .' I fumbled for the appropriate response. 'That is . . . that's a strategic move?'

'It's meant to be. As we said before, it gives you room, Siena. I'll earn decent money, and with money you – we – can manoeuvre.'

Oh, my God. Charlie had still got the wrong end of the stick. I pushed him away and sat up straight. 'Charlie, didn't you understand?'

Appalled, I stared at him across the gender gap, the

marriage gap, the baby gap, whatever gap you could name. A gap so big we could not bridge it. A desolate vista of the long, cold days ahead flashed before me, of the inconsolable grief of not having Charlie. Of the second divorce. 'Charlie, it wasn't a question of being paid off.'

'Siena ... Siena ... Listen to me. I know it's not about money. It's about you. What you are, what you can manage. Your independence and territory, and all the buzz words you can think of. Of course I know.'

Limp with relief, I muttered, 'Sorry.'

He pulled me down beside him. 'Read my lips.'

In a burst of thankfulness and full heart, I kissed them. 'Why didn't you tell me before about accepting the Liversedge deal?'

'I was angry with you. I was angry with myself.'

'Charlie, you were right to believe in Jackie Woodruff,' I said quickly.

He squinted down at me. 'I'm not angry any more.'

I considered what this meant. Charlie was saying he had finessed one side of the bargain. Now, it really was make-your-mind-up time. 'Charlie, that was unbelievably generous.'

'Yes and no. It won't be exactly a penance. Siena, you must do as you like. If I can't make you come round to my way of thinking, then I'll have to live with it.'

'Won't you *hate* being shut up with a whole lot of smug, arrogant bastards chasing fat fees? I quote.'

Charlie stroked my chin with a finger. 'New challenge. Perhaps I'll turn into a smug, arrogant bastard.'

I shivered. 'I don't think so.'

Then again, perhaps he might. Perhaps I might turn into the female equivalent. *A Marybelle Hammond?* Age and disappointment had a knack of changing people. I had seen it too often in my clients to mistake the mission creep of sourness and spoilt expectation.

Charlie's finger proceeded to go walkabout and I lost my train of thought. In fact, happiness and thankfulness made me lose interest in the subject altogether.

I lay very still while Charlie slept. I was soft, floating, expanded.

Happy? Oh, yes. With a happiness that far superseded physical delight.

Far away, up in Bill's orchard, there was the roar of the codling moth, the aphid and the air-borne disease doing battle with the apple trees, and I strained to listen in to that noisy clamour: a dangerous, risky, yet unstoppable process that swelled the apple buds on the branches. ('It's a night-and-day vigil,' said Bill.)

In the hotel wardrobe, on the racks in Trimester Studios, in Jackie Woodruff's nursery, clothes hung on racks, empty and shapeless. There was silence.

Siena. You must do as you wish.

In the end . . . in the end . . . there was no option but to take Charlie's hand and step into that clamour.

Charlie grew heavier and heavier. Flesh pressing into my flesh – his knees, hips and shoulders making indents on my body that pricked and wept and . . . waited.

Waited for the baby that one day, I was sure (could I be sure?), yes, I was sure would be born.

*

New York, Sunday afternoon, and anyone who was anyone – anyone, that is, who had any sense of preserving life – had fled: the late-summer heatwave encircled the city in a vice, and it was so hot that the sidewalks felt liquid underfoot.

It was hard going, setting one's face into the teeth of the heat, but Charlie and I dodged in and out of the sun and the shadows cast by the buildings, as we had in childhood avoiding the cracks between paving stones.

We turned into a street with a cluster of antique shops. One stood out, with a gaudy awning in pink and white, and we stopped to inspect the objects in its window. There was a pretty Swedish chair – Gustavian period, upholstered in silk the colour of old gold. On a pedestal next to it was a vase, a ridiculous concoction of fruit and flowers, topped with a pair of red cherries. The label underneath read: 'English, Rockingham, nineteenth century'.

But the centrepiece of the window display was a clock. It was ormolu, with hands shaped like arrows, and two playful bronze cherubs leaning against the face. One pointed towards the painted Roman numerals . . . taking joy and pleasure from being associated with such a beautiful object. The label read: 'Austrian, 1779'.

'It's a lovely piece,' said the dealer, when we went in to inquire. He lifted it out of the window, spread a square of blue velvet on the counter and eased the clock on to it. 'Very fine indeed.'

I reached over, 'May I?', and touched one of the cherubs. He was cool and smooth, his youth untouched and impervious to the passing of the hours, which he helped to record.

'Its maker, a Johannes Bruckner, was highly sought after. He worked mainly in Vienna and his clocks were bought by the Elector and the Archbishop.' He turned the clock to show us Bruckner's name engraved on the inner mechanism, and my eye was caught by the words '*Ich spüre nur die Zeit*.' I ran my finger along the engraving, feeling the tiny indents made by the letters.

'Do you know what it means?' Charlie asked.

The dealer repeated the German slowly, thoughtfully. 'I have an idea ... roughly, "I feel only time."' He was pleased with his erudition.

The clock's beauty, elegance and clarity took my breath away. I imagined it positioned, elegant and confident, on the shelf in the room overlooking the river ... time flowing through it, the river flowing outside, through the sun and the wind and the rain.

The dealer hesitated when Charlie asked him the price, 'It's not cheap,' and named a staggering sum. All three of us knew it was hopeless. 'I could do a little reduction,' he offered.

I asked where it came from.

'Give me a minute.' He fussed with his computer, and scanned through the records. 'It belonged to a Mr and Mrs Beeching from Guildford, Surrey, England.' He pronounced 'Guildford' incorrectly. 'It was sold at auction with the rest of their estate. Before that . . .' He reeled off a list of provenances that charted the clock's progress from Austria to France and, eventually, to England.

In the street, the shadows of afternoon spilled over the sidewalks. 'We can't afford it, but could I write down the German, please?' I extracted my notebook from my bag and wrote: '*Ich spüre nur die Zeit.*'

Charlie and I looked at each other and smiled.

ELIZABETH BUCHAN

If you enjoyed this book, there are several ways you can read more by the same author and make sure you get the inside track on all Penguin books.

Order any of the following titles direct:

0141009799 THE GOOD WIFE	£6.99

'Compelling, compassionate, and aglow with moments of
laugh-or-cry humour'
Mail on Sunday

0140290087 REVENGE OF THE MIDDLE-AGED WOMAN	£6.99

'Wise, melancholy, funny and sophisticated. Buchan's new novel is
more satisfying than a romance'
The Times

0140290079 SECRETS OF THE HEART	£6.99

'A finely written, intelligent romance'
Mail on Sunday

Simply call Penguin c/o Bookpost on **01624 677237** and have your credit/debit card ready.
Alternatively e-mail your order to **bookshop@enterprise.net.** Postage and package is free
in mainland UK. Overseas customers must add £2 per book. Prices and availability subject
to change without notice.

---

*Visit www.penguin.com and find out first about forthcoming titles, read
exclusive material and author interviews, and enter exciting competitions.
You can also browse through thousands of Penguin books and buy online.*

IT'S NEVER BEEN EASIER TO READ MORE WITH PENGUIN

---

*Frustrated by the quality of books available at Exeter station for his journey back to
London one day in 1935, Allen Lane decided to do something about it. The Penguin
paperback was born that day, and with it first-class writing became available to a mass
audience for the very first time. This book is a direct descendant of those original Penguins
and Lane's momentous vision. What will you read next?*